[Vol. 1]

WRITTEN BY
JASON HENDERSON AND TONY SALVAGGIO

ILLUSTRATED BY
SHANE GRANGER

HAMBURG // LONDON // LOS ANGELES // TOKYO

PSY★COMM

VOLUME [1]

CONTENTS

CHAPTER [1]..5

CHAPTER [2]..25

CHAPTER [3]..43

CHAPTER [4]..6

CHAPTER [5]..79

CHAPTER [6]..105

CHAPTER [7]..129

CHAPTER [8]..15

CHAPTER [9]..165

INDEX..189

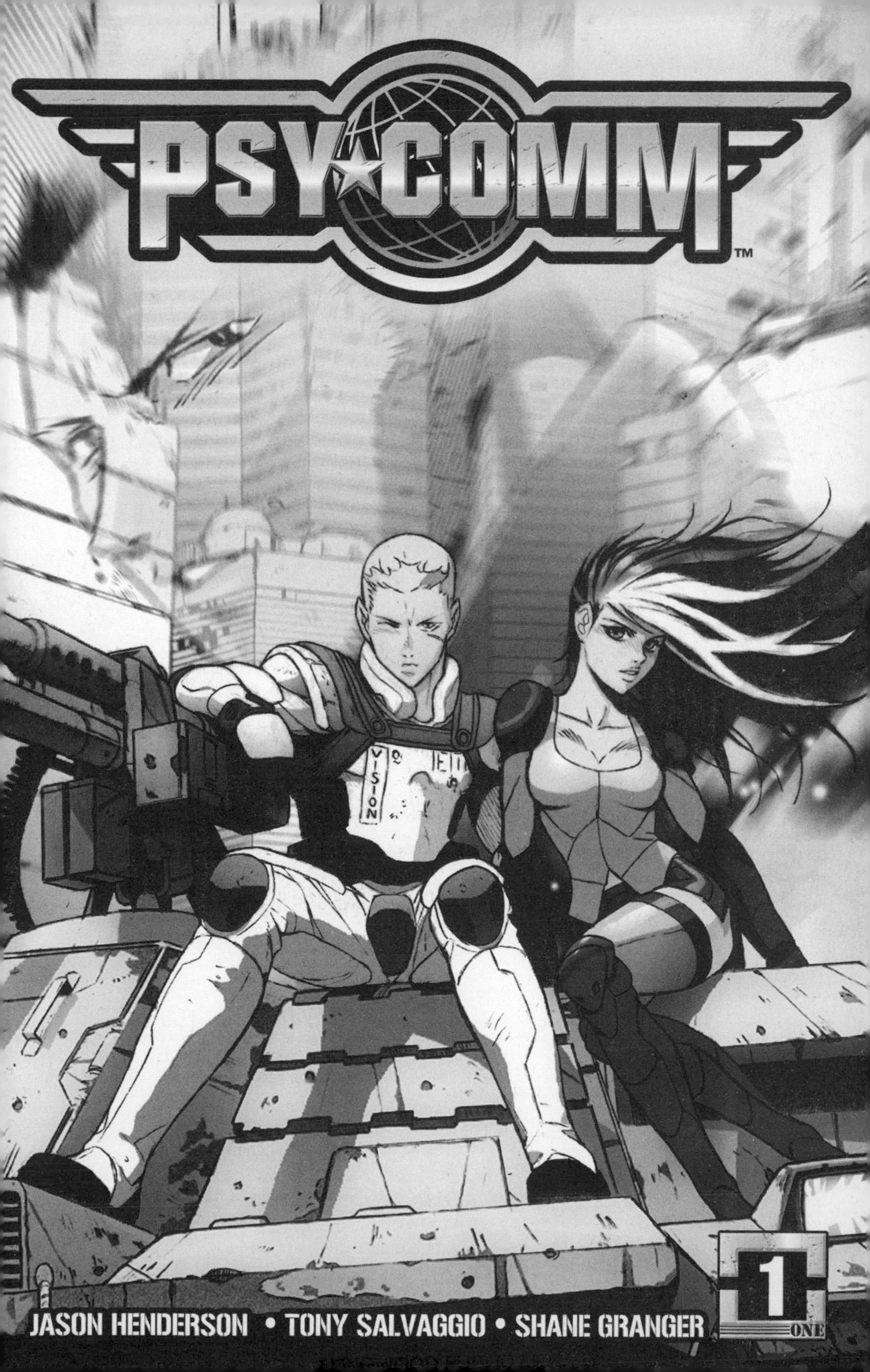
PSY★COMM™
VISION
1
ONE
JASON HENDERSON • TONY SALVAGGIO • SHANE GRANGER

Psy-Comm Vol. 1
Written By Jason Henderson and Tony Salvaggio
Illustrated by Shane Granger

Inks - Jeremy Freeman
Tones - Chi Wang
Kaplan Edition Writer - Bonnie Flaherty
Copy Editor - Hope Donovan
Production Artist - Mike Estacio
Additional Design - Louis Csontos
Cover Designers - Jorge Negrete and Louis Csontos
Editor - Bryce P. Coleman

Editorial Director, Kaplan Publishing - Jennifer Farthing
Project Editor, Kaplan Publishing - Eric Titner
Production Editor, Kaplan Publishing - Fred Urfer

Digital Imaging Manager - Chris Buford
Pre-Production Supervisor - Erika Terriquez
Art Director - Anne Marie Horne
Production Manager - Elisabeth Brizzi
Managing Editor - Vy Nguyen
VP of Production - Ron Klamert
Editor-in-Chief - Rob Tokar
Publisher - Mike Kiley
President and C.O.O. - John Parker
C.E.O. and Chief Creative Officer - Stuart Levy

Published by Kaplan Publishing, a division of Kaplan, Inc.
1 Liberty Plaza, 24th Floor
New York, NY 10006

A  Manga

TOKYOPOP and 🐸 are trademarks or registered trademarks of TOKYOPOP Inc.

TOKYOPOP Inc.
5900 Wilshire Blvd. Suite 2000
Los Angeles, CA 90036

E-mail: info@TOKYOPOP.com
Come visit us online at www.TOKYOPOP.com

ISBN-13: 978-1-4277-5496-7
ISBN-10: 1-4277-5496-9
First printing: July 2007
10 9 8 7 6 5 4 3 2 1
Printed in the USA

Kaplan Publishing books are available at special quantity discounts to use for sales promotions, employee premiums, or educational
purposes. Please email our Special Sales Department to order or for more information at kaplanpublishing@kaplan.com, or write to
Kaplan Publishing, 1 Liberty Plaza, 24th Floor, NY, NY, 10006.

PSY★COMM
CHAPTER [1]

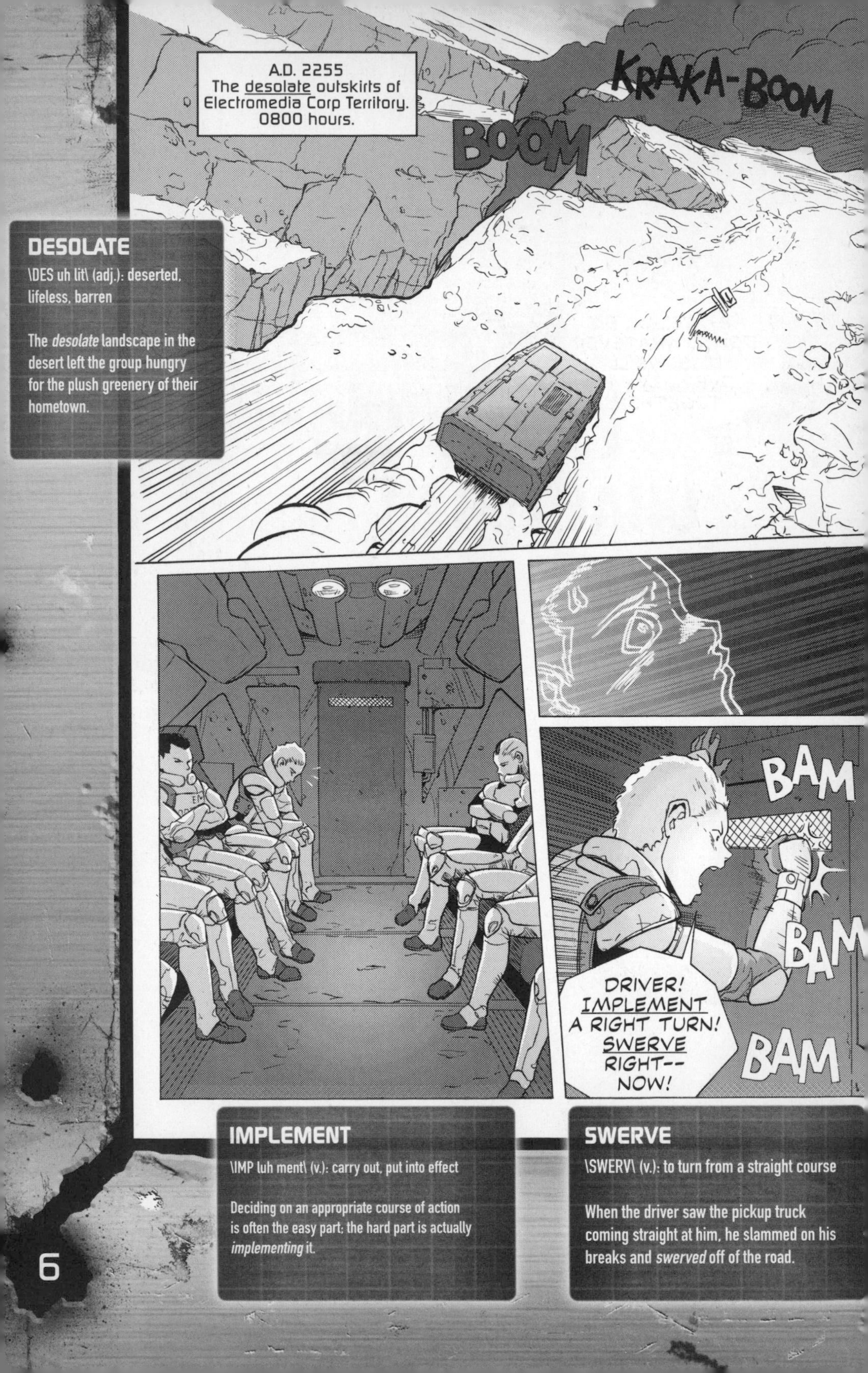
A.D. 2255
The desolate outskirts of Electromedia Corp Territory. 0800 hours.
BOOM
KRAKA-BOOM
BAM
BAM
BAM
DRIVER! IMPLEMENT A RIGHT TURN! SWERVE RIGHT-- NOW!

DESOLATE

\DES uh lit\ (adj.): deserted, lifeless, barren

The *desolate* landscape in the desert left the group hungry for the plush greenery of their hometown.

IMPLEMENT

\IMP luh ment\ (v.): carry out, put into effect

Deciding on an appropriate course of action is often the easy part; the hard part is actually *implementing* it.

SWERVE

\SWERV\ (v.): to turn from a straight course

When the driver saw the pickup truck coming straight at him, he slammed on his breaks and *swerved* off of the road.

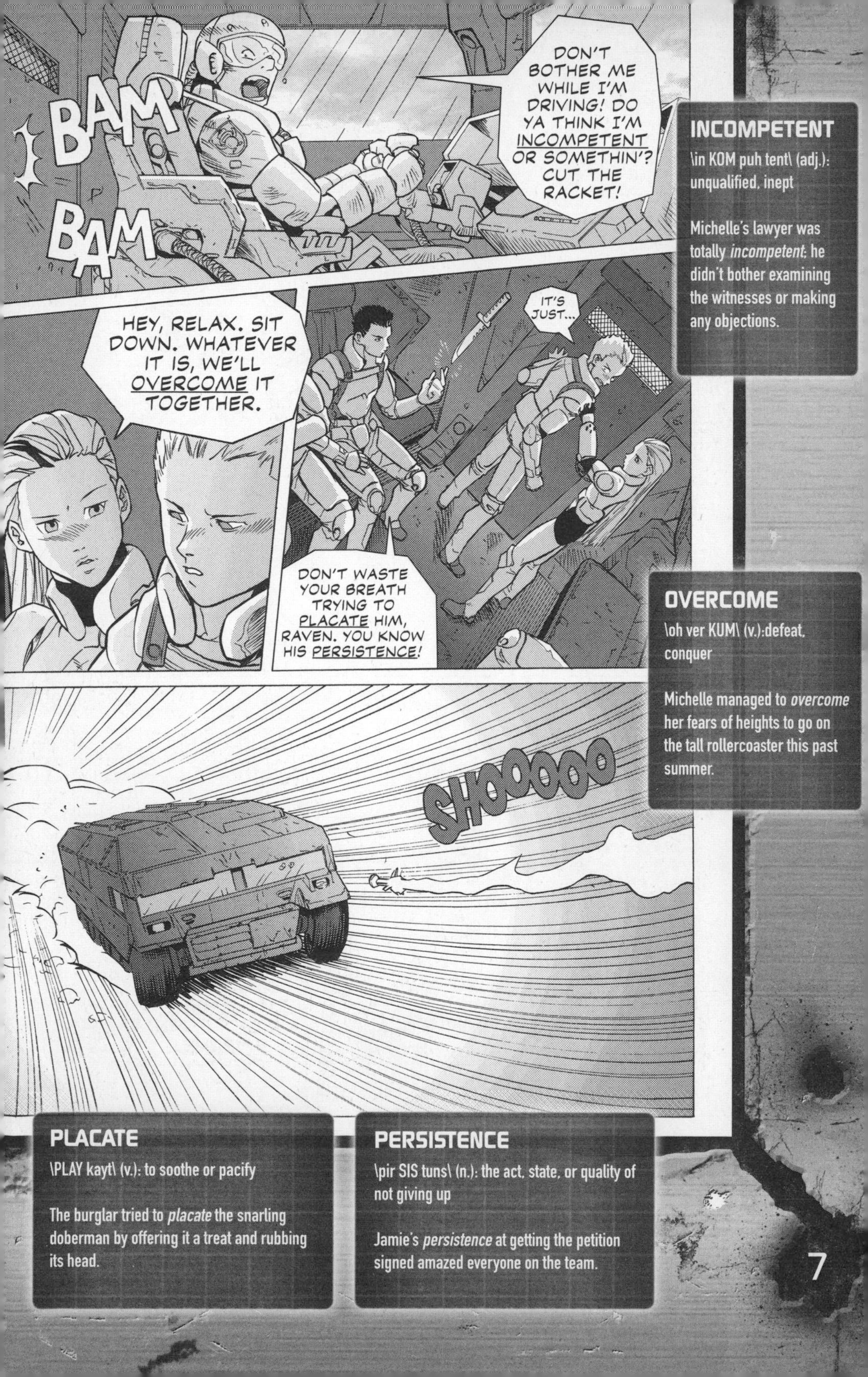
BAM
BAM
DON'T BOTHER ME WHILE I'M DRIVING! DO YA THINK I'M INCOMPETENT OR SOMETHIN'? CUT THE RACKET!
HEY, RELAX. SIT DOWN. WHATEVER IT IS, WE'LL OVERCOME IT TOGETHER.
IT'S JUST...
DON'T WASTE YOUR BREATH TRYING TO PLACATE HIM, RAVEN. YOU KNOW HIS PERSISTENCE!
SHOOOOO

INCOMPETENT

\in KOM puh tent\ (adj.): unqualified, inept

Michelle's lawyer was totally *incompetent*; he didn't bother examining the witnesses or making any objections.

OVERCOME

\oh ver KUM\ (v.):defeat, conquer

Michelle managed to *overcome* her fears of heights to go on the tall rollercoaster this past summer.

PLACATE

\PLAY kayt\ (v.): to soothe or pacify

The burglar tried to *placate* the snarling doberman by offering it a treat and rubbing its head.

PERSISTENCE

\pir SIS tuns\ (n.): the act, state, or quality of not giving up

Jamie's *persistence* at getting the petition signed amazed everyone on the team.

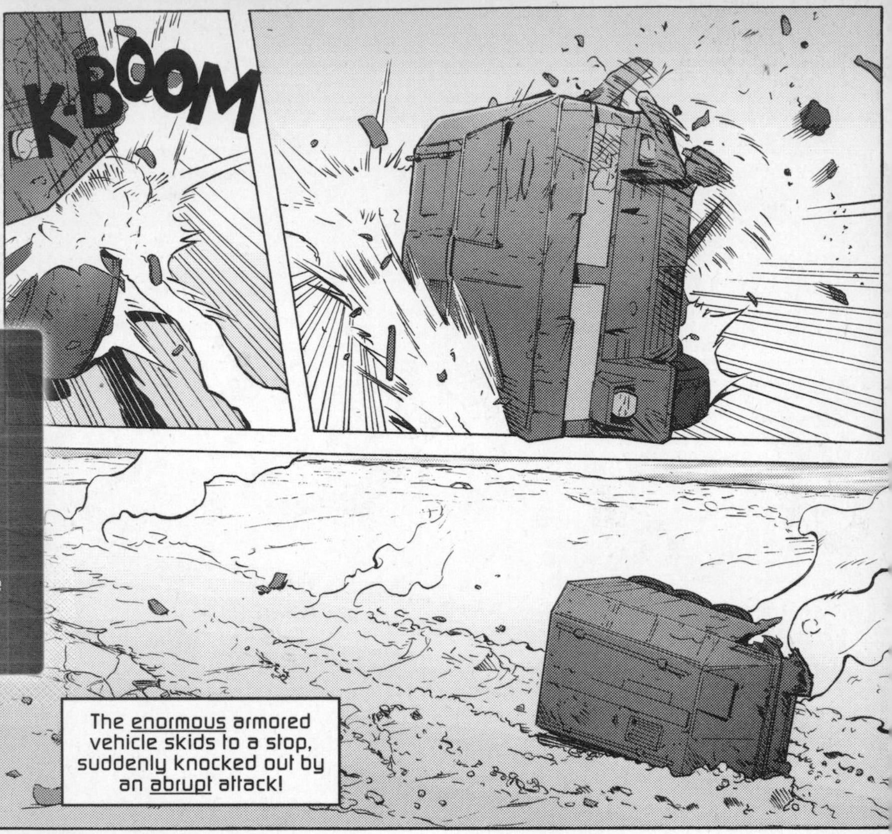
K-BOOM
The enormous armored vehicle skids to a stop, suddenly knocked out by an abrupt attack!
BOOM
The Psychic Commandos defiantly burst through the carg door, eager to locate their attackers.

ENORMOUS

\ee NOR muss\ (adj.): very great in size or degree

The *enormous* sculpture of the elephant dwarfed the delighted children.

ABRUPT

\ab RUPT\ (adj.): sudden; curt

The lion was thrown off-guard by the *abrupt* change in direction of the elk herd.

DEFIANT

\de FIY ant\ (adj.): boldly resisting

The *defiant* soldier ignored the general's orders.

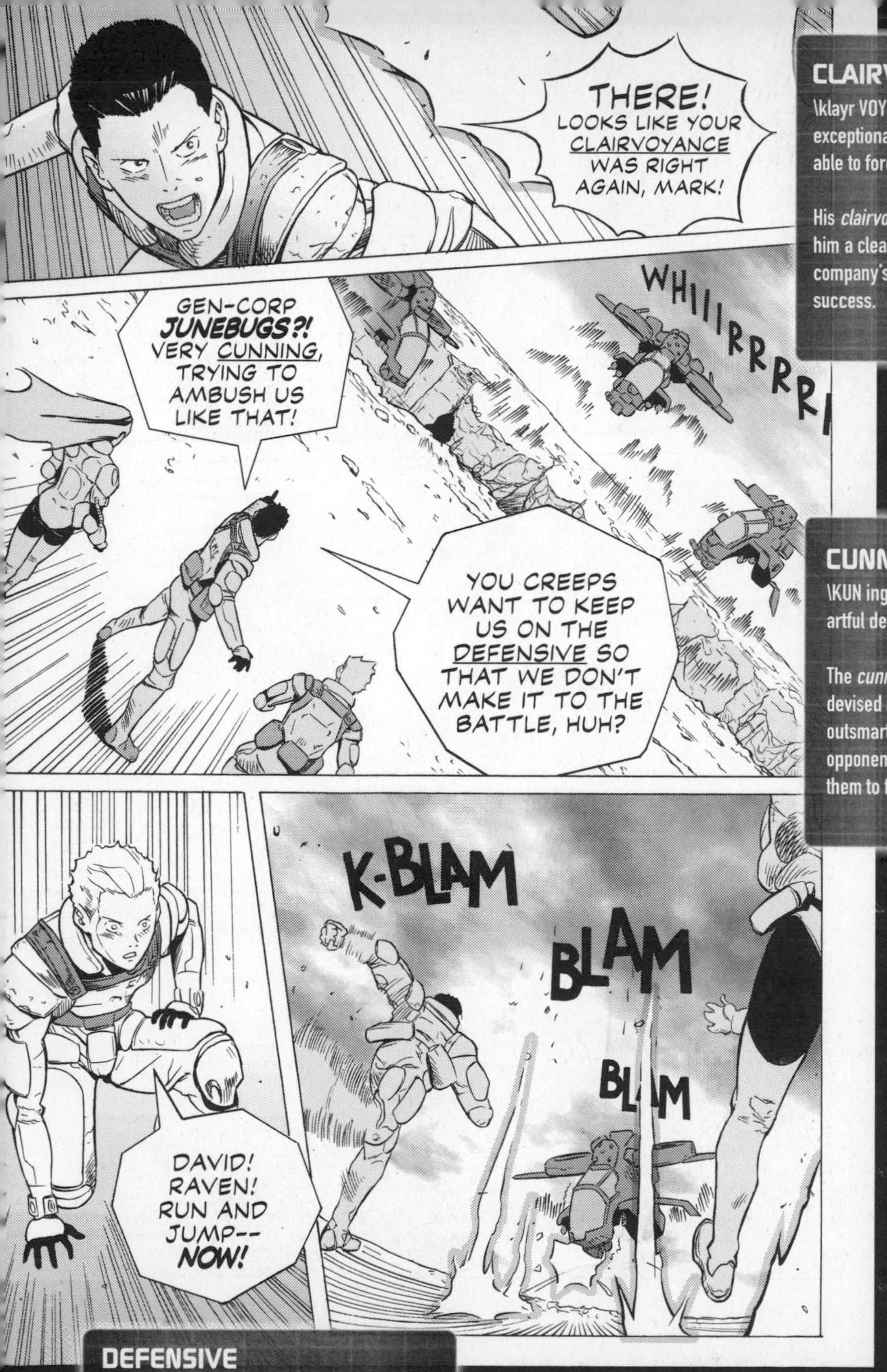
THERE! LOOKS LIKE YOUR CLAIRVOYANCE WAS RIGHT AGAIN, MARK!
WHIIIRRRRRI
GEN-CORP JUNEBUGS?! VERY CUNNING, TRYING TO AMBUSH US LIKE THAT!
YOU CREEPS WANT TO KEEP US ON THE DEFENSIVE SO THAT WE DON'T MAKE IT TO THE BATTLE, HUH?
K-BLAM
BLAM
BLAM
DAVID! RAVEN! RUN AND JUMP-- NOW!

CLAIRVOYANCE

\klayr VOY ens\ (adj.): exceptionally insightful, able to foresee the future

His *clairvoyance* allowed him a clear vision of the company's imminent success.

CUNNING

\KUN ing\ (adj.): given to artful deception

The *cunning* general devised a way to outsmart both his opponents and force them to fight each other.

DEFENSIVE

\de FEN siv\ (adj.): protective

When they learned of the impending attack, the residents of the city took *defensive* measures to protect themselves from annihilation.

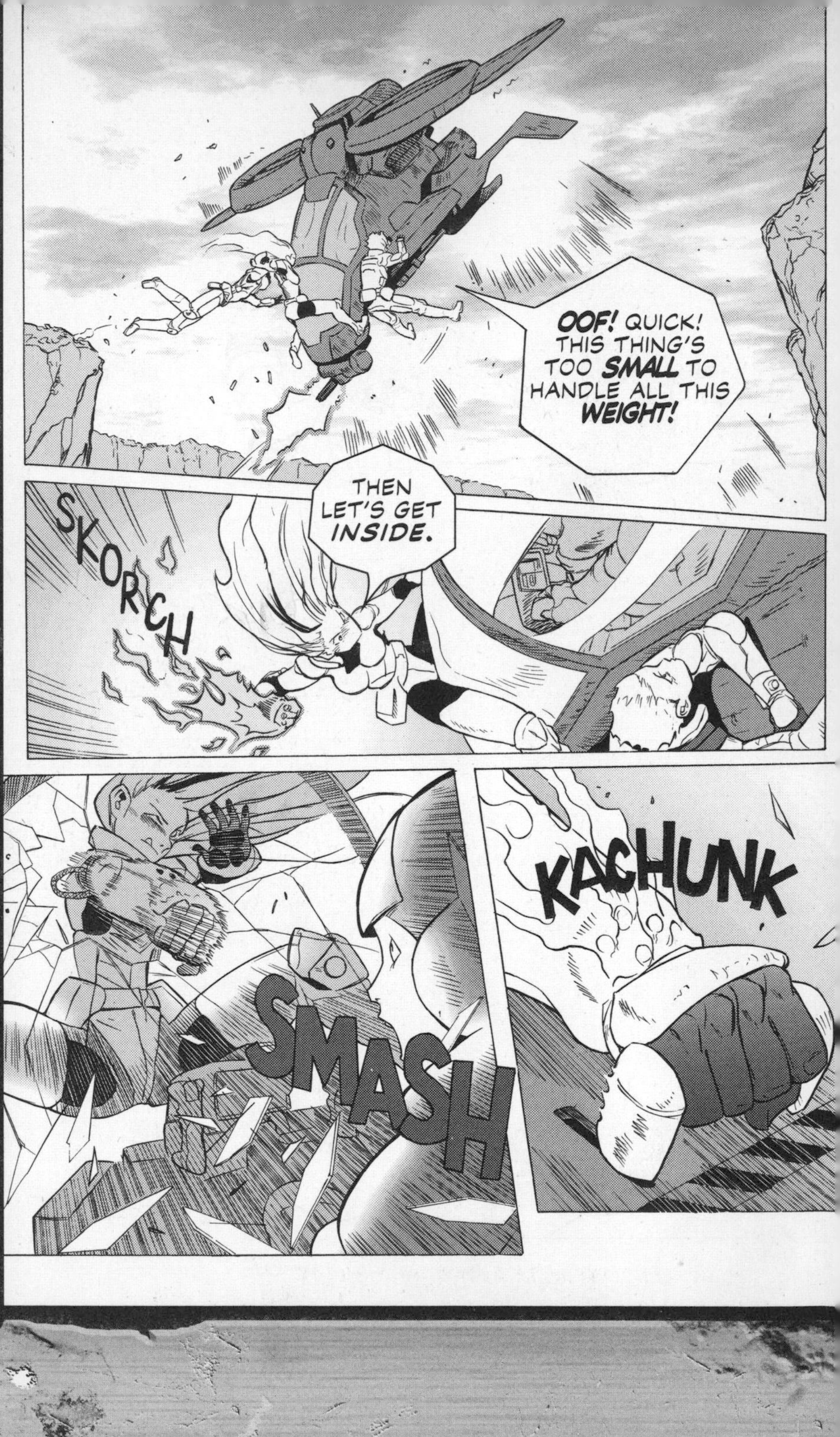
OOF! QUICK! THIS THING'S TOO SMALL TO HANDLE ALL THIS WEIGHT!
THEN LET'S GET INSIDE.
SKORCH
SMASH
KACHUNK

THWAK
YEAH, YOU DIDN'T ANTICIPATE THAT ONE, DID YOU?

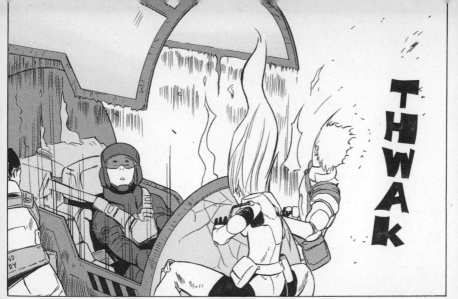

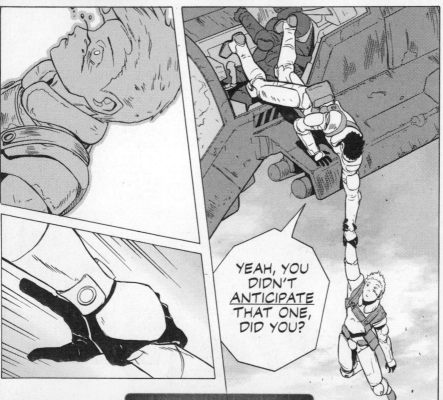

ANTICIPATE

\an TISS uh payt\ (v.): to realize beforehand, to look forward to

Although the CD was greatly *anticipated* because of the tremendous success of the artist's debut, it proved to be sadly disappointing.

RELINQUISH

\re LIN kwish\ (v.): to renounce or surrender something

The toddler was forced to *relinquish* the toy when the girl who owned it asked for it back.

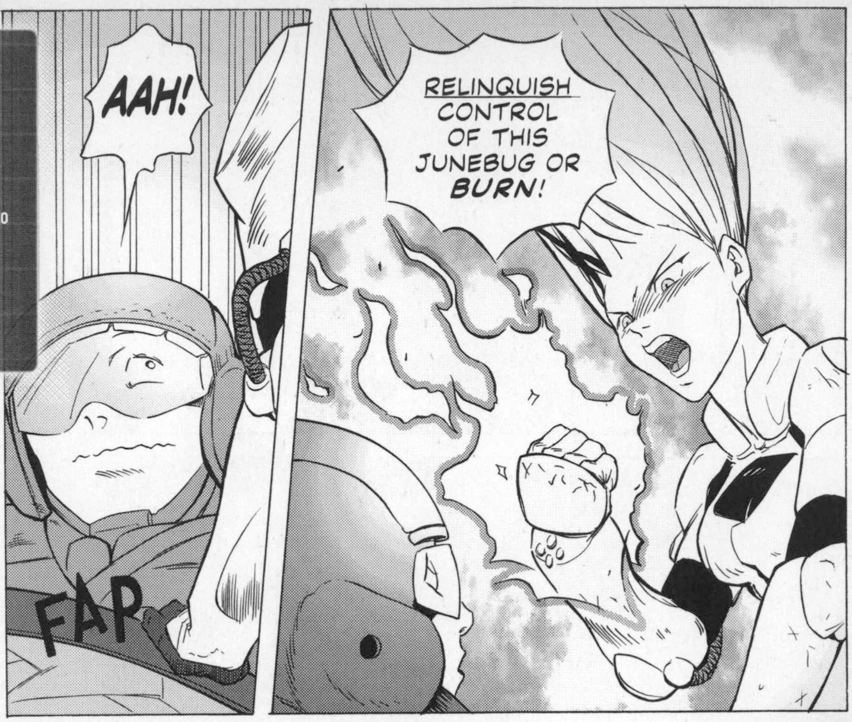
AAH!
FAP
RELINQUISH CONTROL OF THIS JUNEBUG OR BURN!

DAUNTING

\DAWN ting\ (adj.): discouraging

While running the New York Marathon may be a *daunting* task to some, the event consistently draws thousands of participants.

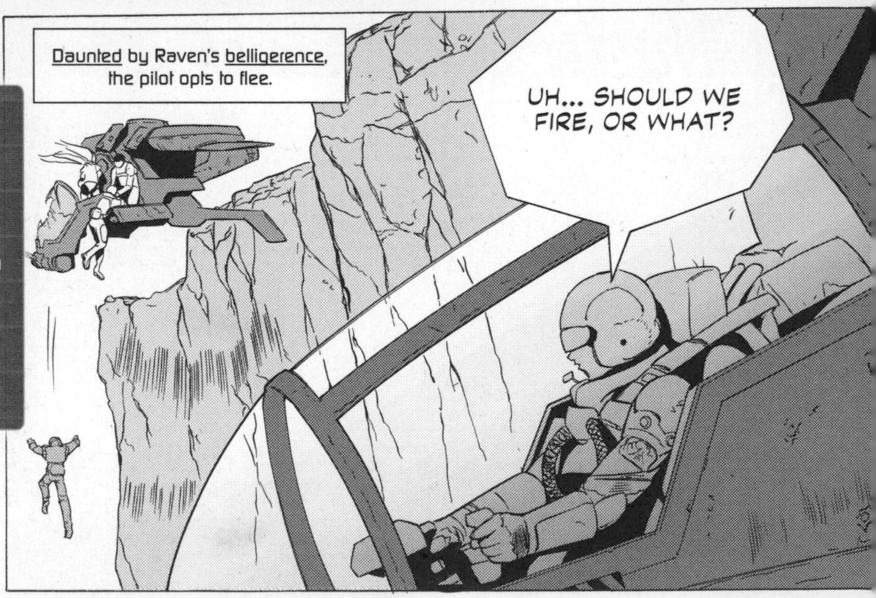
Daunted by Raven's belligerence, the pilot opts to flee.
UH... SHOULD WE FIRE, OR WHAT?

BELLIGERENT

\be LIJ er ent\ (adj.): hostile, inclined to fight

Although he had a reputation for being peaceable, Gerald could actually become quite *belligerent* when he felt he was being mocked.

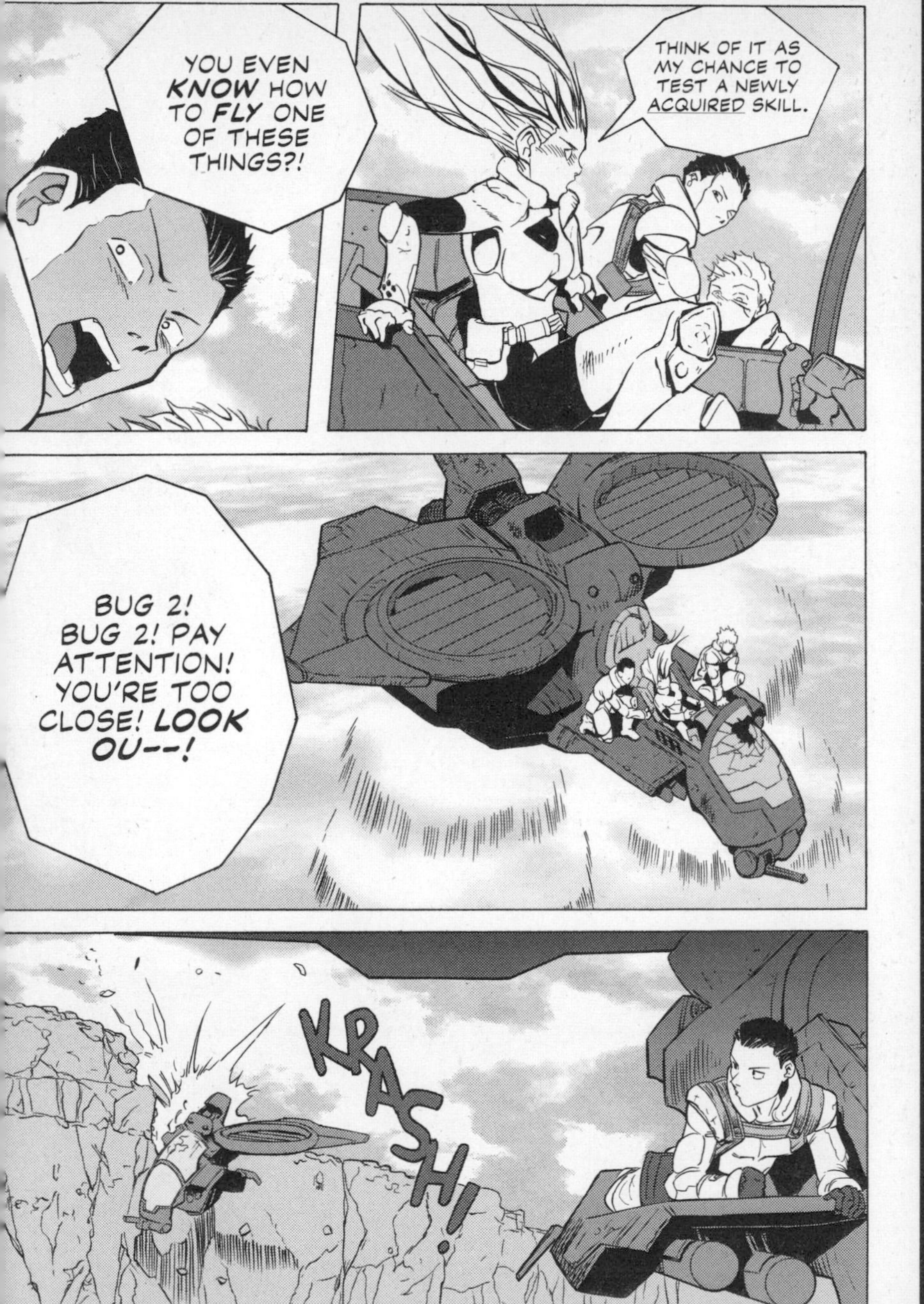
YOU EVEN KNOW HOW TO FLY ONE OF THESE THINGS?!
THINK OF IT AS MY CHANCE TO TEST A NEWLY ACQUIRED SKILL.
BUG 2! BUG 2! PAY ATTENTION! YOU'RE TOO CLOSE! LOOK OU--!
KRASH!

ACQUIRE

\ah KWIYR\ (v.): to gain possession of

After this weekend's movie marathon, Lenora *acquired* a taste for Italian movies; she now wants to see all of them.

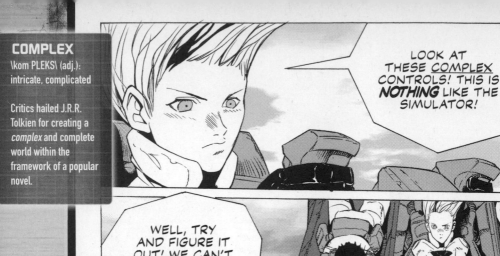

COMPLEX

\kom PLEKS\ (adj.): intricate, complicated

Critics hailed J.R.R. Tolkien for creating a *complex* and complete world within the framework of a popular novel.

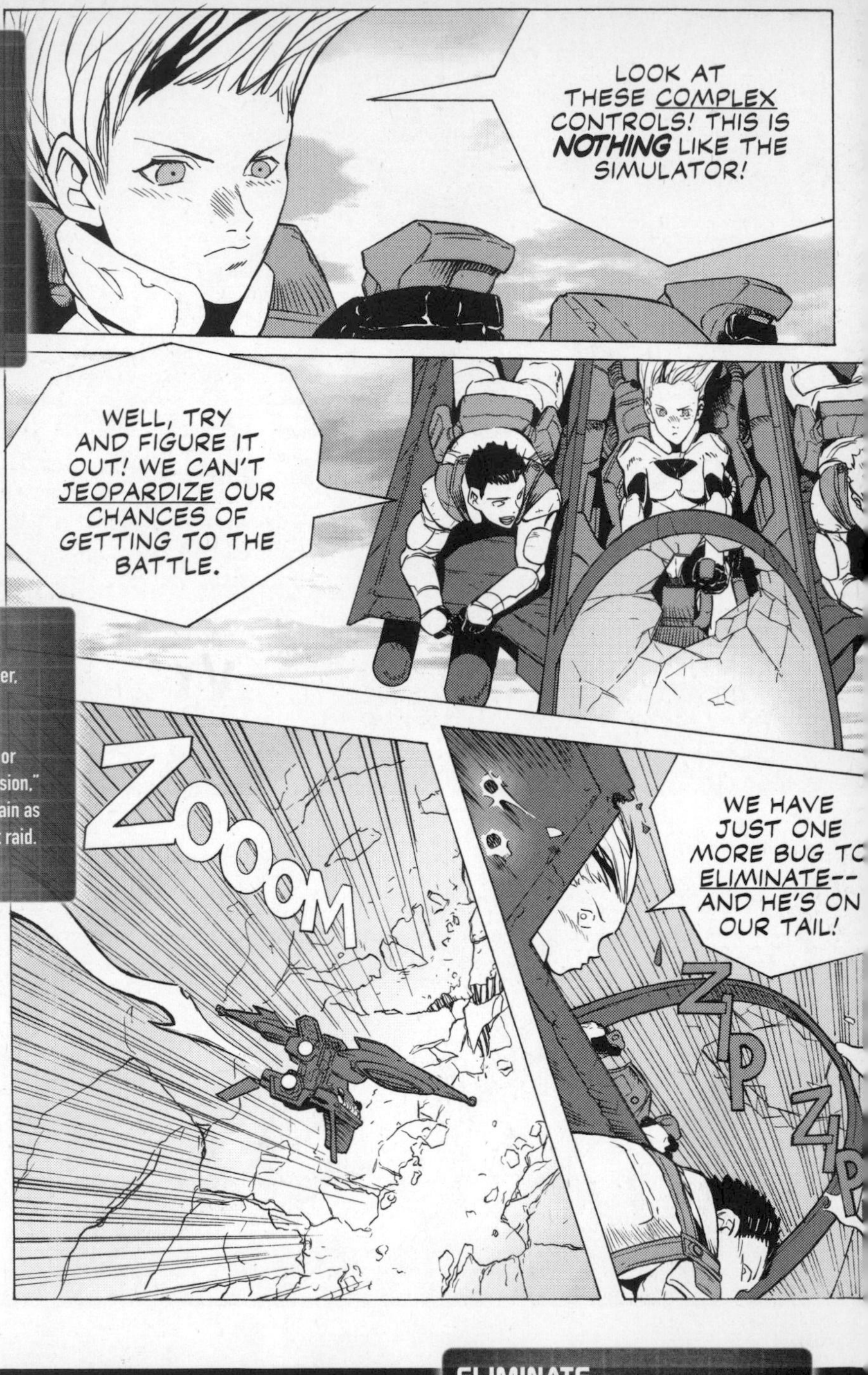
LOOK AT THESE COMPLEX CONTROLS! THIS IS NOTHING LIKE THE SIMULATOR!
WELL, TRY AND FIGURE IT OUT! WE CAN'T JEOPARDIZE OUR CHANCES OF GETTING TO THE BATTLE.
ZOOOM
WE HAVE JUST ONE MORE BUG TO ELIMINATE-- AND HE'S ON OUR TAIL!
ZIP
ZIP

JEOPARDIZE

\JEP er diyz\ (v.): endanger, expose to injury

"Keep your voices down or you'll *jeopardize* the mission," cautioned the army captain as he led his unit on a night raid.

ELIMINATE

\ee LIM uh nayt\ (v.): get rid of; remove

One of television's first reality shows placed a group of strangers on an island and forced them to *eliminate* a contestant each week until there was only one person left.

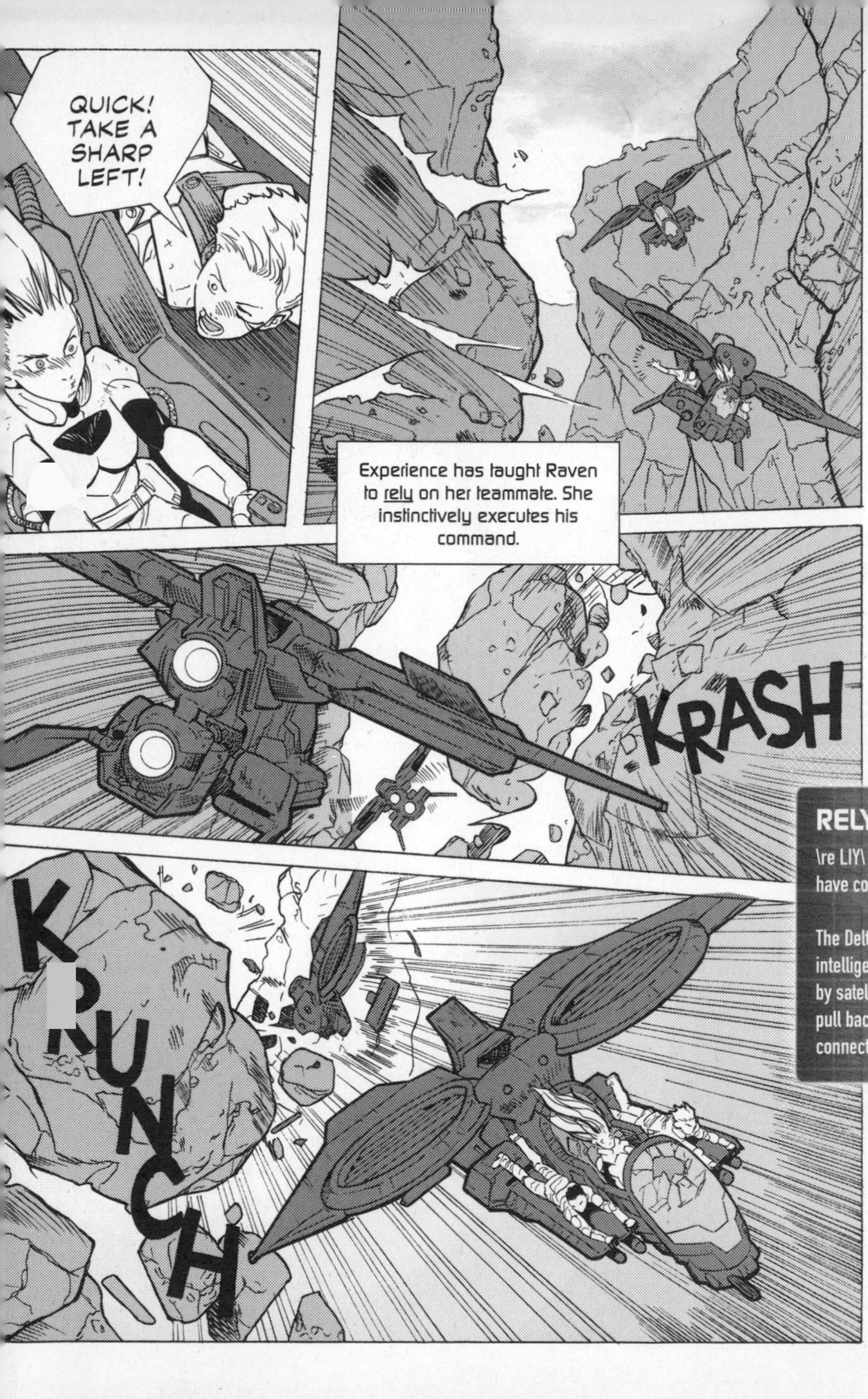
QUICK! TAKE A SHARP LEFT!
Experience has taught Raven to rely on her teammate. She instinctively executes his command.
KRASH
KRUNCH

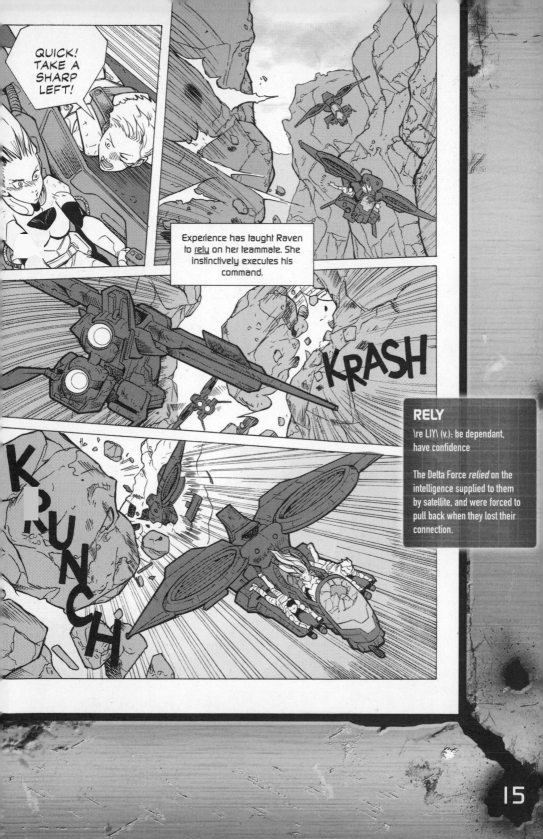

RELY

\re LIY\ (v.): be dependant, have confidence

The Delta Force *relied* on the intelligence supplied to them by satellite, and were forced to pull back when they lost their connection.

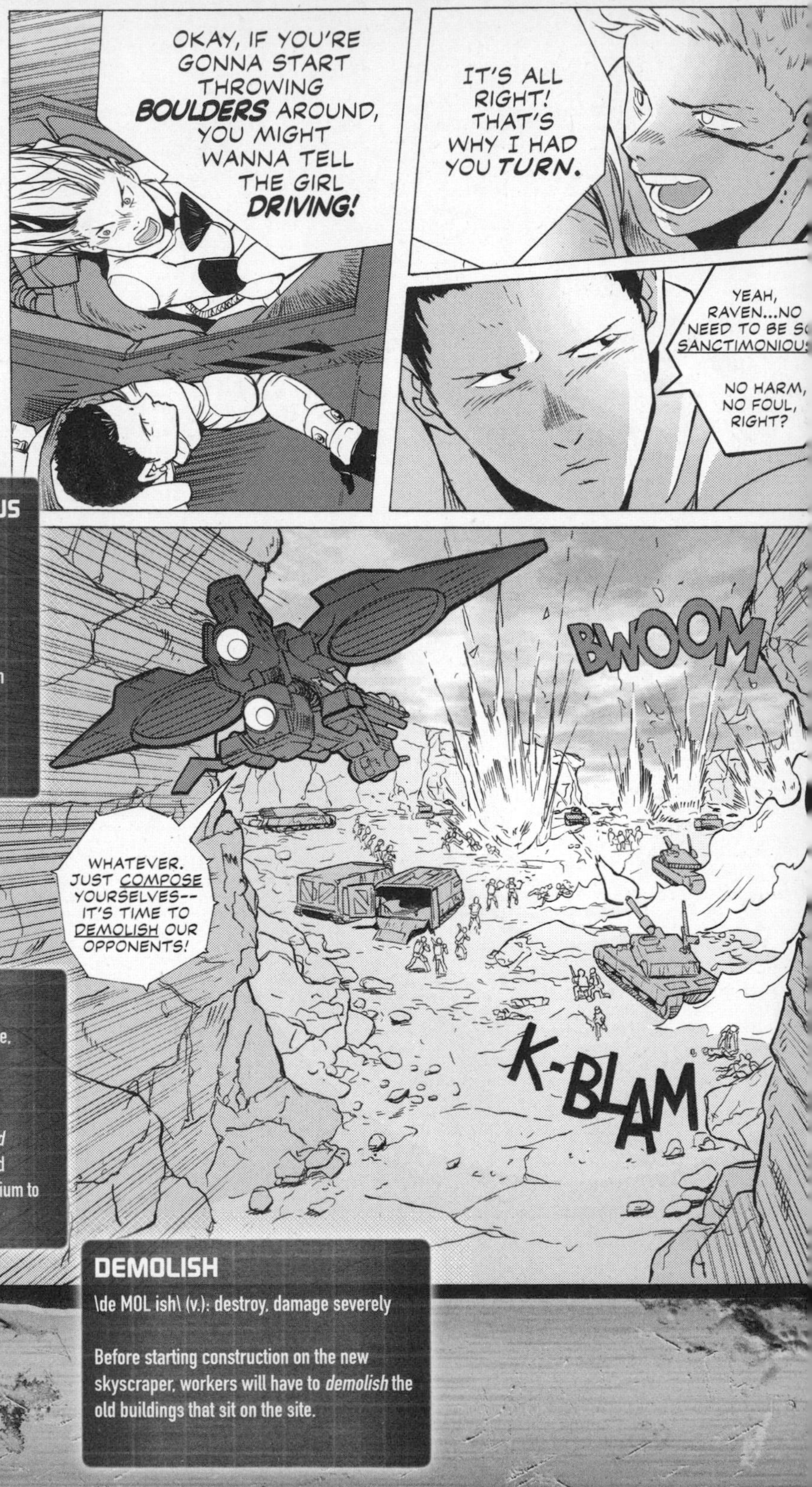
OKAY, IF YOU'RE GONNA START THROWING **BOULDERS** AROUND, YOU MIGHT WANNA TELL THE GIRL **DRIVING!**
IT'S ALL RIGHT! THAT'S WHY I HAD YOU **TURN.**
YEAH, RAVEN...NO NEED TO BE S SANCTIMONIOU
NO HARM, NO FOUL, RIGHT?
BWOOM
WHATEVER. JUST COMPOSE YOURSELVES-- IT'S TIME TO DEMOLISH OUR OPPONENTS!
K-BLAM

SANCTIMONIOUS

\sangk ti MOH nee us\ (adj.): excessively righteous

Sanctimonious anger ripped across the room when the politician questioned his party's agenda.

COMPOSED

\kom POS d\ (adj.): serene, calm

Friends noticed the valedictorian's *composed* appearance as he walked confidently up to the podium to address the crowd.

DEMOLISH

\de MOL ish\ (v.): destroy, damage severely

Before starting construction on the new skyscraper, workers will have to *demolish* the old buildings that sit on the site.

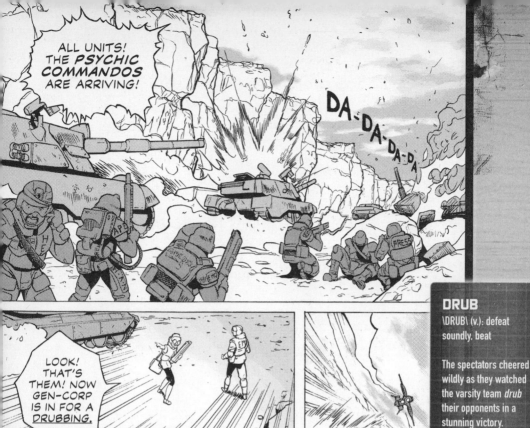

ALL UNITS! THE PSYCHIC COMMANDOS ARE ARRIVING!
DA-DA-DA-DA
LOOK! THAT'S THEM! NOW GEN-CORP IS IN FOR A DRUBBING.
THAT'S RIGHT, LADIES AND GENTLEMEN OF ELECTROMEDIA CORP! THE SIRENS DON'T LIE! THE PSY-COMMS HAVE ARRIVED AT THE SCENE AND--WAIT A SECOND! IT APPEARS THAT SOME OF OUR INDOMITABLE TROOPS HAVE COMMANDEERED A GEN-CORP JUNEBUG!
THINGS JUST GOT A LOT MORE INTERESTING, PEOPLE!

DRUB

\DRUB\ (v.): defeat soundly. beat

The spectators cheered wildly as they watched the varsity team *drub* their opponents in a stunning victory.

INDOMITABLE

\in DOM ih tu bul\ (adj.): fearless, unconquerable

Samson was *indomitable* in battle until the treacherous Delilah cut off his hair, taking away his strength.

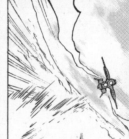

LIABILITY
\liy uh BIL uh tee\ (n.): handicap, something holding one back

Although some businesses consider it a *liability* to be situated close to a competitor, many industries believe that they will attract more customers if they stay together.

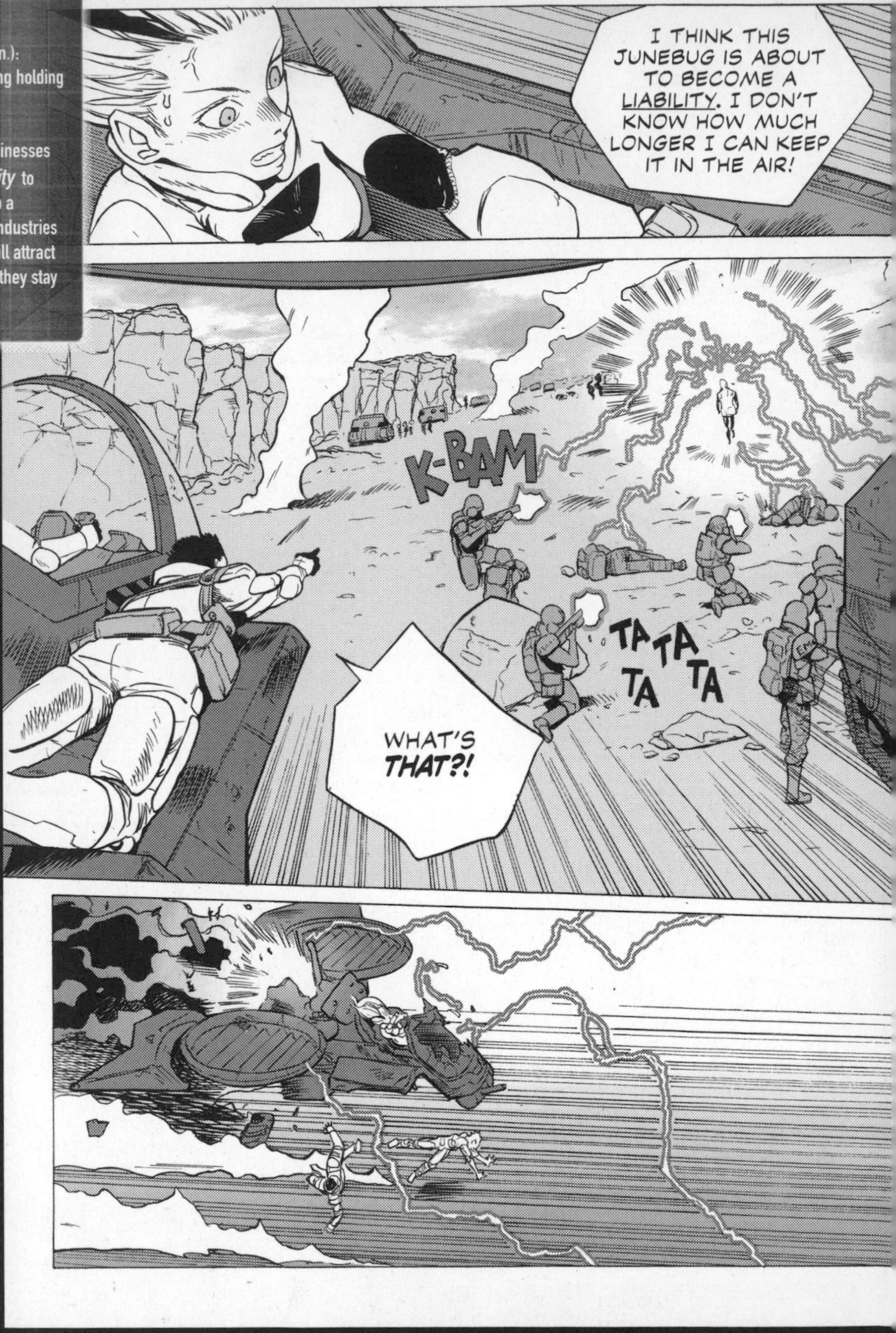
I THINK THIS JUNEBUG IS ABOUT TO BECOME A LIABILITY. I DON'T KNOW HOW MUCH LONGER I CAN KEEP IT IN THE AIR!
K-BAM
TA TA TA TA TA
WHAT'S THAT?!

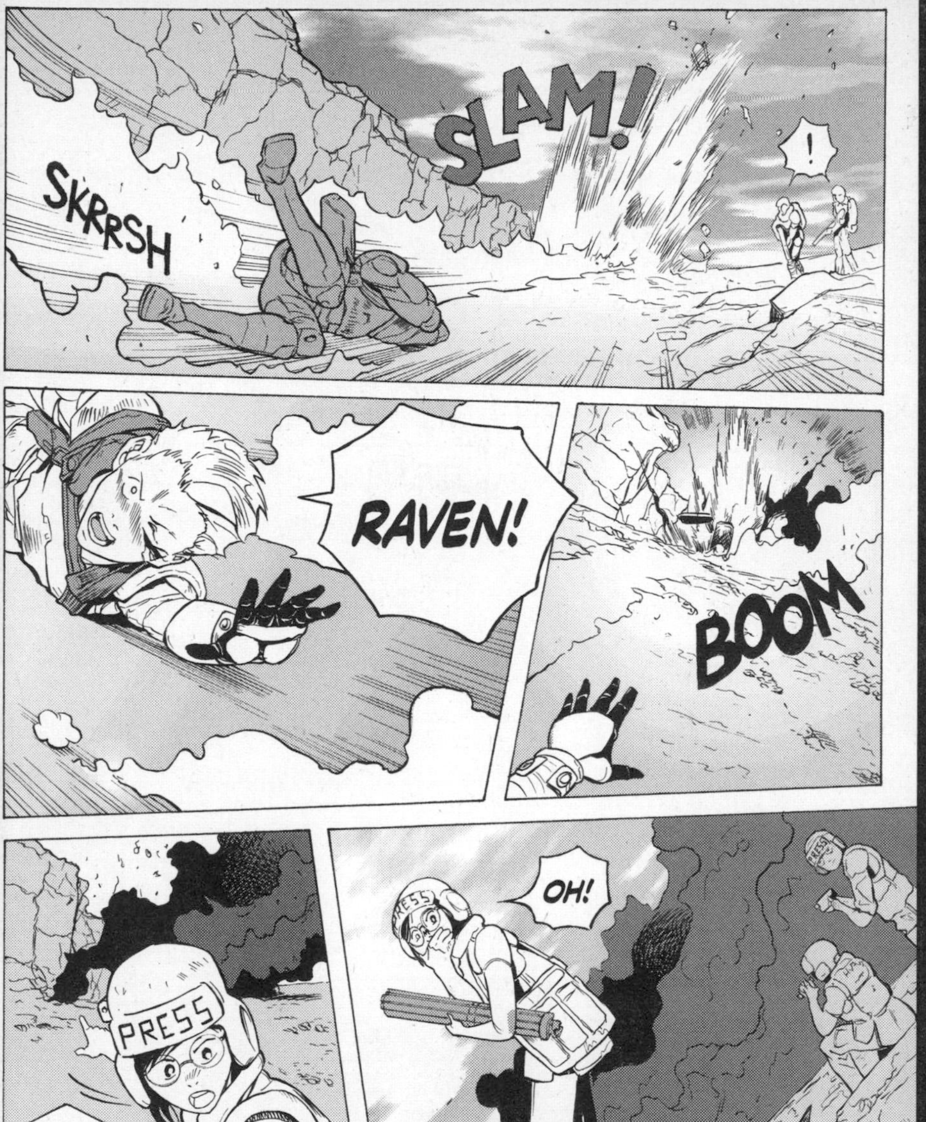
SKRRSH
SLAM!
!
RAVEN!
BOOM
PRESS
HUND, DID YOU SEE THAT?! DO YOU THINK THERE'LL BE ANYTHING TO SALVAGE? HUND??
PRESS
OH!
PRESS
PRESS

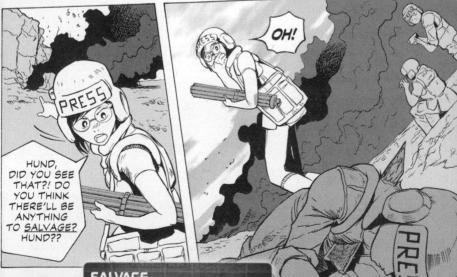

SALVAGE

\SAL vij\ (v.): to recover, save from loss

Historians have been attempting to *salvage* the remains of the Titanic for years, but attempts to raise the ship to the surface have failed.

SUPERFICIAL

\soo per FISH ul\ (adj.): hasty; shallow and phony

The politician was friendly, but in a *superficial*, unconvincing way.

INTREPID

\in TREP id\ (adj.): fearless

The *intrepid* explorer entered the ominous-looking cave without a moment's hesitation.

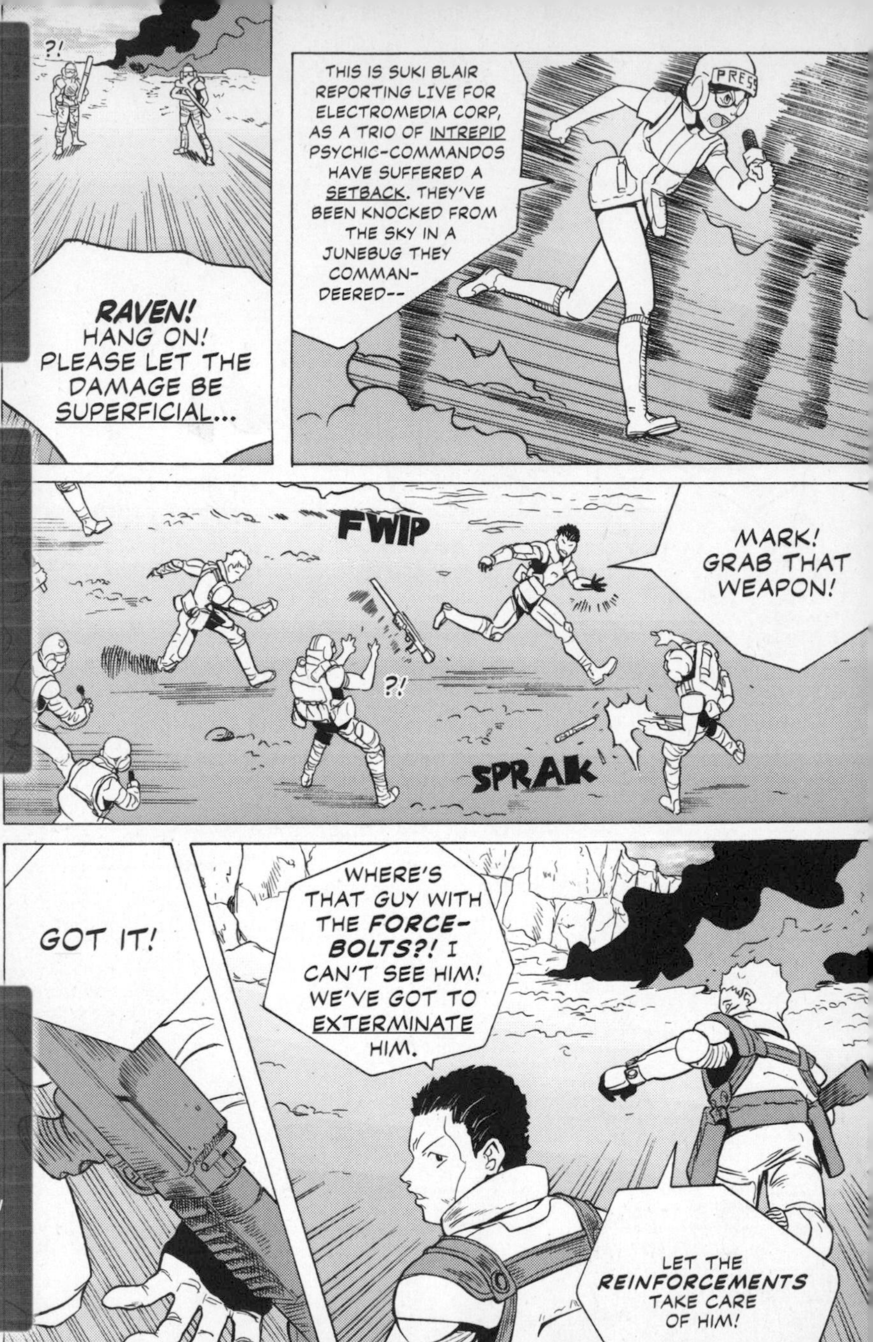
?!
RAVEN! HANG ON! PLEASE LET THE DAMAGE BE SUPERFICIAL...
THIS IS SUKI BLAIR REPORTING LIVE FOR ELECTROMEDIA CORP, AS A TRIO OF INTREPID PSYCHIC-COMMANDOS HAVE SUFFERED A SETBACK. THEY'VE BEEN KNOCKED FROM THE SKY IN A JUNEBUG THEY COMMAN-DEERED--
PRESS
FWIP
MARK! GRAB THAT WEAPON!
?!
SPRAK
GOT IT!
WHERE'S THAT GUY WITH THE FORCE-BOLTS?! I CAN'T SEE HIM! WE'VE GOT TO EXTERMINATE HIM.
LET THE REINFORCEMENTS TAKE CARE OF HIM!

SETBACK

\SET back\ (n.): change from better to worse

Despite several financial *setbacks* in the last two years, we hope to post new profits in the near future.

EXTERMINATE

\ek STUR mu nayt\ (v.): destroy completely, annihilate

When the office manager noticed that the building was infested with vermin, he hired an expert to *exterminate* them.

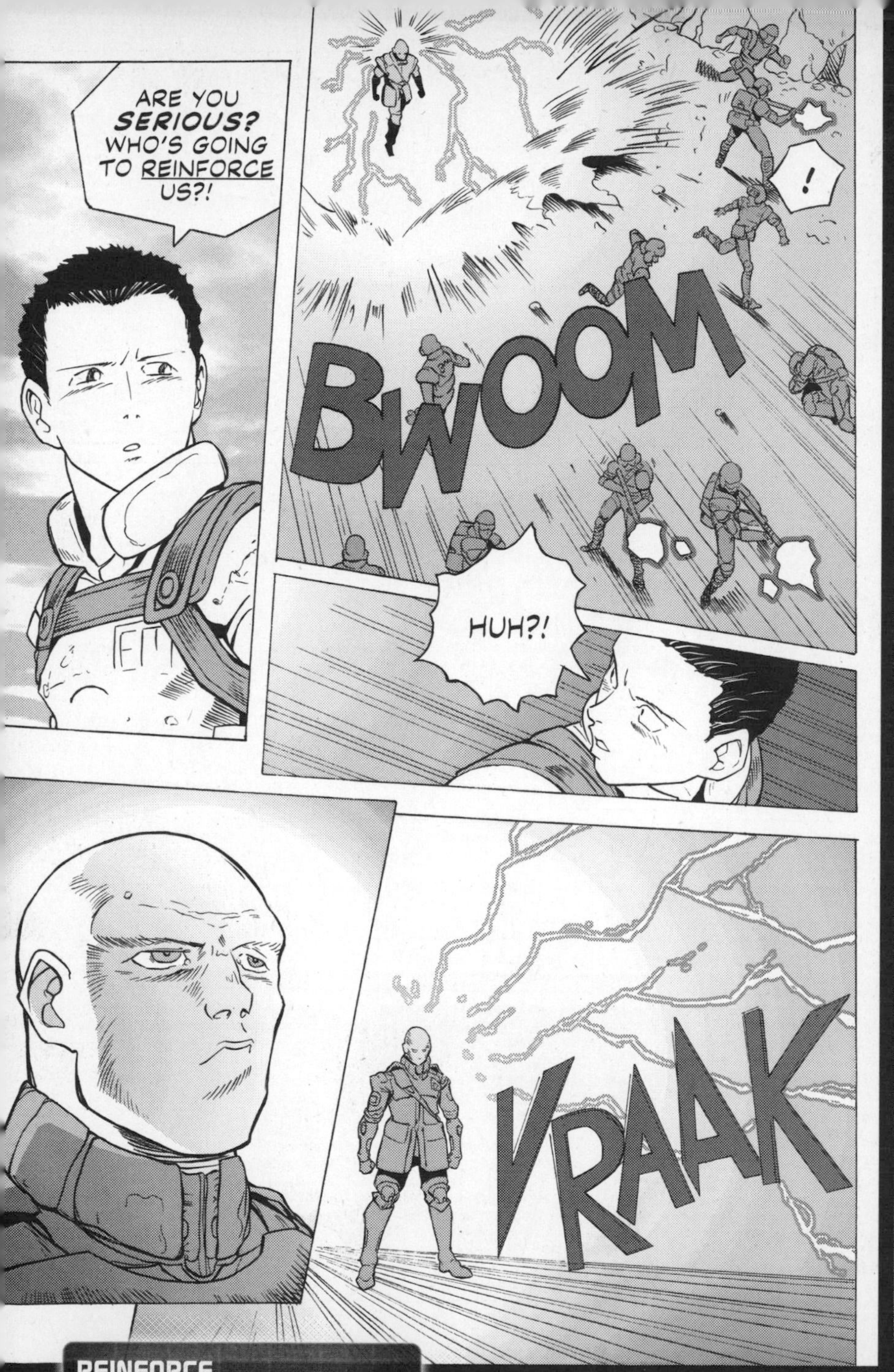
ARE YOU SERIOUS? WHO'S GOING TO REINFORCE US?!
!
BWOOM
HUH?!
VRAAK

REINFORCE

\ree in FORSS\ (v.): strengthen

Linda *reinforced* her argument by quoting several authoritative sources that all agree with her.

WHAM

THANKS--I DON'T THINK I WOULD'VE BEEN ABLE TO COUNTERACT THAT ATTACK ON MY OWN.

SURE, ANYTIME

COUNTERACT
\kown ter ACT\ (v.): to oppose the effects by contrary action

Dr. Byron started administering antibiotics to *counteract* the effects of the virus sweeping through the town.

M-MARK...
RAVEN! I DIDN'T... I ***COULDN'T*** SEE THIS. I'M SORRY...
MEDIA Corp.
OH, NO!
THE COMMANDO'S DEMEANOR TELLS THIS REPORTER ALL SHE NEEDS TO KNOW. HIS COMRADE IS GONE.

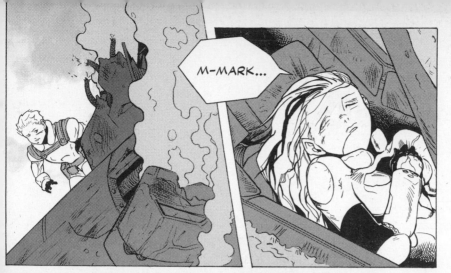

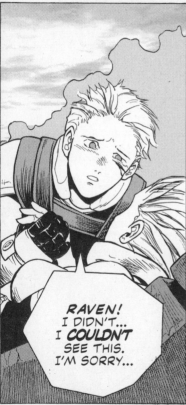

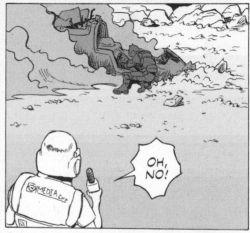

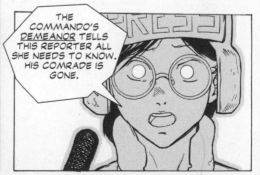

DEMEANOR

\de MEE ner\ (n.): the way a person behaves

Many psychologists believe that a person's *demeanor* during an interview—how they sit, where they hold their arms, etc.—can provide a deep insight into their character.

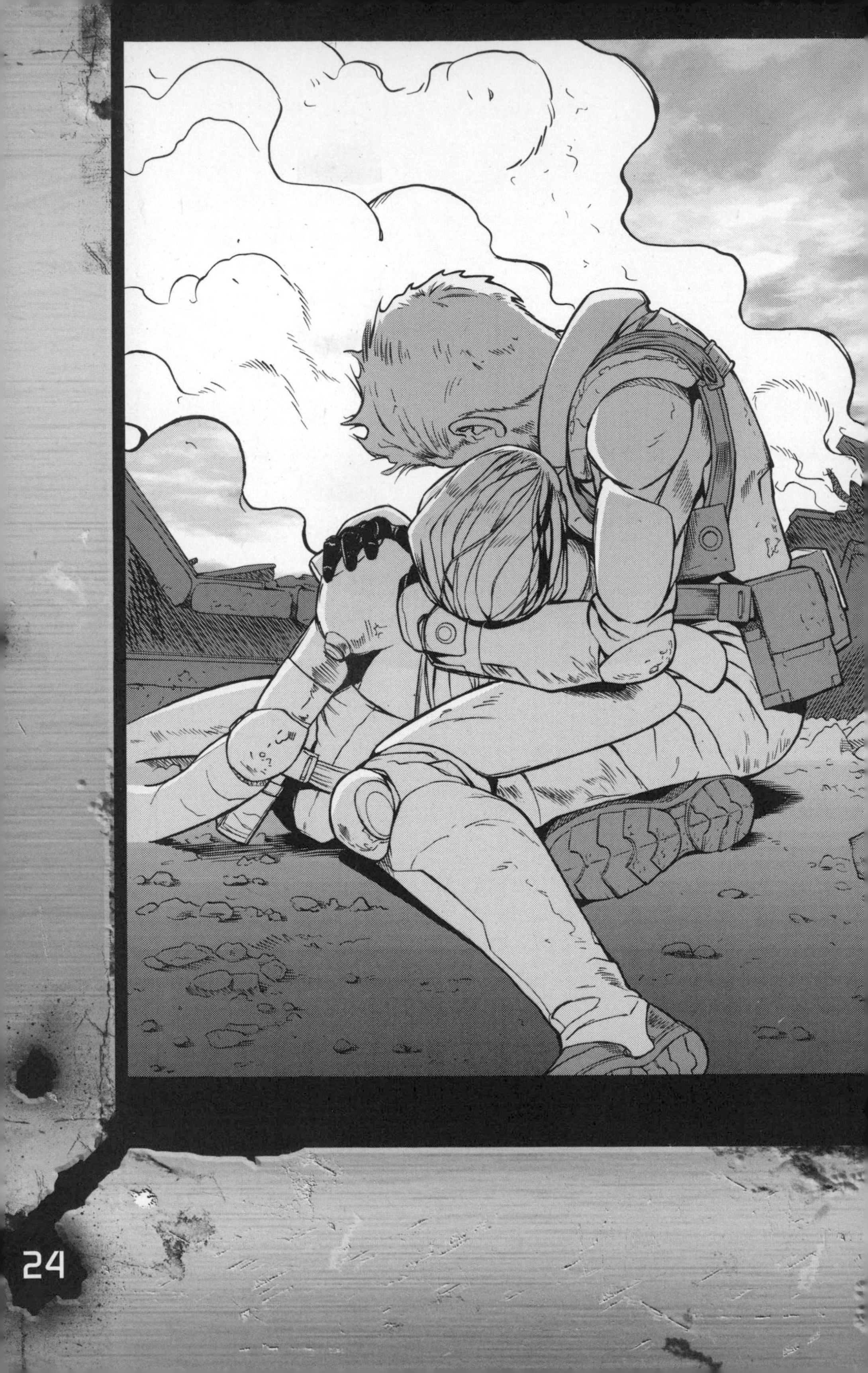

PSY★COMM

CHAPTER [2]

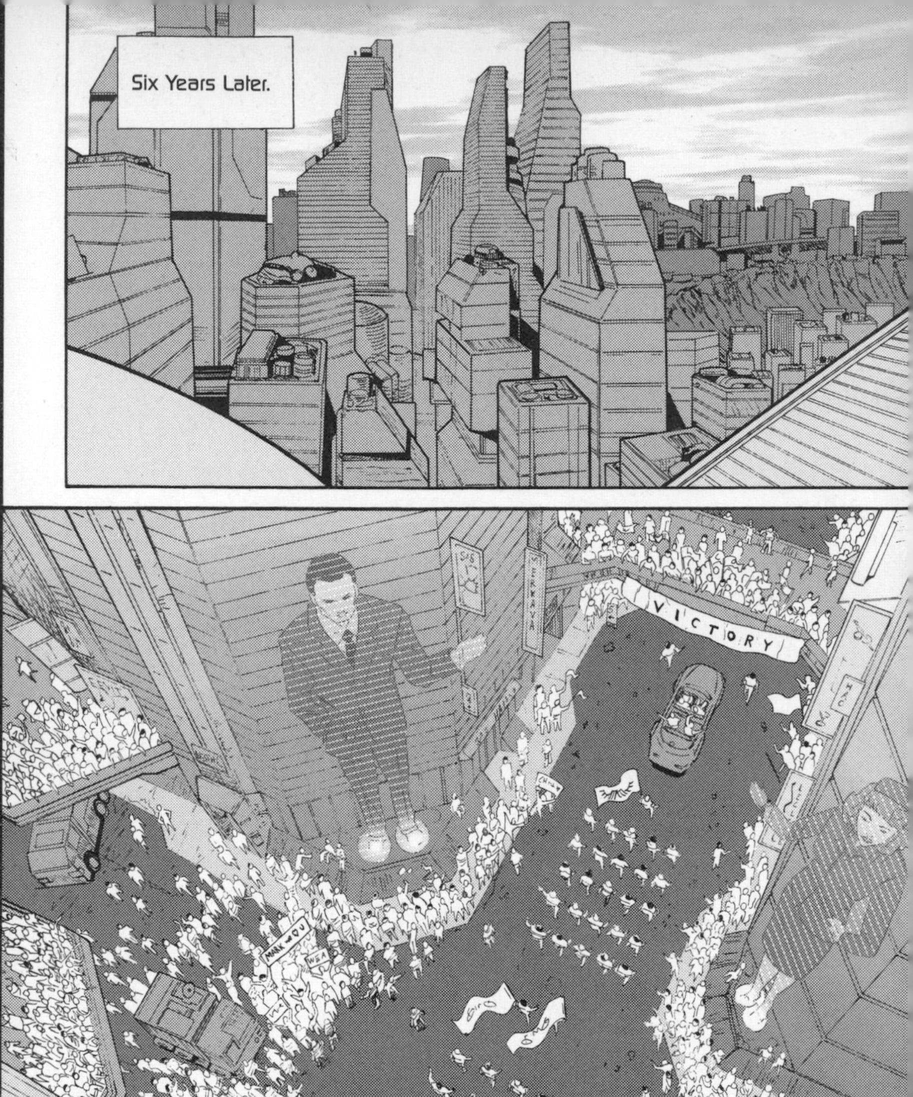
Six Years Later.
VICTORY
Throngs of adoring citizens have gathered to greet their heroes.

THRONG

\THRONG\ (n.): a large group of people, crowd

Glenda squeezed through the *throngs* of people trying to reach the box office before it closed.

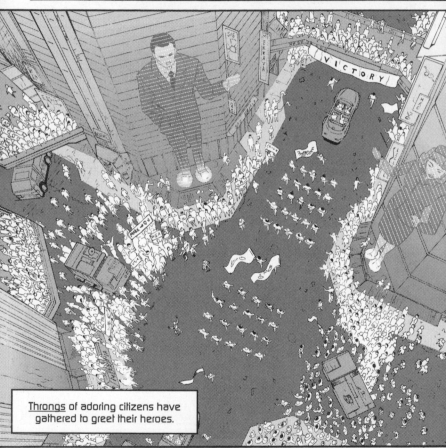

ELECTROMEDIA CORP WELCOMES HOME ITS CHAMPIONS! REMEMBER, VICTORY FOR ELECTROMEDIA MEANS PROSPERITY FOR ALL!

TUNE YOUR MEDIA CHIPS TO FF068 FOR ALL THE DETAILS OF OUR OVERPOWERING VICTORY

GEE, BOB, LOOKS LIKE A GOOD TIME FOR A REFRESHING SOLAR COLA! IT'S THE PERFECT DRINK TO ENJOY WHILE OUR HEROES REGALE US WITH THEIR WAR TALES

FANTASTIC! I REALLY LOVE ALL THE FANFARE.

PROSPERITY

\pross PER ih tee\ (n.): wealth or success

While some people have achieved wealth in life, the pursuit of *prosperity* can mean sacrificing enjoyment and leisure.

OVERPOWERING

\oh ver POW er ing\ (adj.): overwhelming

Although the foolish man prattled on senselessly, Sandra held back an *overpowering* urge to quiet him down.

REGALE

\re GAYL\ (v.): amuse, entertain

The celebrity *regaled* the crowd with tales about the mistakes and goofs in the movie.

FANFARE

\FAN fayr\ (n.): a showy public display

The actor enjoyed the *fanfare* he received at every premiere in a new city.

27

FEIGN

\FAYN\ (v.): to pretend, give a false impression; to invent falsely

Although Sean *feigned* indifference, he was very much interested in the contents of the envelope.

ENHANCE

\in HANSS\ (v.): to improve, bring to a greater level of intensity

They can sure use a hand in *enhancing* the quality of the food in the cafeteria.

CRASS

\KRASS\ (adj.): crude, unrefined

Miss Manner watched in horror as her *crass* date belched loudly and snapped his fingers at the waiter.

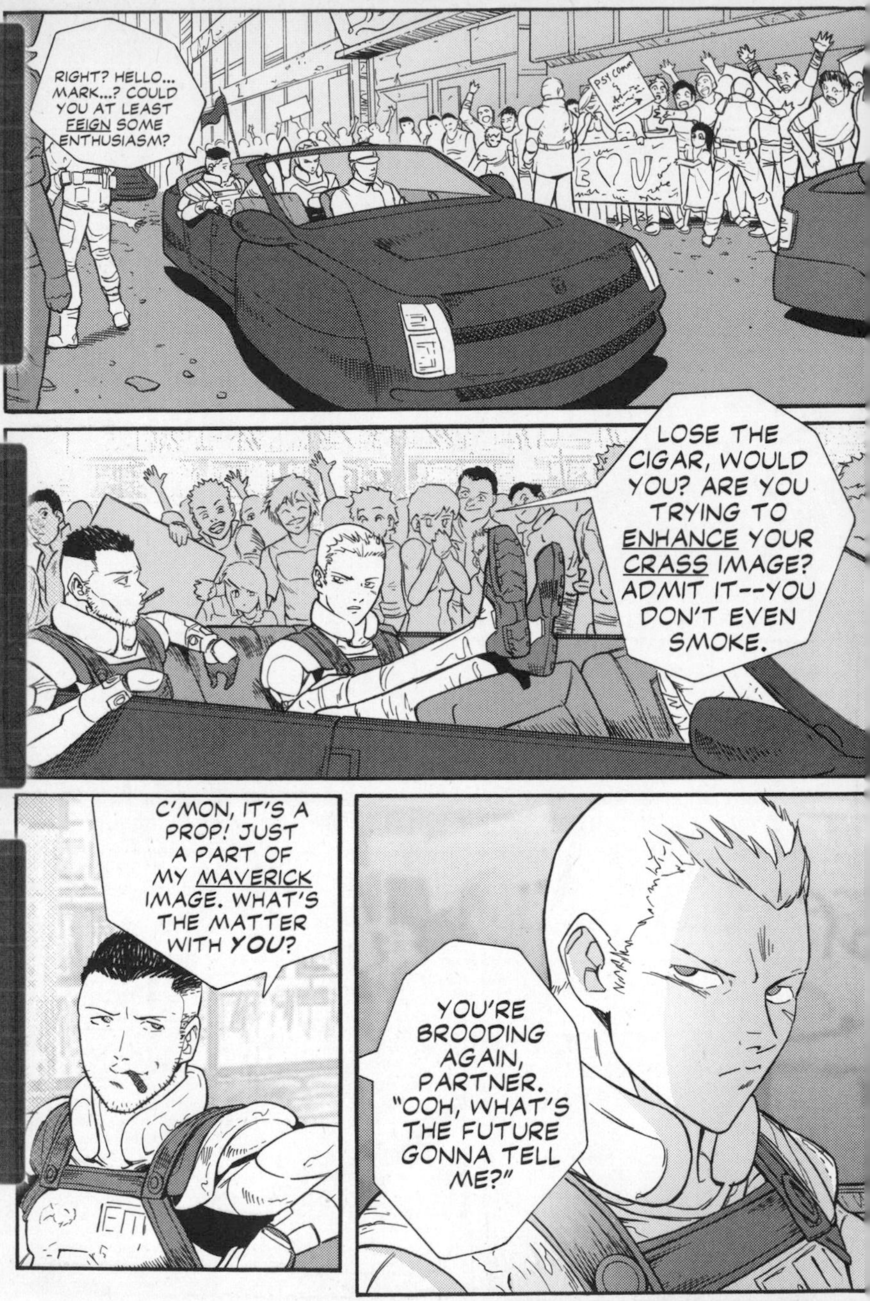
RIGHT? HELLO... MARK...? COULD YOU AT LEAST FEIGN SOME ENTHUSIASM?
LOSE THE CIGAR, WOULD YOU? ARE YOU TRYING TO ENHANCE YOUR CRASS IMAGE? ADMIT IT--YOU DON'T EVEN SMOKE.
C'MON, IT'S A PROP! JUST A PART OF MY MAVERICK IMAGE. WHAT'S THE MATTER WITH *YOU*?
YOU'RE BROODING AGAIN, PARTNER. "OOH, WHAT'S THE FUTURE GONNA TELL ME?"

MAVERICK

\MAV uh rik\ (n.): one who breaks away from group conformity and forges a new course

While possessing greater skill than the rest of the squad, the soldier had a reputation for being a *maverick* and therefore didn't advance in rank as quickly as the others.

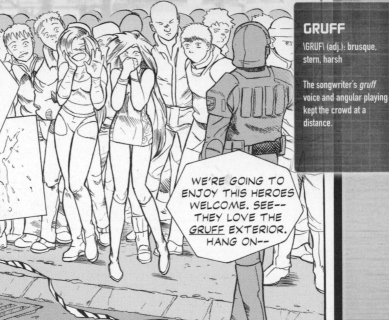

WELL, LET ME TELL YOU WHAT'S IN OUR FUTURE, OKAY?
WE'RE GOING TO ENJOY THIS HEROES WELCOME. SEE-- THEY LOVE THE GRUFF EXTERIOR. HANG ON--
HERE, LADIES! CALL MY MEDIA GUY. HE'LL SET SOMETHING UP!
REMEMBER, WE'VE GOT TO TRY AND STAY AWAKE WHILE THE COMMANDER REPRIMANDS US FOR WHATEVER WE'RE SUPPOSED TO HAVE DONE WRONG TODAY. THAT GUY'S ALWAYS LOOKING FOR A SCAPEGOAT, AND WE'RE USUALLY IT.

GRUFF

\GRUF\ (adj.): brusque, stern, harsh

The songwriter's *gruff* voice and angular playing kept the crowd at a distance.

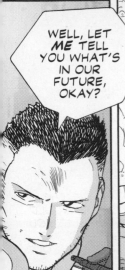

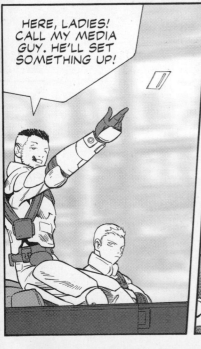

REPRIMAND

\REP ruh mand\ (v.): rebuke, admonish

Sarah didn't want to *reprimand* her son, but she needed to make sure he understood and obeyed her rules.

SCAPEGOAT

\SKAYP goht\ (n.): someone blamed for every problem

Because Charlie never bothered coming to the office, his coworkers used him as the *scapegoat* for all their mistakes.

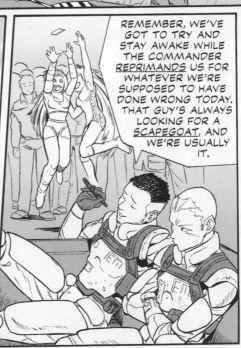

TURMOIL

\TUR moyl\ (n.): state of extreme confusion or agitation

In the *turmoil* of the fire drill, Jackie had forgotten where she left her wallet and cell phone.

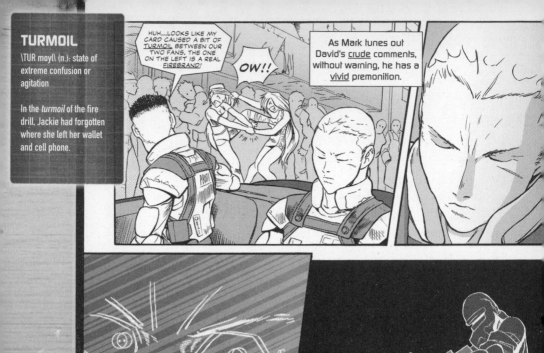

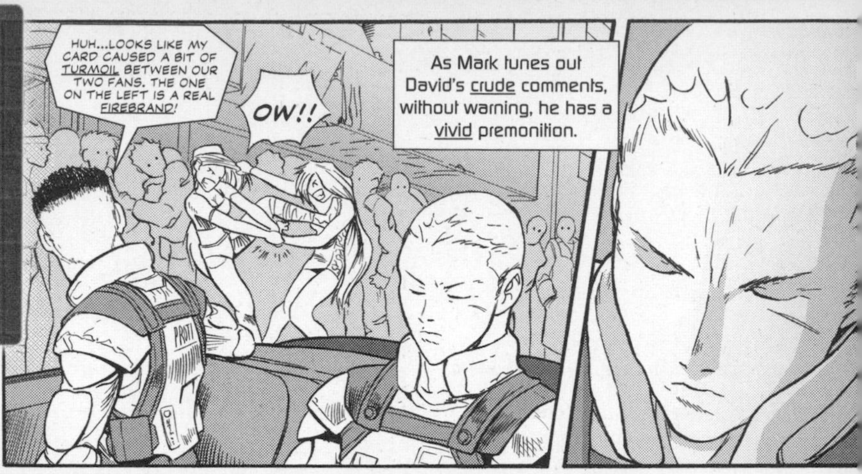
HUH...LOOKS LIKE MY CARD CAUSED A BIT OF TURMOIL BETWEEN OUR TWO FANS. THE ONE ON THE LEFT IS A REAL FIREBRAND!
OW!!
As Mark tunes out David's crude comments, without warning, he has a vivid premonition.

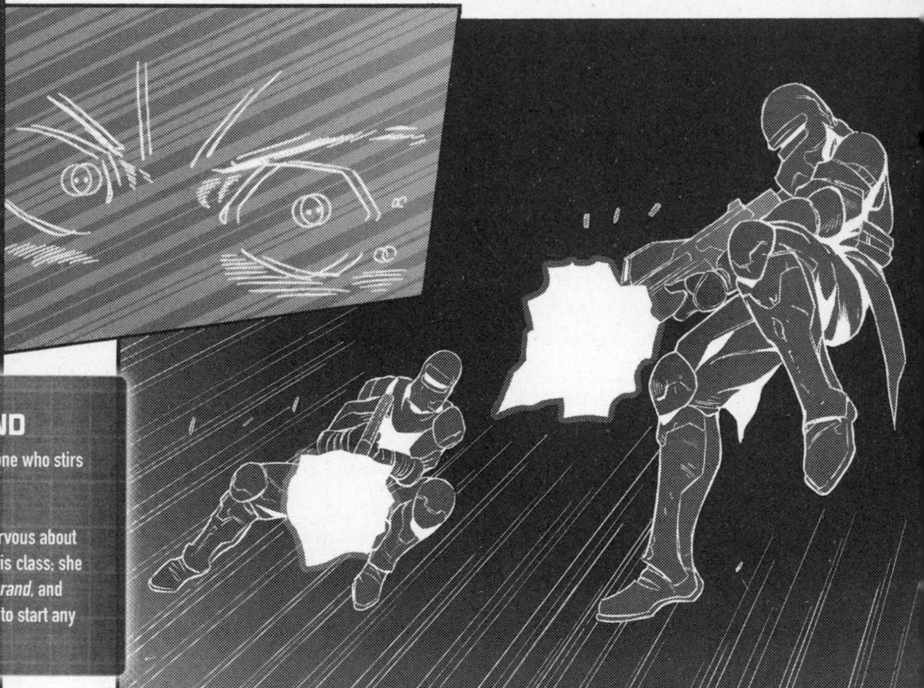

FIREBRAND

\FIYR brand\ (n.): one who stirs up trouble

Mr. Phelps was nervous about having Regine in his class; she was a known *firebrand*, and he didn't want her to start any trouble.

CRUDE

\KROOD\ (adj.): unrefined, natural; blunt, offensive

After two months of ignoring Billy's *crude* remarks, Denise summoned the courage to ask him to stop.

VIVID

\VIV id\ (adj.): bright and intense in color; strongly perceived

The *vivid* colors of the rose garden were visible from miles away.

DAVID! GET DOWN-- DUCK!
FWMP
KRANG
KRANG
KATAKA TAKA

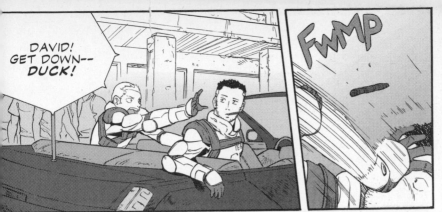

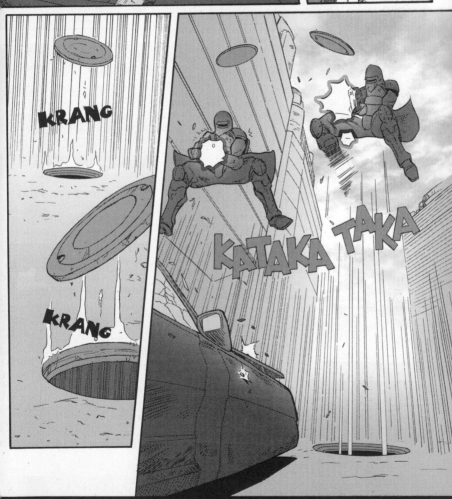

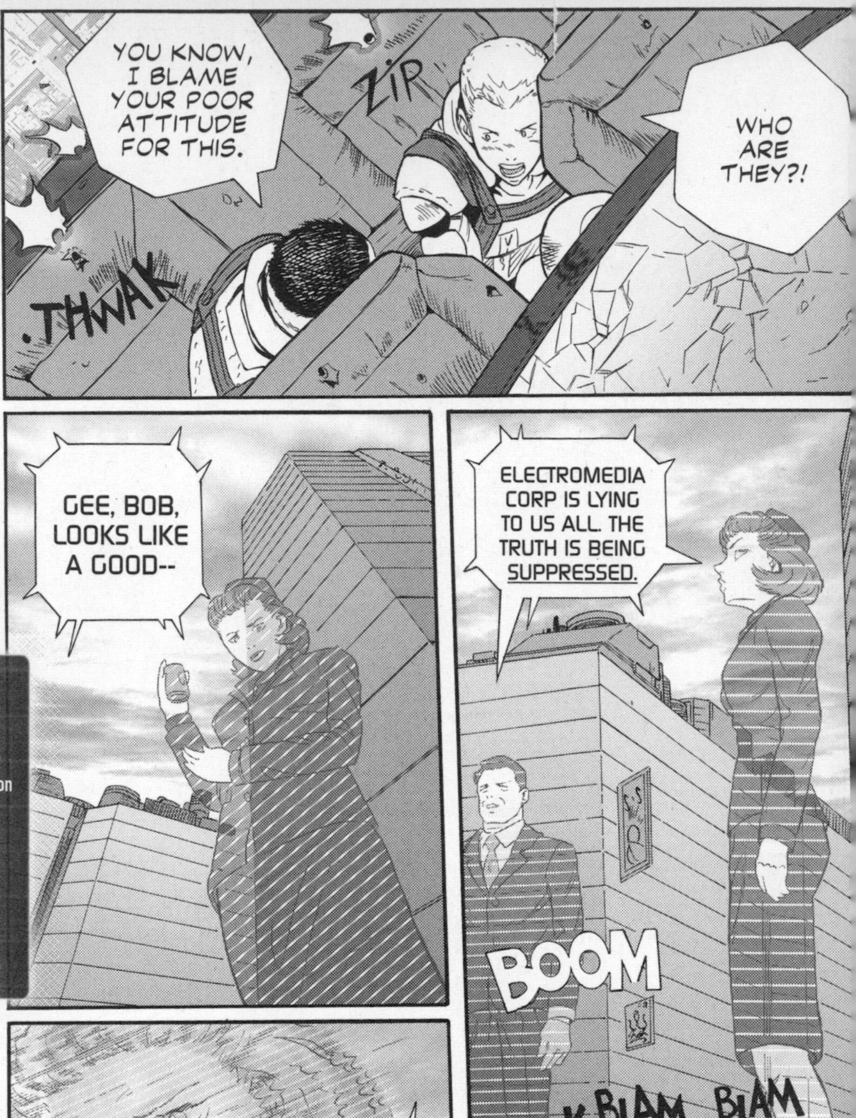

YOU KNOW, I BLAME YOUR POOR ATTITUDE FOR THIS.
ZIP
WHO ARE THEY?!
THWAK
GEE, BOB, LOOKS LIKE A GOOD--
ZRRKK-- LOOKS LIKE A G-GOOD--
ELECTROMEDIA CORP IS LYING TO US ALL. THE TRUTH IS BEING SUPPRESSED.
BOOM
K-BLAM
BLAM

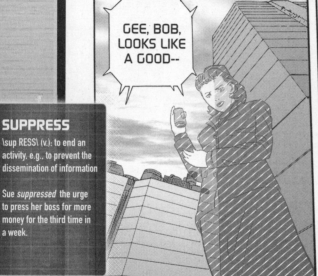

SUPPRESS

\sup RESS\ (v.): to end an activity, e.g., to prevent the dissemination of information

Sue *suppressed* the urge to press her boss for more money for the third time in a week.

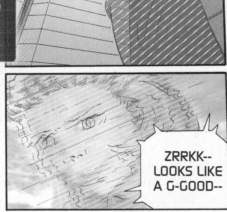

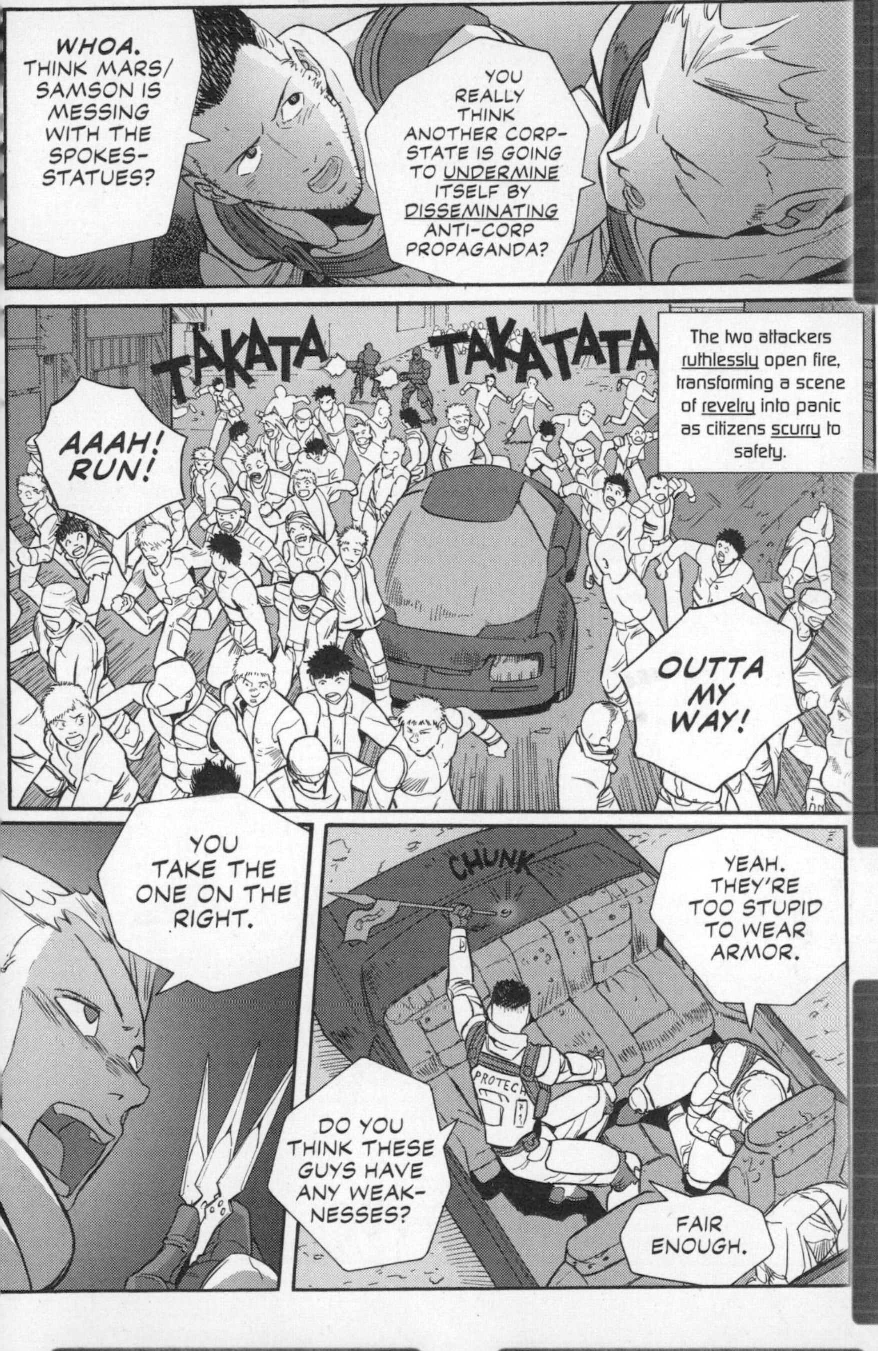
WHOA. THINK MARS/ SAMSON IS MESSING WITH THE SPOKES-STATUES?
YOU REALLY THINK ANOTHER CORP-STATE IS GOING TO UNDERMINE ITSELF BY DISSEMINATING ANTI-CORP PROPAGANDA?
TAKATA
TAKATATA
The two attackers ruthlessly open fire, transforming a scene of revelry into panic as citizens scurry to safety.
AAAH! RUN!
OUTTA MY WAY!
YOU TAKE THE ONE ON THE RIGHT.
CHUNK
YEAH. THEY'RE TOO STUPID TO WEAR ARMOR.
DO YOU THINK THESE GUYS HAVE ANY WEAK-NESSES?
FAIR ENOUGH.

UNDERMINE

\un der MIYN\ (v.): to sabotage, thwart

Rumors of his infidelities *undermined* the star's marriage, which eventually ended in divorce.

DISSEMINATE

\dih SEM uh nayt\ (v.): to spread far and wide

The wire service *disseminates* information so rapidly that events seem to get reported before they happen.

RUTHLESS

\ROOTH less\ (adj.): merciless, compassionless

The Terminator was a perfectly *ruthless* killer, not possessing any emotions or compassion for its victims.

REVELRY

\REV ul ree\ (n.): boisterous festivity

An atmosphere of *revelry* filled the school after its basketball team's surprising victory.

SCURRY

\SKUR ree\ (v.): scamper, run lightly

Robin had trouble sleeping through the noise of squirrels *scurrying* across the roof.

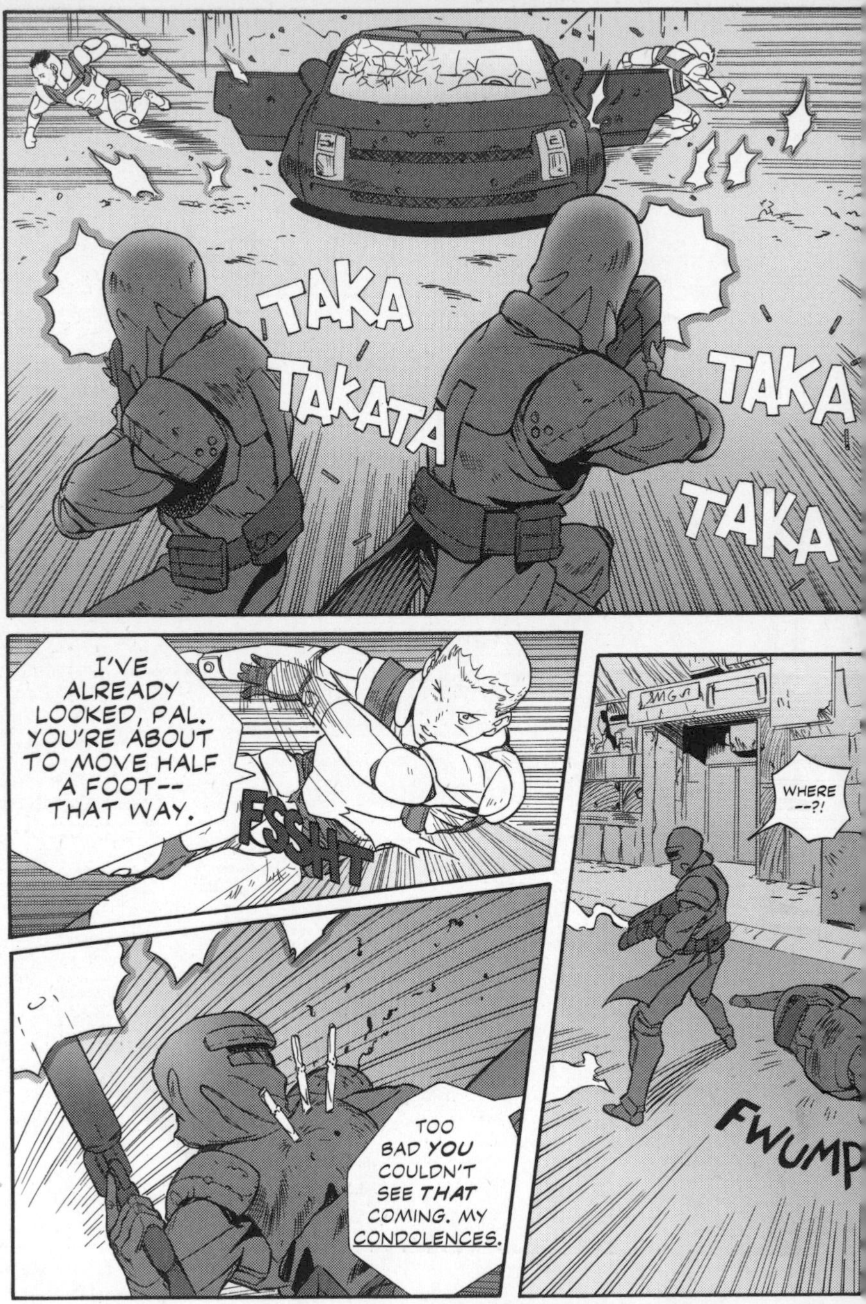
TAKA
TAKATA
TAKA
TAKA
I'VE ALREADY LOOKED, PAL. YOU'RE ABOUT TO MOVE HALF A FOOT-- THAT WAY.
FSSHT
TOO BAD *YOU* COULDN'T SEE *THAT* COMING. MY CONDOLENCES.
WHERE --?!
FWUMP

CONDOLENCE

\kon DOH lens\ (n.): sympathy for a person's misfortune

After Fred's grandmother passed away we visited his house to offer our *condolences*.

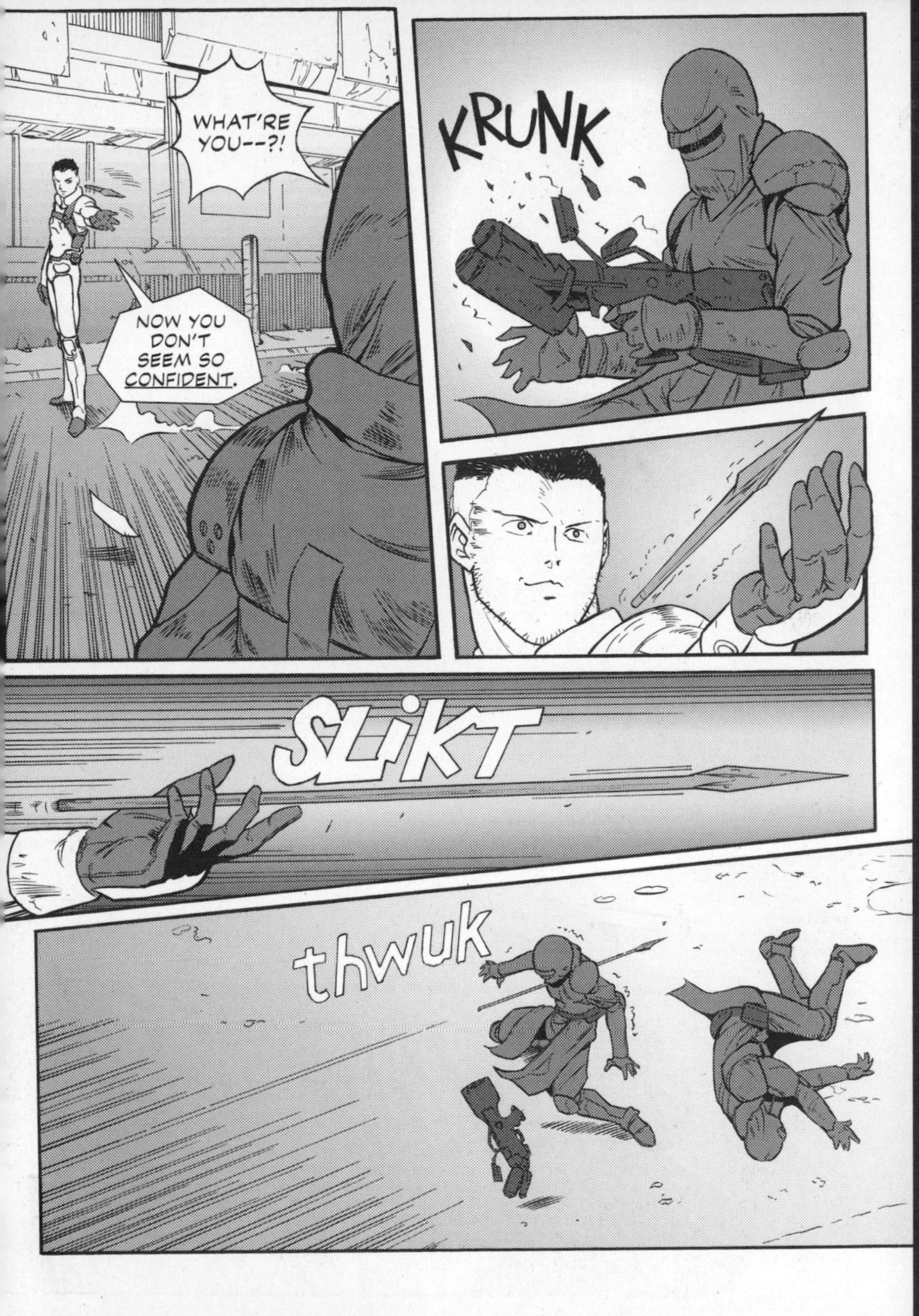
WHAT'RE YOU--?!
NOW YOU DON'T SEEM SO CONFIDENT.
KRUNK
SLIKT
thwuk

CONFIDENT

\KON fi dent\ (adj.): self-assured

Confident that she was going to ace the exam, Cynthia strode into class with a broad smile across her face.

UNFETTER

\un FET er\ (v.): to free from restrictions

The dog owners fighting the ordinance believe they should have the right to *unfetter* their dogs occasionally, rather than keep them on leashes at all times.

NONCHALANT

\non shuh LAHNT\ (adj.): calm, casual, seemingly unexcited

Humphrey Bogart often played characters who were remarkably *nonchalant*, remaining calm and composed even in the most difficult situations.

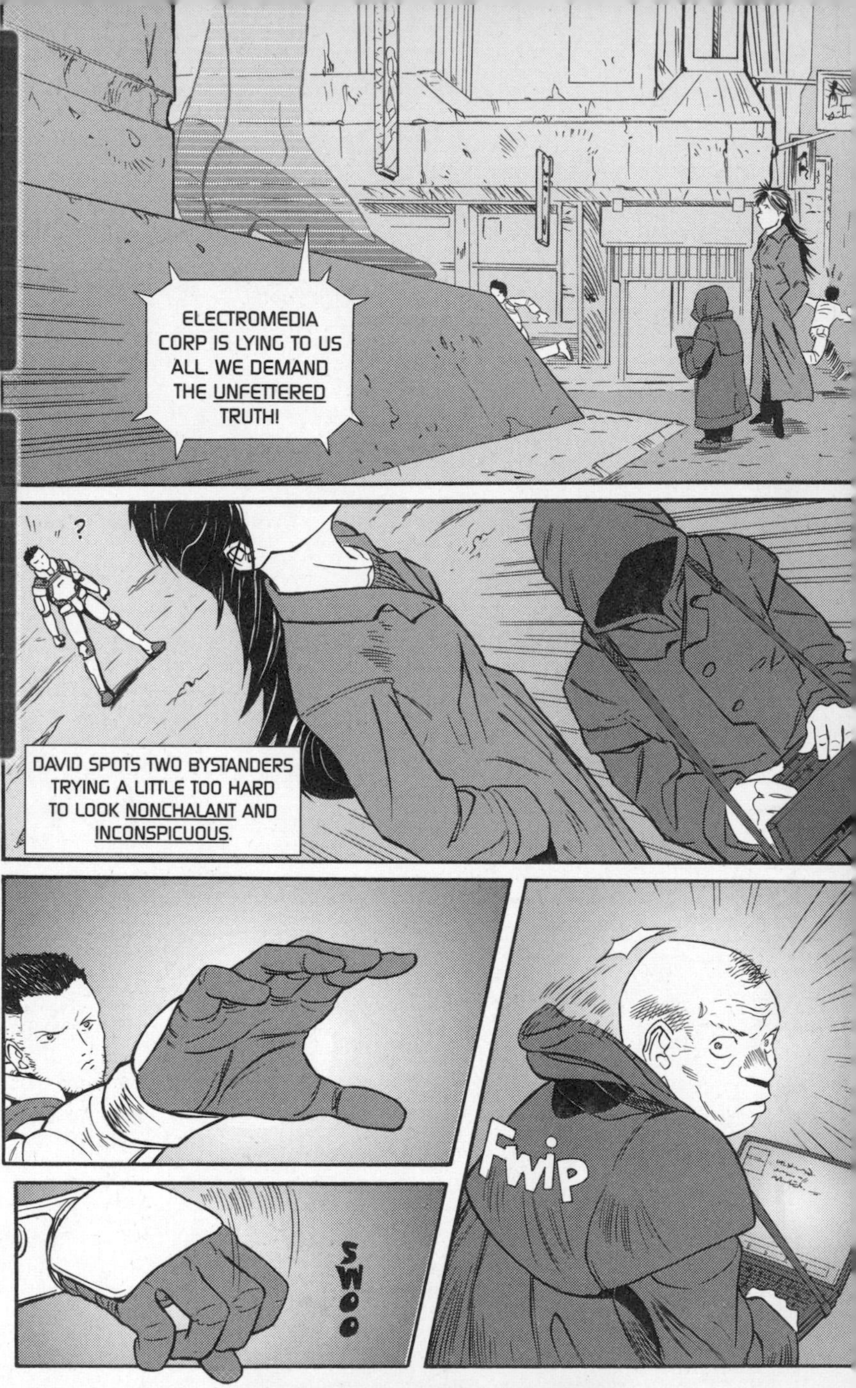
ELECTROMEDIA CORP IS LYING TO US ALL. WE DEMAND THE UNFETTERED TRUTH!
?
DAVID SPOTS TWO BYSTANDERS TRYING A LITTLE TOO HARD TO LOOK NONCHALANT AND INCONSPICUOUS.
SWOO
Fwip

INCONSPICUOUS

\in con SPIK yoo us\ (adj.): not easily noticeable

Jason didn't want his roommate to notice the new phone he had bought, so he placed it in as *inconspicuous* a corner as possible.

HEY! YOU TWO! GET OVER HERE! IT'S FUTILE TO RUN.
MERKA
RUMMBLE
RIP
RIP
AH!

FUTILE

\FYOO tiyl\ (adj.): useless; hopeless

"It is *futile* to resist," claimed the invading general. "our armies outnumber yours five to one."

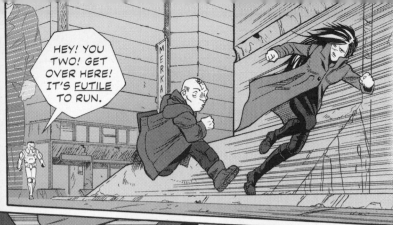

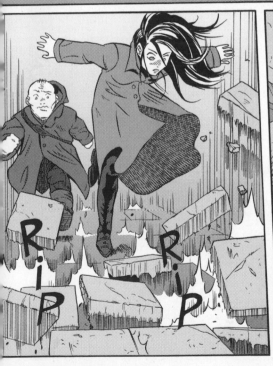

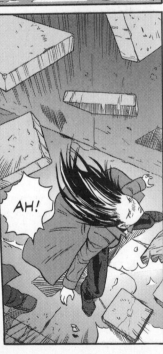

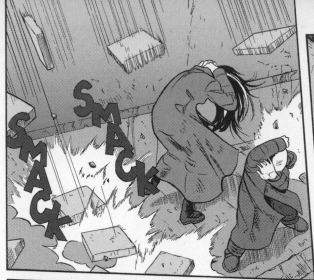

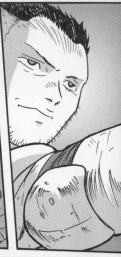

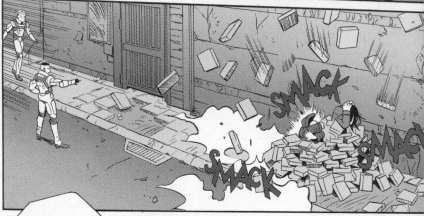

SMACK
SMACK
SMACK
SMACK
YOU CAN'T DO THIS! I HAVE **RIGHTS!** WE ALL HAVE RIGHTS! ELECTROMEDIA IS NOT THE BENEVOLENT CORPORATION YOU THINK IT IS.
DAVID, WAIT. **STOP!** YOU'RE GONNA **KILL** THEM! DON'T B SO MERCILESS

BENEVOLENT

\bu NEV uh lint\ (adj.): friendly and helpful

Ben and Eve volunteer at the shelter, which is typical of their *benevolent* nature.

MERCILESS

\MER see less\ (adj.): without pity

The *merciless* dictator ordered an entire village to be imprisoned for yelling at him when he rode through their town.

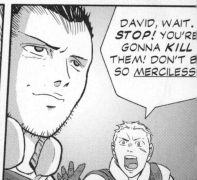

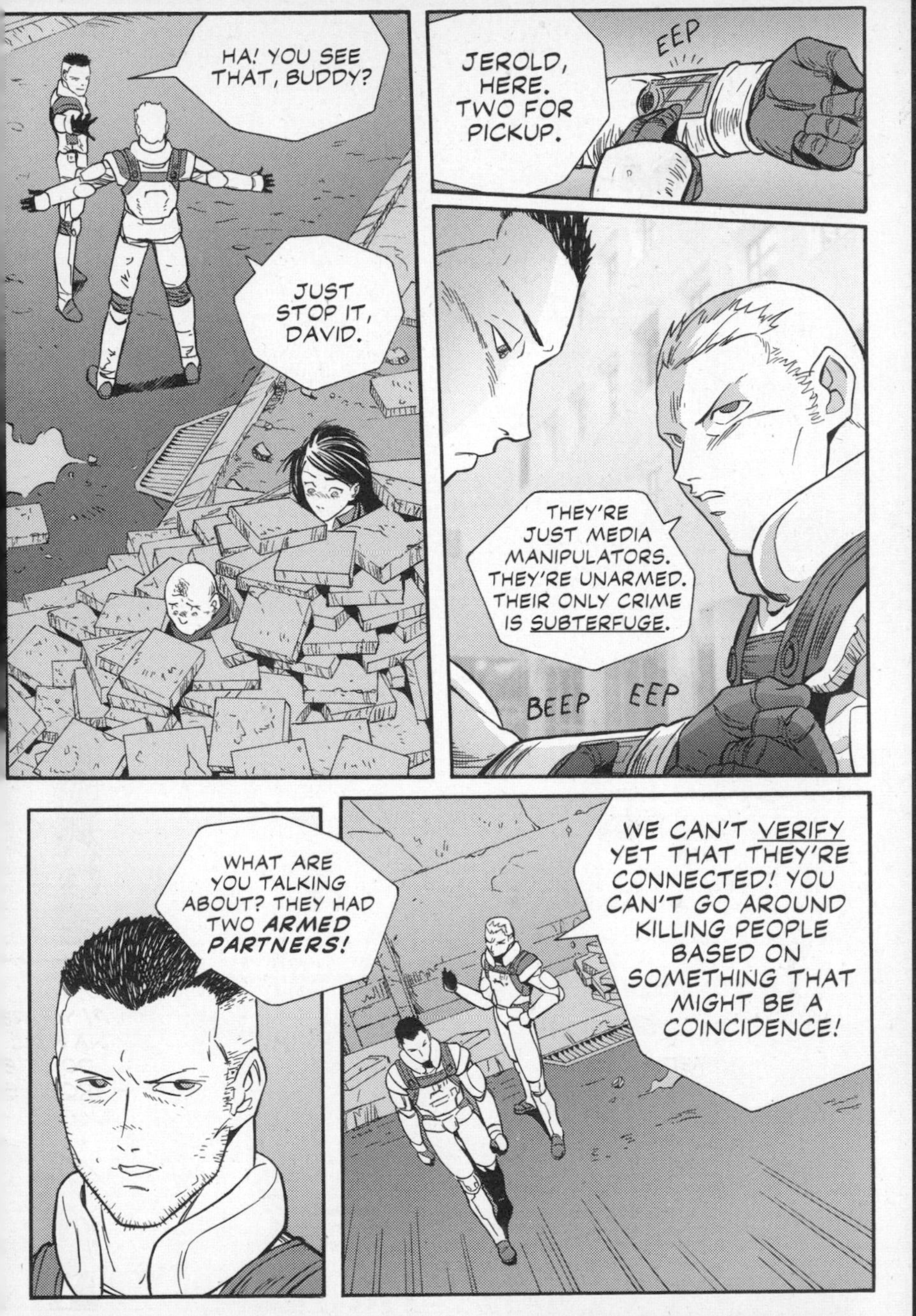
HA! YOU SEE THAT, BUDDY?
JUST STOP IT, DAVID.
EEP
JEROLD, HERE. TWO FOR PICKUP.
THEY'RE JUST MEDIA MANIPULATORS. THEY'RE UNARMED. THEIR ONLY CRIME IS SUBTERFUGE.
BEEP EEP
WHAT ARE YOU TALKING ABOUT? THEY HAD TWO ARMED PARTNERS!
WE CAN'T VERIFY YET THAT THEY'RE CONNECTED! YOU CAN'T GO AROUND KILLING PEOPLE BASED ON SOMETHING THAT MIGHT BE A COINCIDENCE!

SUBTERFUGE

\SUB ter fyooj\ (n.): deceptive strategy

Spies who are not skilled in the art of *subterfuge* are generally exposed before too long.

VERIFY

\VER ih fiy\ (v.): substantiate, confirm

Before we can go any further with the experiment, we need to *verify* that the results we've obtained are in fact accurate.

YOU KNOW MY POWERS OF PERCEPTION CAN'T EXTEND TO THE LONG-TERM FUTURE. AND I DON'T ALWAYS CATCH THE SHORT-TERM STUFF...
...BUT SOMETIMES YOU SCARE ME, MAN.
LOOK, IF THINGS WERE GONNA GO REAL BAD, YOU'D HAVE TOLD ME BY NOW.
DAVID, THAT DOESN'T MAKE ANY--
HEY! YOU TWO CONCEITED MAGGOTS DONE JAWING?
YOU TWO WOULDN'T HAVE SENSE ENOUGH TO COME IN OUT OF THE RAIN IF I DIDN'T TELL YOU!

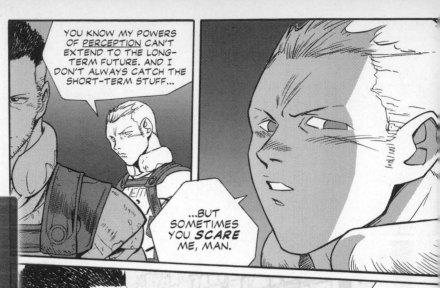

PERCEPTION

\per SEP shun\ (n.): act of seeing or comprehending: ability to see or understand

The errors in carrying out the plan were the result of poor *perception* of the desired result.

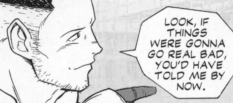

CONCEITED

\kon SEET id\ (adj.): holding an unduly high opinion of oneself, vain

The author was too *conceited* to acknowledge that any revision to the novel was necessary.

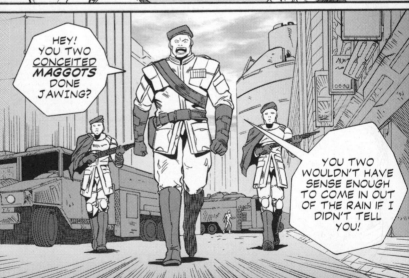

NO NEED TO TREAT US TO ONE OF YOUR FAMOUS HARANGUES, SIR. I THINK WE CAN PRETTY MUCH STOP THE RAIN AT THIS POINT.
KLAK
DON'T GOAD ME, DAVID! LET ME MAKE THIS CRYSTAL CLEAR. YOU ARE STARS TO THE PEOPLE OF THIS CITY. THAT MEANS YOUR FLESH IS EXPENSIVE, AND THE BIG BOSSES CAN'T STAND TO WASTE MONEY ON THEIR INVESTMENTS.
POKE
BUT MORE THAN THAT, IF YOU DON'T TAKE A THREAT SERIOUSLY-- THEY DON'T. THERE'S A REASON WE HAVE THESE WARS THE WAY WE DO.
WE DON'T LIKE SEEING THE POPULACE UPSET...OR HURT. IT'S YOUR JOB TO PACIFY THE CIVILIANS. NOW, ARE WE CLEAR, MISTER?
YES, SIR.
I SAID, ARE WE CLEAR?!
YES, SIR!

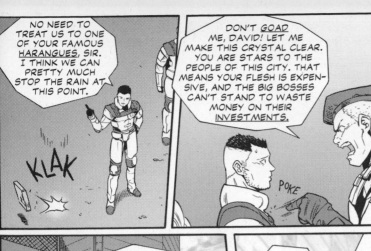

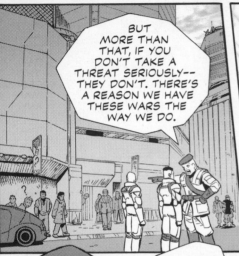

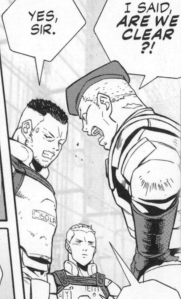

HARANGUE

\hu RANG\ (n.): pompous speech, tirade

Although Richard's criticism of the company threatened to derail the board meeting, the chairman let him finish his *harangue* before adjourning.

GOAD

\GOAD\ (v.): to prod or urge

Denise *goaded* her sister Leigh into running the marathon with her.

INVESTMENT

\in VEST mint\ (n.): a commitment of time, support, or money

After working so intensely on the initial research and proposal, Adrian felt that he had already made a significant *investment* in the project's success.

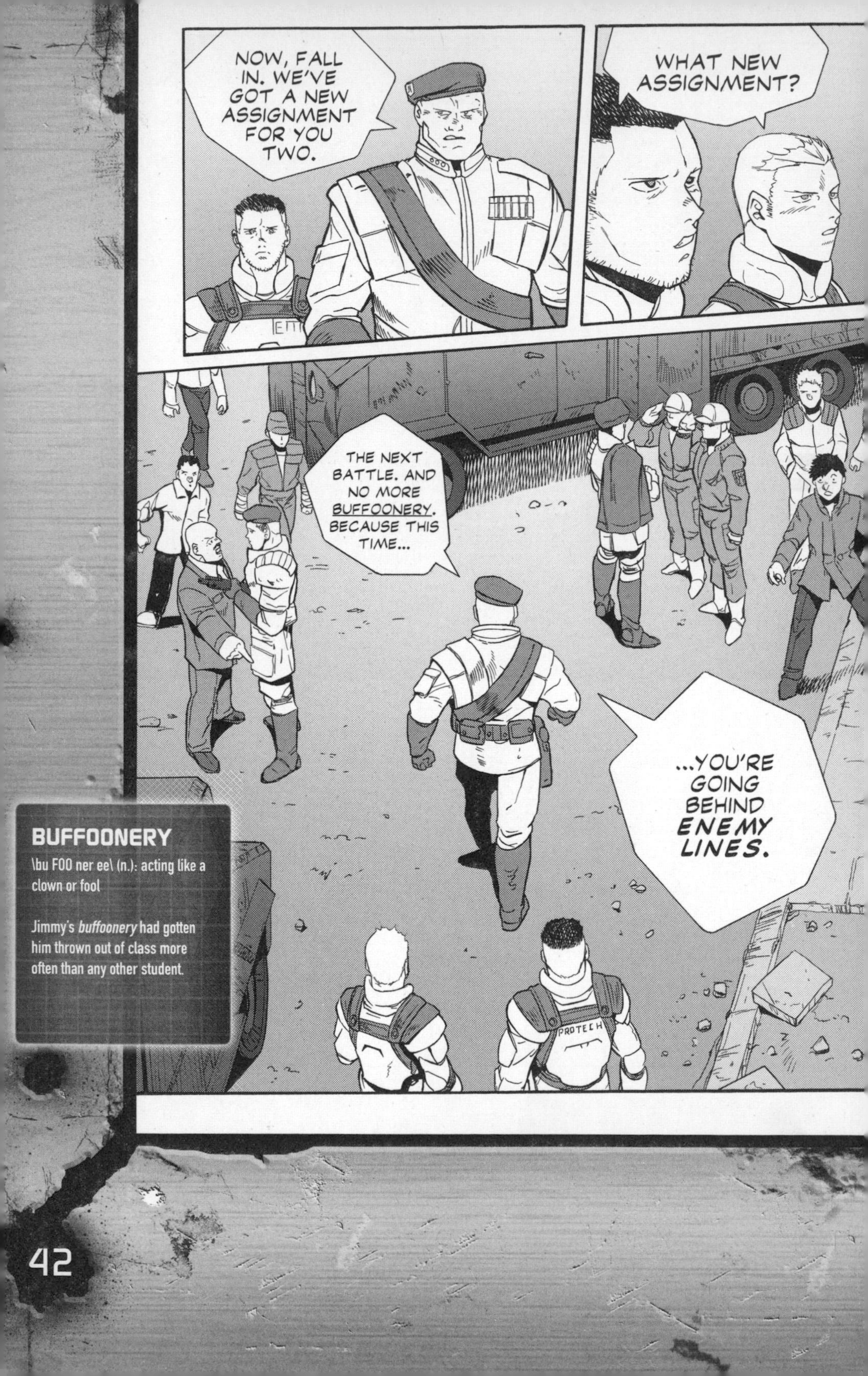
NOW, FALL IN. WE'VE GOT A NEW ASSIGNMENT FOR YOU TWO.
WHAT NEW ASSIGNMENT?
THE NEXT BATTLE. AND NO MORE BUFFOONERY. BECAUSE THIS TIME...
...YOU'RE GOING BEHIND ENEMY LINES.
PROTECH

BUFFOONERY

\bu FOO ner ee\ (n.): acting like a clown or fool

Jimmy's *buffoonery* had gotten him thrown out of class more often than any other student.

PSY★COMM

CHAPTER [3]

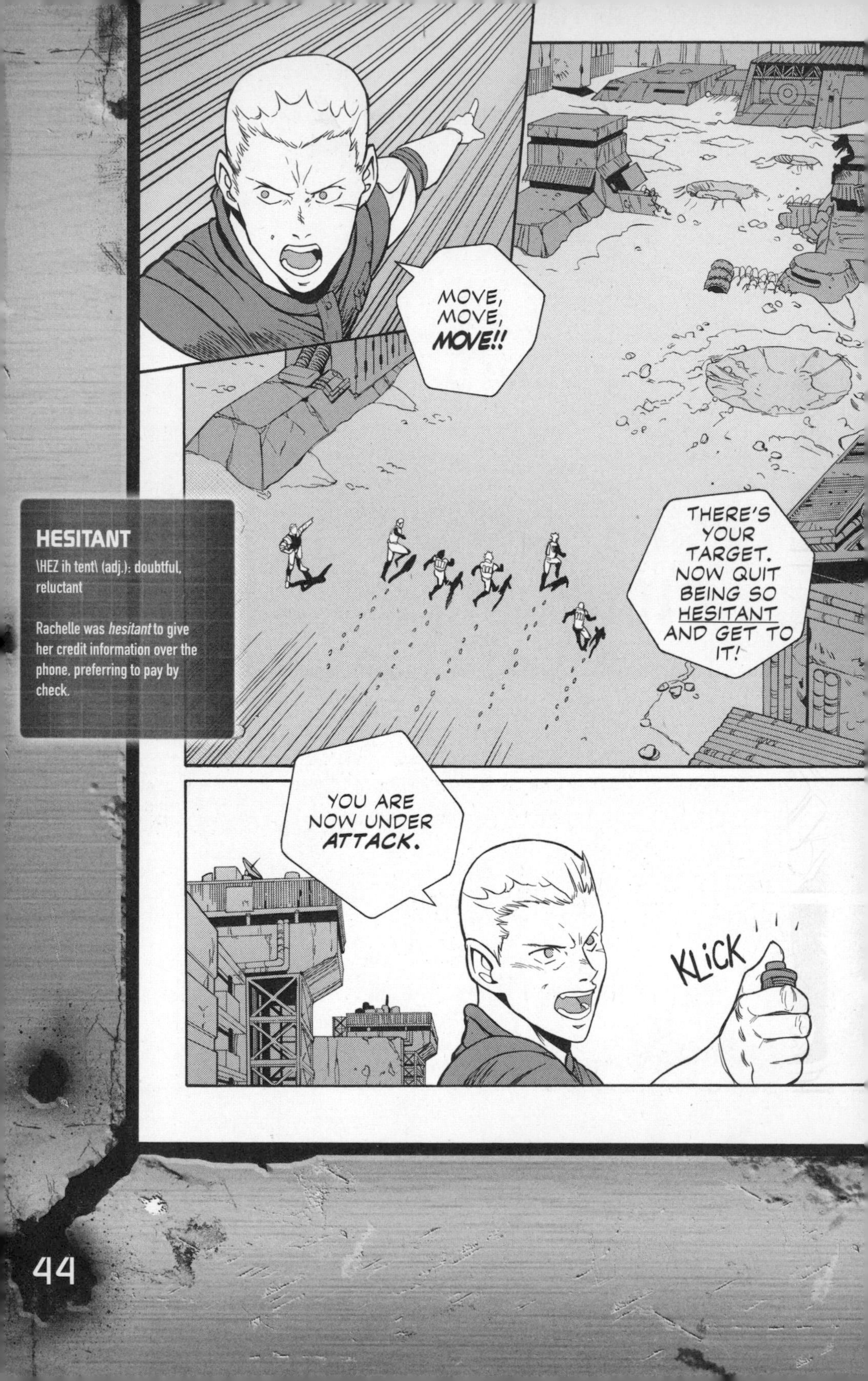
MOVE, MOVE, MOVE!!
THERE'S YOUR TARGET. NOW QUIT BEING SO HESITANT AND GET TO IT!
YOU ARE NOW UNDER ATTACK.
KLICK

HESITANT

\HEZ ih tent\ (adj.): doubtful, reluctant

Rachelle was *hesitant* to give her credit information over the phone, preferring to pay by check.

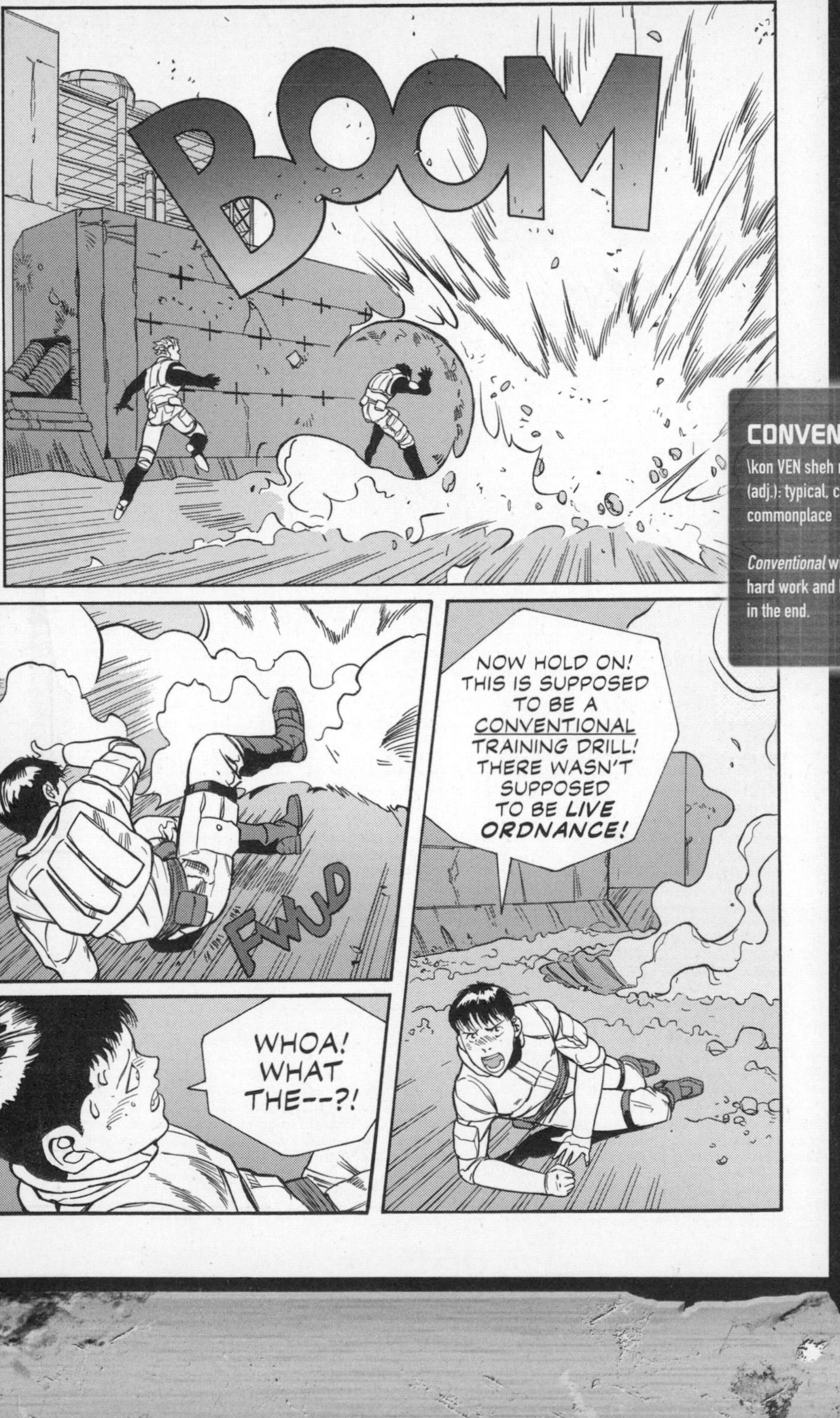
BOOM
FWUD
WHOA! WHAT THE--?!
NOW HOLD ON! THIS IS SUPPOSED TO BE A CONVENTIONAL TRAINING DRILL! THERE WASN'T SUPPOSED TO BE *LIVE ORDNANCE!*

CONVENTIONAL

\kon VEN sheh null\
(adj.): typical, customary, commonplace

Conventional wisdom holds that hard work and honesty pays off in the end.

WHAT DO YOU THINK THIS IS, SOME KID'S PRANK?
YOU'VE GOTTA BE READY FOR ANYTHING!
REMEMBER YOUR TARG-- UH, STEP OVER HERE.
BOOM
!!
DON'T WORRY, NOVICE. I KNEW IT WOULD MISS YOU.
AS LONG AS YOU WERE ON MY LEFT.

PRANK

\PRANK\ (n.): practical joke

Gary was notorious for playing tricks and *pranks* on all his coworkers.

NOVICE

\NAHV is\ (n.): beginner, apprentice

Although Jen is only a *novice* at sailing, she shows great potential.

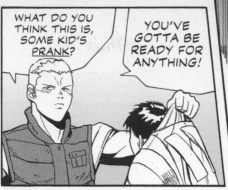

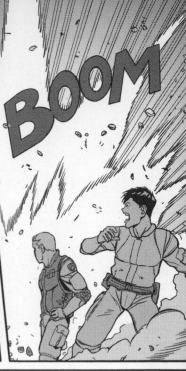

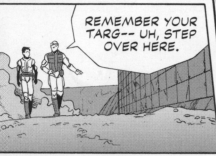

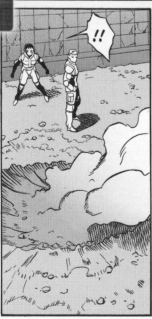

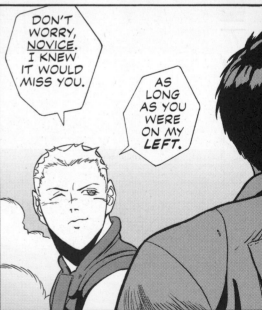

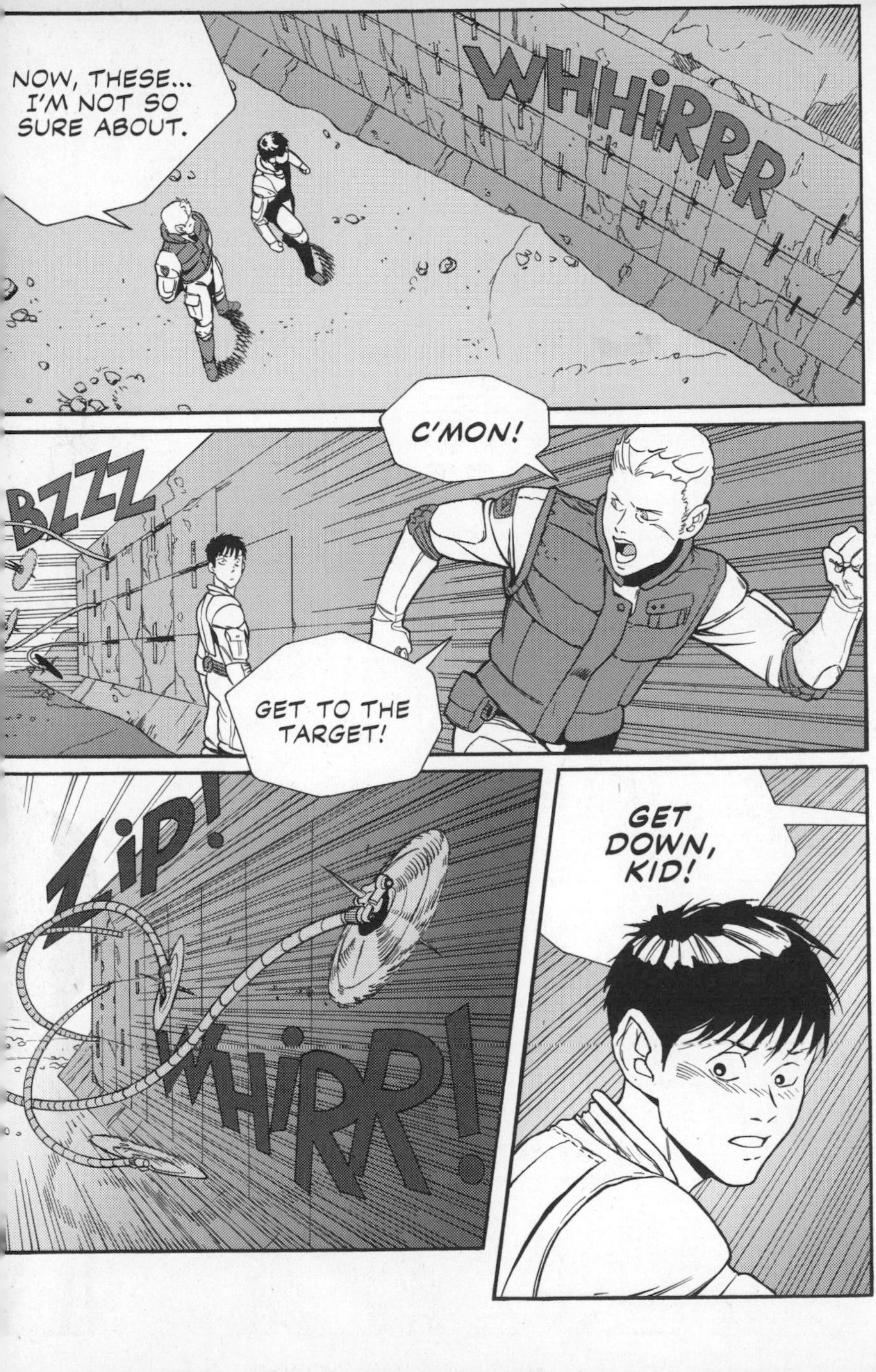
NOW, THESE... I'M NOT SO SURE ABOUT.
WHHIRRR
C'MON!
BZZZ
GET TO THE TARGET!
ZIP!
WHIRR!
GET DOWN, KID!

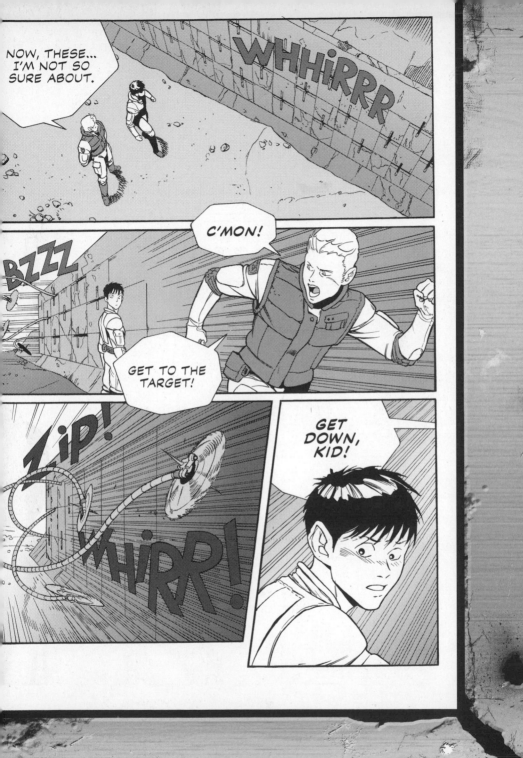

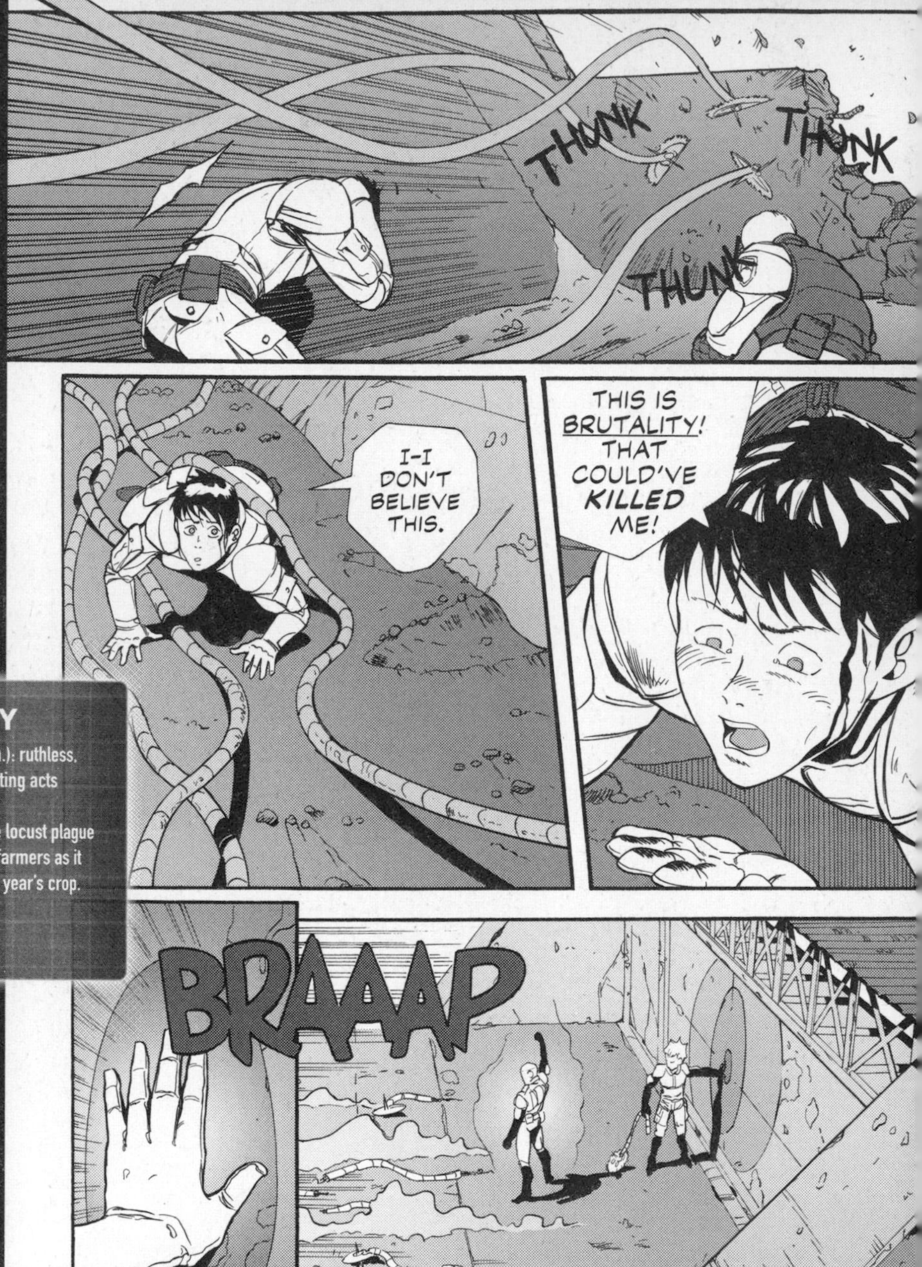
THUNK
THUNK
THUNK
I-I DON'T BELIEVE THIS.
THIS IS BRUTALITY! THAT COULD'VE KILLED ME!
BRAAAP

BRUTALITY

\broo TAL ih tee\ (n.): ruthless, cruel, and unrelenting acts

The *brutality* of the locust plague overwhelmed the farmers as it destroyed a whole year's crop.

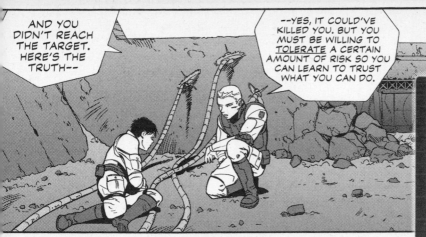

AND YOU DIDN'T REACH THE TARGET. HERE'S THE TRUTH--
--YES, IT COULD'VE KILLED YOU. BUT YOU MUST BE WILLING TO TOLERATE A CERTAIN AMOUNT OF RISK SO YOU CAN LEARN TO TRUST WHAT YOU CAN DO.
LISTEN UP! YOU ALL HAVE YOUR OWN ABILITIES, AND YOU NEED TO NURTURE THEM. BUT THAT'S NOT ALWAYS ENOUGH. IF YOU'RE WITH A FUTURE-SEER, AND HE SAYS DUCK--YOU DUCK! IF YOU'RE A SEER NEXT TO A SHIELD-MAKER, HAVE HIM MAKE A SHIELD.
FIP
FIP
YOU NEED TO BE COLLABORATORS. IF YOU LEARN TO WORK TOGETHER, YOU'LL SURVIVE...IF YOU'RE LUCKY. INHIBIT YOUR FEARS AND DO YOUR BEST TO PROTECT YOUR COMRADES.
OR, AT LEAST TRY. RIGHT, RAVEN?

TOLERATE

\TOL uh rayt\ (v.): to endure, permit; to respect others

Peter was unable to *tolerate* the noise from below any longer, so he went downstairs to ask his neighbor not to play the drums at four in the morning.

NURTURE

\NOOR chur\ (v.): to help develop, cultivate

Scientists today believe that dinosaurs lived in groups so mothers could better *nurture* their babies when they were born.

COLLABORATOR

\ku LAB u RAY tor\ (n.): someone who helps on a task

Lucy was Chuck's *collaborator* on the file; he did the research and she wrote the briefs.

INHIBIT

\in HIB it\ (v.): to hold back, prevent, restrain

John's harsh criticism *inhibited* the free exchange of ideas on the project.

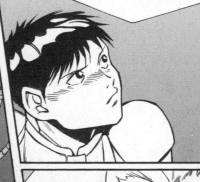

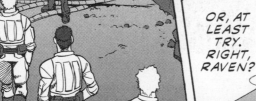

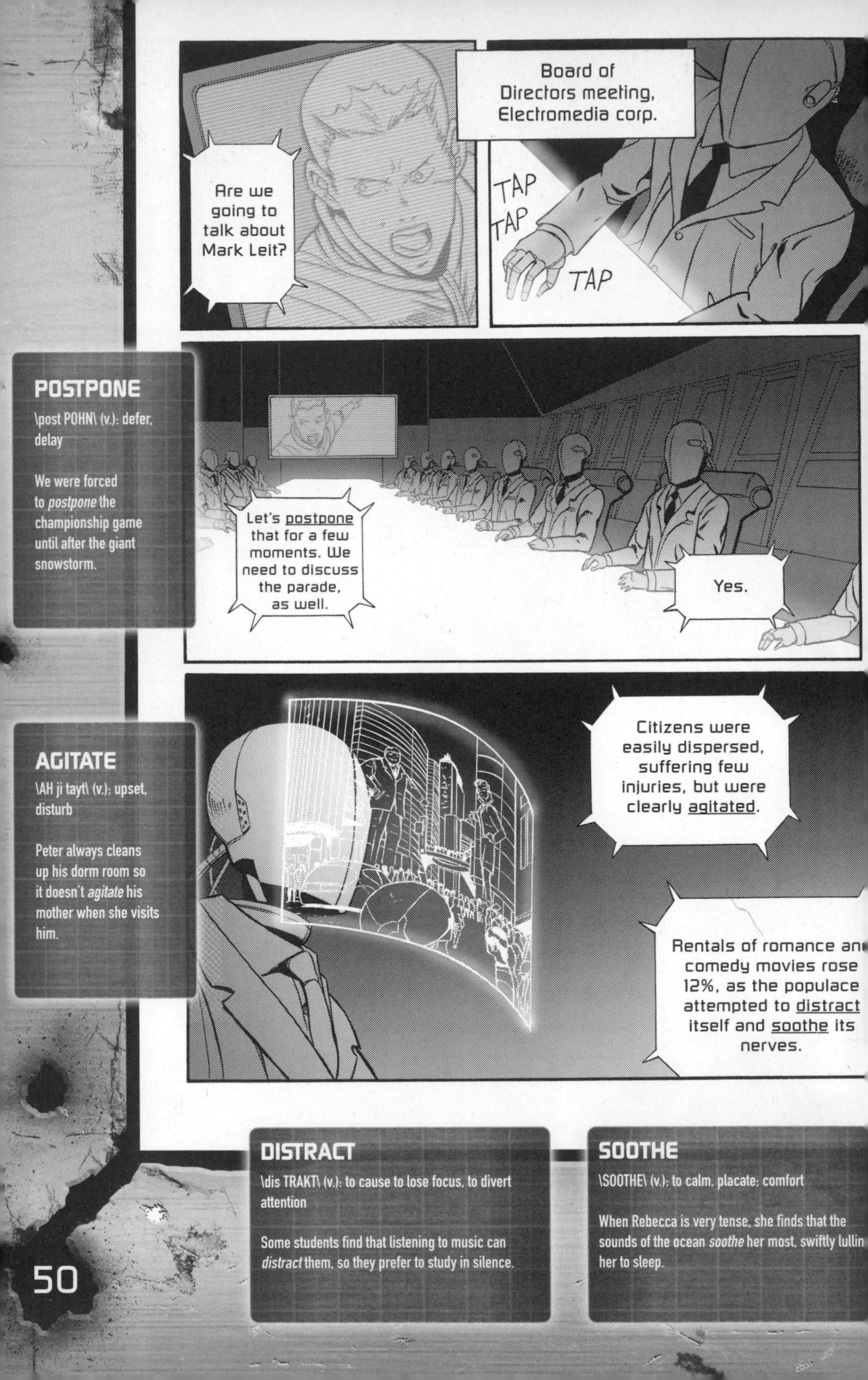
Board of Directors meeting, Electromedia corp.
TAP TAP TAP
Are we going to talk about Mark Leit?
Let's postpone that for a few moments. We need to discuss the parade, as well.
Yes.
Citizens were easily dispersed, suffering few injuries, but were clearly agitated.
Rentals of romance and comedy movies rose 12%, as the populace attempted to distract itself and soothe its nerves.

POSTPONE

\post POHN\ (v.): defer, delay

We were forced to *postpone* the championship game until after the giant snowstorm.

AGITATE

\AH ji tayt\ (v.): upset, disturb

Peter always cleans up his dorm room so it doesn't *agitate* his mother when she visits him.

DISTRACT

\dis TRAKT\ (v.): to cause to lose focus, to divert attention

Some students find that listening to music can *distract* them, so they prefer to study in silence.

SOOTHE

\SOOTHE\ (v.): to calm, placate; comfort

When Rebecca is very tense, she finds that the sounds of the ocean *soothe* her most, swiftly lullin her to sleep.

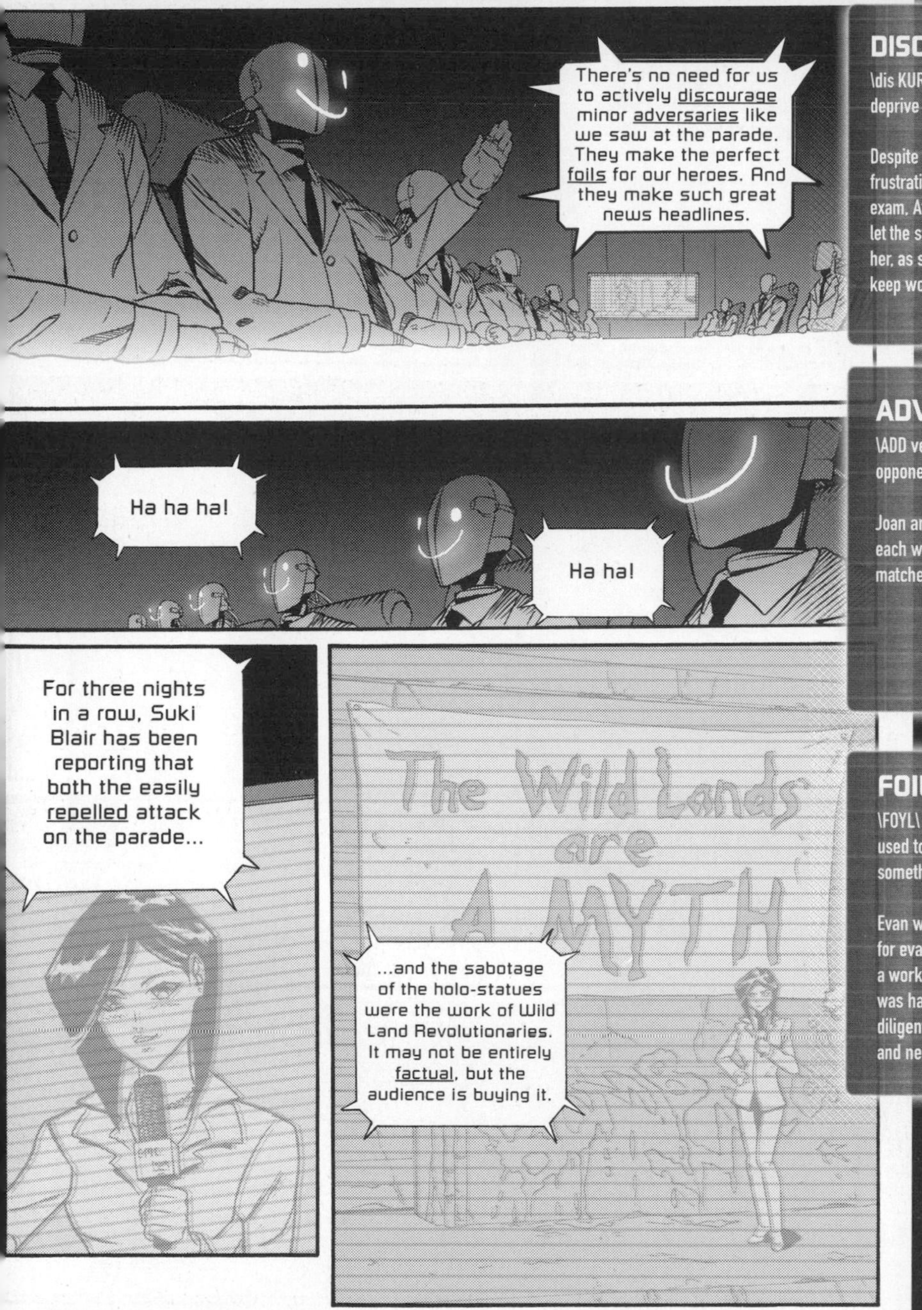
There's no need for us to actively discourage minor adversaries like we saw at the parade. They make the perfect foils for our heroes. And they make such great news headlines.
Ha ha ha!
Ha ha!
For three nights in a row, Suki Blair has been reporting that both the easily repelled attack on the parade...
The Wild Lands are A MYTH
...and the sabotage of the holo-statues were the work of Wild Land Revolutionaries. It may not be entirely factual, but the audience is buying it.

DISCOURAGE

\dis KUR ij\ (v.): dishearten, deprive of hope or spirit

Despite five hours of frustrating study for her exam, Athena refused to let the struggle *discourage* her, as she committed to keep working.

ADVERSARY

\ADD ver SEH ree\ (n.): opponent, enemy

Joan and her *adversary* each won two fencing matches.

FOIL

\FOYL\ (n.): something used to contrast against something else

Evan was the perfect *foil* for evaluating Jeremy as a worker; while Jeremy was hard working and diligent, Evan was lazy and negligent.

REPEL

re PEL\ (v.): to rebuff, repulse; disgust, offend

So far, the castle defenders have managed to *repel* the attackers, but they will not be able to hold out much longer.

FACTUAL

\FAK choo ul\ (adj.): real

"I have *factual* evidence that this man committed the crime!" declared the prosecuting attorney.

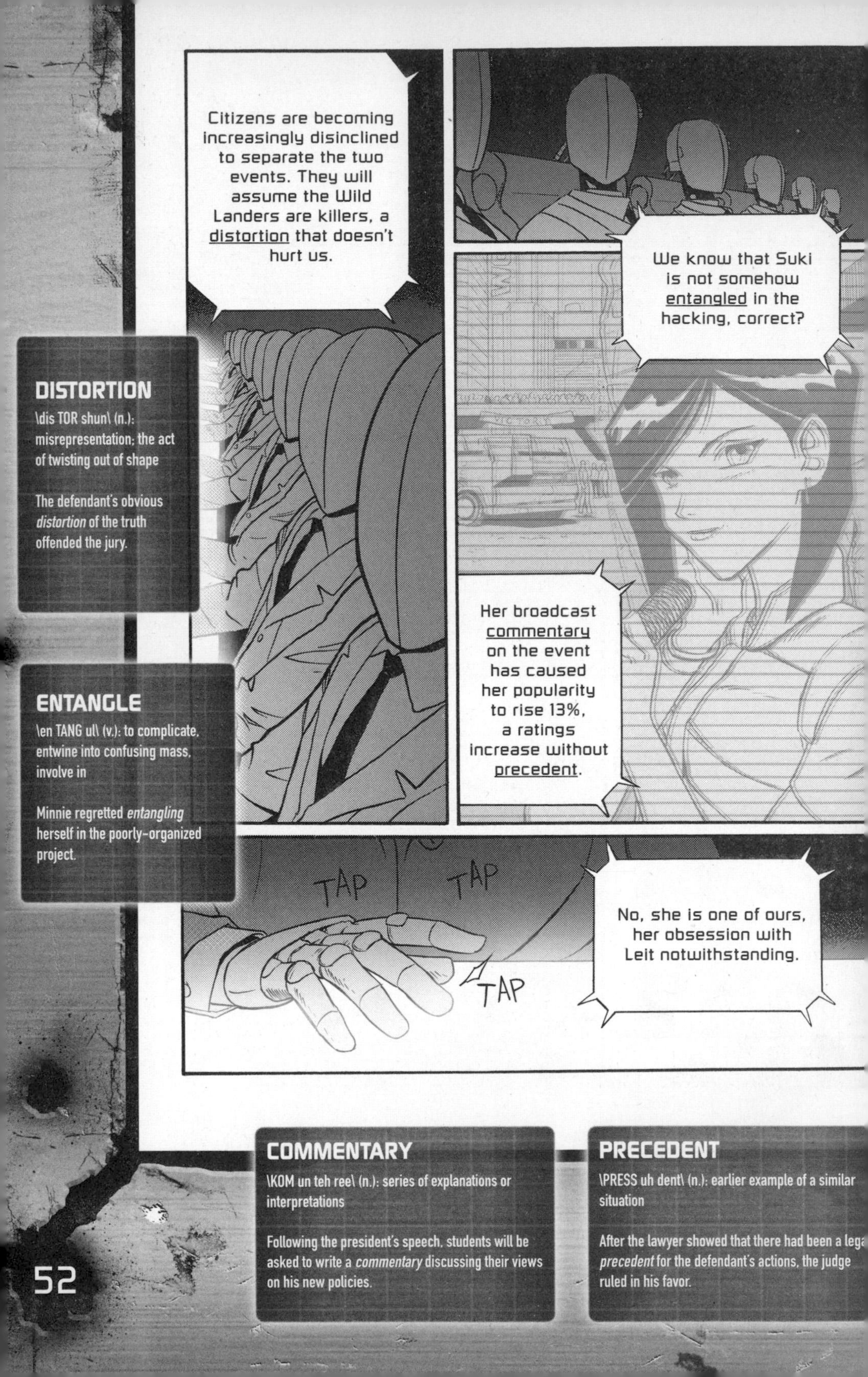
Citizens are becoming increasingly disinclined to separate the two events. They will assume the Wild Landers are killers, a distortion that doesn't hurt us.
We know that Suki is not somehow entangled in the hacking, correct?
Her broadcast commentary on the event has caused her popularity to rise 13%, a ratings increase without precedent.
TAP
TAP
TAP
No, she is one of ours, her obsession with Leit notwithstanding.

DISTORTION

\dis TOR shun\ (n.): misrepresentation; the act of twisting out of shape

The defendant's obvious *distortion* of the truth offended the jury.

ENTANGLE

\en TANG ul\ (v.): to complicate, entwine into confusing mass, involve in

Minnie regretted *entangling* herself in the poorly-organized project.

COMMENTARY

\KOM un teh ree\ (n.): series of explanations or interpretations

Following the president's speech, students will be asked to write a *commentary* discussing their views on his new policies.

PRECEDENT

\PRESS uh dent\ (n.): earlier example of a similar situation

After the lawyer showed that there had been a lega *precedent* for the defendant's actions, the judge ruled in his favor.

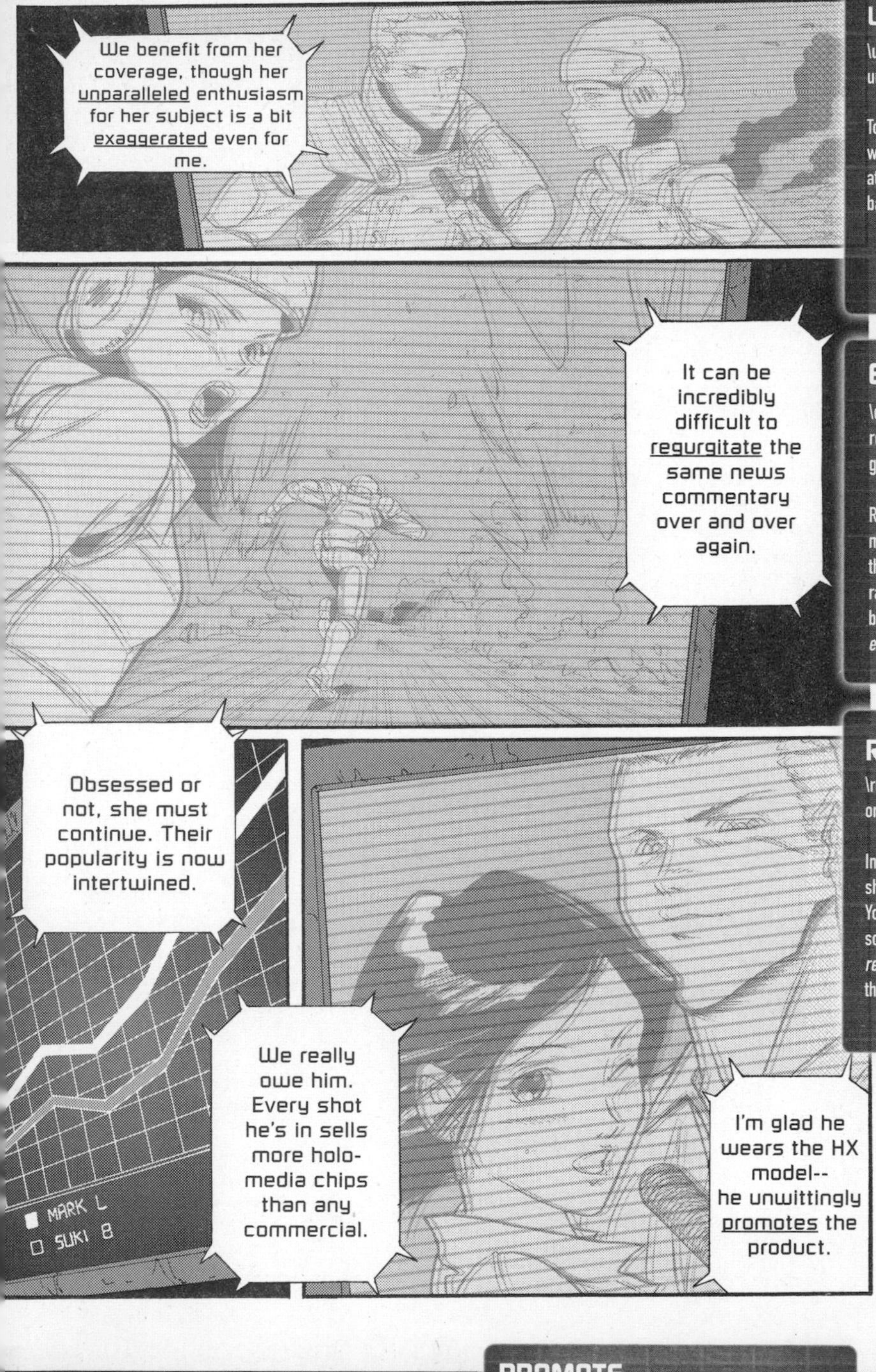
We benefit from her coverage, though her unparalleled enthusiasm for her subject is a bit exaggerated even for me.
It can be incredibly difficult to regurgitate the same news commentary over and over again.
Obsessed or not, she must continue. Their popularity is now intertwined.
MARK L
SUKI 8
We really owe him. Every shot he's in sells more holo-media chips than any commercial.
I'm glad he wears the HX model--he unwittingly promotes the product.

UNPARALLELED

\un PAR uh leld\ (adj.): unequaled; without match

To many, Michael Jordan was an *unparalleled* athlete who redefined basketball stardom.

EXAGGERATE

\eg ZAJ uh rayt\ (v.): to represent something as greater than it actually is

Roger knew that there must have been several thousand people at the rally because Sandra had been there and she never *exaggerates.*

REGURGITATE

\re GURJ uh tayt\ (v.): rush or surge back

Instead of making sure she knew the material, Yolanda memorized some key phrases and *regurgitated* them back to the teacher.

PROMOTE

\pru MOHT\ (v.): to contribute to the progress of

The whole team did its best to *promote* the school's new fundraising effort.

AGGRESSIVE

\uh GRESS iv\ (adj.): actively hostile; assertive, bold

While football may be an *aggressive* sport, the captain of the team is a quiet guy off the field.

ARCHETYPAL

\ark TY pul\ (adj.): representing an ideal example of a type

Gibson, an *archetypal* procrastinator, never began his papers until the night before they were due.

TRAIT

\TRAYT\ (n.): distinguishing feature; quality

While Mary Ann and Georgie share many *traits*, their identical sense of humor stands out most.

FATHOM

\FAH thom\ (v.): comprehend, penetrate the meaning of

Andrea couldn't *fathom* how a person could cheat on a test; every instinct told her it was wrong.

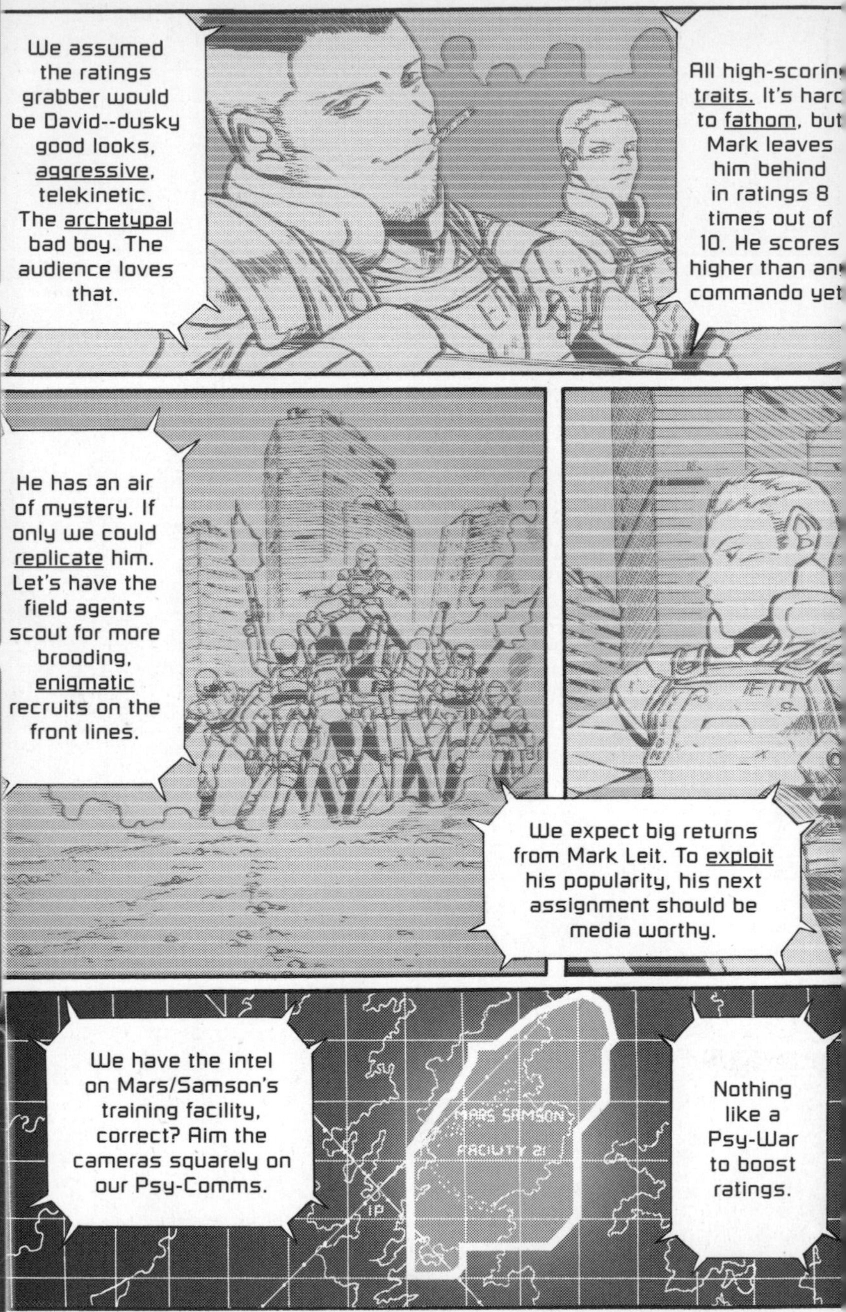

We assumed the ratings grabber would be David--dusky good looks, aggressive, telekinetic. The archetypal bad boy. The audience loves that.
All high-scorin traits. It's har to fathom, but Mark leaves him behind in ratings 8 times out of 10. He scores higher than an commando yet
He has an air of mystery. If only we could replicate him. Let's have the field agents scout for more brooding, enigmatic recruits on the front lines.
We expect big returns from Mark Leit. To exploit his popularity, his next assignment should be media worthy.
We have the intel on Mars/Samson's training facility, correct? Aim the cameras squarely on our Psy-Comms.
MARS SAMSON
FACILITY 21
IP
Nothing like a Psy-War to boost ratings.

REPLICATE

\REP lih kayt\ (v.): to duplicate, repeat

If we're going to *replicate* last year's profit margins, we're going to have to work harder.

ENIGMATIC

\en ig MAT ik\ (adj.): puzzling

The professor answered the questions about the upcoming exam in *enigmatic* terms, leaving the class more confused than they had been before.

EXPLOIT

\ek SPLOYT\ (v.): take advantage of

The brilliant tactician studied his enemy's method to discover a weakness that he could easily *explo* in battle.

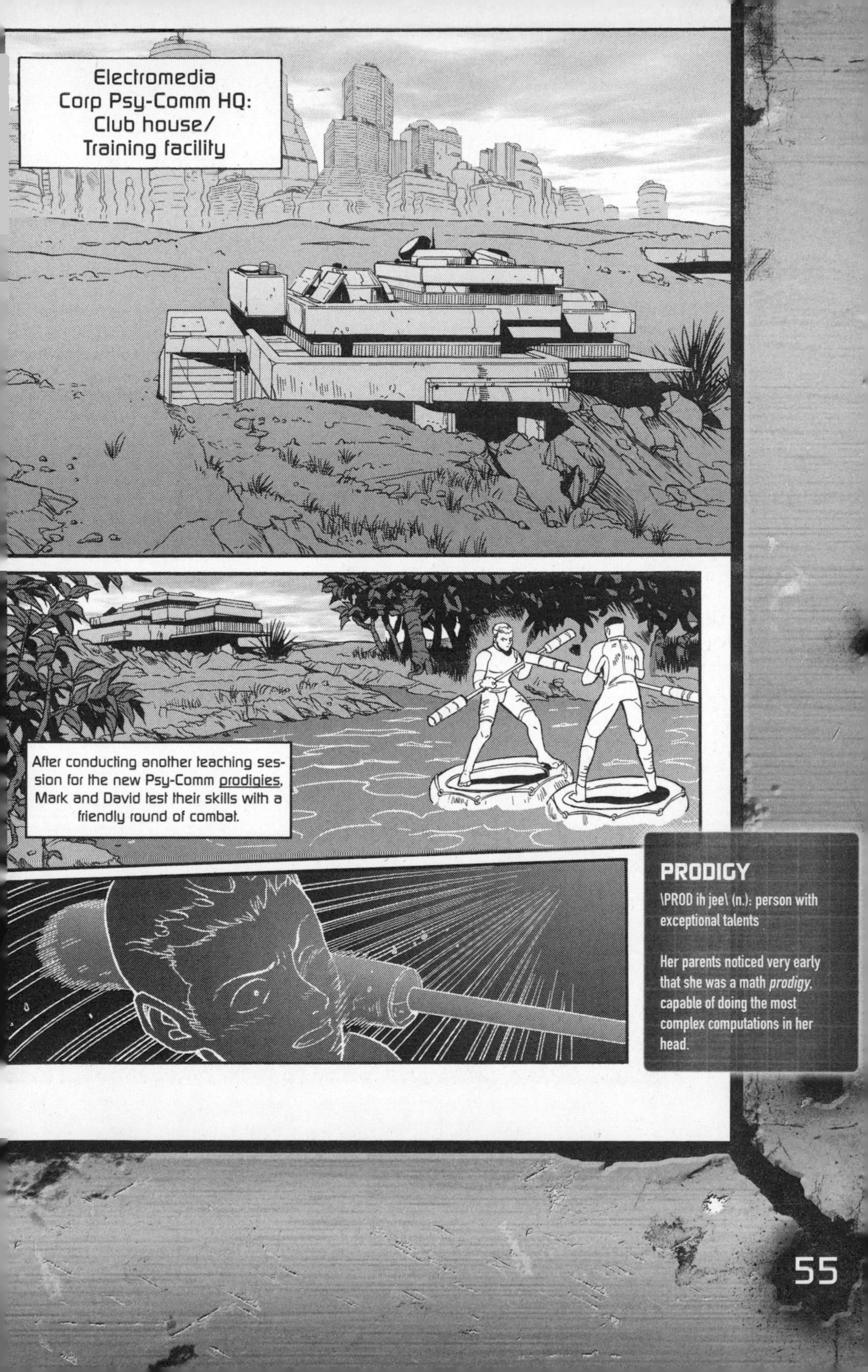
Electromedia Corp Psy-Comm HQ: Club house/ Training facility
After conducting another teaching session for the new Psy-Comm prodigies, Mark and David test their skills with a friendly round of combat.

PRODIGY

\PROD ih jee\ (n.): person with exceptional talents

Her parents noticed very early that she was a math *prodigy*, capable of doing the most complex computations in her head.

FWOOSH
OH, THE BOY SEES THE *FUTURE!*
SPLASH
BUT HOW EXTENSIVE IS THAT VISION, MARK?!
I CAN MOVE ANYTHING-- EVEN WATER! MY ACTIONS WON'T ALWAYS BE PREDICTABLE, EVEN FOR YOU.

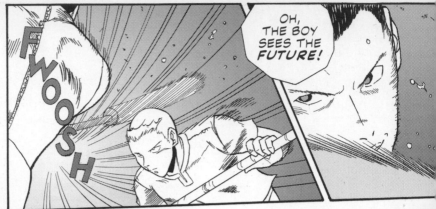

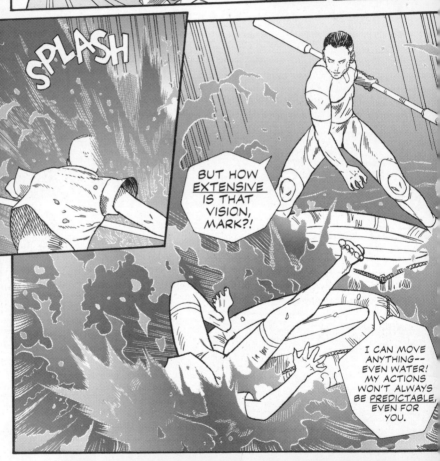

EXTENSIVE

\ek STEN siv\ (adj.): large in range, comprehensive

After reading a short article about String Theory in physics, she wanted to study the topic in *extensive* detail.

PREDICTABLE

\pre DIKT uh bul\ (adj.): expected beforehand

Tired of silly, *predictable* movies, the studio decided to hire a screenwriter to devise an original story that defied all expectations.

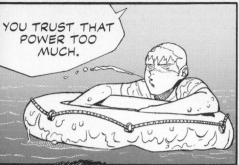

YOU TRUST THAT POWER TOO MUCH.
STAY TWO STEPS AHEAD-- OR IT'S GOING TO GET YOU KILLED.
ALL RIGHT, ALL RIGHT! YOU'VE PROVED YOUR POINT! I'M NOT ALWAYS COMPLETELY INSIGHTFUL. YOU DON'T NEED TO BE SO SMUG ABOUT IT.
DRIP
COMMAND-- PATH!

INSIGHTFUL

\in SIYT ful\ (adj.): clever, perceptive; intuitive

I never submit an article before giving it to my roommate to edit, since he always offers *insightful* advice.

SMUG

\SMUG\ (adj.): excessively self-satisfied

After completing the obstacle course in less time than any of his peers, Roger walked back to his seat with a *smug* expression on his face.

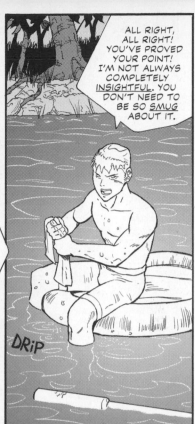

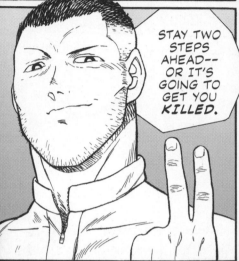

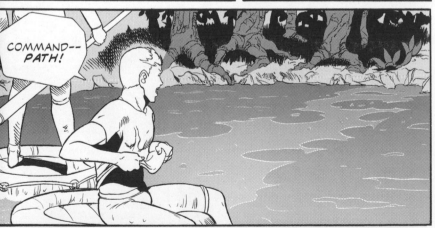

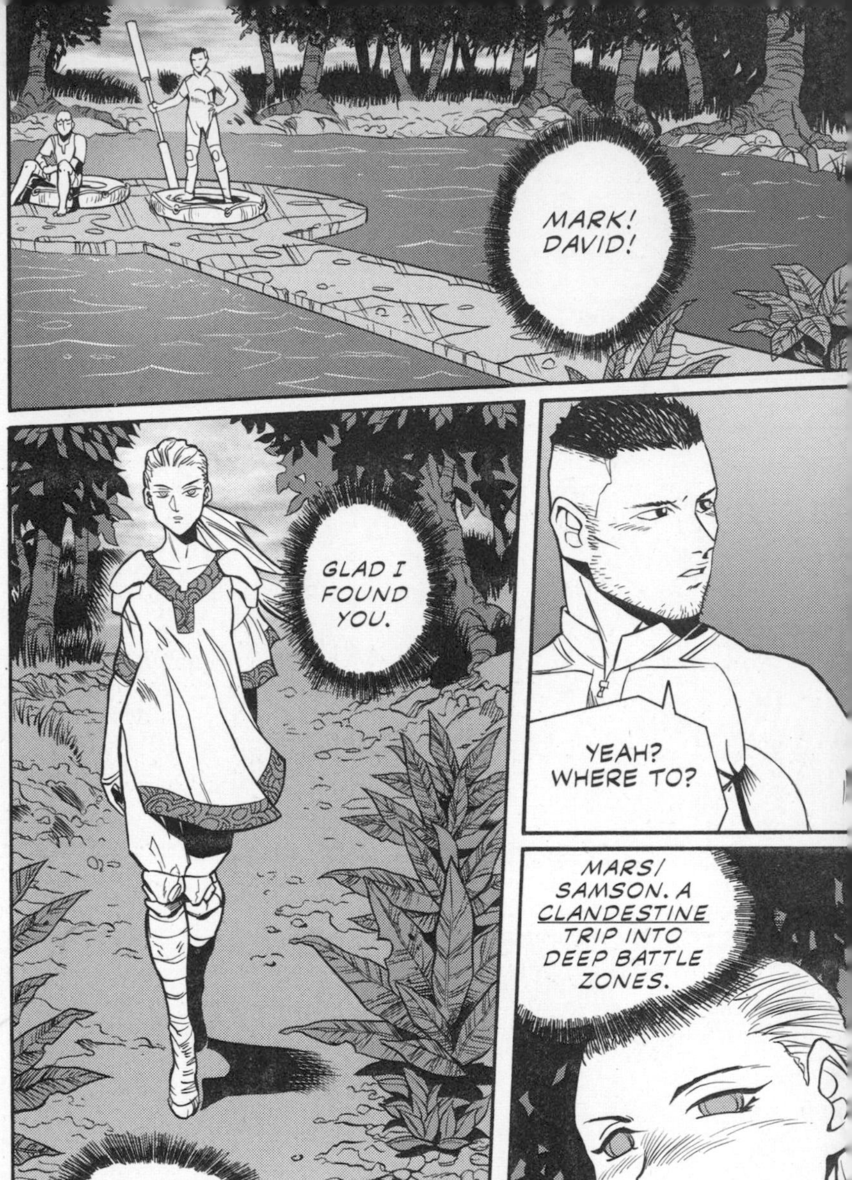
MARK! DAVID!
GLAD I FOUND YOU.
WE'RE LEAVING SOON.
YEAH? WHERE TO?
MARS/ SAMSON. A CLANDESTINE TRIP INTO DEEP BATTLE ZONES.

CLANDESTINE

\klan DES tin\ (adj.): secretive, concealed for a darker purpose

The double agent paid many *clandestine* visits to the president's office in the dead of the night.

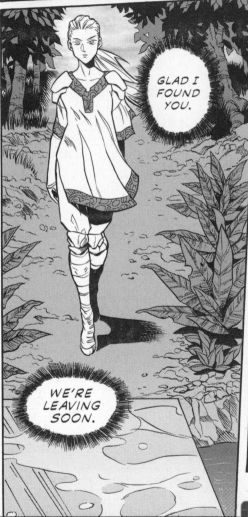

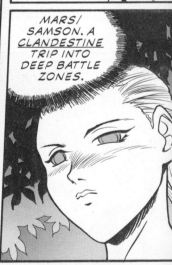

YOU'RE DOING RECON BEHIND ENEMY LINES ON A STEALTH MISSION. IT'S HAZARDOUS WORK, WHICH USUALLY MEANS GREAT RATINGS.
DID YOU HEAR THAT THEY CONVICTED THOSE RADICAL MEDIA MANIPULATORS FROM THE PARADE ATTACK?
EXECUTION'S NEXT WEEK.
THOSE OUTCASTS. THEY'RE NOTHING MORE THAN PARIAHS, TRYING TO TAKE ADVANTAGE OF THE CITIZENS.
UH-HUH, RIGHT...DON'T YOU THINK YOU SOUND A LITTLE BIASED?

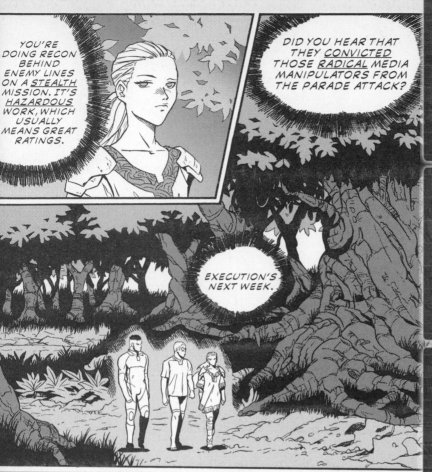

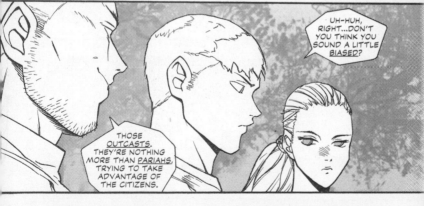

STEALTH

\STELTH\ (n.): act of moving in a covert way

The special unit traveled by *stealth* so the enemy scouts would not detect their position.

HAZARDOUS

\HAZ er duss\ (adj.): dangerous, risky, perilous

Though filtering has removed many *hazardous* toxins from the reservoir, the water may not yet be drinkable.

CONVICTED

\kon VICT\ (v.): to find guilty of a crime

If the jury chooses to *convict* the defendant, the attorney will appeal to a higher court.

RADICAL

\RAD ih kul\ (adj.): extreme, marked departure from the norm

Bored with her appearance, Lucinda decided to make a *radical* change and dyed her hair bright purple.

OUTCAST

OWT kast\ (n.): someone rejected from a society

he *outcast* decided that the only way to rejoin the group was to give in to their demands.

PARIAH

\puh RIY uh\ (n.): outcast

She needlessly worried that her short hair would make her a social *pariah* at the school dance.

BIASED

\BY ust\ (adj.): prejudiced

The defendant's lawyer filed a motion to move the case to a new town because the people in this one were all *biased* against her client.

REMORSEFUL

\re MORS ful\ (adj.): feeling sorry for wrongdoing

Molly realized that Scott was truly *remorseful* for insulting her and decided to forgive him.

EXCULPATE

\EK skul payt\ (v.): to clear of blame or fault, vindicate

The adversarial legal system is intended to convict those who are guilty and to *exculpate* those who are innocent.

HINDRANCE

\HIN drens\ (n.): impediment, clog; stumbling block

Not wishing to be a *hindrance* while their mother was preparing for the party, the children packed a picnic lunch and went to the park.

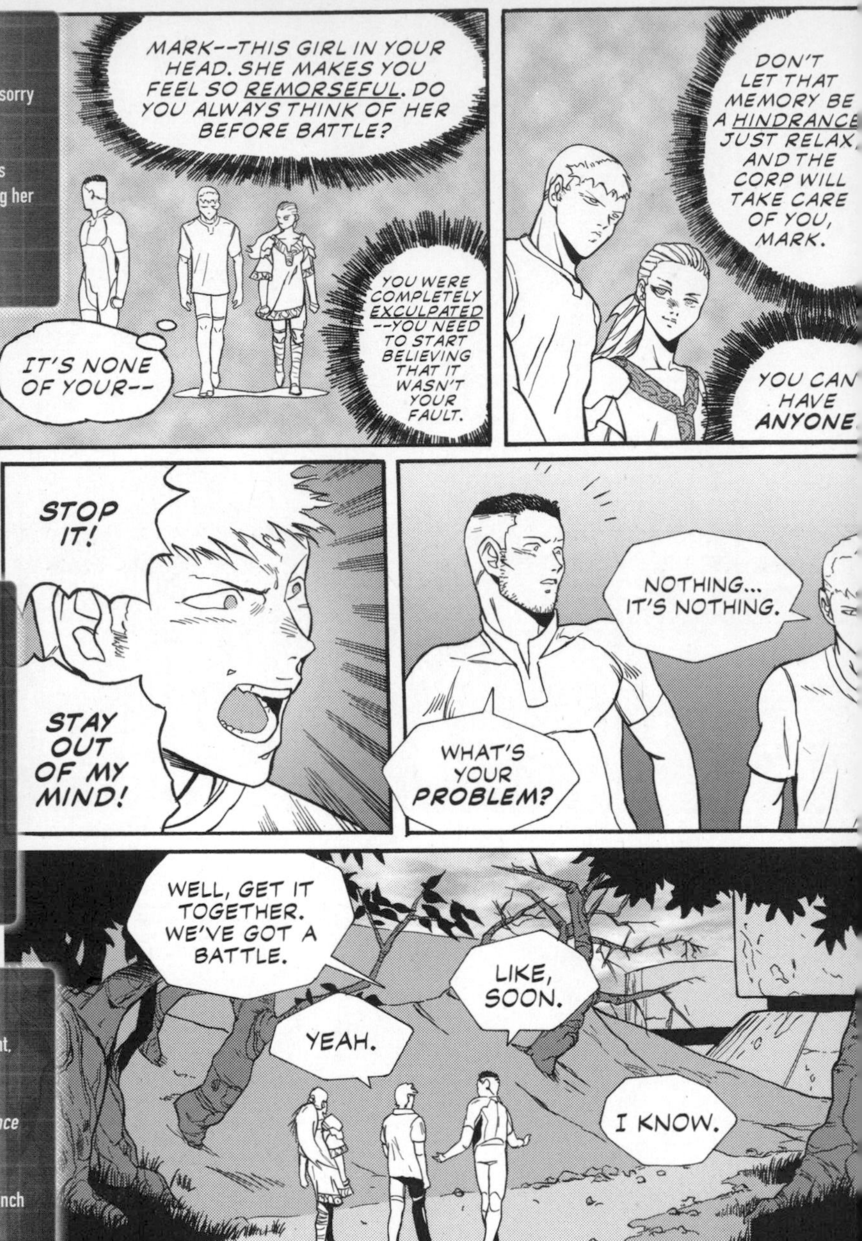
MARK--THIS GIRL IN YOUR HEAD. SHE MAKES YOU FEEL SO REMORSEFUL. DO YOU ALWAYS THINK OF HER BEFORE BATTLE?
IT'S NONE OF YOUR--
YOU WERE COMPLETELY EXCULPATED --YOU NEED TO START BELIEVING THAT IT WASN'T YOUR FAULT.
DON'T LET THAT MEMORY BE A HINDRANCE JUST RELAX, AND THE CORP WILL TAKE CARE OF YOU, MARK.
YOU CAN HAVE ANYONE
STOP IT!
STAY OUT OF MY MIND!
WHAT'S YOUR PROBLEM?
NOTHING... IT'S NOTHING.
WELL, GET IT TOGETHER. WE'VE GOT A BATTLE.
LIKE, SOON.
YEAH.
I KNOW.

PSY★COMM
CHAPTER [4]

STIFLE

\STY ful\ (v.): to smother or suffocate; suppress

Much as she longed to express her anger at the dictator, Maria *stifled* her protests for fear of being arrested.

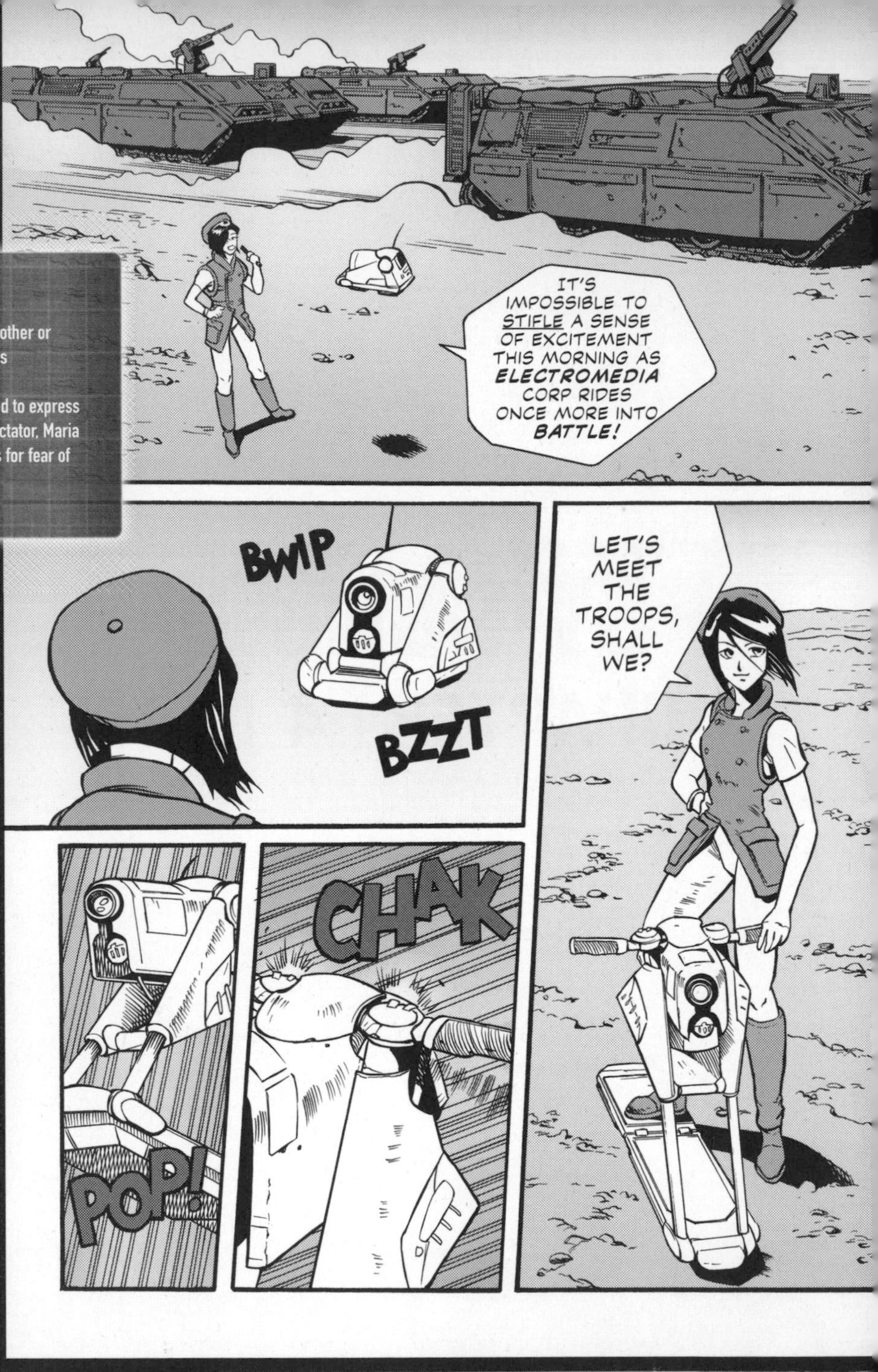

IT'S IMPOSSIBLE TO STIFLE A SENSE OF EXCITEMENT THIS MORNING AS ELECTROMEDIA CORP RIDES ONCE MORE INTO BATTLE!
BWIP
BZZT
POP!
CHAK
LET'S MEET THE TROOPS, SHALL WE?

ZOOOM
SUSPENDED IN MIDAIR, SUKI SURVEYS THE LINE OF ARMORED TANKS WAITING TO DEPLOY FOR REASONS THAT ARE ENTIRELY VAGUE TO THE SOLDIERS INSIDE.
MAN, WISH I HAD ONE OF THOSE HOLO-RECORDERS.
GET ENOUGH POINTS AND NO PROBLEM. I ONLY NEED FIVE MORE.
HEY THERE!! READY TO ENFORCE THE WILL OF ELECTROMEDIA AND REAP THE REWARDS OF VICTORY?
WE'RE LOUD AND PROUD *ELECTROMEDIA CORSICANS!*

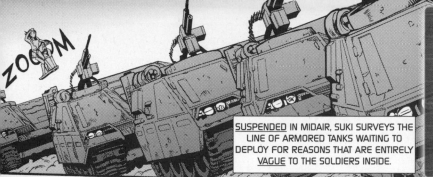

SUSPEND

\su SPEND\ (v.): to defer, interrupt; dangle, hang

Construction of the building was suspended when the contractor ran out of bricks.

VAGUE

\VAYG\ (adj.): inexplicit, ambiguous, indistinct

We had to go back to the professor for further directions because the ones posted at the class website were too *vague* to follow.

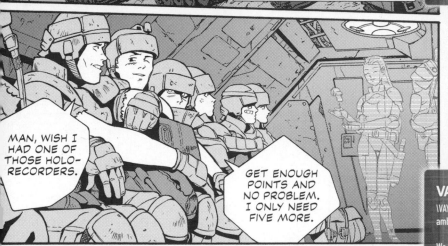

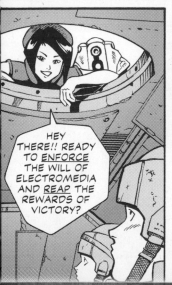

ENFORCE

en FORS\ (v.): to compel others to adhere or observe

While it is the job of the legislative branch of government to create the laws, it is the job of the judicial branch to *enforce* them.

REAP

\REEP\ (v.): to obtain a return, often a harvest

While the grasshopper starved in the winter, the ant *reaped* the benefits of his hard labor, having so much food left over from his summer gathering.

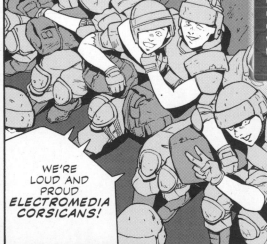

Psy-Comm
Recon unit
LRR-7.

OKAY! THIS IS OUR STOP!

BAM

BAM

BROM

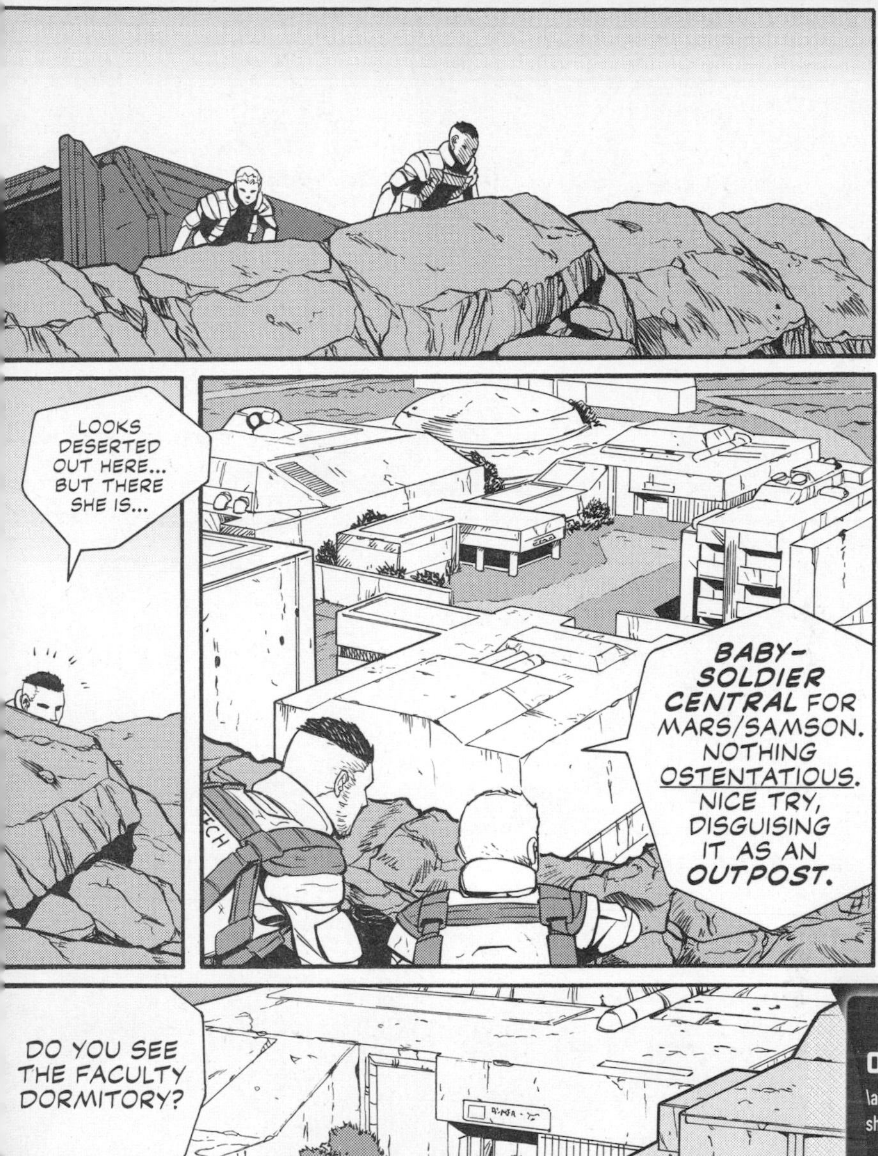
LOOKS DESERTED OUT HERE... BUT THERE SHE IS...
BABY-SOLDIER CENTRAL FOR MARS/SAMSON. NOTHING OSTENTATIOUS. NICE TRY, DISGUISING IT AS AN OUTPOST.
DO YOU SEE THE FACULTY DORMITORY?

OSTENTATIOUS

\ah sten TAY shus\ (adj.): showy

The billionaire's 200-room palace was considered by many to be an overly *ostentatious* display of wealth.

SCHOLARLY

\SKOL ur lee\ (adj.): related to higher learning

Dr. Lee studied English literature for fifteen years and published articles in a variety of *scholarly* journals.

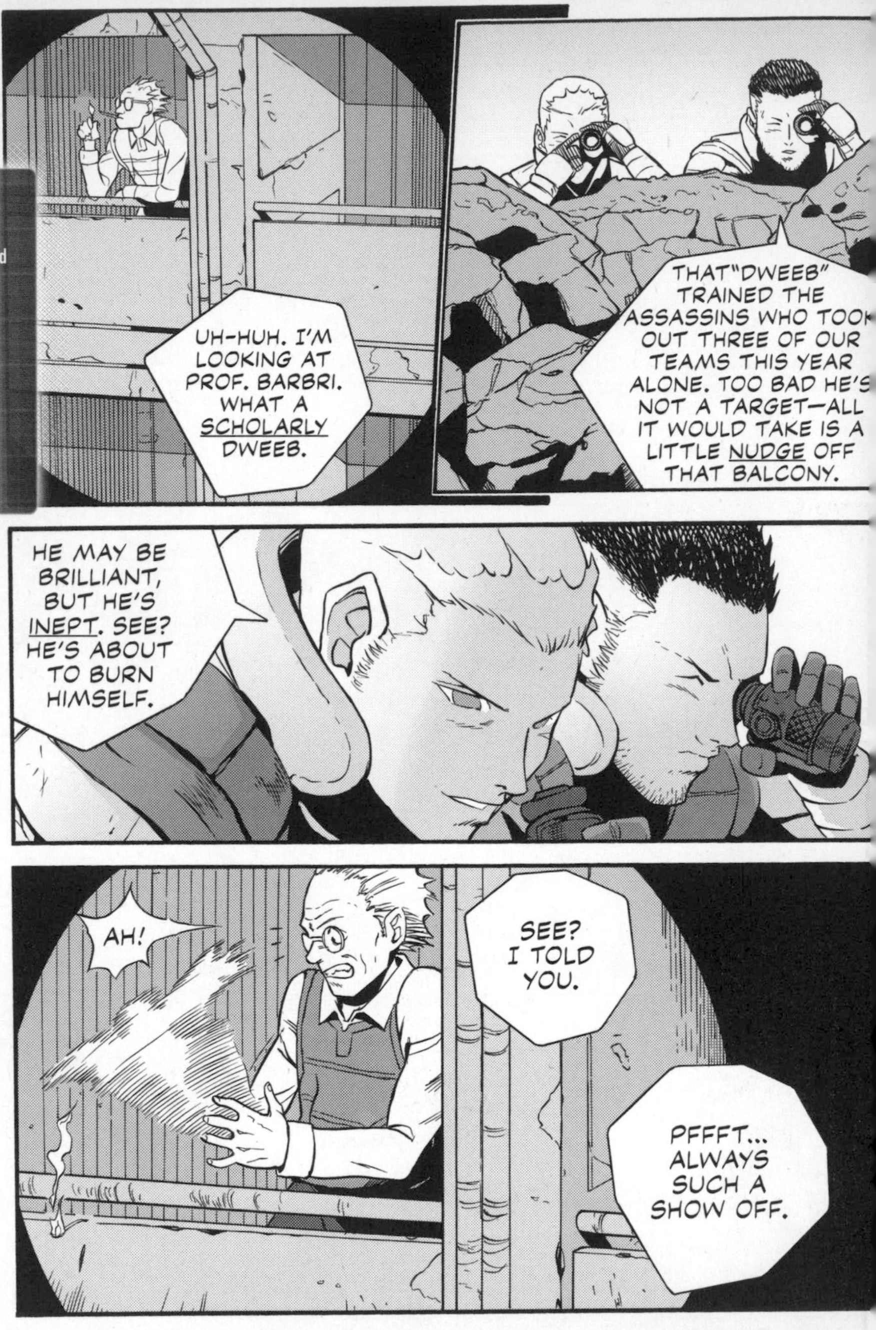

UH-HUH. I'M LOOKING AT PROF. BARBRI. WHAT A SCHOLARLY DWEEB.
THAT "DWEEB" TRAINED THE ASSASSINS WHO TOOK OUT THREE OF OUR TEAMS THIS YEAR ALONE. TOO BAD HE'S NOT A TARGET—ALL IT WOULD TAKE IS A LITTLE NUDGE OFF THAT BALCONY.
HE MAY BE BRILLIANT, BUT HE'S INEPT. SEE? HE'S ABOUT TO BURN HIMSELF.
AH!
SEE? I TOLD YOU.
PFFFT... ALWAYS SUCH A SHOW OFF.

NUDGE

\NUJ\ (n.): gentle push

In his hurry to get to the front of the line, Mark kept *nudging* all the people around him and asking them to let him through.

INEPT

\in EPT\ (adj.): clumsy, awkward; incapable; foolish, nonsensical

While capable of designing elegant clothing on paper, he was *inept* when it came to the real work of cutting the fabric and stitching the garments.

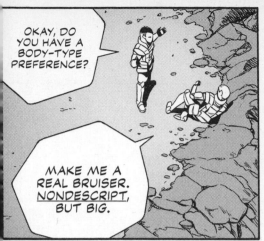

OKAY, DO YOU HAVE A BODY-TYPE PREFERENCE?
MAKE ME A REAL BRUISER. NONDESCRIPT, BUT BIG.
YOU'D **NEVER** PULL OFF BRUISER, BUT I'LL SEE WHAT I CAN DO.
I'LL JUST PULL TOGETHER THE AIR MOLECULES AROUND US AND REDIRECT THEIR REFLECTIONS...NOTHING TOO DEMANDING...
...EMBELLISH OUR HAIR COLOR, BODY SHAPES, FACES...
...AND **VOILA!** PEOPLE ONLY SEE WHAT I WANT THEM TO SEE.
NOW LET'S GO MAKE TROUBLE FOR MARS/ SAMSON.

NONDESCRIPT

\non des KRIPT\ (adj.): lacking interesting or distinctive qualities

The celebrity showed up wearing sunglasses and a *nondescript* black outfit.

DEMANDING

\de MAN ding\ (adj.): requiring much effort and attention

Joe had to quit his part-time job in order to keep up with his *demanding* schedule at school.

EMBELLISH

\em BELL ish\ (v.): to ornament; make attractive with decorations or details; add details to a statement

Sanjev's story is too short: It needs to be *embellished* with more details about life among the penguins.

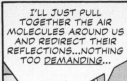

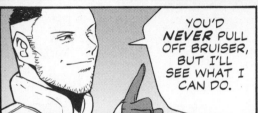

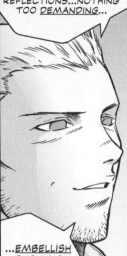

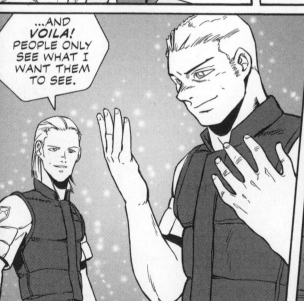

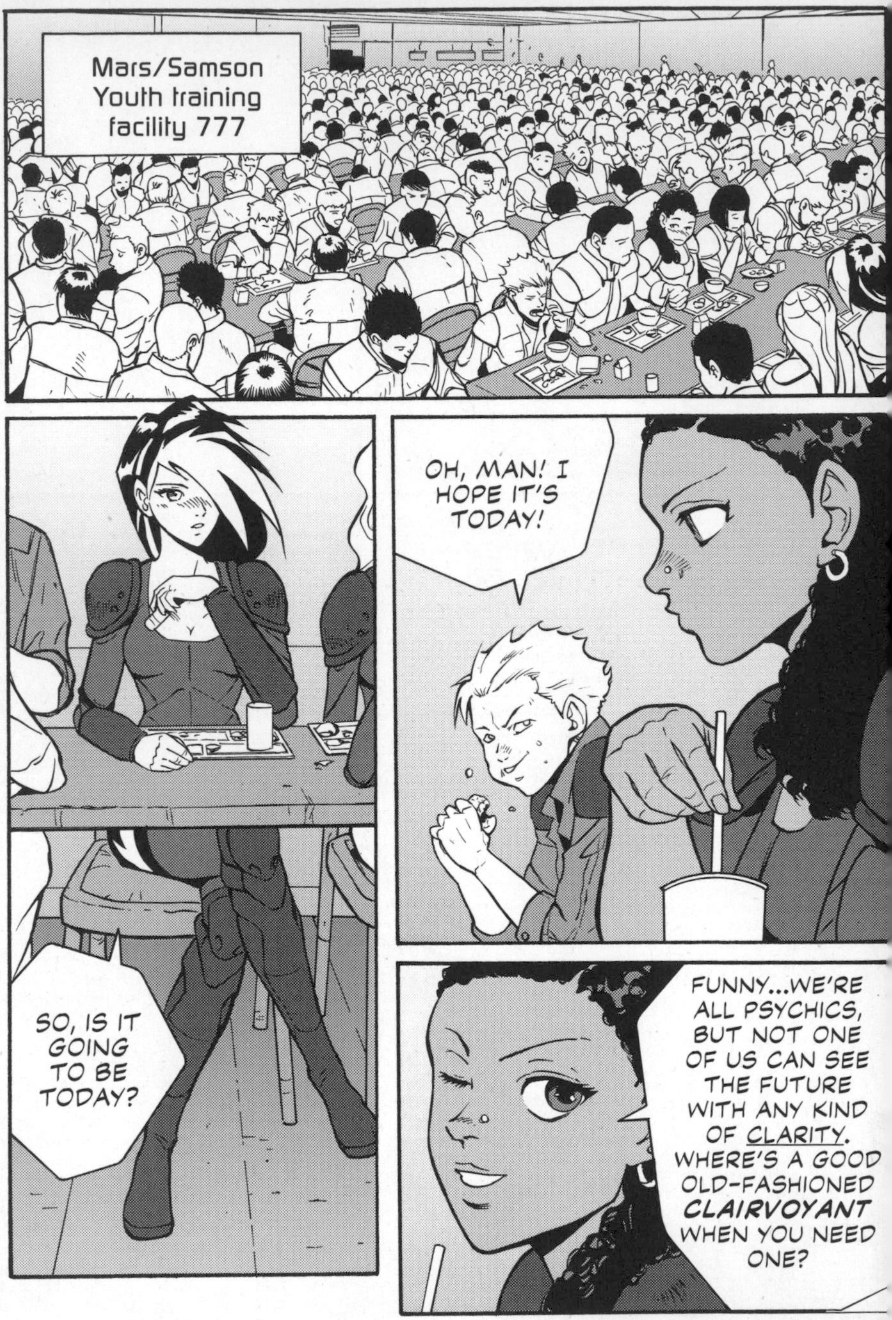
Mars/Samson Youth training facility 777
SO, IS IT GOING TO BE TODAY?
OH, MAN! I HOPE IT'S TODAY!
FUNNY...WE'RE ALL PSYCHICS, BUT NOT ONE OF US CAN SEE THE FUTURE WITH ANY KIND OF CLARITY. WHERE'S A GOOD OLD-FASHIONED CLAIRVOYANT WHEN YOU NEED ONE?

CLARITY

\KLAR it ee\ (n.): clearness; clear understanding

Henrietta explained the plan to Greg with the utmost *clarity*, but he still failed to understand.

HEY! CHECK THIS OUT!
WELL I'M GOING TO GO FIND OUT WHAT'S UP.
JUST GATHER THE STATIC ELECTRICITY AROUND IT AND STIMULATE IT A BIT--
C'MON! CHARGE, BABY-- CHARGE!
SPLAT
OOPS.
CAL! YOU'RE SUCH A FOOL! I DON'T KNOW WHY I SOCIALIZE WITH YOU!
IT'S OKAY, GUYS.
I'LL JUST MAKE THE MILK DROPLETS...

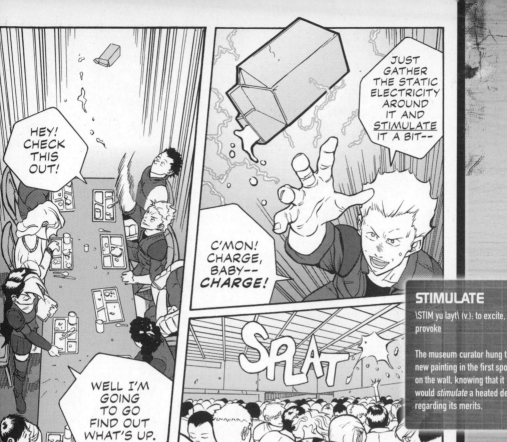

STIMULATE

\STIM yu layt\ (v.): to excite, provoke

The museum curator hung the new painting in the first spot on the wall, knowing that it would *stimulate* a heated debate regarding its merits.

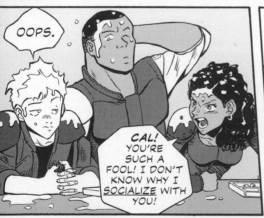

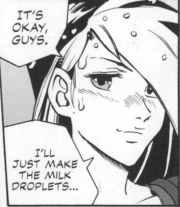

SOCIALIZE

\so shu LIYZ\ (v.): take part in group activities

Reggie felt that it was more important to finish his homework than to go out and *socialize* with his friends.

...HEAVIER THAN EVERYTHING ELSE.

MORE EFFICIENT THAN PROFESSIONAL CLEANING!

OH!

I'M SORRY... UM, EXCUSE ME.

EFFICIENT

\ee FISH int\ (adj.): effective with a minimum of unnecessary effort or waste

When designing an electrical system, engineers seek to achieve the most *efficient* design possible, to ensure that they don't waste any power.

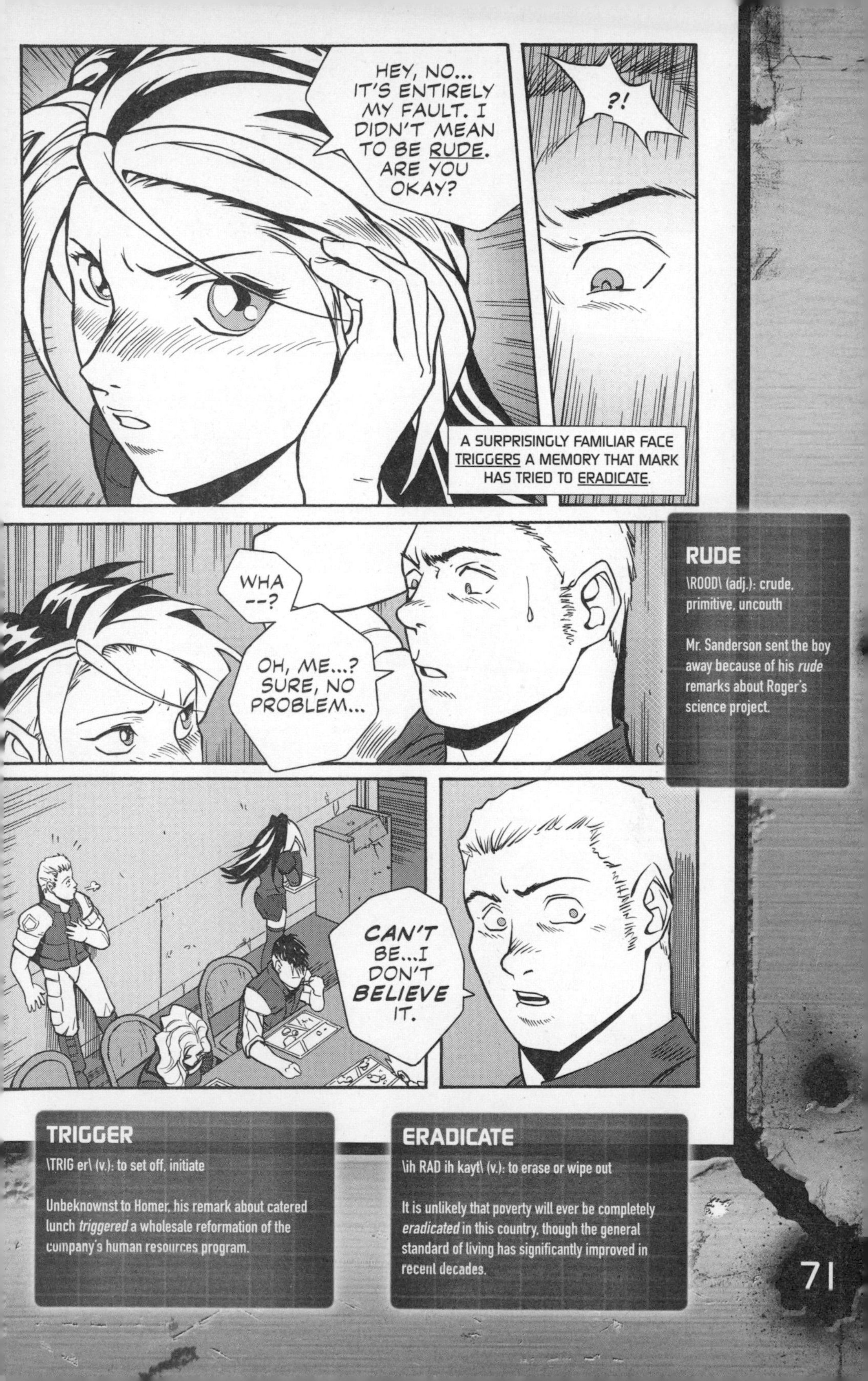
HEY, NO... IT'S ENTIRELY MY FAULT. I DIDN'T MEAN TO BE RUDE. ARE YOU OKAY?
?!
A SURPRISINGLY FAMILIAR FACE TRIGGERS A MEMORY THAT MARK HAS TRIED TO ERADICATE.
WHA --?
OH, ME...? SURE, NO PROBLEM...
CAN'T BE...I DON'T BELIEVE IT.

RUDE

\ROOD\ (adj.): crude, primitive, uncouth

Mr. Sanderson sent the boy away because of his *rude* remarks about Roger's science project.

TRIGGER

\TRIG er\ (v.): to set off, initiate

Unbeknownst to Homer, his remark about catered lunch *triggered* a wholesale reformation of the company's human resources program.

ERADICATE

\ih RAD ih kayt\ (v.): to erase or wipe out

It is unlikely that poverty will ever be completely *eradicated* in this country, though the general standard of living has significantly improved in recent decades.

SLUGGISH

\SLUG ish\ (adj.): lazy, inactive

Helga's *sluggish* husband sits on the couch all day watching television instead of looking for a job.

HARASS

\\hu RASS\ (v.): irritate, torment

Susan wondered whether the department store was trying to *harass* her since, despite her repeated pleas, it kept sending her catalogue after catalogue.

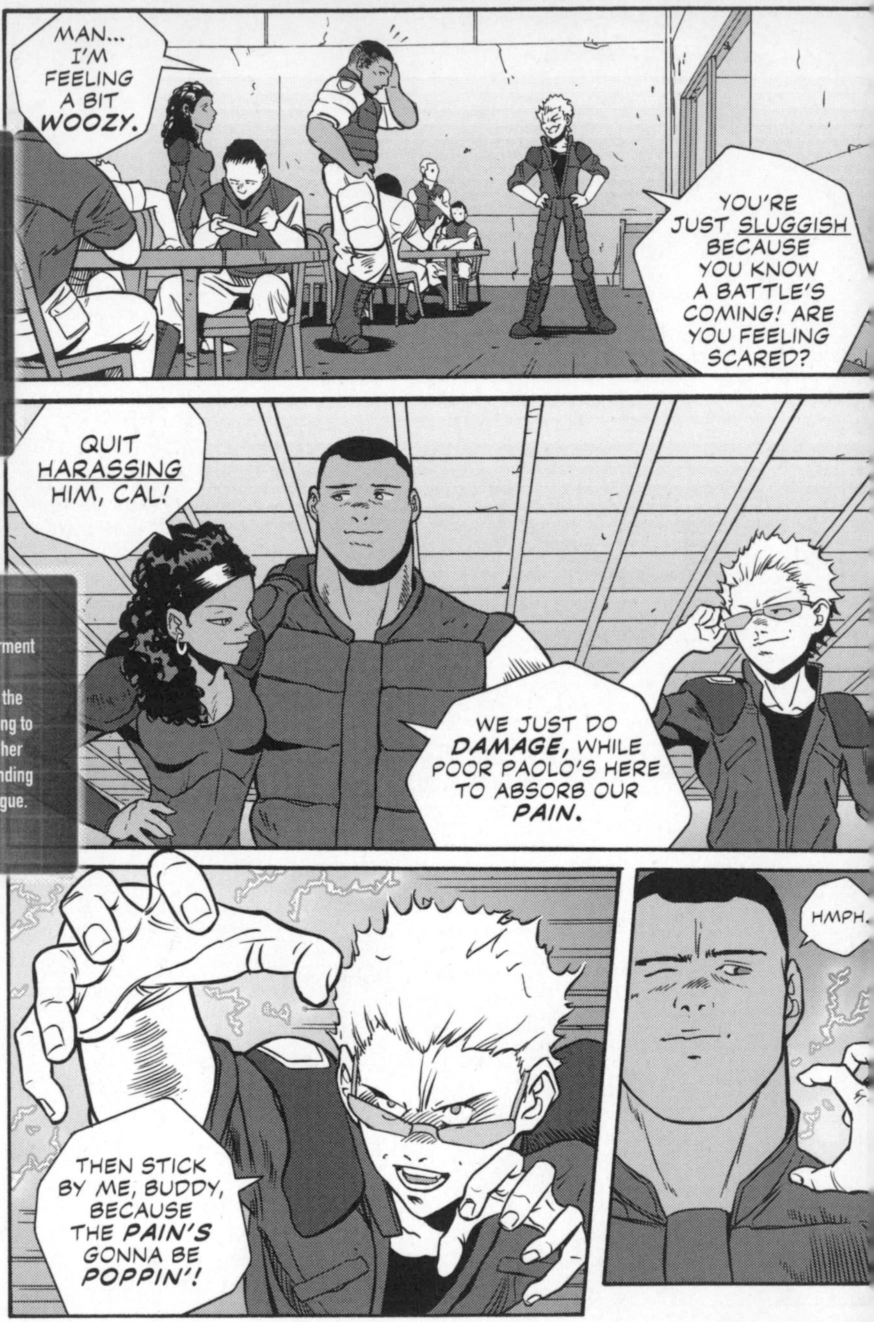
MAN... I'M FEELING A BIT **WOOZY.**
YOU'RE JUST SLUGGISH BECAUSE YOU KNOW A BATTLE'S COMING! ARE YOU FEELING SCARED?
QUIT HARASSING HIM, CAL!
WE JUST DO **DAMAGE,** WHILE POOR PAOLO'S HERE TO ABSORB OUR **PAIN.**
THEN STICK BY ME, BUDDY, BECAUSE THE ***PAIN'S*** GONNA BE ***POPPIN'!***
HMPH.

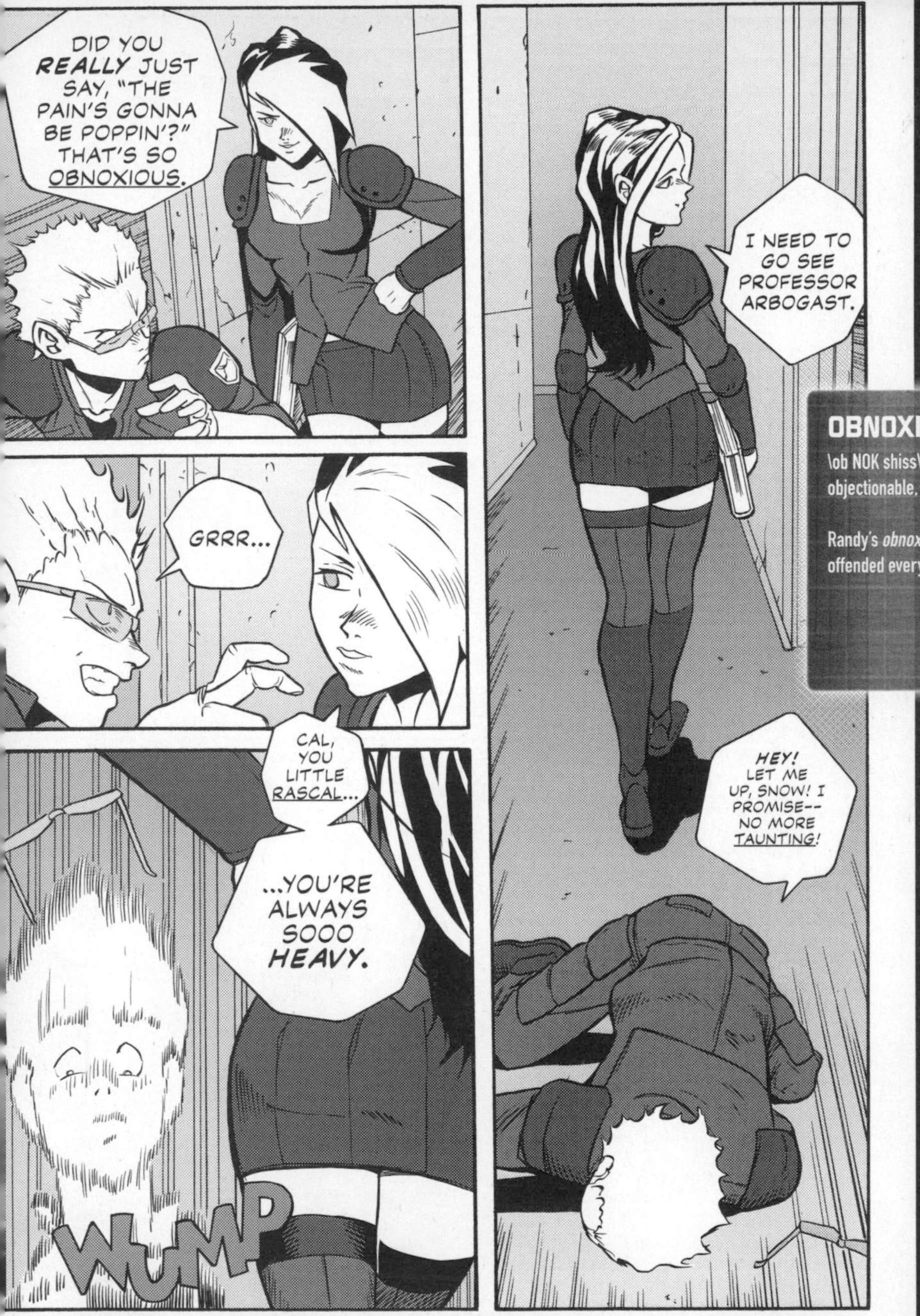
DID YOU **REALLY** JUST SAY, "THE PAIN'S GONNA BE POPPIN'?" THAT'S SO OBNOXIOUS.
GRRR...
CAL, YOU LITTLE RASCAL...
...YOU'RE ALWAYS SOOO **HEAVY.**
WUMP
I NEED TO GO SEE PROFESSOR ARBOGAST.
HEY! LET ME UP, SNOW! I PROMISE-- NO MORE TAUNTING!

OBNOXIOUS

\ob NOK shiss\ (adj.): objectionable, offensive

Randy's *obnoxious* comments offended everyone at the party.

RASCAL

\RAS kul\ (n.): playful, mischievous person; a scoundrel

"You little *rascals*! I'll get you for this!" shouted Mr. Wilson as Dennis and Joey ran from his broken window.

TAUNT

\TAWNT\ (v.): to ridicule, to mock, insult

Gary sat crying in a corner of the playground because the other children had *taunted* him for wearing pink polka dot suspenders.

OBSTACLE

\AHB stukl\ (n.): impediment

Despite the many *obstacles* barring his way toward success, the ambitious young man was determined to succeed.

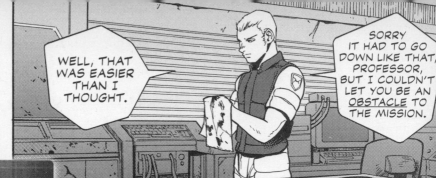

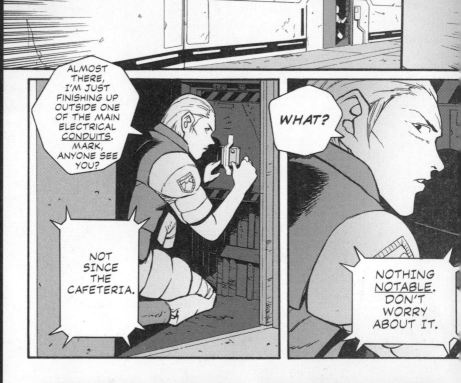

WELL, THAT WAS EASIER THAN I THOUGHT.
SORRY IT HAD TO GO DOWN LIKE THAT, PROFESSOR, BUT I COULDN'T LET YOU BE AN OBSTACLE TO THE MISSION.
ALMOST THERE, I'M JUST FINISHING UP OUTSIDE ONE OF THE MAIN ELECTRICAL CONDUITS. MARK, ANYONE SEE YOU?
NOT SINCE THE CAFETERIA.
WHAT?
NOTHING NOTABLE. DON'T WORRY ABOUT IT.

CONDUIT

\KON doo it\ (n.): tube, pipe, or similar passage

The *conduit* carried excess rainwater down to the ocean, preventing flooding.

NOTABLE

\NO tu bul\ (adj.): remarkable, worthy of notice

Sean didn't bother explaining the rules of the game again because no *notable* changes had been made since the last game.

AS SNOW TENTATIVELY ENTERS THE CELEBRATED PROFESSOR'S LABORATORY, SHE QUICKLY DISCERNS THAT SOMETHING IS AMISS IN HER MENTOR'S USUALLY ORDERLY WORK SPACE.
HMM...
PROFESSOR ARBOGAST?
CRiiiii

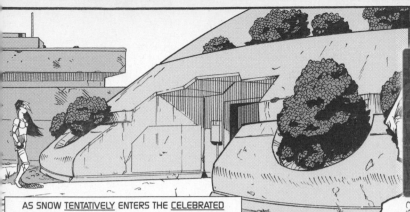

TENTATIVE

\TEN tu tiv\ (adj.): not fully worked out; uncertain

The published meeting schedule is, unfortunately, only a *tentative* plan.

CELEBRATED

\SELL uh bray ted\ (adj.): known and praised widely

The class quivered with excitement in anticipation of the *celebrated* author's upcoming speech.

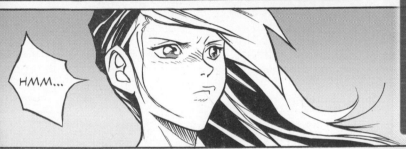

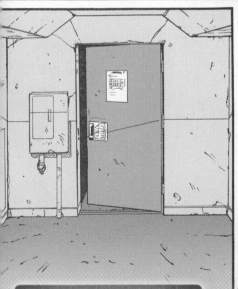

ORDERLY

\OR der lee\ (adj.): neat, systematic

"Please line up in an *orderly* fashion so everyone may get a ticket" the manager announced to the crowd outside the theater.

DISCERN

\di SURN\ (v.): to perceive something using the senses or intellect

It is easy to *discern* the difference between real butter and butter-flavored topping.

BUMP

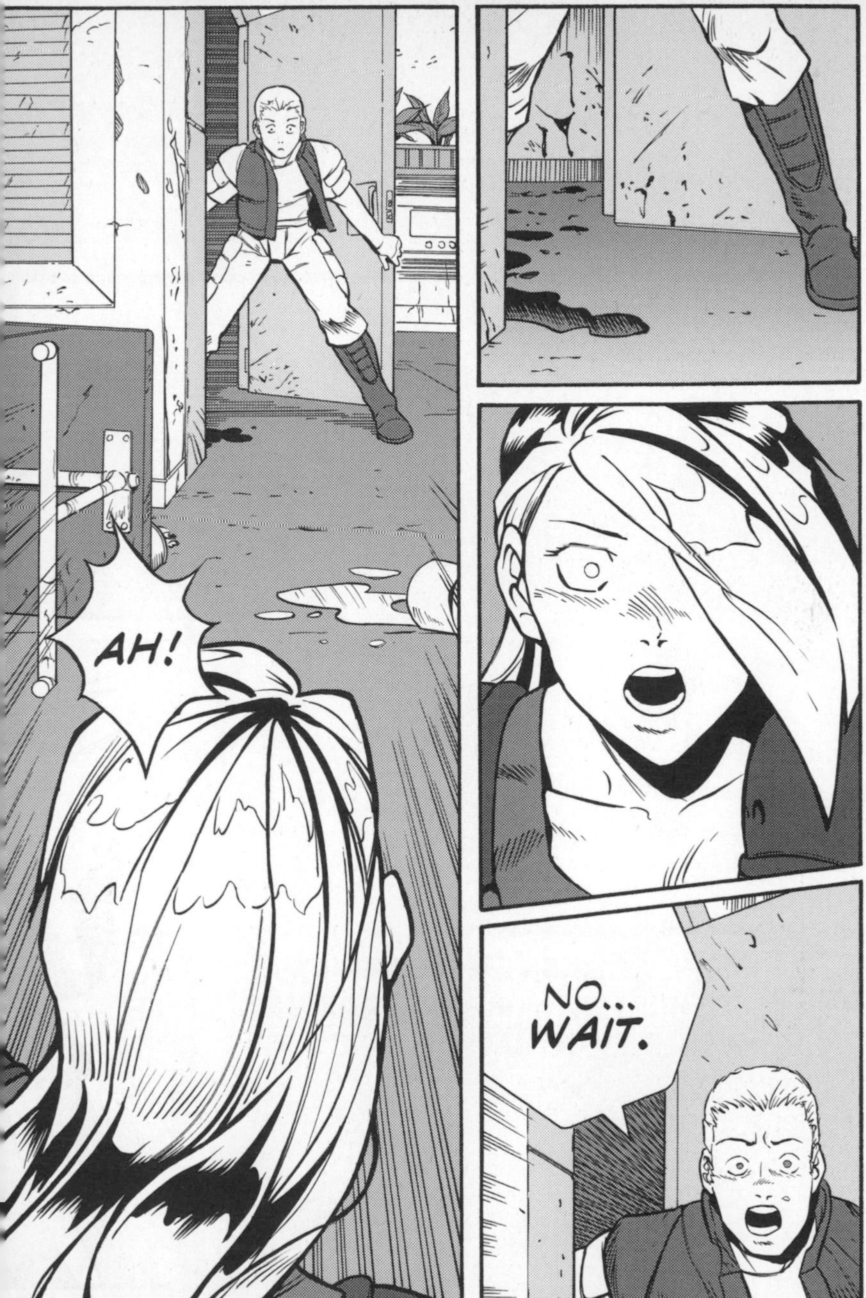
AH!
NO... WAIT.

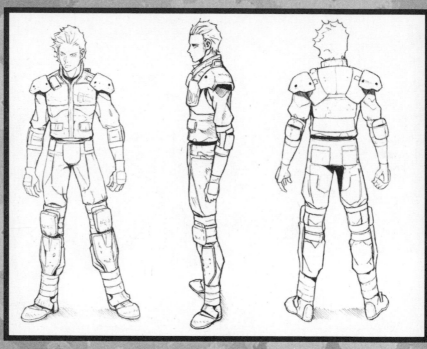

**EARLY DESIGN SKETCH FOR MARK LEIT:
A SHORTER, MORE MILITARY HAIR STYLE
WOULD EVENTUALLY REPLACE THIS LOOK.**

PSY★COMM

CHAPTER [5]

EVAPORATE

\ee VAP uh rayt\ (v.): to vanish quickly

You need to watch the pot carefully, since the sauce will begin to burn once the water *evaporates*.

INEVITABLE

\in EV ih tu bul\ (adj.): certain, unavoidable

With an active effort to cut costs and raise productivity, bankruptcy is far from *inevitable*.

Snow's doubts begin to evaporate as the inevitable confrontation between the naive ps
comm and her battle-proven peer commences
HOLD IT RIGHT THERE! WHAT WERE YOU DOING IN THAT OFFICE? IS--IS THAT BLOOD?!

NAÏVE

\niy EEV\ (adj.): lacking experience and understanding

Although the newly elected politician was very *naïve* about political maneuvering in Washington, it only took her a few weeks to learn the tricks of Congress.

PEER

\PEER\ (n.): contemporary, equal, match

Adults often blame their children's inappropriate actions on pressure from their *peers*.

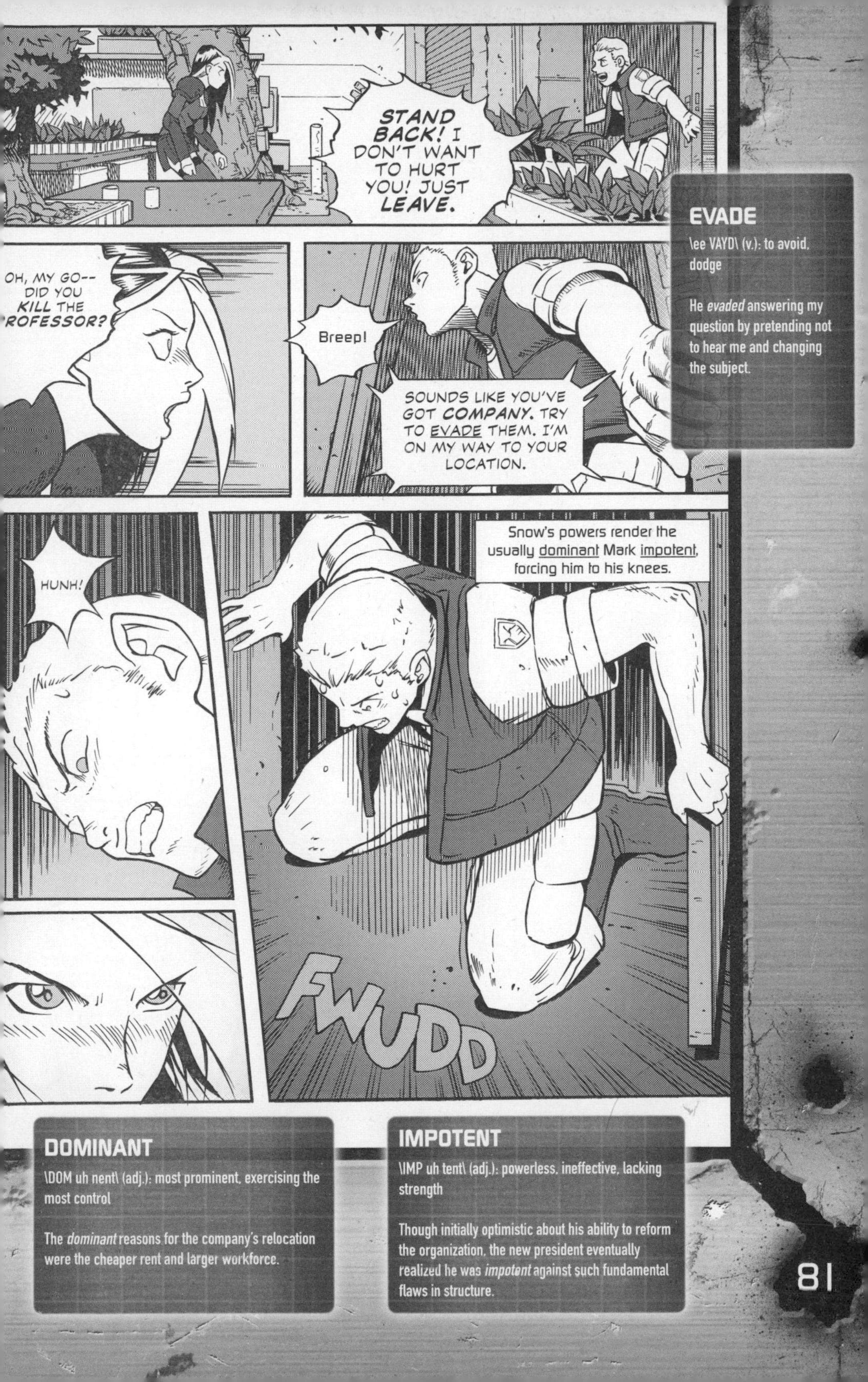
STAND BACK! I DON'T WANT TO HURT YOU! JUST LEAVE.
OH, MY GO-- DID YOU KILL THE ROFESSOR?
Breep!
SOUNDS LIKE YOU'VE GOT COMPANY. TRY TO EVADE THEM. I'M ON MY WAY TO YOUR LOCATION.
HUNH!
Snow's powers render the usually dominant Mark impotent, forcing him to his knees.
FWUDD

EVADE

\ee VAYD\ (v.): to avoid, dodge

He *evaded* answering my question by pretending not to hear me and changing the subject.

DOMINANT

\DOM uh nent\ (adj.): most prominent, exercising the most control

The *dominant* reasons for the company's relocation were the cheaper rent and larger workforce.

IMPOTENT

\IMP uh tent\ (adj.): powerless, ineffective, lacking strength

Though initially optimistic about his ability to reform the organization, the new president eventually realized he was *impotent* against such fundamental flaws in structure.

DAVID! I'VE G-GOT A PSYCHIC KID PINNING ME DOWN...SHE'S A ***LEVEL 3 GRAV-CONTROLLER,*** AT LEAST! I'M IN GREENHOUSE F-7! PLEASE CONFIRM THAT YOU'RE ON YOUR WAY!
HEY! WHO ARE YOU TALKING TO? KEEP QUIET AND LOSE ANY NOTION YOU MAY HAVE OF ESCAPE!
LISTEN, I CAN MAKE THAT ARMOR CRUSH TH AIR OUT OF YOU! NOW DO YOU COMPREHEND THE GRAVITY OF YOUR SITUATION? ***NOW BE QUIET AND STAY STILL!***
HURRY UP, DAVID! MY DISGUISE JUST CUT OUT! WHEN YOU COME IN...SH-SHIFT THE ROOTS OF THE BIG TREE AT MY 12--***HURK!***

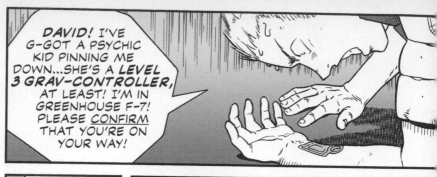

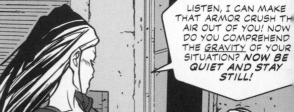

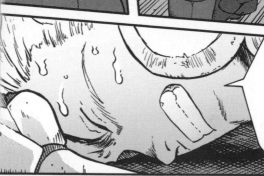

CONFIRM

\kon FIRM\ (v.): verify

Many airlines require their passengers to call a day in advance and *confirm* their reservation for their flight.

NOTION

\NO shin\ (n.): idea or conception

Requiring school uniforms is a *notion* that has been tossed back and forth in governments, but has never been implemented on a national scale in the United States..

GRAVITY

\GRAH vih tee\ (adj.): importance, seriousness

Phyllis, not grasping the *gravity* of the situation, strode into the police station whistling and smiling.

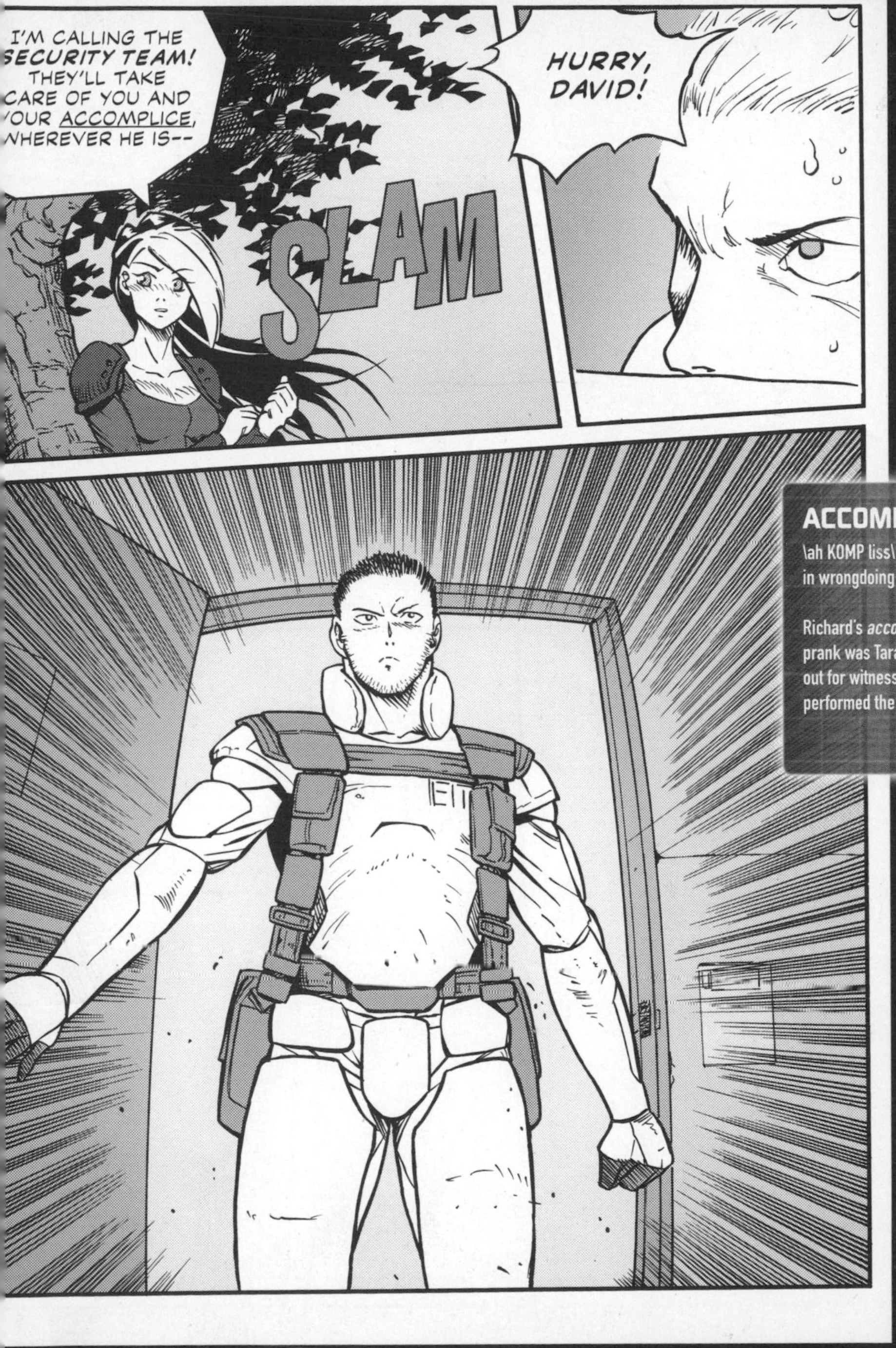
I'M CALLING THE SECURITY TEAM! THEY'LL TAKE CARE OF YOU AND YOUR ACCOMPLICE, WHEREVER HE IS--
SLAM
HURRY, DAVID!

ACCOMPLICE

\ah KOMP liss\ (n.): an associate in wrongdoing

Richard's *accomplice* in the prank was Tara, who watched out for witnesses while he performed the deed.

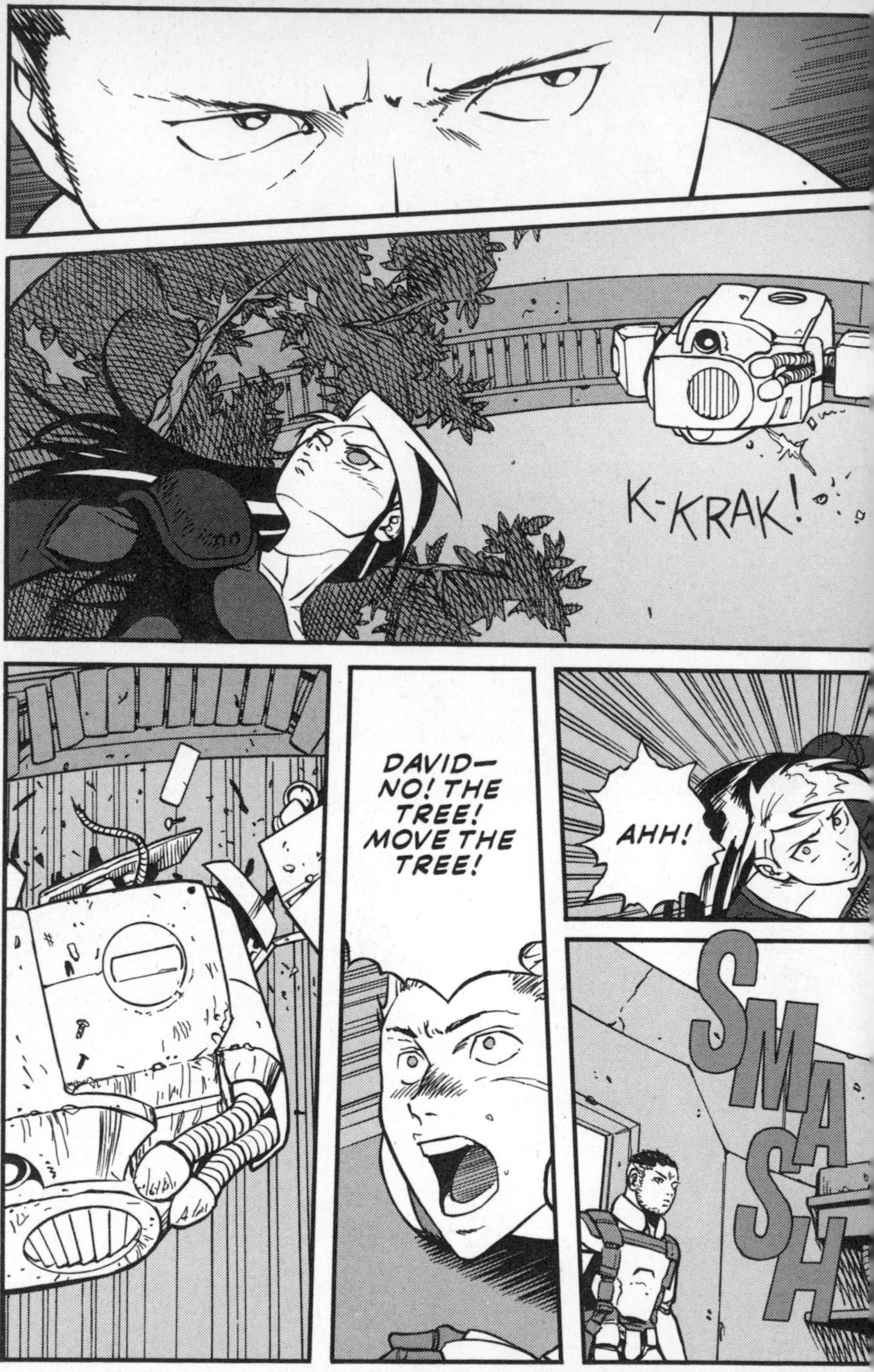
K-KRAK!
DAVID— NO! THE TREE! MOVE THE TREE!
AHH!
SMASH

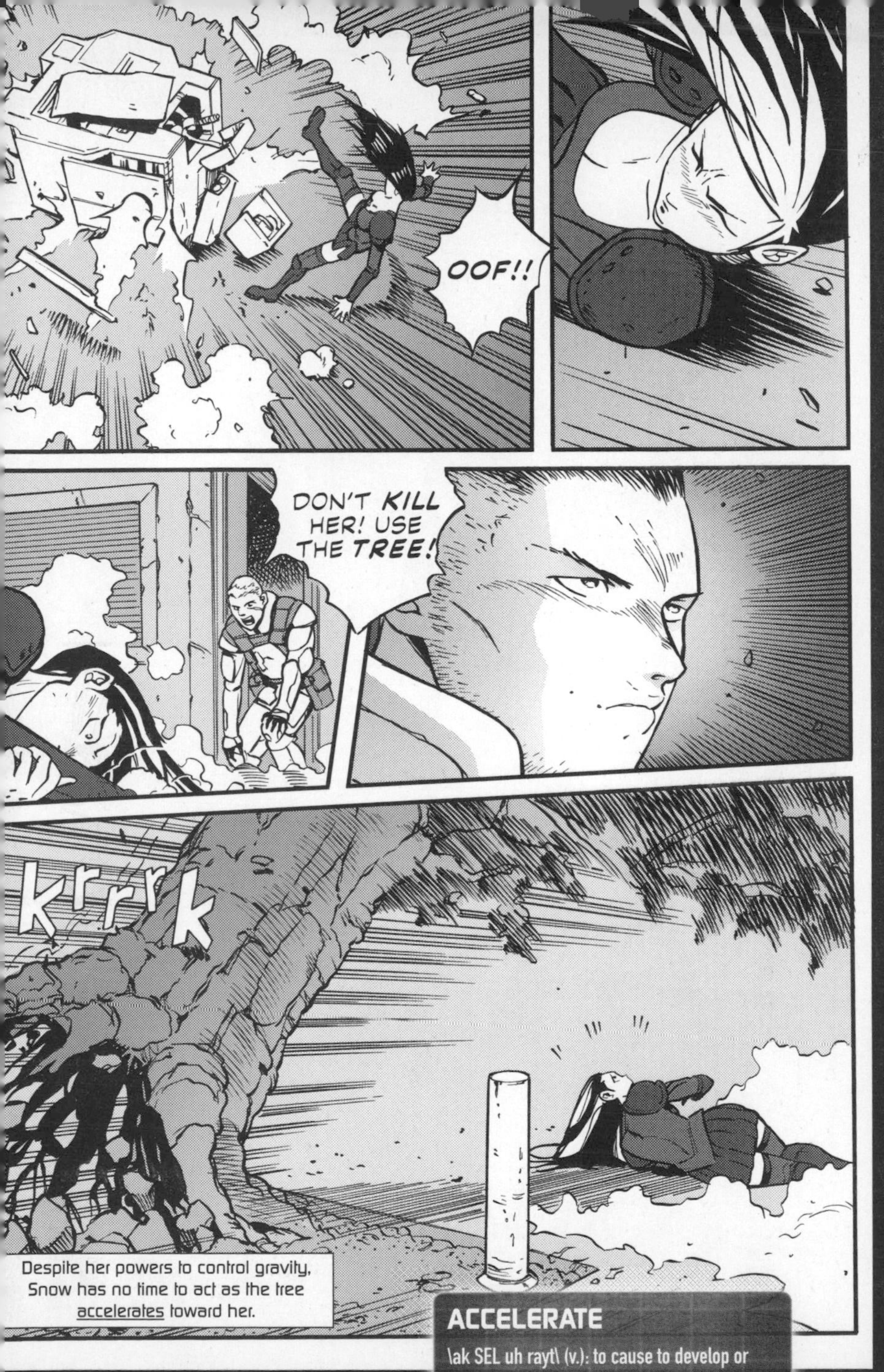
OOF!!
DON'T KILL HER! USE THE TREE!
krrrk
Despite her powers to control gravity, Snow has no time to act as the tree accelerates toward her.

ACCELERATE

\ak SEL uh rayt\ (v.): to cause to develop or progress more quickly

Professor Kinget stopped answering questions during the lecture so he could *accelerate* the pace of the class.

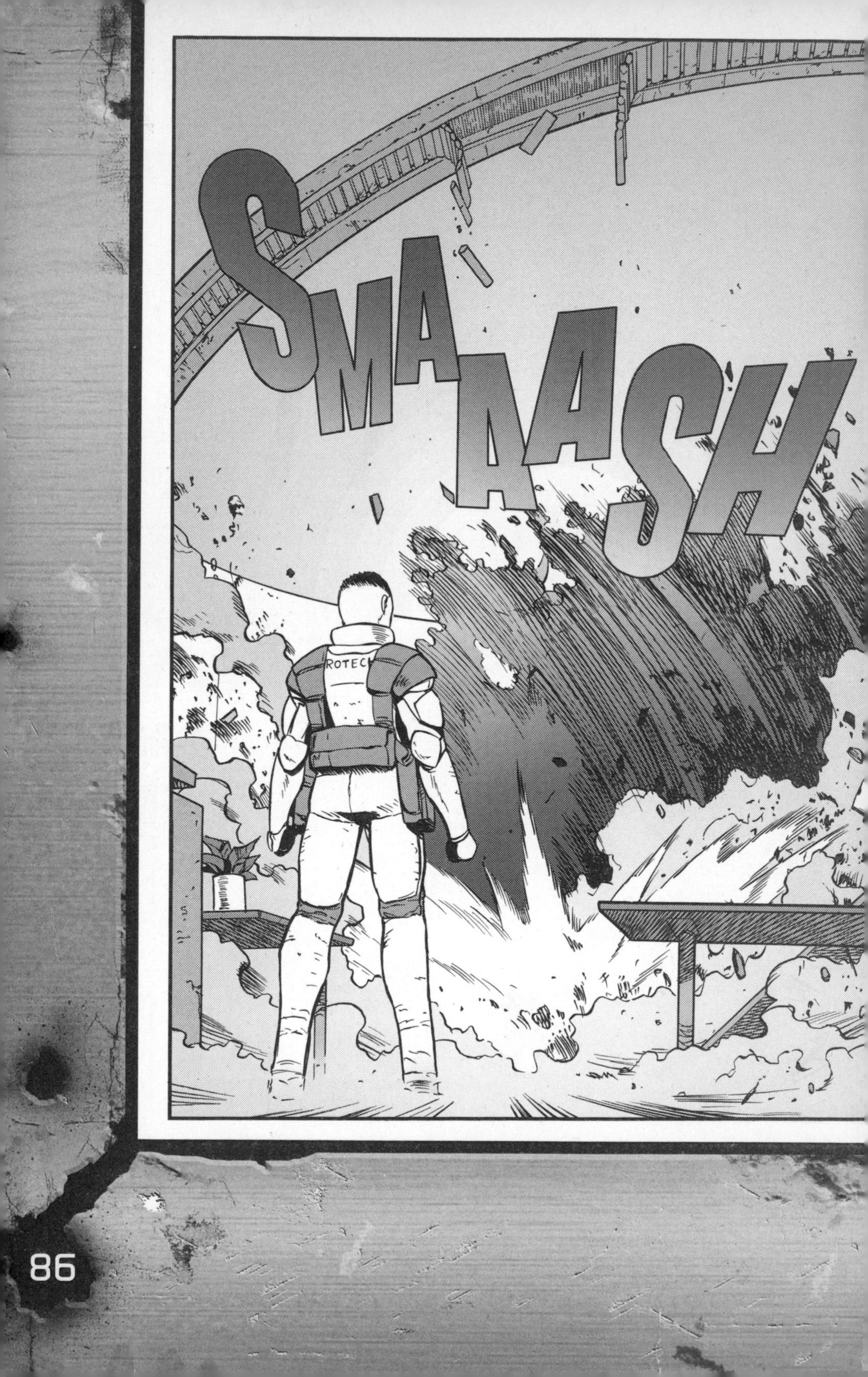
SMAASH
ROTECH

OOOOOGAAAAH

WHAT'S THAT AWFUL NOISE?

DID SHE TRIP SOME KIND OF *ALARM*?

NO. THAT'S THE *COMBAT SIREN*. THEY'RE BEING CALLED INTO *BATTLE*.

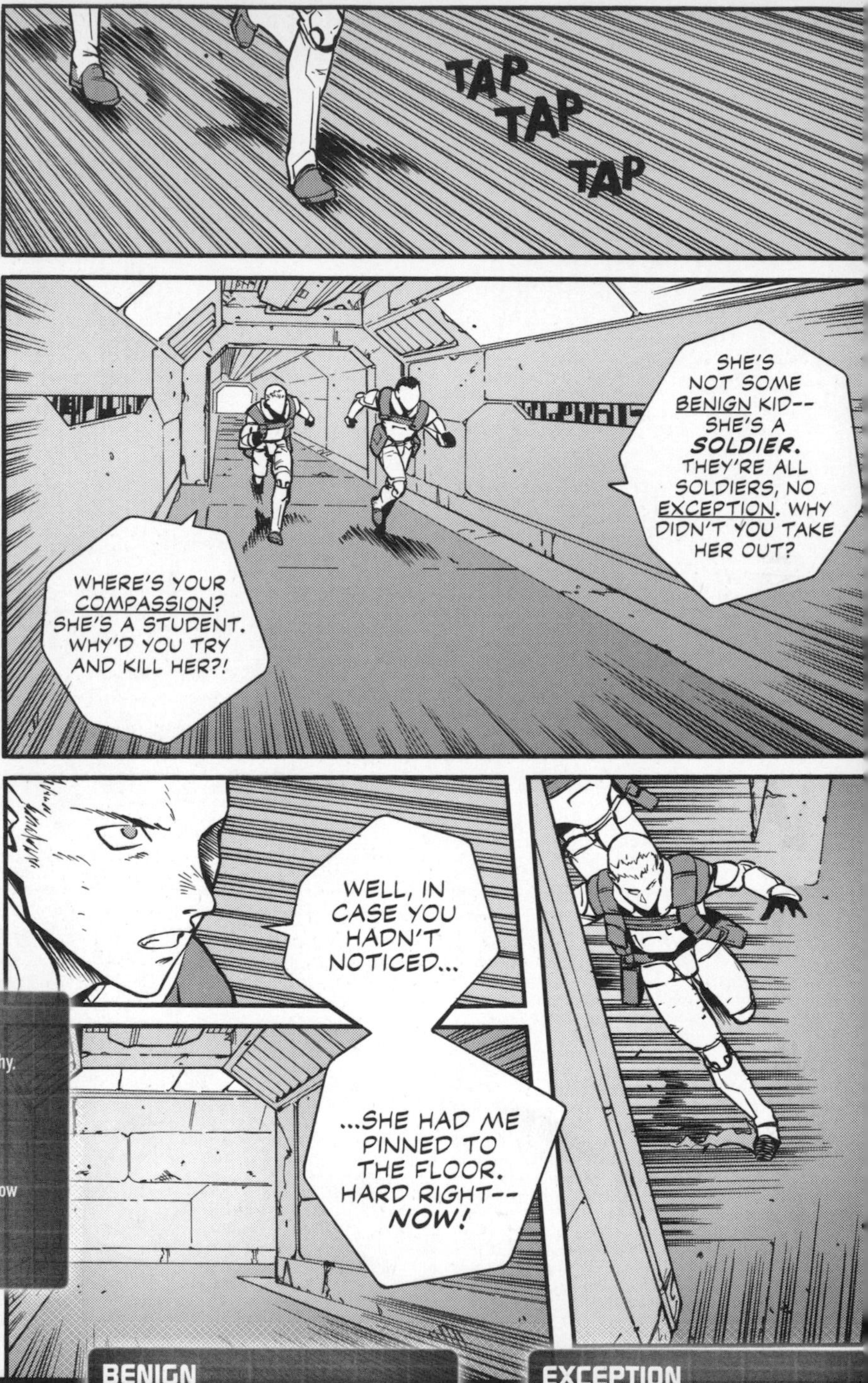
TAP
TAP
TAP
WHERE'S YOUR COMPASSION? SHE'S A STUDENT. WHY'D YOU TRY AND KILL HER?!
SHE'S NOT SOME BENIGN KID-- SHE'S A ***SOLDIER.*** THEY'RE ALL SOLDIERS, NO EXCEPTION. WHY DIDN'T YOU TAKE HER OUT?
WELL, IN CASE YOU HADN'T NOTICED...
...SHE HAD ME PINNED TO THE FLOOR. HARD RIGHT-- ***NOW!***

COMPASSION

\kum PASH in\ (n.): sympathy, helpfulness or mercy

In a touching show of *compassion*, the little girl presented the grieving widow with a flower.

BENIGN

\bi NIYN\ (adj.): gentle, harmless

Although many children in the neighborhood feared the old dog, he was actually quite *benign*.

EXCEPTION

\ek SEP shun\ (n.): a case that doesn't conform to generalization

With the *exception* of Yolanda, none of the studen in the class had previously seen Death of a Salesman.

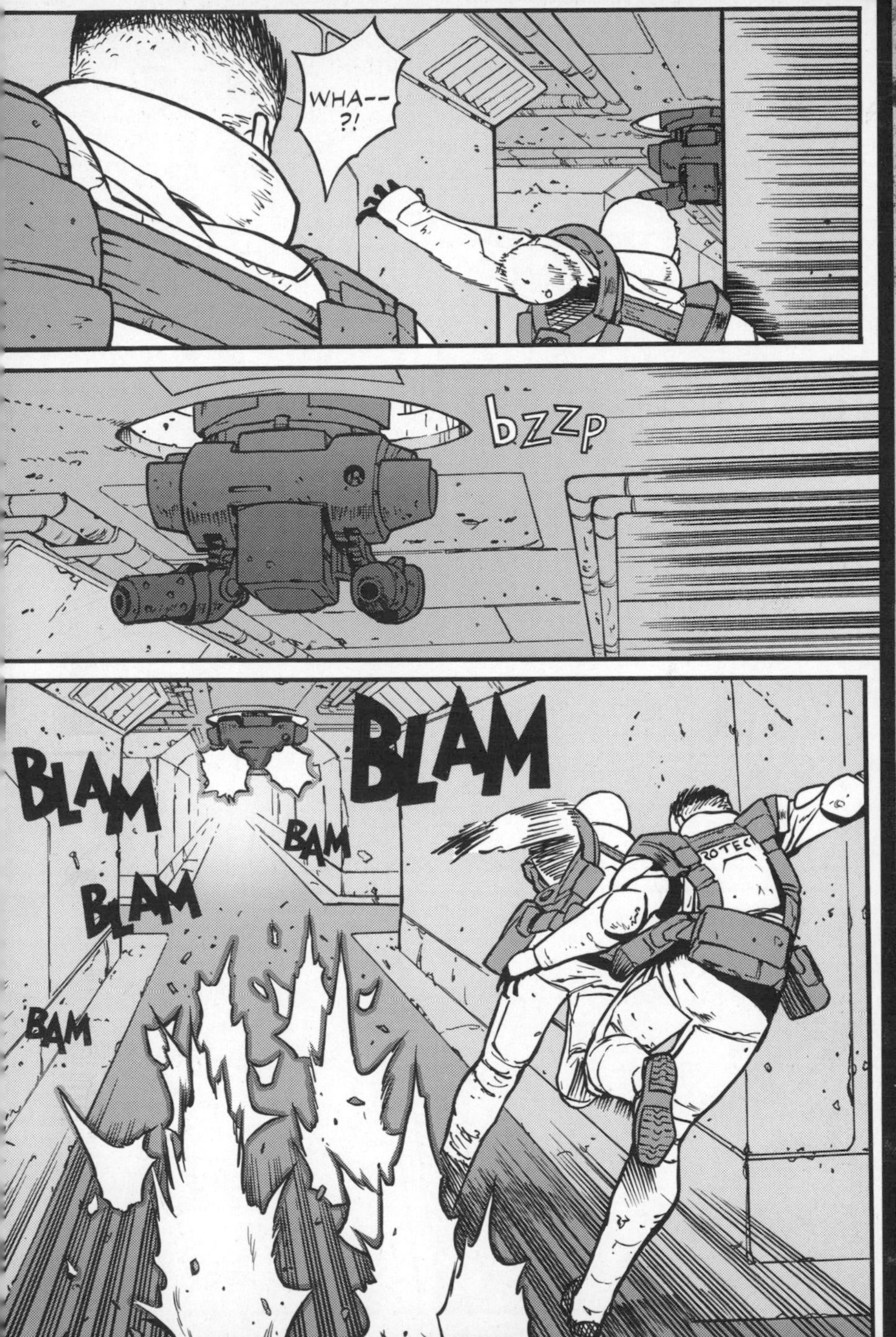

WHA-- ?!
bzzp
BLAM
BLAM
BAM
BLAM
BAM

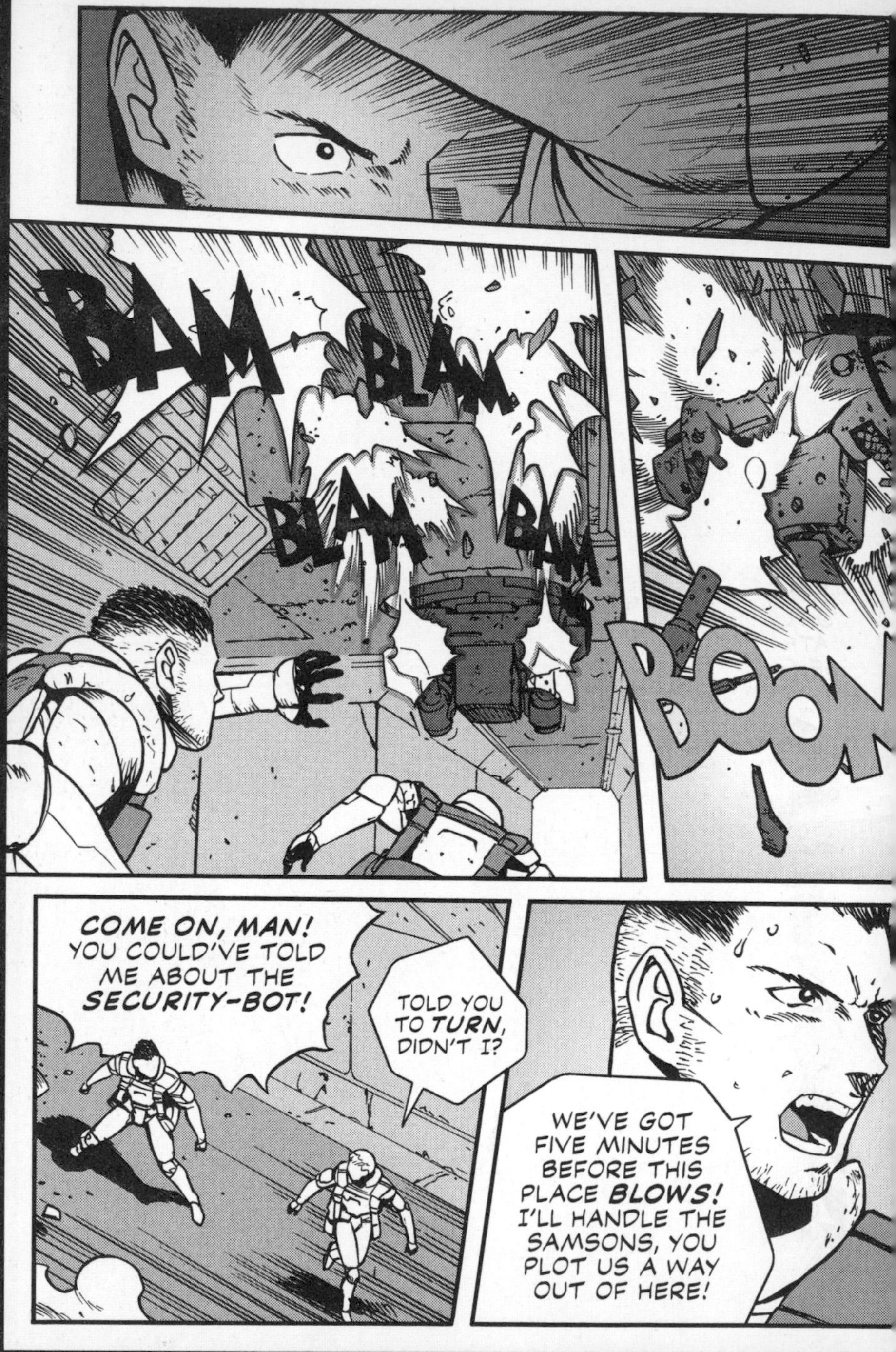
BAM
BLAM
BLAM
BAM
BOOM
COME ON, MAN! YOU COULD'VE TOLD ME ABOUT THE SECURITY-BOT!
TOLD YOU TO TURN, DIDN'T I?
WE'VE GOT FIVE MINUTES BEFORE THIS PLACE BLOWS! I'LL HANDLE THE SAMSONS, YOU PLOT US A WAY OUT OF HERE!

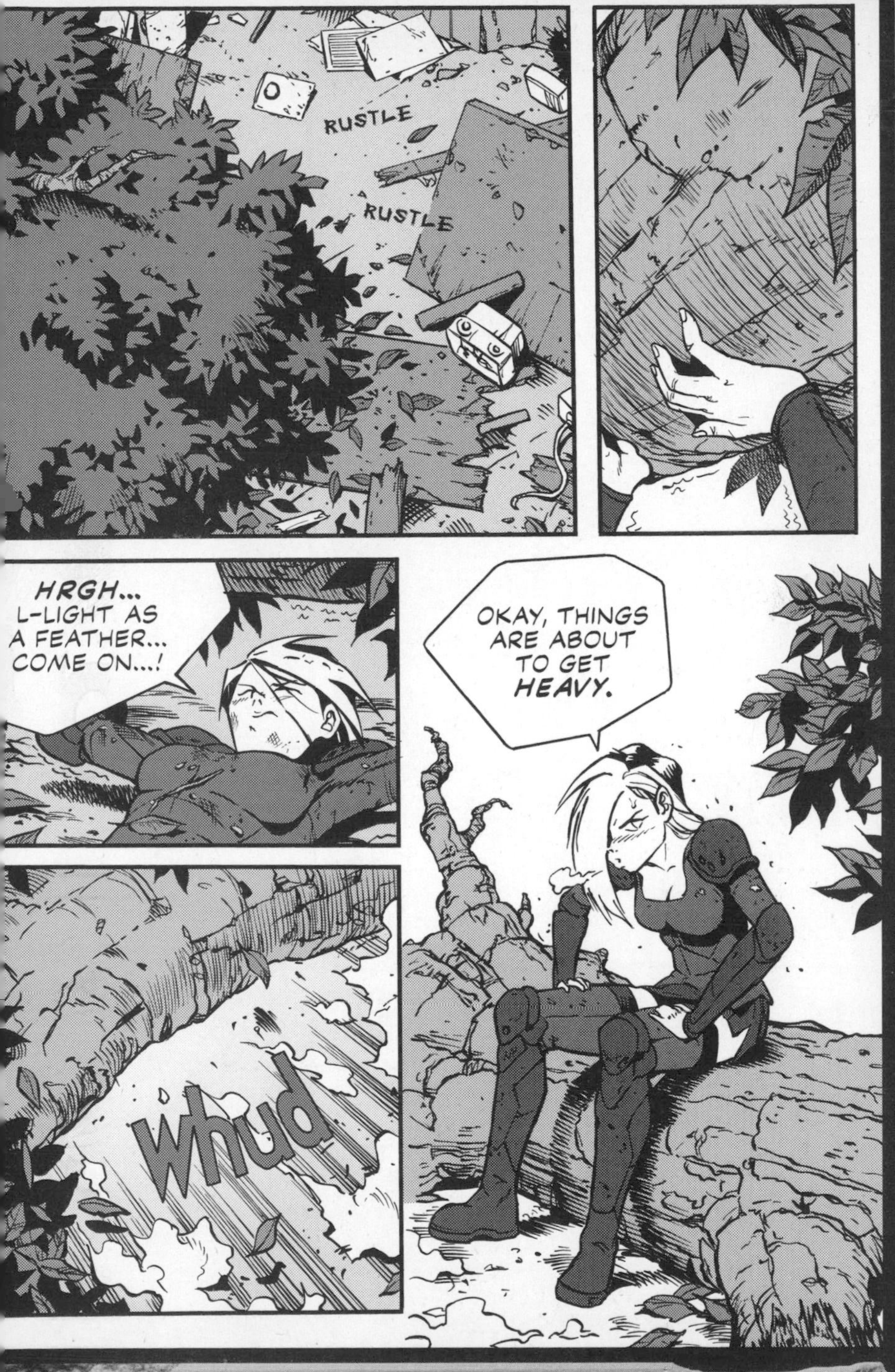
RUSTLE
RUSTLE
HRGH... L-LIGHT AS A FEATHER... COME ON...!
OKAY, THINGS ARE ABOUT TO GET HEAVY.
whud

GUYS? I'M JUST OUTSIDE GREENHOUSE F-7.

MEET ME HALFWAY. WE'VE GOT <u>INTRUDERS</u> WHO ARE TRYING TO <u>FLEE</u>.

TAK

TAK

INTRUDER

\in TROO der\ (n.): a trespasser

My uncle just bought a new watchdog to chase away any *intruders*.

FLEE

\FLEE\ (v.): run away from, escape

Many of the first immigrants to North America were *fleeing* religious persecution in their home countries.

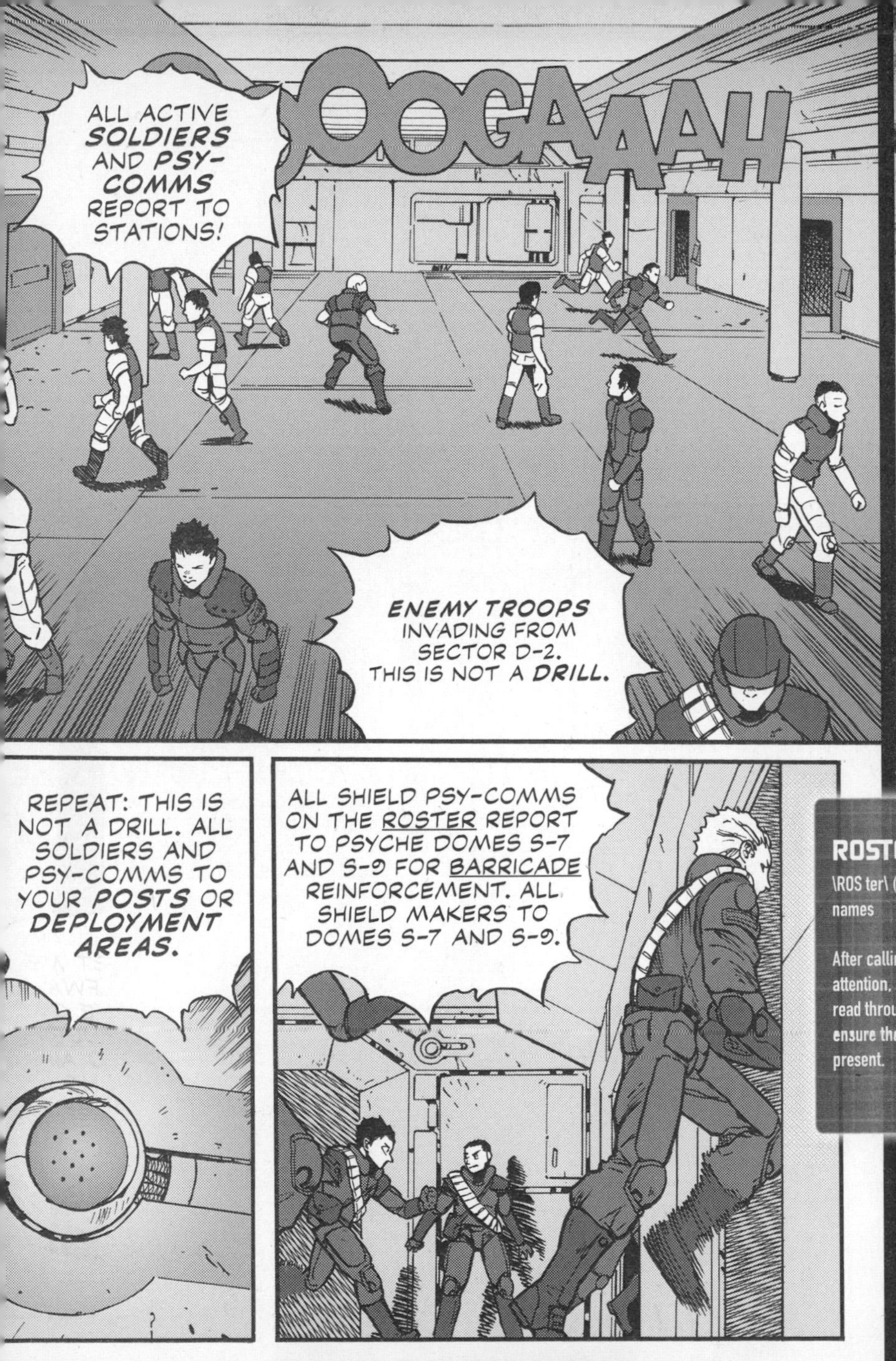
ALL ACTIVE SOLDIERS AND PSY-COMMS REPORT TO STATIONS!
OOGAAAH
ENEMY TROOPS INVADING FROM SECTOR D-2. THIS IS NOT A DRILL.
REPEAT: THIS IS NOT A DRILL. ALL SOLDIERS AND PSY-COMMS TO YOUR POSTS OR DEPLOYMENT AREAS.
ALL SHIELD PSY-COMMS ON THE ROSTER REPORT TO PSYCHE DOMES S-7 AND S-9 FOR BARRICADE REINFORCEMENT. ALL SHIELD MAKERS TO DOMES S-7 AND S-9.

ROSTER

\ROS ter\ (n.): a list of names

After calling the unit to attention, Lieutenant Cole read through the *roster* to ensure that everyone was present.

BARRICADE

\BAR ih kayd\ (n.): obstacle, barrier

During the French Revolution, students set up *barricades* in Paris to keep the army from moving through the streets.

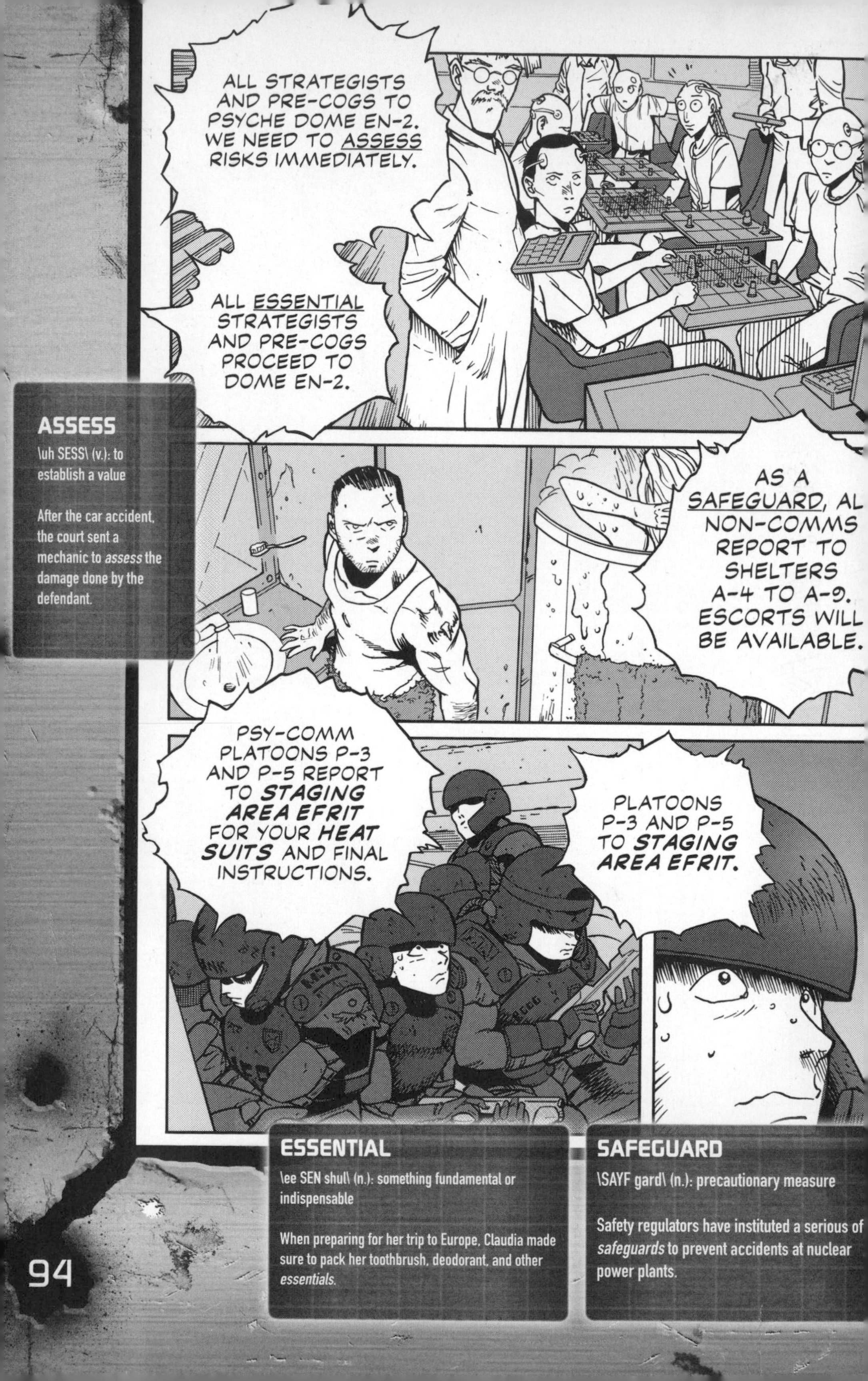
ALL STRATEGISTS AND PRE-COGS TO PSYCHE DOME EN-2. WE NEED TO ASSESS RISKS IMMEDIATELY.
ALL ESSENTIAL STRATEGISTS AND PRE-COGS PROCEED TO DOME EN-2.
AS A SAFEGUARD, AL NON-COMMS REPORT TO SHELTERS A-4 TO A-9. ESCORTS WILL BE AVAILABLE.
PSY-COMM PLATOONS P-3 AND P-5 REPORT TO STAGING AREA EFRIT FOR YOUR HEAT SUITS AND FINAL INSTRUCTIONS.
PLATOONS P-3 AND P-5 TO STAGING AREA EFRIT.

ASSESS

\uh SESS\ (v.): to establish a value

After the car accident, the court sent a mechanic to *assess* the damage done by the defendant.

ESSENTIAL

\ee SEN shul\ (n.): something fundamental or indispensable

When preparing for her trip to Europe, Claudia made sure to pack her toothbrush, deodorant, and other *essentials*.

SAFEGUARD

\SAYF gard\ (n.): precautionary measure

Safety regulators have instituted a serious of *safeguards* to prevent accidents at nuclear power plants.

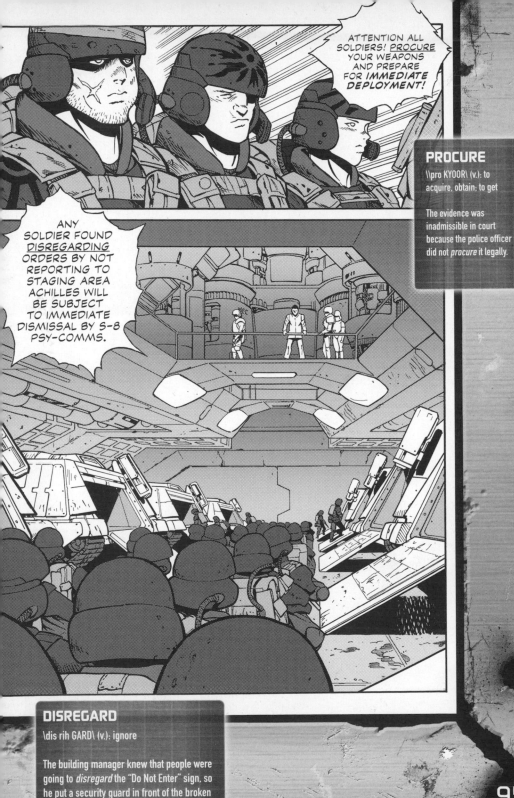

ATTENTION ALL SOLDIERS! *PROCURE* YOUR WEAPONS AND PREPARE FOR *IMMEDIATE DEPLOYMENT*!

ANY SOLDIER FOUND <u>DISREGARDING</u> ORDERS BY NOT REPORTING TO STAGING AREA ACHILLES WILL BE SUBJECT TO *IMMEDIATE* DISMISSAL BY S-8 PSY-COMMS.

PROCURE

\\pro KYOOR\ (v.): to acquire, obtain; to get

The evidence was inadmissible in court because the police officer did not *procure* it legally.

DISREGARD

\dis rih GARD\ (v.): ignore

The building manager knew that people were going to *disregard* the "Do Not Enter" sign, so he put a security guard in front of the broken elevator.

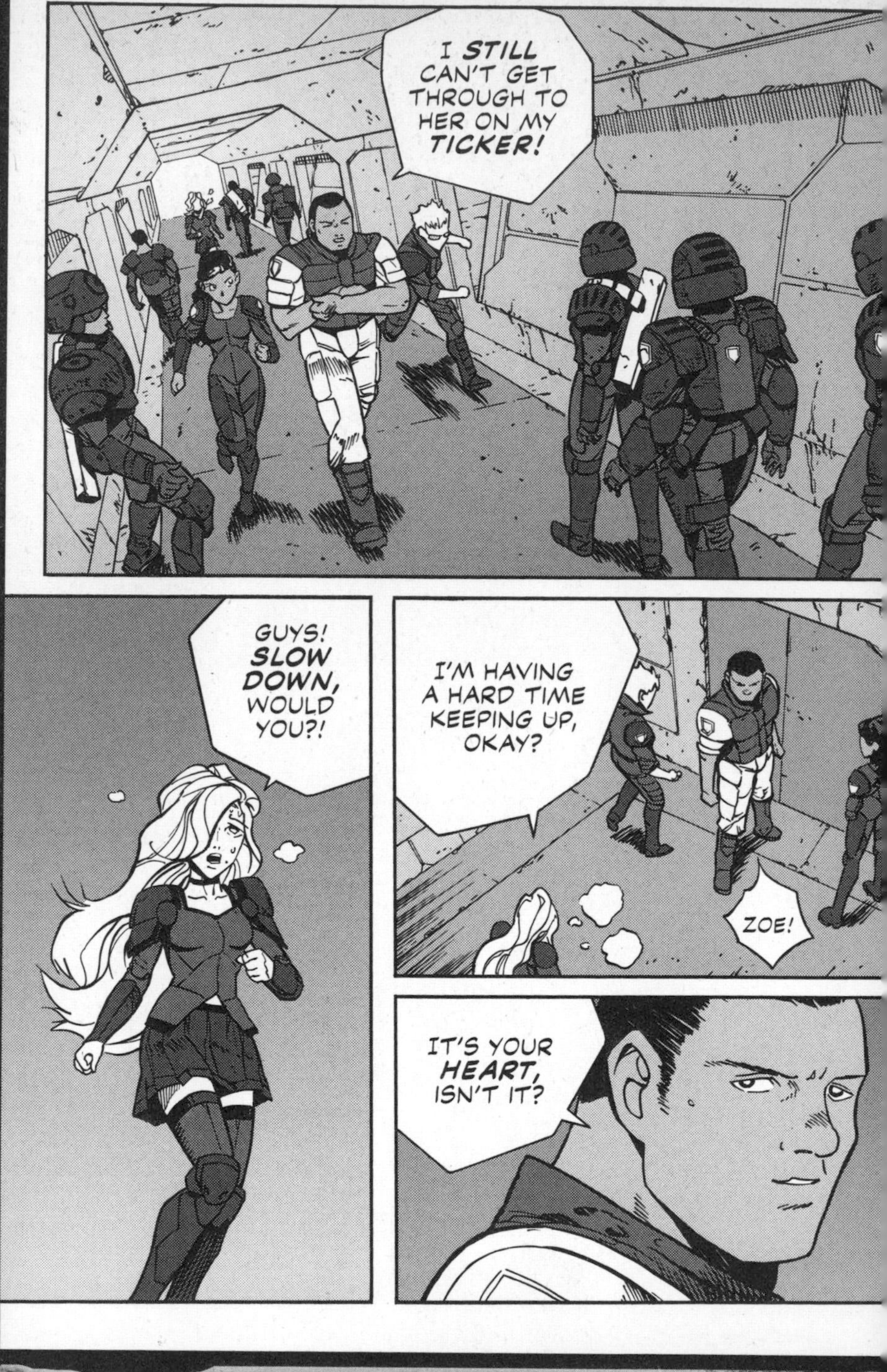
I STILL CAN'T GET THROUGH TO HER ON MY TICKER!
GUYS! SLOW DOWN, WOULD YOU?!
I'M HAVING A HARD TIME KEEPING UP, OKAY?
ZOE!
IT'S YOUR HEART, ISN'T IT?

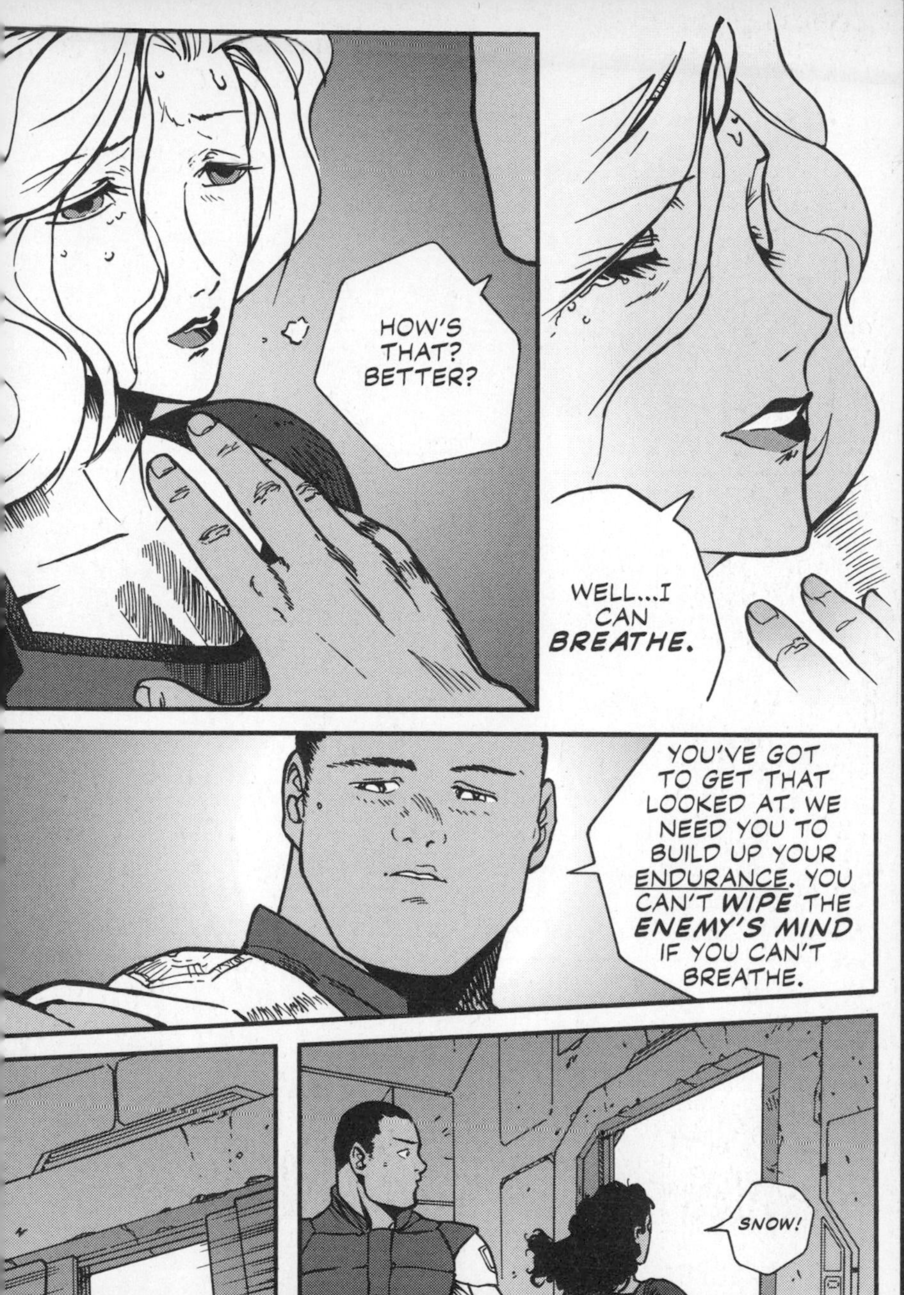

HOW'S THAT? BETTER?
WELL...I CAN *BREATHE.*
YOU'VE GOT TO GET THAT LOOKED AT. WE NEED YOU TO BUILD UP YOUR ENDURANCE. YOU CAN'T *WIPE* THE *ENEMY'S MIND* IF YOU CAN'T BREATHE.
SSHHP
SNOW!

ENDURANCE

\en DOOR uns\ (n.): ability to withstand hardships

To prepare for the marathon, Bekki built up her *endurance* by running ten miles every day.

WRATH

\RATH\ (n.): forceful anger

Hillary feared her father's *wrath* when she told him that she wrecked his car.

SNOW! HEY, ARE YOU ALL RIGHT?!
WHAT'S GOING ON?!
I RAN...INTO SOME SPIES. PROFESSOR ARBOGAST IS D-DEAD!
I WAS TOO LATE...I COULDN'T STOP THEM.
IF I CATC THEM, THEY'LL GE A TASTE OF CAL'S WRATH!
THEN AGAIN...I'M GUESSING OUR BOTANY EXAM IS CANCELLED. IF THIS ISN'T AN "EXTENUATING CIRCUMSTANCE," I DON'T KNOW WHAT IS.
SHUT UP, CAL! SNOW, ARE YOU OKAY TO GO OUT? WE CAN'T BE LATE FOR OUR FIRST FULL-SCALE CONFLICT.
SHE'S RIGH THE SARG WILL KILL US!

EXTENUATING

\ek STEN yoo ayt ing\ (adj.): partially excusing

Mr. Szen, due to the *extenuating* circumstances, allowed Brian an extra week to finish the assignment.

CONFLICT

\KON flikt\ (n.): a clash, a battle

The *conflict* between Debbie and Gerry heightened as the former friends began to insult each other publicly.

BEEP
WHAT THE--?!
BEEP
ALERT! EXPLOSIVES FOUND IN AREA D-3! DIVERT ALL PERSONNEL! EXPLO--
OH, NO... NO--
KABOOM

DIVERT

\di VURT\ (v.): to turn aside, to distract

To keep the child quiet during the doctor's examination, the nurse *diverted* his attention with puppets.

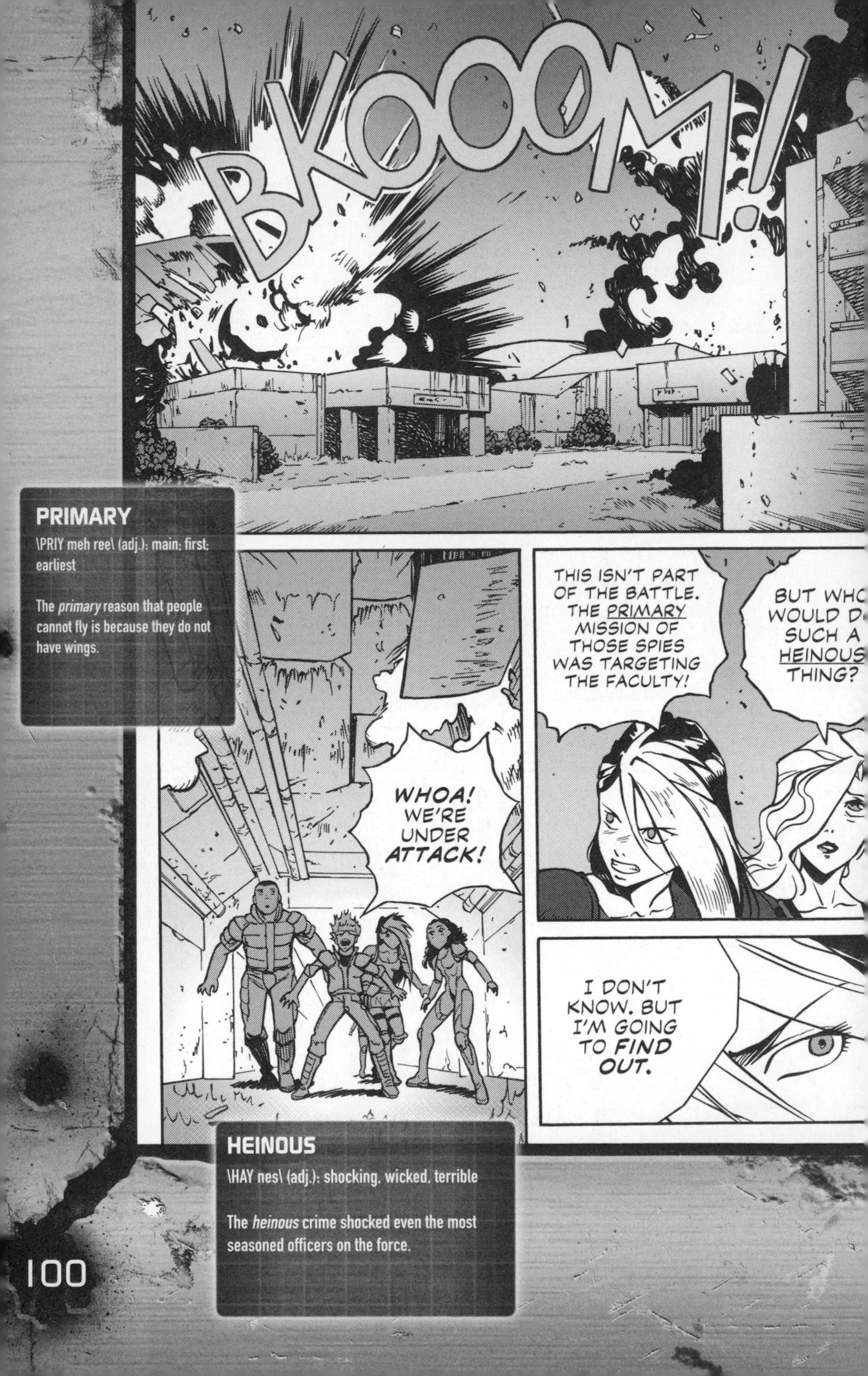
BKOOOM!!
WHOA! WE'RE UNDER ATTACK!
THIS ISN'T PART OF THE BATTLE. THE PRIMARY MISSION OF THOSE SPIES WAS TARGETING THE FACULTY!
BUT WHO WOULD D SUCH A HEINOUS THING?
I DON'T KNOW. BUT I'M GOING TO FIND OUT.

PRIMARY

\PRIY meh ree\ (adj.): main; first; earliest

The *primary* reason that people cannot fly is because they do not have wings.

HEINOUS

\HAY nes\ (adj.): shocking, wicked, terrible

The *heinous* crime shocked even the most seasoned officers on the force.

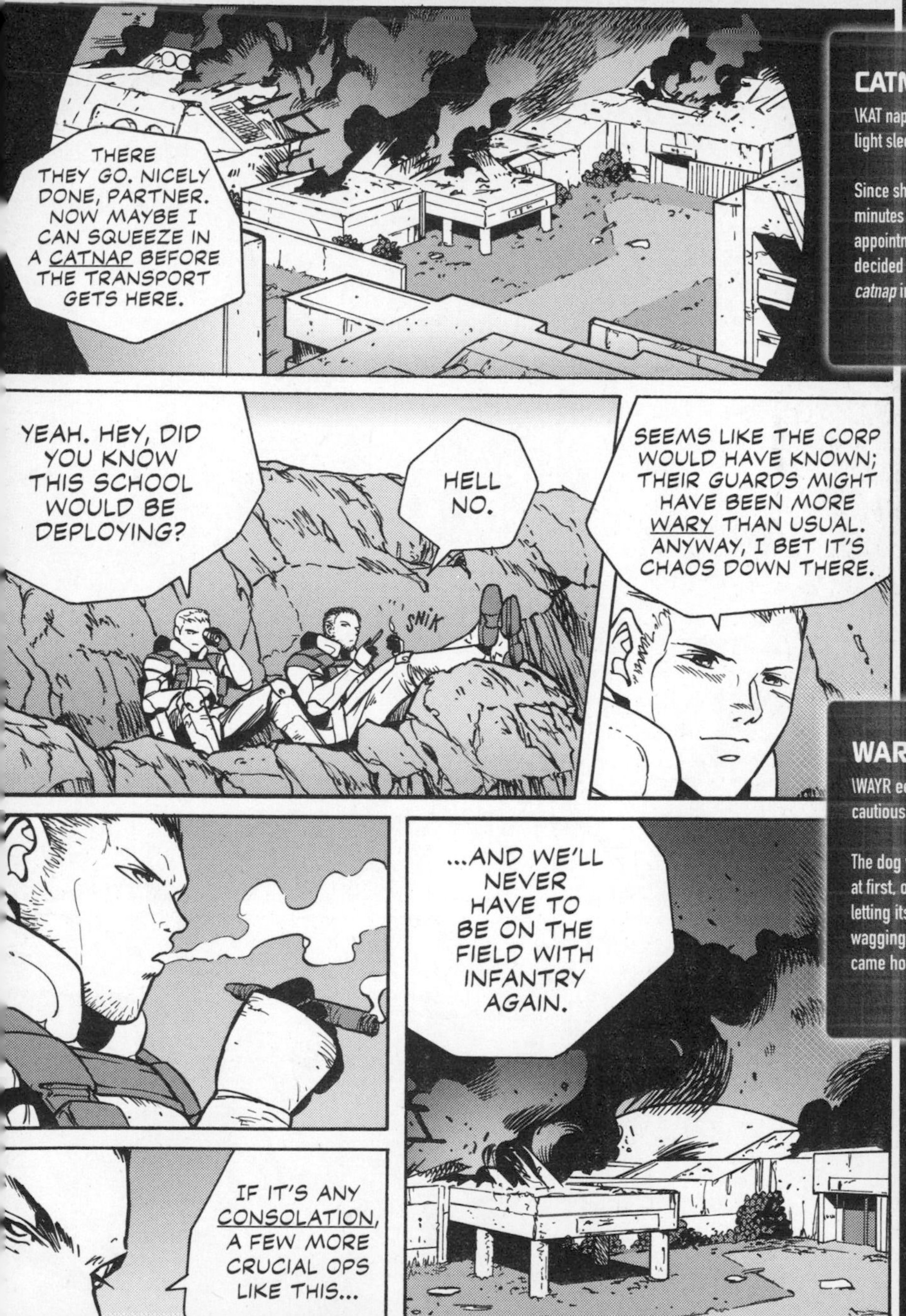
THERE THEY GO. NICELY DONE, PARTNER. NOW MAYBE I CAN SQUEEZE IN A CATNAP BEFORE THE TRANSPORT GETS HERE.
YEAH. HEY, DID YOU KNOW THIS SCHOOL WOULD BE DEPLOYING?
HELL NO.
SNIK
SEEMS LIKE THE CORP WOULD HAVE KNOWN; THEIR GUARDS MIGHT HAVE BEEN MORE WARY THAN USUAL. ANYWAY, I BET IT'S CHAOS DOWN THERE.
IF IT'S ANY CONSOLATION, A FEW MORE CRUCIAL OPS LIKE THIS...
...AND WE'LL NEVER HAVE TO BE ON THE FIELD WITH INFANTRY AGAIN.

CATNAP

\KAT nap\ (n.): short, light sleep

Since she had twenty minutes before her next appointment, Cheryl decided to take a *catnap* in her office.

WARY

\WAYR ee\ (adj.): careful, cautious

The dog was *wary* of Bola at first, only gradually letting its guard down and wagging its tail when Bola came home at night.

CONSOLATION

\kon so LAY shun\ (n.): the act of providing comfort or solace for a loss or hardship

The vast inheritance offered little *consolation* to the grief-stricken widow.

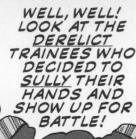

WELL, WELL! LOOK AT THE DERELICT TRAINEES WHO DECIDED TO SULLY THEIR HANDS AND SHOW UP FOR BATTLE!
WHAT'S WRONG WITH YOU?!
YOU SEE THESE TROOPS WAITING TO DEPLOY?! YOU THINK BECAUSE YOU'RE THE PROFESSOR'S PROTEGES THAT YOU'RE SPECIAL?!
BE NICE, SARGE.
JUST FORGET WE'RE LATE.
UHH...
RIGHT THIS WAY, LADIES!

DERELICT

\DER uh likt\ (adj.): neglectful of one's obligations; abandoned

Davey's father scolded him for being *derelict* in his household chores; the garbage hadn't been thrown out in a week.

SULLY

\SUL ee\ (v.): soil, stain, tarnish, taint

Reginald was upset to discover that the child's sticky red lollipop had *sullied* his new cashmere overcoat.

PROTÉGÉ

\PRO tuh zhay\ (n.): one receiving personal direction and care from a mentor

Although David was initially a *protégé* of Pauline, he soon broke loose and developed his own style of writing.

OH, GOD. MY STOMACH FEELS... URP.
rrrmmmbb
67
TRITO
C-TECH
ALL RIGHT, YOU PRECIOUS SWEETHEARTS-- LISTEN UP! THAT RUMBLING YOU FEEL IS THE TIRES ON THE ROAD...
...AND THAT KNOT YOU FEEL IS YOUR STOMACH. NOW THERE'S ONE THING YOU MAGGOTS NEED TO KEEP IN MIND!
REMEMBER YOUR FUNDAMENTAL TRAINING, WATCH FOR CUES FROM THE EXPERIENCED SOLDIERS, AND YOU WILL COME HOME ALIVE!

PRECIOUS

\PRESH us\ (adj.): valuable; beloved

Although Michelle had a lot of expensive jewelry, the copper bracelet that belonged to her grandmother was her most *precious* possession.

FUNDAMENTAL

\fun da MEN tul\ (adj.): basic, essential

One of the *fundamental* tenets of the Declaration of Independence is that all men are created equal.

CUE

\KYOO\ (n.): reminder, prompting

Sally nervously sat backstage waiting for the director to give her the *cue* to start singing.

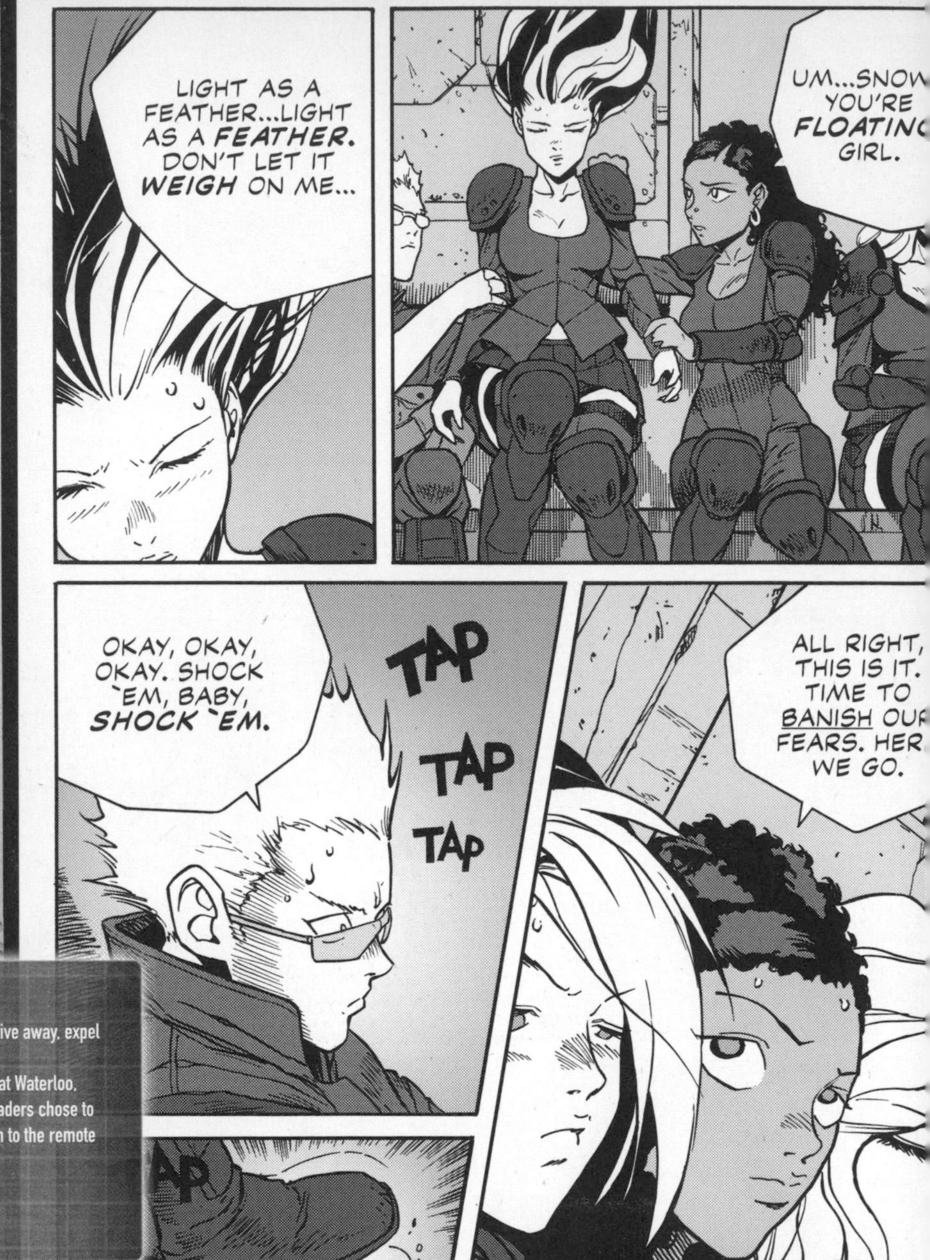
LIGHT AS A FEATHER...LIGHT AS A FEATHER. DON'T LET IT WEIGH ON ME...
UM...SNOW YOU'RE FLOATIN GIRL.
OKAY, OKAY, OKAY. SHOCK `EM, BABY, SHOCK `EM.
TAP
TAP
TAP
ALL RIGHT, THIS IS IT. TIME TO BANISH OU FEARS. HER WE GO.
TAP
TAP

BANISH

\BAN ish\ (v.): drive away, expel

After his defeat at Waterloo, the European leaders chose to *banish* Napoleon to the remote island of Elba.

PSY★COMM

CHAPTER [6]

CONVENIENT

\kon VEEN yent\ (adj.): favorable to one's comfort or needs

The hardest part about working with a big group is finding a time that is *convenient* for everyone.

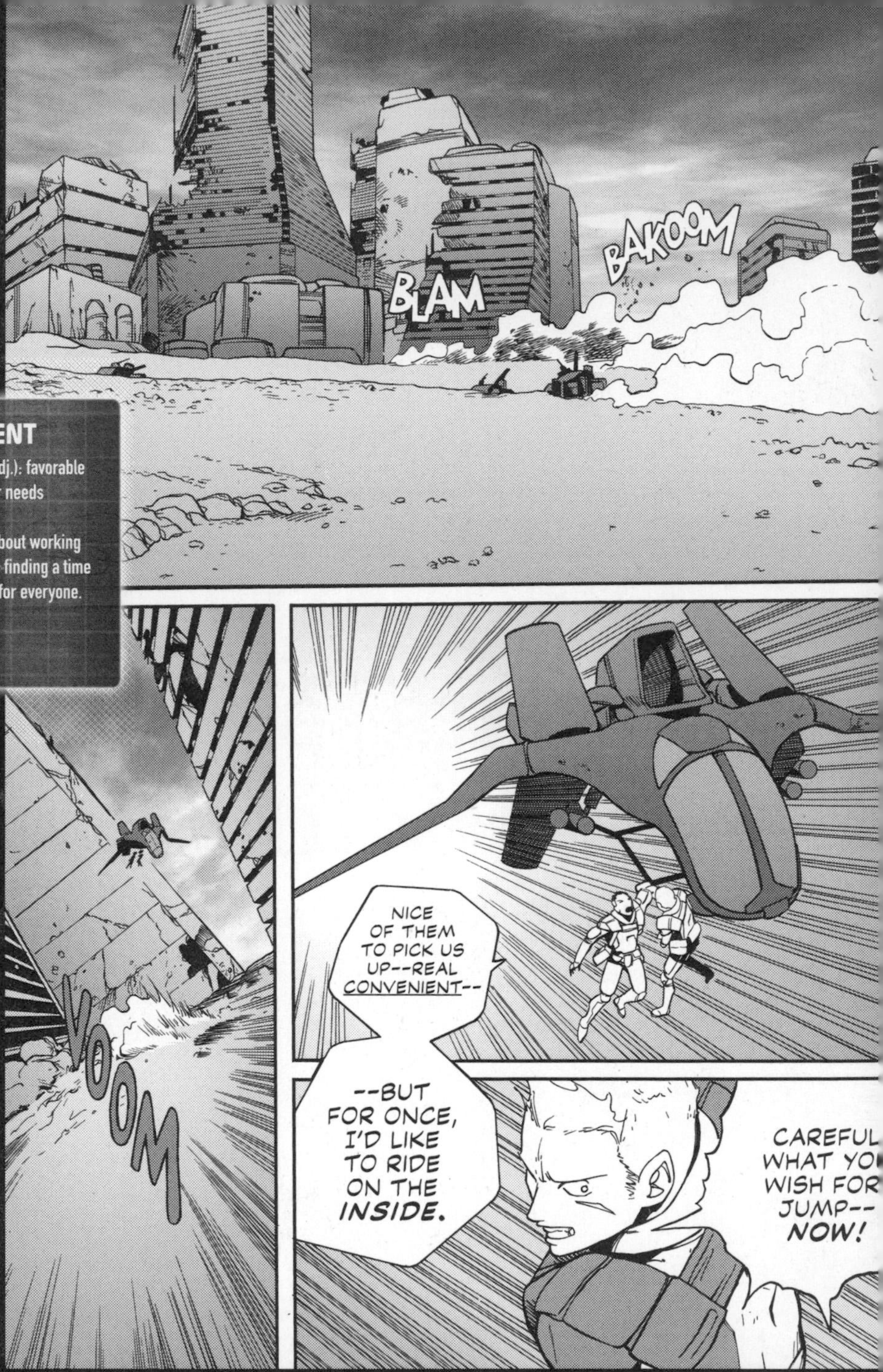
BLAM
BAKOOM
VOOM
NICE OF THEM TO PICK US UP--REAL CONVENIENT--
--BUT FOR ONCE, I'D LIKE TO RIDE ON THE INSIDE.
CAREFUL WHAT YO WISH FOR JUMP-- NOW!

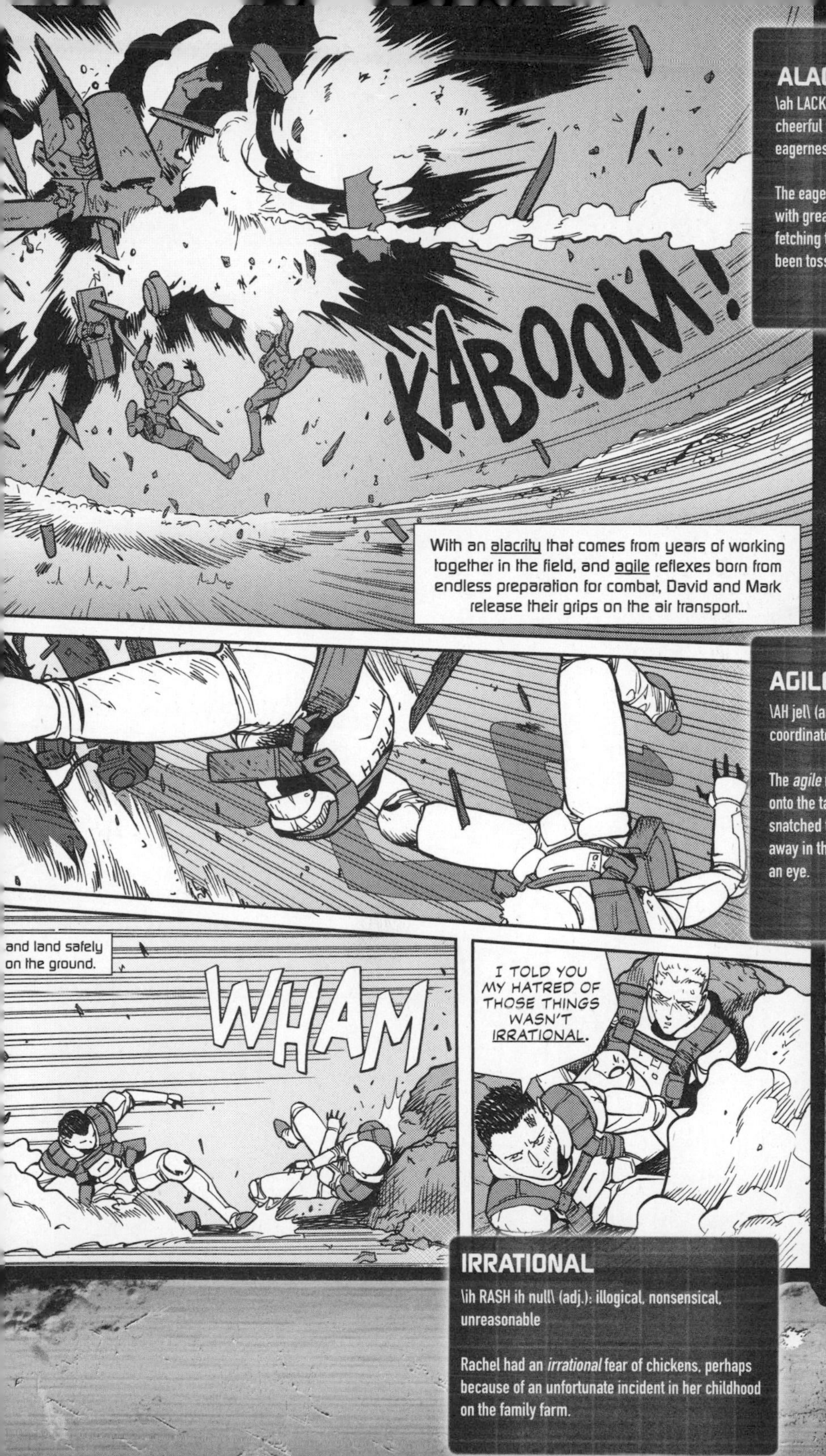
KABOOM!
With an alacrity that comes from years of working together in the field, and agile reflexes born from endless preparation for combat, David and Mark release their grips on the air transport...
and land safely on the ground.
WHAM
I TOLD YOU MY HATRED OF THOSE THINGS WASN'T IRRATIONAL.

ALACRITY

\ah LACK ri tee\ (n.): cheerful willingness, eagerness; speed

The eager dog obeyed with great *alacrity*, fetching the stick that had been tossed for him.

AGILE

\AH jel\ (adj.): well coordinated, nimble

The *agile* monkey leapt onto the table and snatched the boy's banana away in the blink of an eye.

IRRATIONAL

\ih RASH ih null\ (adj.): illogical, nonsensical, unreasonable

Rachel had an *irrational* fear of chickens, perhaps because of an unfortunate incident in her childhood on the family farm.

BUDDA
BUDDA
BUDDA
OVER THERE! A SOLITARY TANK AND SOME COMBATANTS.
YEAH, I SEE THEM! I HATE TO BOAST, BUT I THINK THEIR ARMOR IS GOING TO BE USELESS AGAINST THIS!
KRR
?!

BOAST

\BOHST\ (v.): speak with excessive pride

"I can beat all of you at that video game any day of the week," *boasted* Derrick last night.

SOLITARY

\SOL ih ter ee\ (adj.): alone; remote, secluded

I love going up to the mountains in the autumn to live in my *solitary* cabin in the woods.

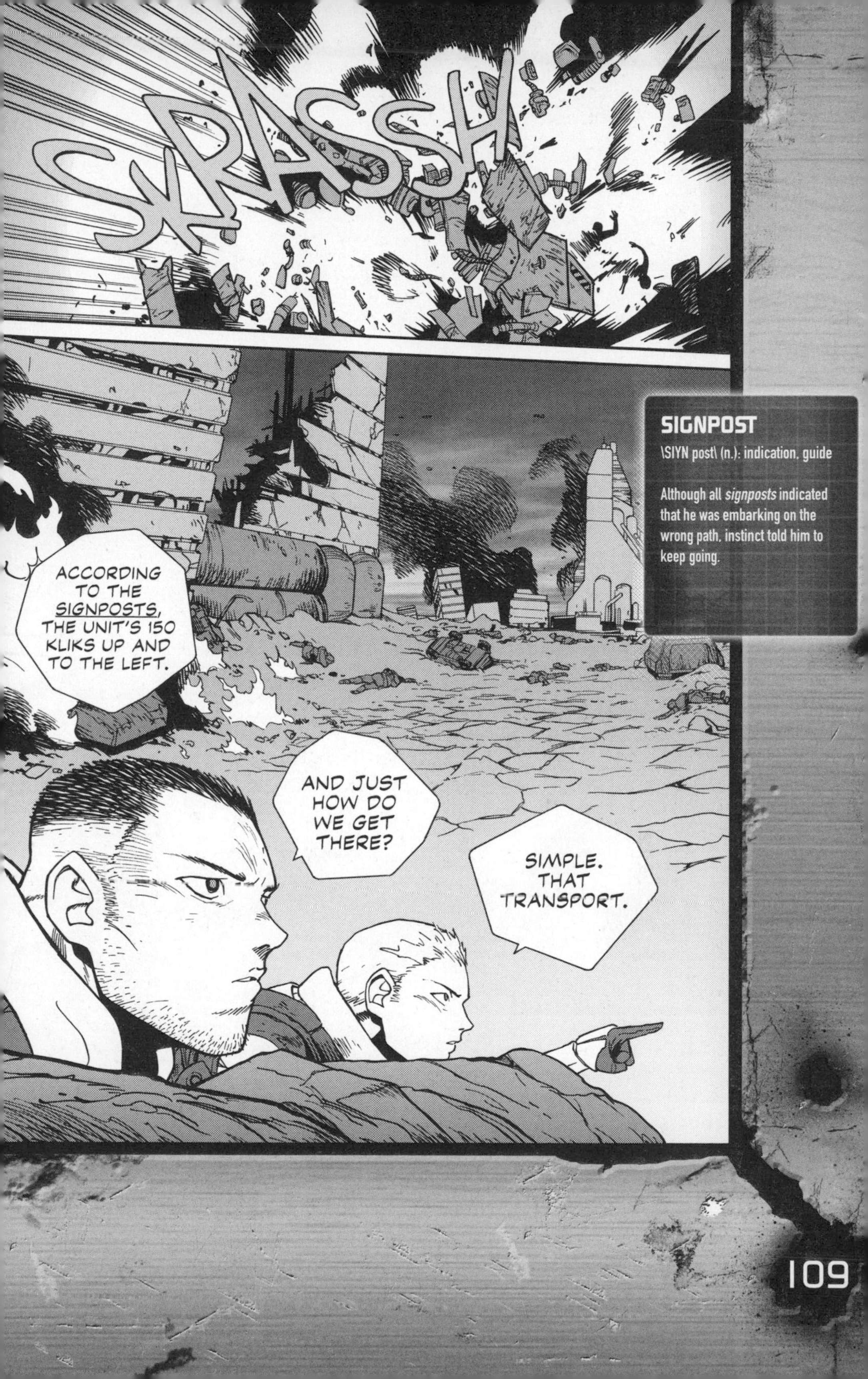
SKRASSH
ACCORDING TO THE SIGNPOSTS, THE UNIT'S 150 KLIKS UP AND TO THE LEFT.
AND JUST HOW DO WE GET THERE?
SIMPLE. THAT TRANSPORT.

SIGNPOST

\SIYN post\ (n.): indication, guide

Although all *signposts* indicated that he was embarking on the wrong path, instinct told him to keep going.

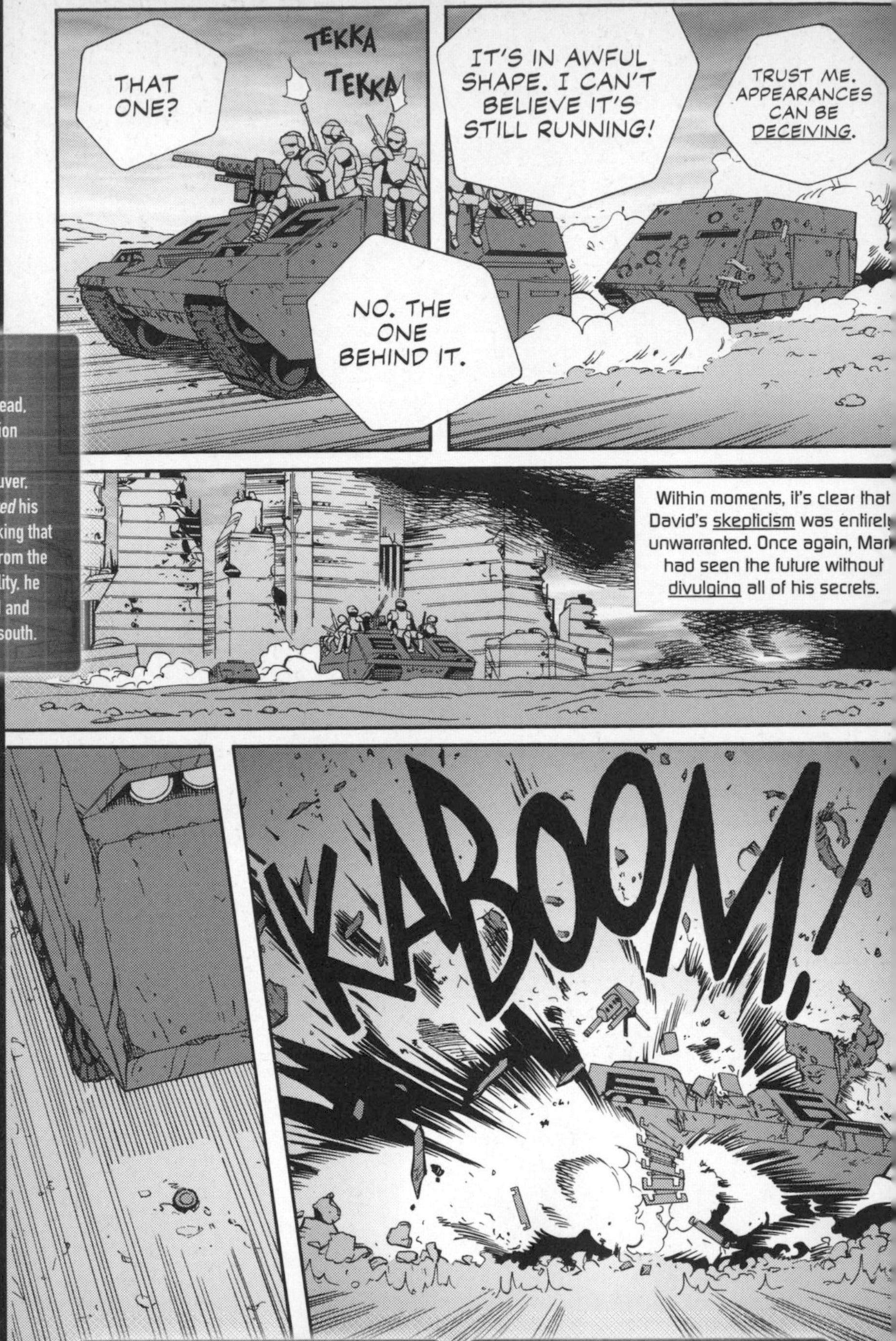
THAT ONE?
TEKKA TEKKA
NO. THE ONE BEHIND IT.
IT'S IN AWFUL SHAPE. I CAN'T BELIEVE IT'S STILL RUNNING!
TRUST ME. APPEARANCES CAN BE DECEIVING.
Within moments, it's clear that David's skepticism was entirely unwarranted. Once again, Mark had seen the future without divulging all of his secrets.
KABOOM!

DECEIVE

\de SEEV\ (v.): mislead, give false impression

In a brilliant maneuver, the general *deceived* his opponent into thinking that he was attacking from the north when, in reality, he had circled around and attacked from the south.

SKEPTICISM

\SKEP tih sizm\ (n.): doubt, disbelief; uncertainty

Despite their onlookers' *skepticism*, the Wright Brothers demonstrated that man was capable of flight.

DIVULGE

\di VULJ\ (v.): to make known

Pat was fired for *divulging* company secrets to its competitors.

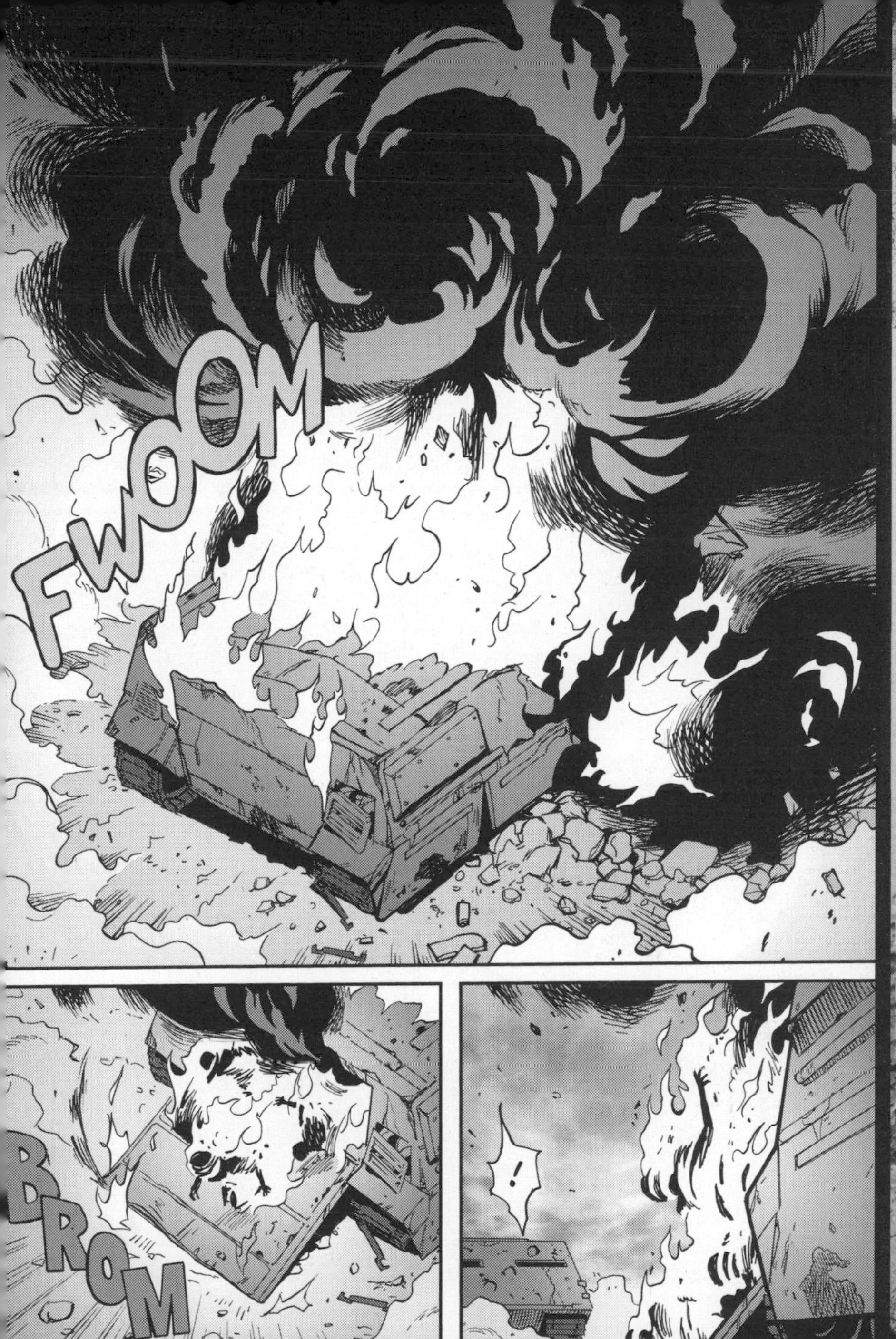
FWOOOM
BROM
!

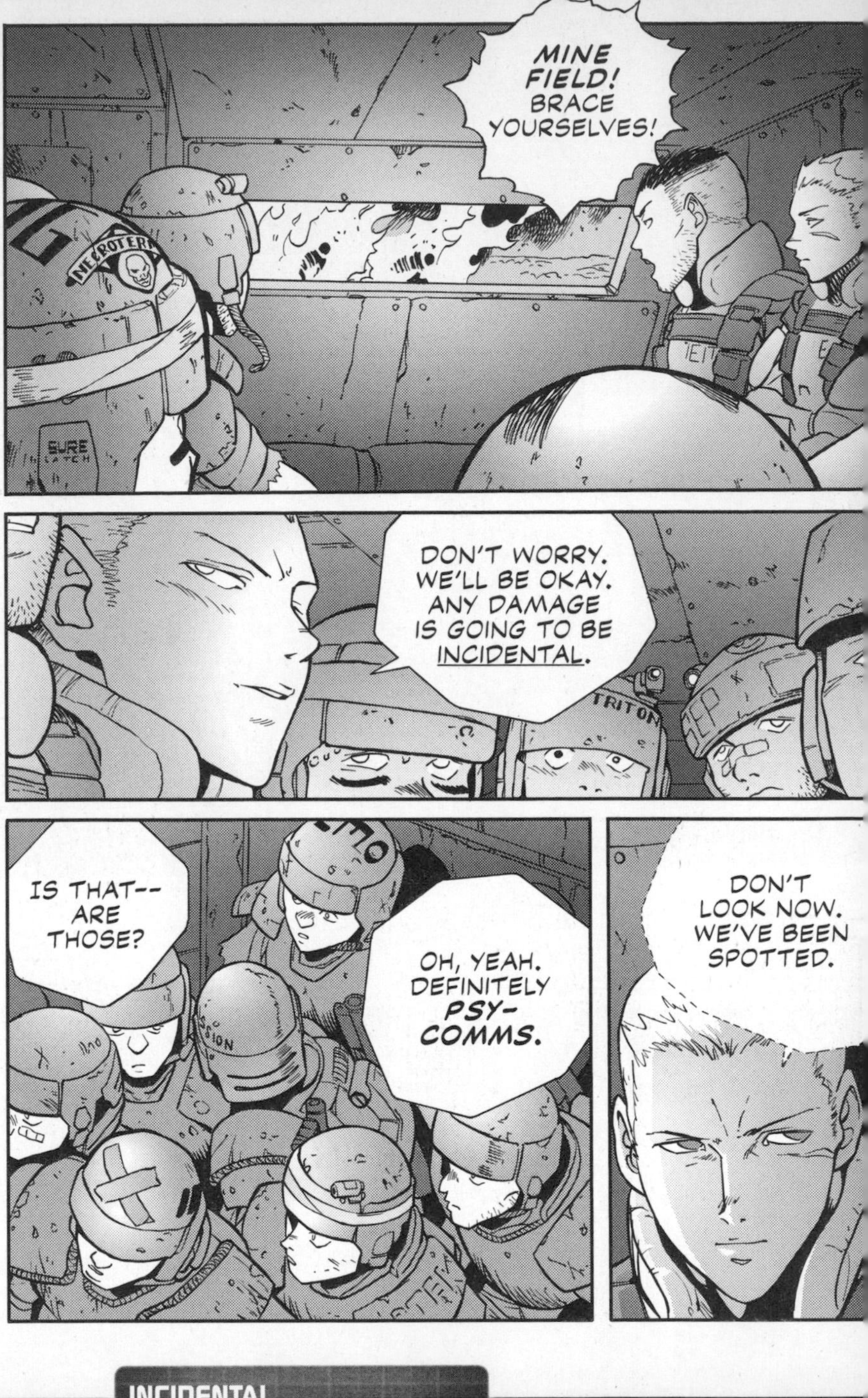
MINE FIELD! BRACE YOURSELVES!
DON'T WORRY. WE'LL BE OKAY. ANY DAMAGE IS GOING TO BE INCIDENTAL.
IS THAT-- ARE THOSE?
OH, YEAH. DEFINITELY PSY-COMMS.
DON'T LOOK NOW. WE'VE BEEN SPOTTED.

INCIDENTAL

\in sih DEN tul\ (adj.): minor, casual

Our trip to the coast will cost seven hundred dollars, not including *incidental* costs like admissions to parks and theatres.

FWAM
WHAT'RE YOU MAGGOTS WAITING FOR... SOME QUAINT INVITATION?! NO ONE'S GOING TO CAJOLE YOU ONTO THE BATTLEFIELD.
GET OUT THERE! SHOW THEM THAT WE'RE NOT A BUNCH OF COWARDS!
AH!

QUAINT

\KWAYNT\ (adj.): charmingly strange

The highlight of the street was the *quaint* little cottage that resided alone amongst the four-story mansions.

CAJOLE

\ka JOL\ (v.): flatter, coax, persuade

The spoiled girl could *cajole* her father into buying her anything.

DEBILITATING

\dee BIL uh tay ting\ (adj.): impairing the strength or energy

The company's relocation was *debilitating* to its employees; they lost all will to work in their new environment.

COLOSSAL

\kuh LOS us\ (adj.): immense, enormous

Joseph made a *colossal* error by skipping school; he failed the final and was forced to retake the course.

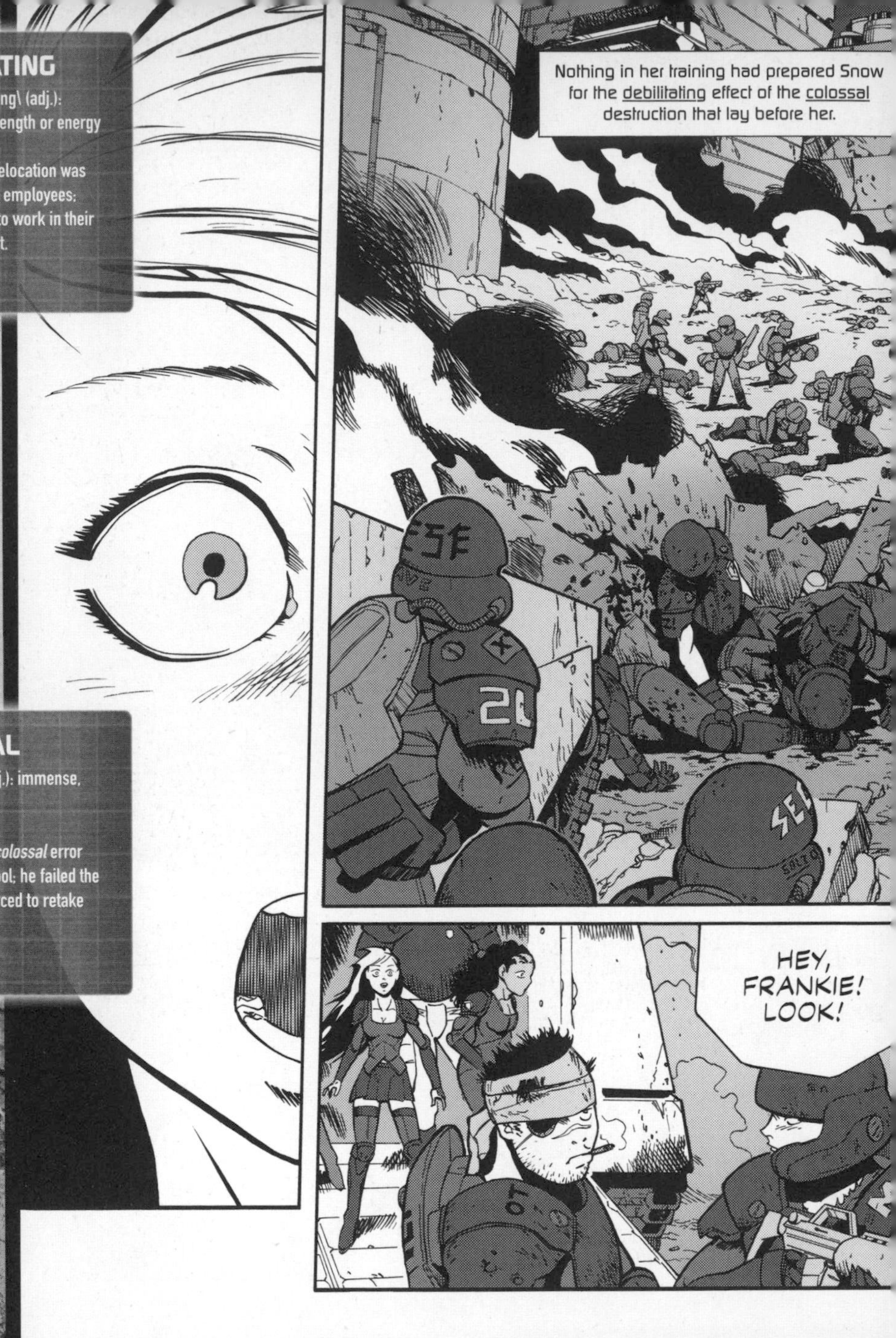
Nothing in her training had prepared Snow for the debilitating effect of the colossal destruction that lay before her.
HEY, FRANKIE! LOOK!

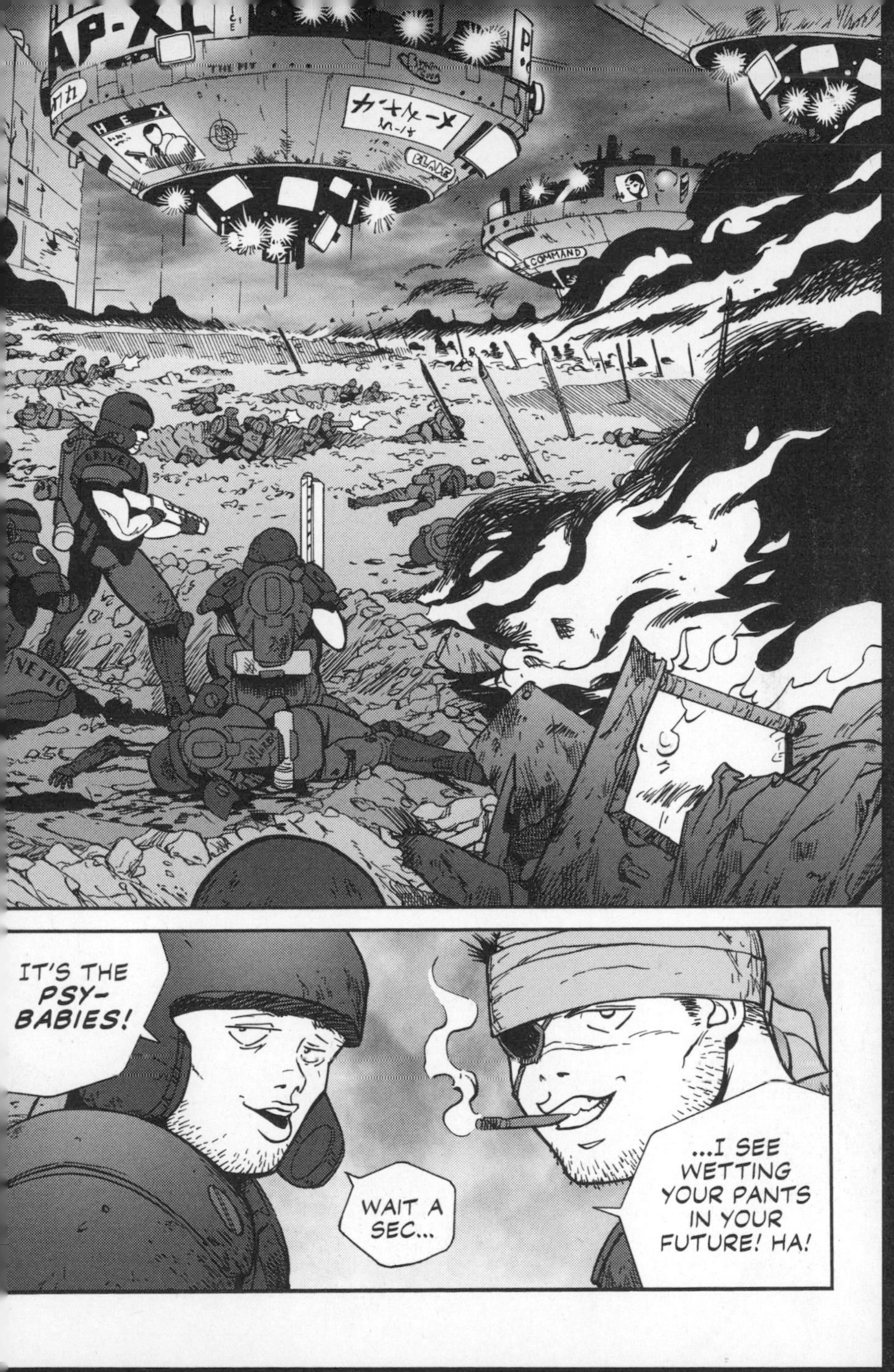
AP-XL
HEX
COMMAND
IT'S THE *PSY-BABIES!*
WAIT A SEC...
...I SEE WETTING YOUR PANTS IN YOUR FUTURE! HA!

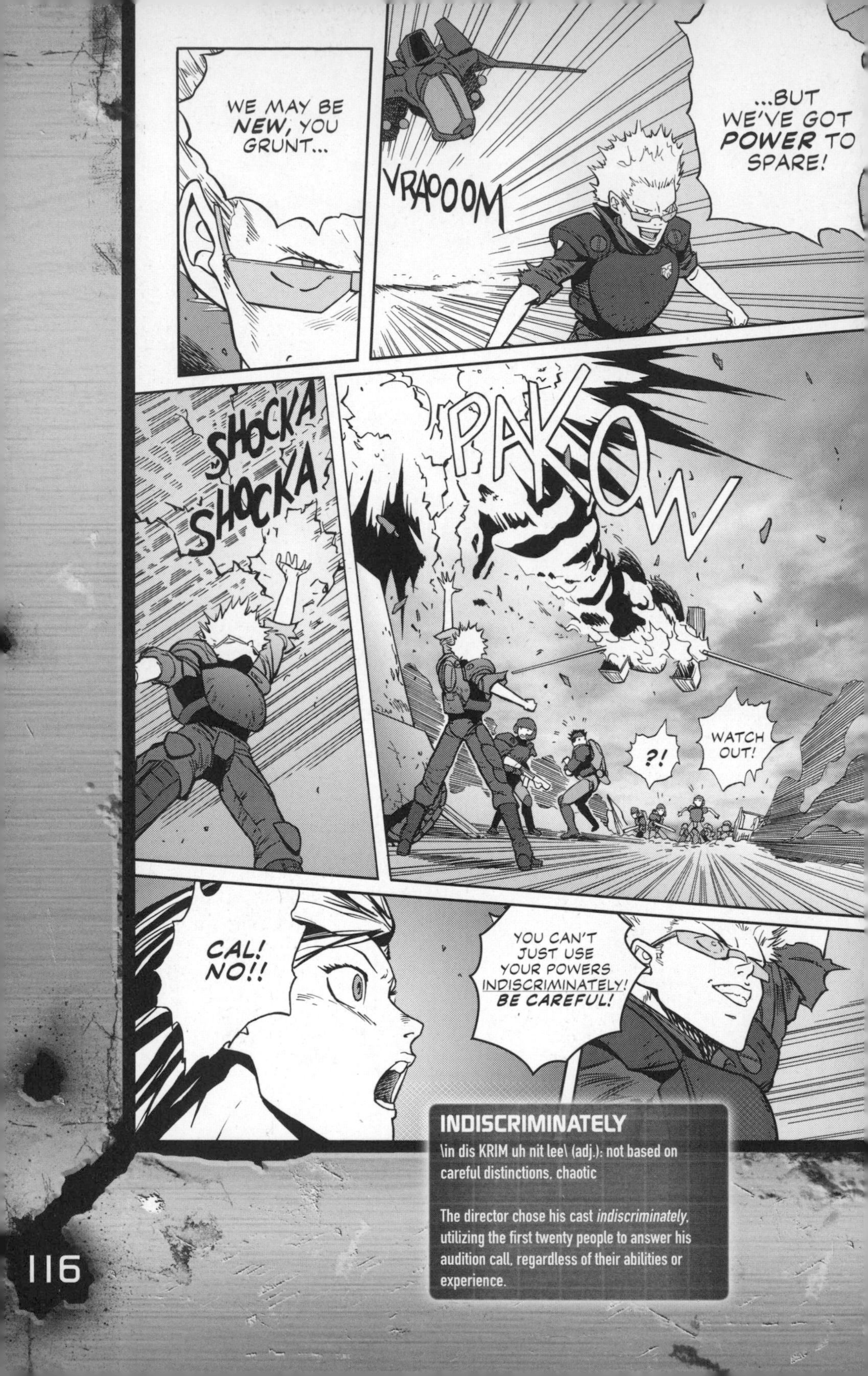
WE MAY BE *NEW,* YOU GRUNT...
VRAOOOM
...BUT WE'VE GOT *POWER* TO SPARE!
SHOCKA SHOCKA
PAKOW
?!
WATCH OUT!
CAL! NO!!
YOU CAN'T JUST USE YOUR POWERS INDISCRIMINATELY! *BE CAREFUL!*

INDISCRIMINATELY

\in dis KRIM uh nit lee\ (adj.): not based on careful distinctions, chaotic

The director chose his cast *indiscriminately*, utilizing the first twenty people to answer his audition call, regardless of their abilities or experience.

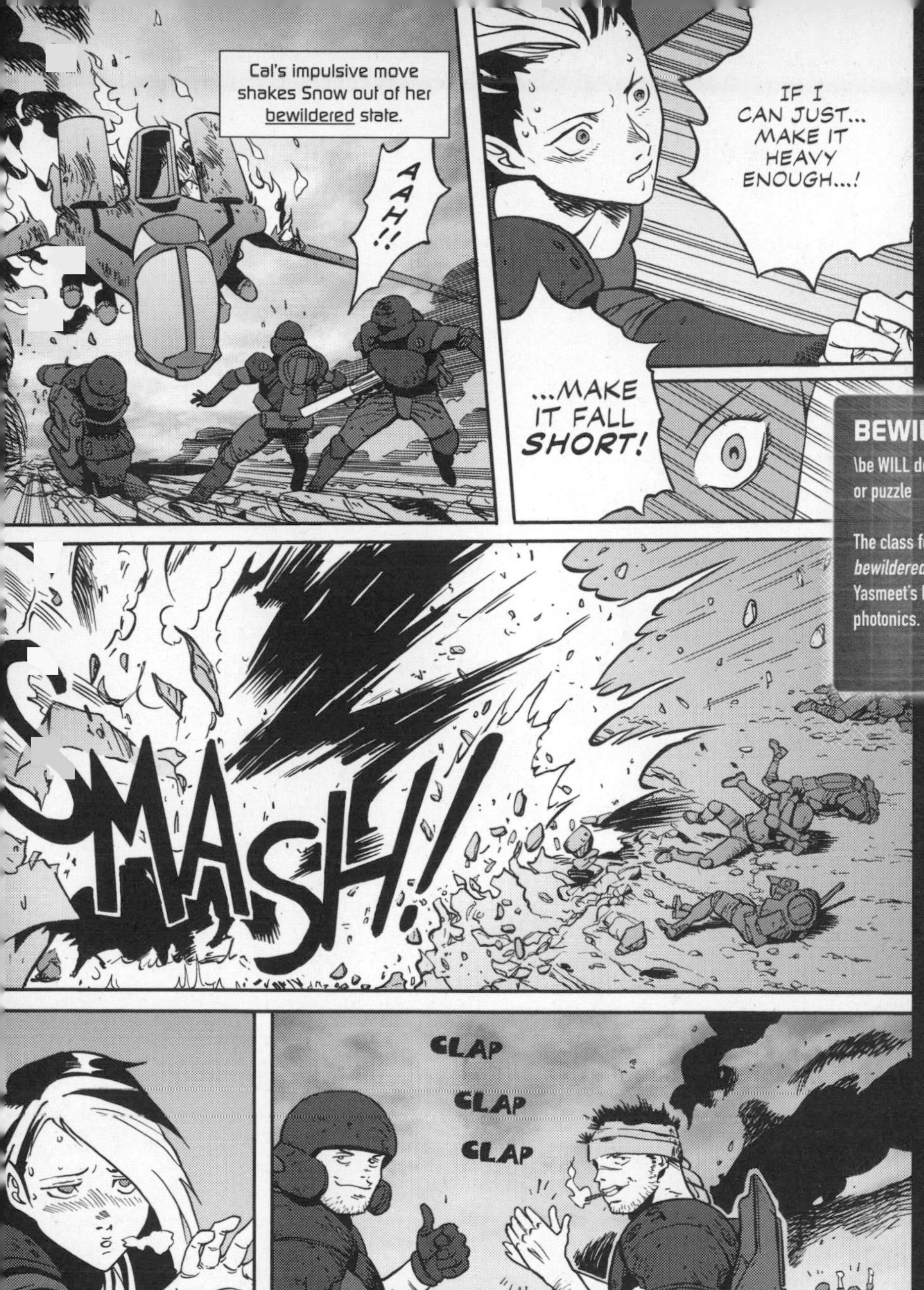
Cal's impulsive move shakes Snow out of her bewildered state.
AAH!!
IF I CAN JUST... MAKE IT HEAVY ENOUGH...!
...MAKE IT FALL SHORT!
SMASH!!
CLAP
CLAP
CLAP

BEWILDER

\be WILL der\ (v.): to confuse or puzzle

The class found themselves *bewildered* by Professor Yasmeet's lecture on advanced photonics.

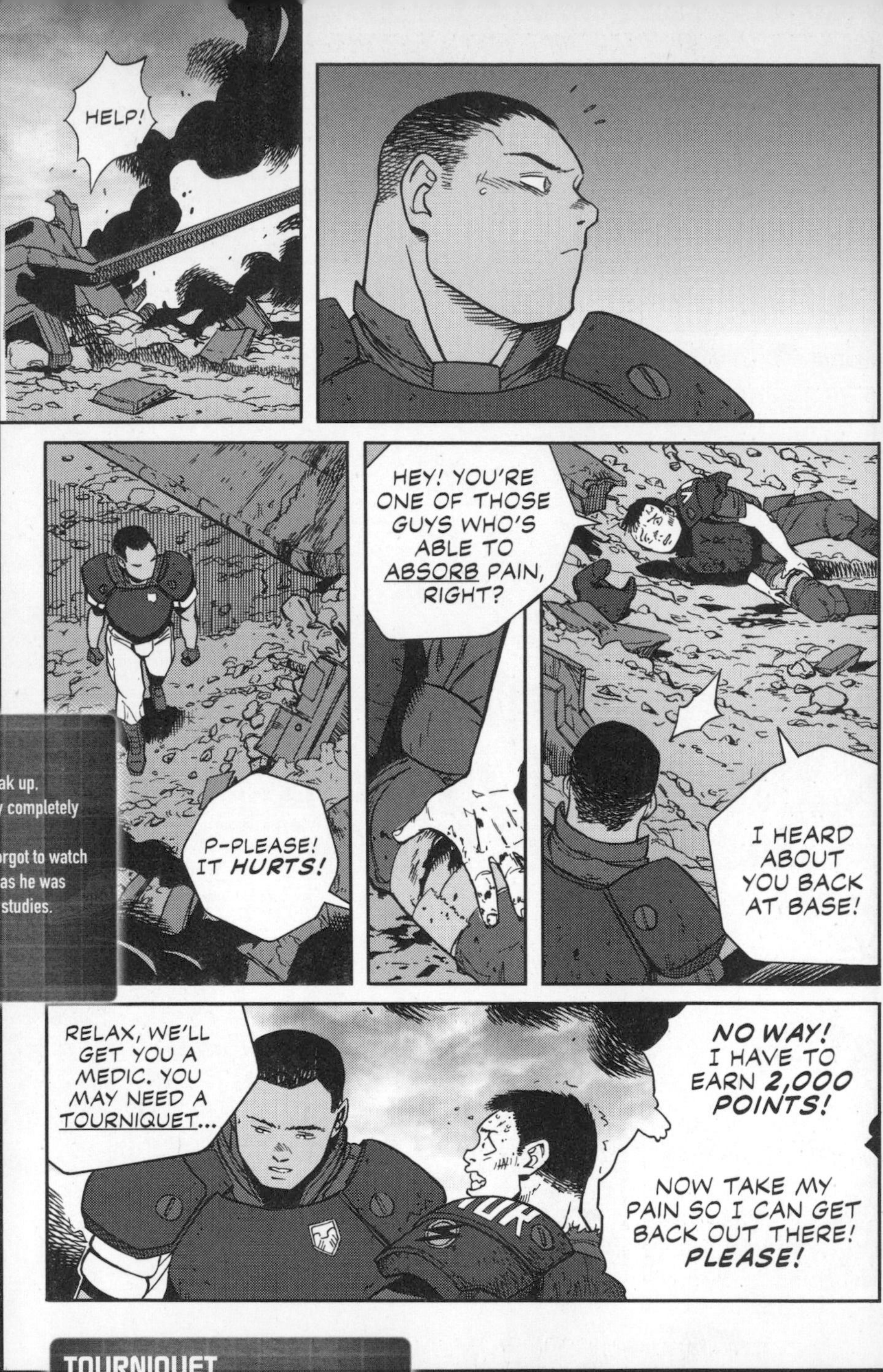
HELP!
P-PLEASE! IT *HURTS!*
HEY! YOU'RE ONE OF THOSE GUYS WHO'S ABLE TO ABSORB PAIN, RIGHT?
I HEARD ABOUT YOU BACK AT BASE!
RELAX, WE'LL GET YOU A MEDIC. YOU MAY NEED A TOURNIQUET...
NO WAY! I HAVE TO EARN *2,000 POINTS!*
NOW TAKE MY PAIN SO I CAN GET BACK OUT THERE! *PLEASE!*

ABSORB

\ab ZORB\ (v.): to soak up, consume; to occupy completely

Jason completely forgot to watch the baseball game, as he was too *absorbed* in his studies.

TOURNIQUET

\TOOR ni kit\ (n.): bandage that pressures an artery in order to stop bleeding

Though advocated in days of old, administering a *tourniquet* to victims of severe cuts is frowned upon by the medical establishment.

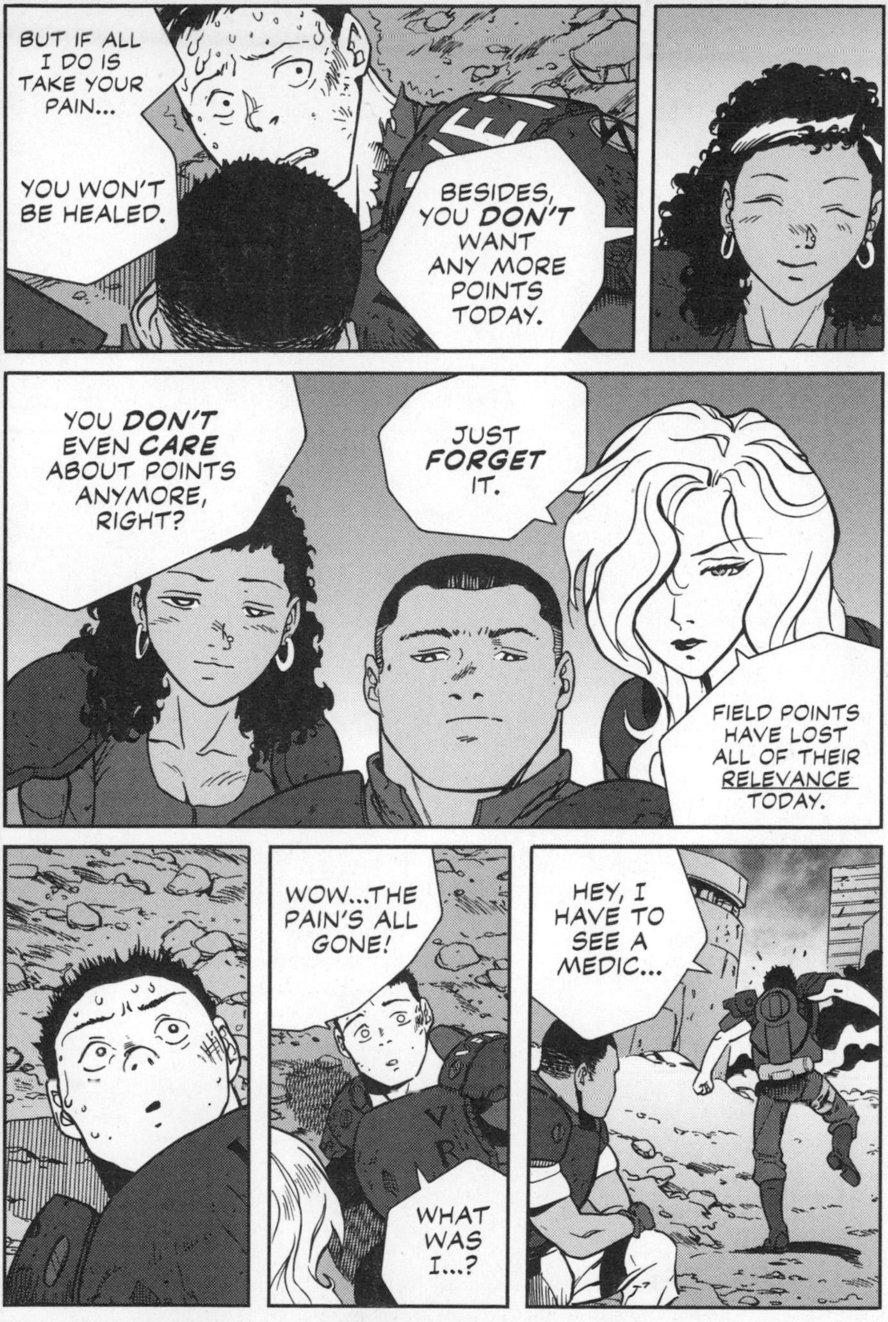
BUT IF ALL I DO IS TAKE YOUR PAIN...
YOU WON'T BE HEALED.
BESIDES, YOU DON'T WANT ANY MORE POINTS TODAY.
YOU DON'T EVEN CARE ABOUT POINTS ANYMORE, RIGHT?
JUST FORGET IT.
FIELD POINTS HAVE LOST ALL OF THEIR RELEVANCE TODAY.
WOW...THE PAIN'S ALL GONE!
WHAT WAS I...?
HEY, I HAVE TO SEE A MEDIC...

RELEVANCE

\REL uh vens\ (n.): pertinence to the matter at hand, applicability

Because the witness's testimony bore no *relevance* to the trial, the jury was instructed to disregard it.

THOSE *PSY-COMMS!* THEY USE THEIR LITTLE *MAGIC TRICKS* AND EARN ALL THE POINTS! IT ISN'T FAIR!

KAPOW

BLAM

BLAM

I DON'T KNOW, MAN. THAT HOT ONE SAVED OUR BACON BACK THERE.

AND SHE'LL GET COMPENSATED WITH A MONTH'S PAY FOR IT, TOO.

DO YOU KNOW WHAT WE'D HAVE TO DO TO MAKE THAT?

YUP.

KILL AN ENEMY *PSY-COMM.*

COMPENSATE

\KOMP en sayt\ (v.): to repay or reimburse

The moving company *compensated* me for the broken furniture.

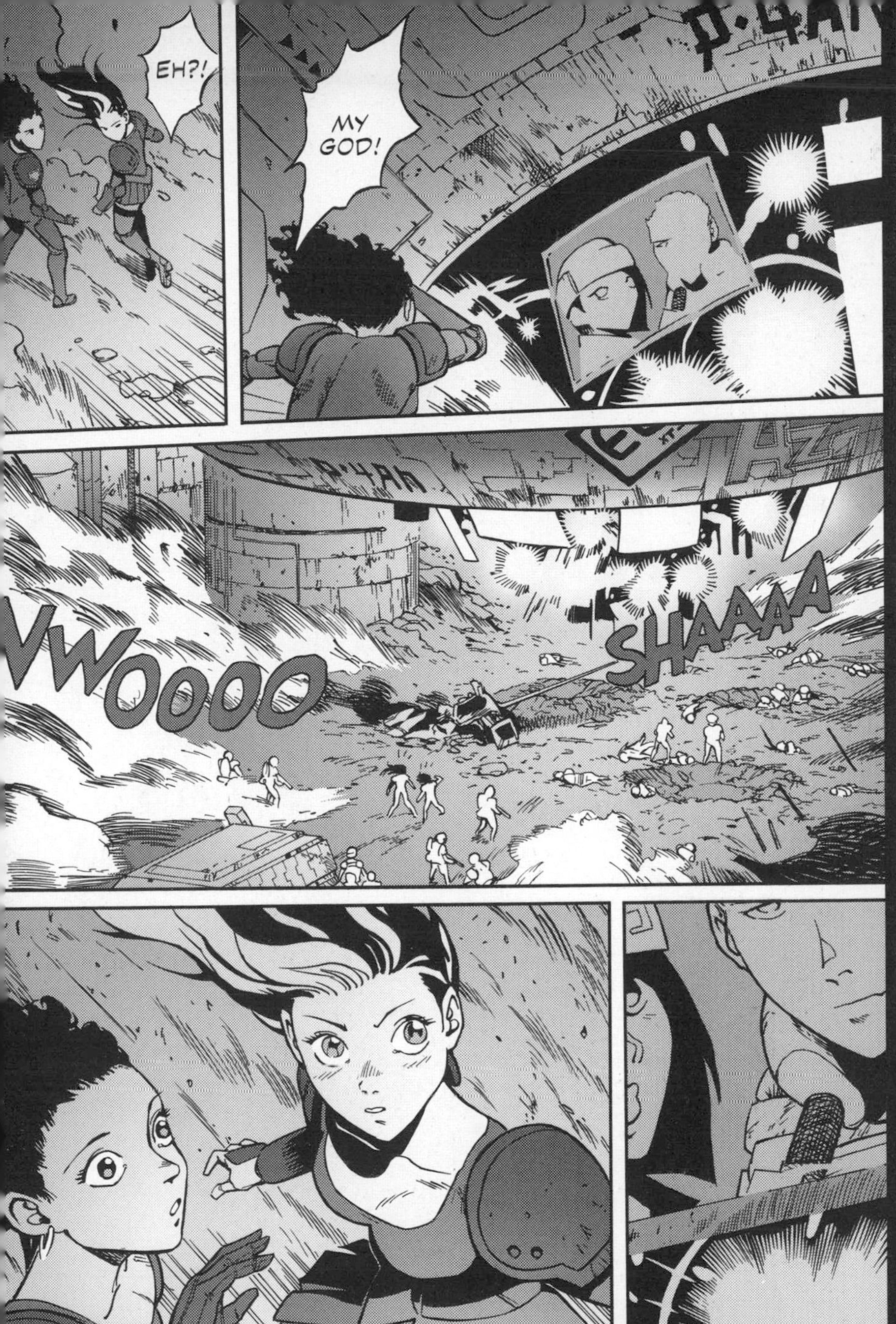
EH?!
MY GOD!
VWOOOO
SHAAAA

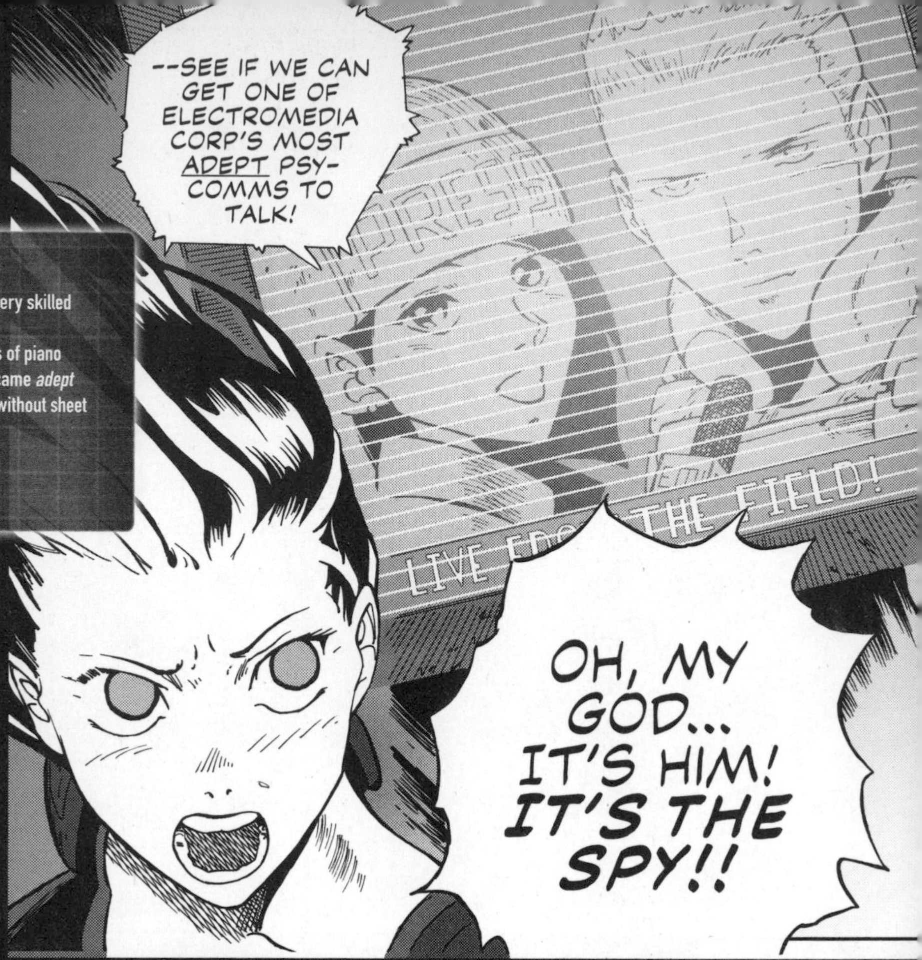
--SEE IF WE CAN GET ONE OF ELECTROMEDIA CORP'S MOST ADEPT PSY-COMMS TO TALK!
OH, MY GOD... IT'S HIM! IT'S THE SPY!!

ADEPT

\ah DEPT\ (adj.): very skilled

After fifteen years of piano practice, Lisa became *adept* at playing songs without sheet music.

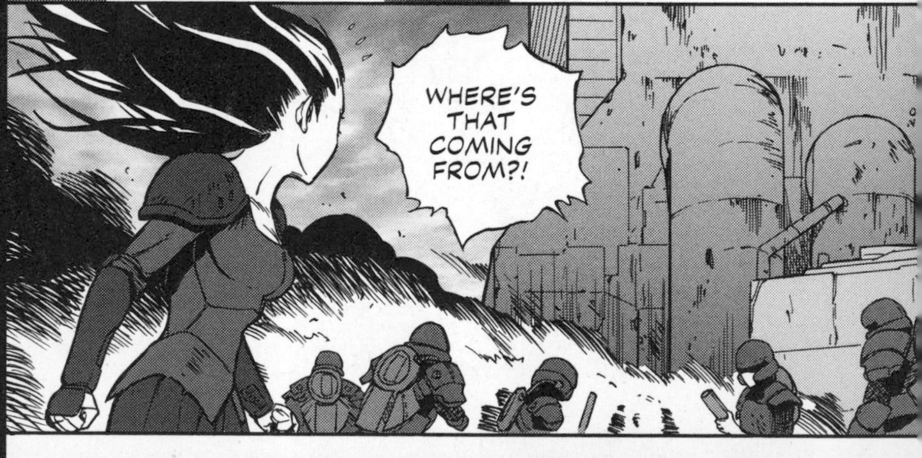
WHERE'S THAT COMING FROM?!

IT'S OKAY... EASY, NOW...
PAOLO! CONSERVE YOUR ENERGY. YOU'RE SUPPOSED TO BE OUR PAIN-ABSORBER!
SEDATIVES FROM THE MEDICS WILL TAKE CARE OF THEM.
PAOLO, YOU CARE TOO MUCH...
P-PLEASE...
IT'S OKAY...
OWW!
ALL RIGHT, I'M COMING.

CONSERVE

\kon SERV\ (v.): use sparingly: protect from loss or harm

The government urged citizens to *conserve* water in the midst of the drought.

SEDATIVE

\SED uh tiv\ (n.): something that calms or soothes

Marie was very tense, so her doctor gave her some *sedatives* to help her sleep.

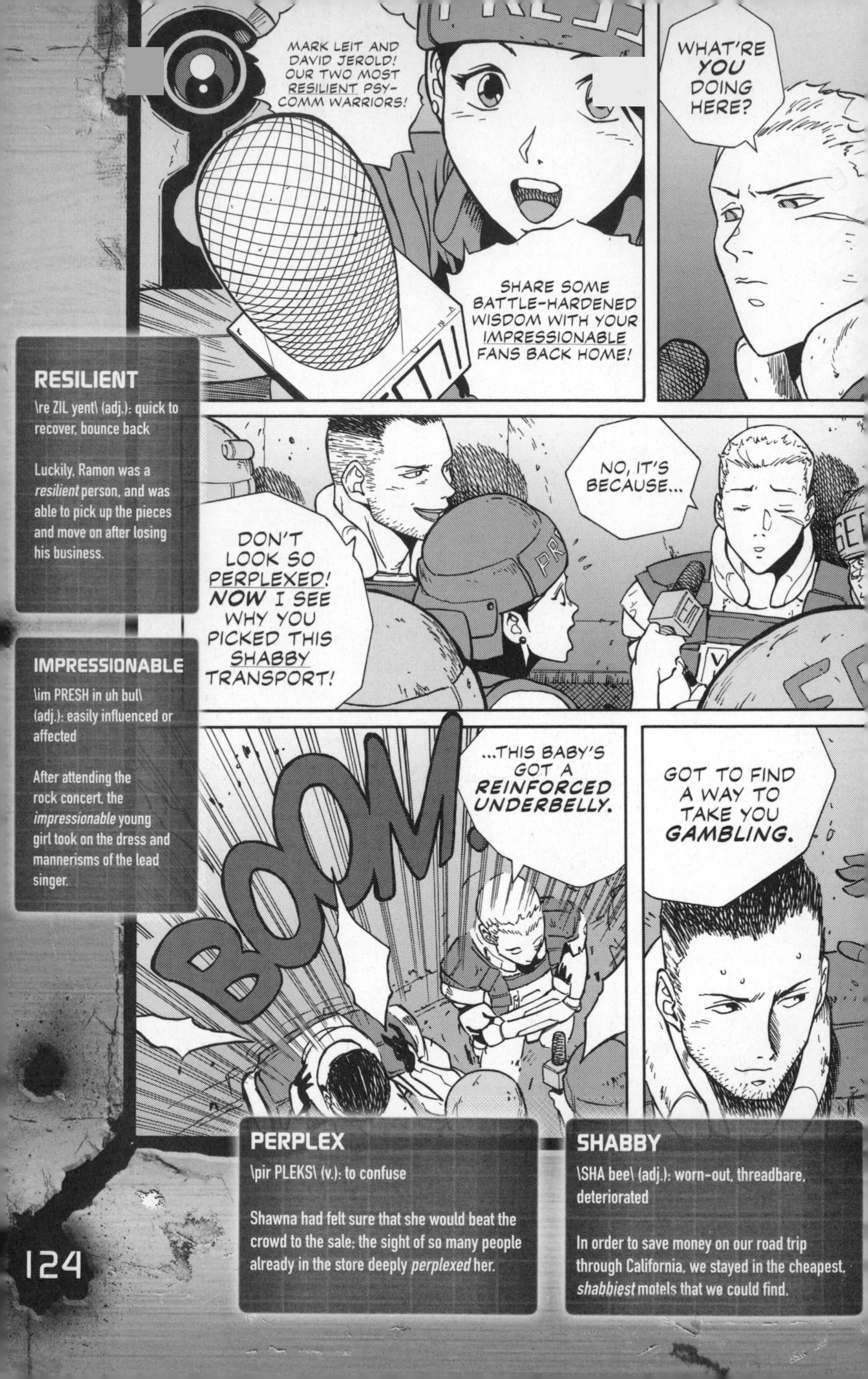
MARK LEIT AND DAVID JEROLD! OUR TWO MOST RESILIENT PSY-COMM WARRIORS!
SHARE SOME BATTLE-HARDENED WISDOM WITH YOUR IMPRESSIONABLE FANS BACK HOME!
WHAT'RE YOU DOING HERE?
DON'T LOOK SO PERPLEXED! NOW I SEE WHY YOU PICKED THIS SHABBY TRANSPORT!
NO, IT'S BECAUSE...
BOOM
...THIS BABY'S GOT A REINFORCED UNDERBELLY.
GOT TO FIND A WAY TO TAKE YOU GAMBLING.

RESILIENT

\re ZIL yent\ (adj.): quick to recover, bounce back

Luckily, Ramon was a *resilient* person, and was able to pick up the pieces and move on after losing his business.

IMPRESSIONABLE

\im PRESH in uh bul\ (adj.): easily influenced or affected

After attending the rock concert, the *impressionable* young girl took on the dress and mannerisms of the lead singer.

PERPLEX

\pir PLEKS\ (v.): to confuse

Shawna had felt sure that she would beat the crowd to the sale; the sight of so many people already in the store deeply *perplexed* her.

SHABBY

\SHA bee\ (adj.): worn-out, threadbare, deteriorated

In order to save money on our road trip through California, we stayed in the cheapest, *shabbiest* motels that we could find.

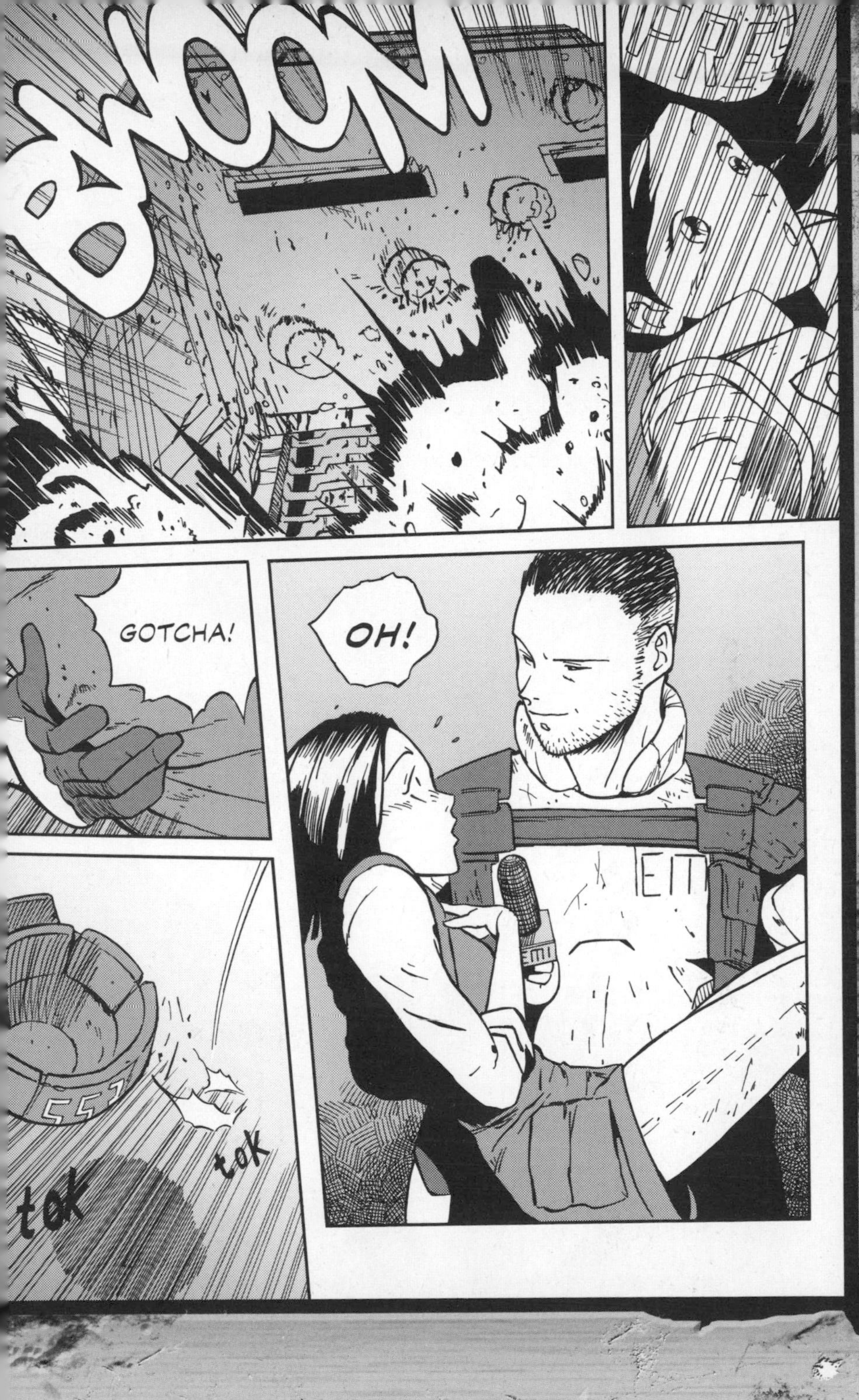
BWOOM
GOTCHA!
tok
tok
OH!

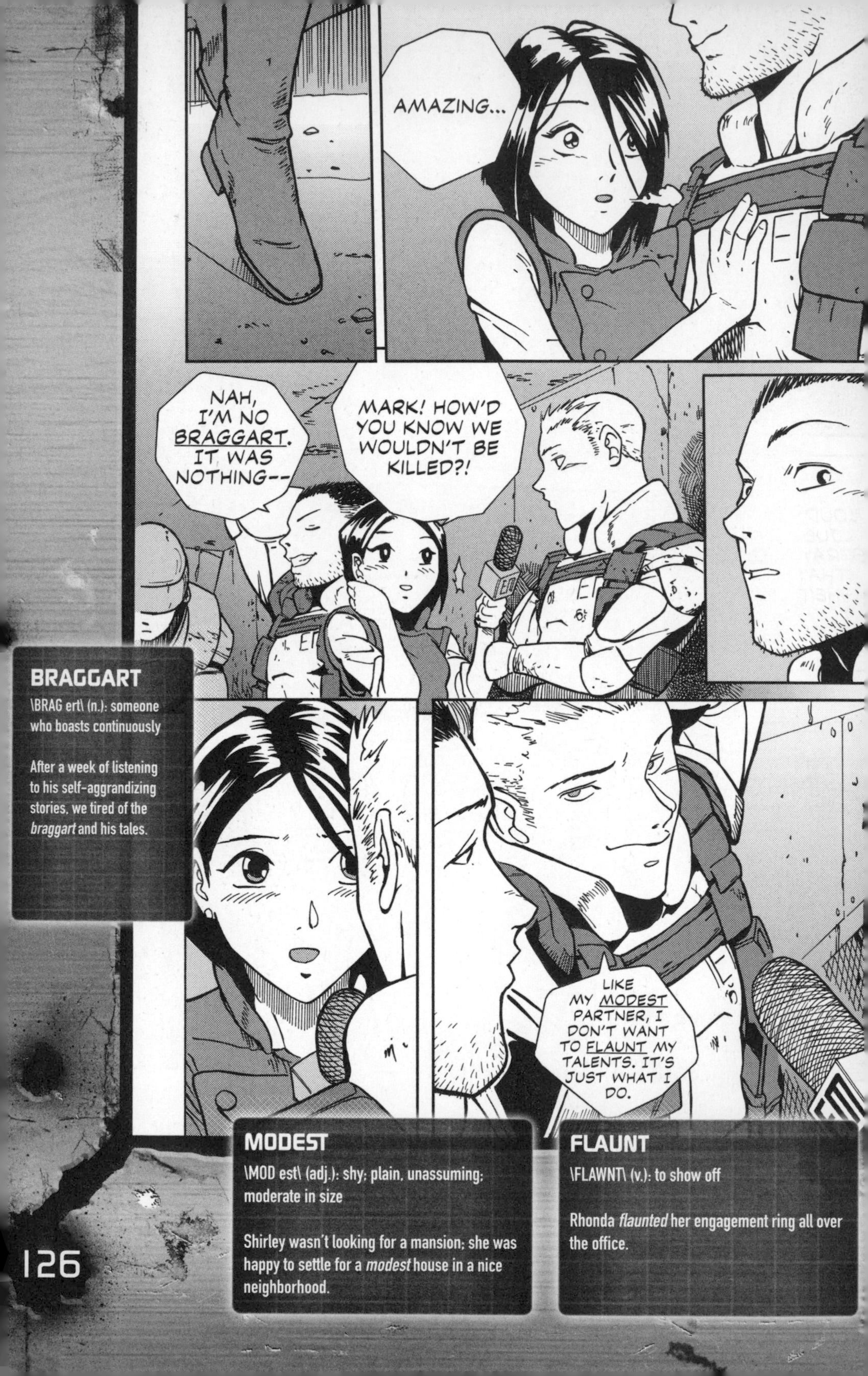
AMAZING...
NAH, I'M NO BRAGGART. IT WAS NOTHING--
MARK! HOW'D YOU KNOW WE WOULDN'T BE KILLED?!
LIKE MY MODEST PARTNER, I DON'T WANT TO FLAUNT MY TALENTS. IT'S JUST WHAT I DO.

BRAGGART

\BRAG ert\ (n.): someone who boasts continuously

After a week of listening to his self-aggrandizing stories, we tired of the *braggart* and his tales.

MODEST

\MOD est\ (adj.): shy; plain, unassuming; moderate in size

Shirley wasn't looking for a mansion; she was happy to settle for a *modest* house in a nice neighborhood.

FLAUNT

\FLAWNT\ (v.): to show off

Rhonda *flaunted* her engagement ring all over the office.

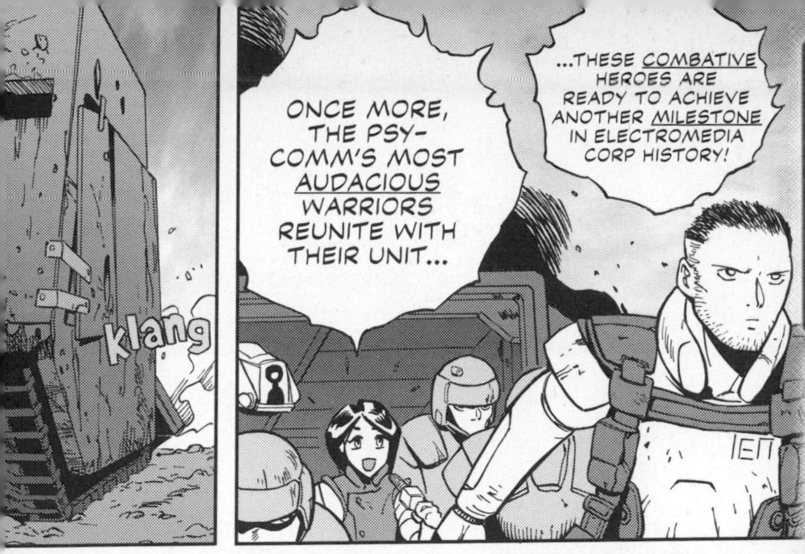
klang
ONCE MORE, THE PSY-COMM'S MOST AUDACIOUS WARRIORS REUNITE WITH THEIR UNIT...
...THESE COMBATIVE HEROES ARE READY TO ACHIEVE ANOTHER MILESTONE IN ELECTROMEDIA CORP HISTORY!

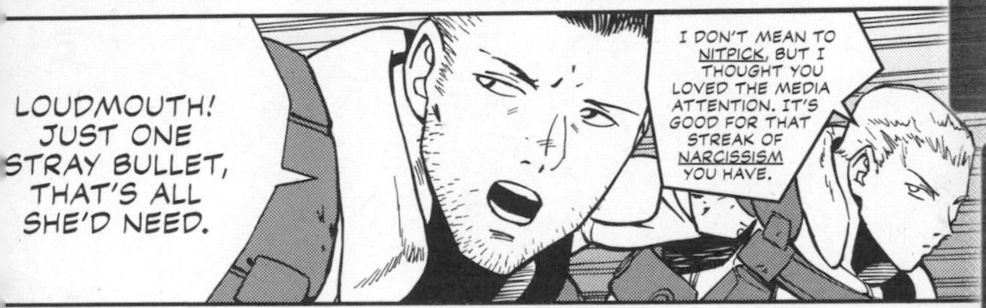
LOUDMOUTH! JUST ONE STRAY BULLET, THAT'S ALL SHE'D NEED.
I DON'T MEAN TO NITPICK, BUT I THOUGHT YOU LOVED THE MEDIA ATTENTION. IT'S GOOD FOR THAT STREAK OF NARCISSISM YOU HAVE.

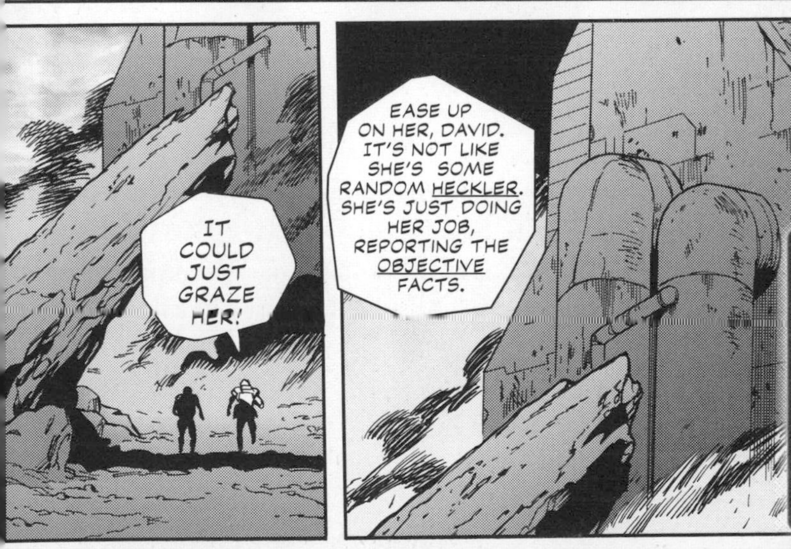
IT COULD JUST GRAZE HER!
EASE UP ON HER, DAVID. IT'S NOT LIKE SHE'S SOME RANDOM HECKLER. SHE'S JUST DOING HER JOB, REPORTING THE OBJECTIVE FACTS.

AUDACIOUS

\aw DAY shis\ (adj.): bold, daring, fearless

The protestors' *audacious* slogans angered the large corporation, but also won them considerable attention and support from onlookers.

COMBATIVE

\kom BAT iv\ (adj.): eager to fight

The *combative* prisoner was put into solitary confinement after starting a third fight.

MILESTONE

\MIYL stohn\ (n.): important event in something or someone's history

The Nineteenth Amendment, which allowed women to vote in elections, was a *milestone* in the advancement of women's rights.

NITPICK

\NIT pik\ (v.): to criticize minor details

Unable to find fault with the general behavior of the company, the difficult stockholder decided instead to *nitpick* and pointed out misspellings in its correspondence.

ECKLER

K ler\ (n.): someone who tried to embarrass annoy others

pite the presence of *hecklers* in the audience, comedian maintained his composure and vered an effective monologue.

OBJECTIVE

\ob jek TIV\ (adj.): impartial, uninfluenced by emotion

When making important decisions, it is important to always remain *objective* and decide based on the facts alone.

NARCISSISM

\NAR sih sizm\ (n.): excessive love or admiration of oneself

Miguel, plagued by *narcissism*, could never admit to others that he had made a mistake.

David
Stealth Gear
integrated shoulder pads
Pistol Mags
integrated holster

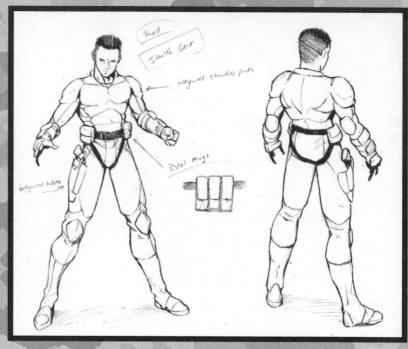

STEALTH GEAR SUIT FOR DAVID JEROLD:
THIS DESIGN WENT UNUSED IN THE FINAL BOOK.
A SLEEK-LOOKING OUTFIT, NONETHELESS.

PSY★COMM
CHAPTER [7]

Hungry for battle points, the trio of foolhardy Mars/Samson desperadoes develop a reckless ploy to take down the most valuable antagonists--the Electromedia Psy-Comms.
SO? CAN YOU TELL WHAT THEY CAN DO?
LOOKS LIKE THE DARKER ONE CAN THROW THINGS. THE LIGHTER ONE, HE'S DODGING STUFF. ON THE VID-DRONE THEY SAY HE HAS SOME KIND OF PRE-SIGHT THING.
LOOK, WE CAN'T SHOOT THESE GUYS UNTIL WE'RE CLOSE ENOUGH TO BE SURE. GOTTA TAKE 'EM WHILE THEY'RE BUSY.
C'MON! WE CAN DO THIS!

FOOLHARDY

\FOOL hard ee\ (adj.): reckless, rash

Lisa tried in vain to dissuade Bart from jumping over the Springfield Ravine with a skateboard; only Homer was able to talk his son out of the *foolhardy* act.

RECKLESS

\REK lis\ (adj.): careless, rash

Gary's license was revoked for *reckless* driving; the police caught him speeding through traffic at twice the speed limit.

PLOY

\PLOY\ (n.): maneuver, plan

To catch the con artist, the detective developed a *ploy* whereby the criminal himself would admit his guilt to witnesses.

ANTAGONIST

\an TAG uh nist\ (n.): foe, adversary, opponent

In some comic books, the heroes are actually somewhat boring while their *antagonists* are considerably more compelling.

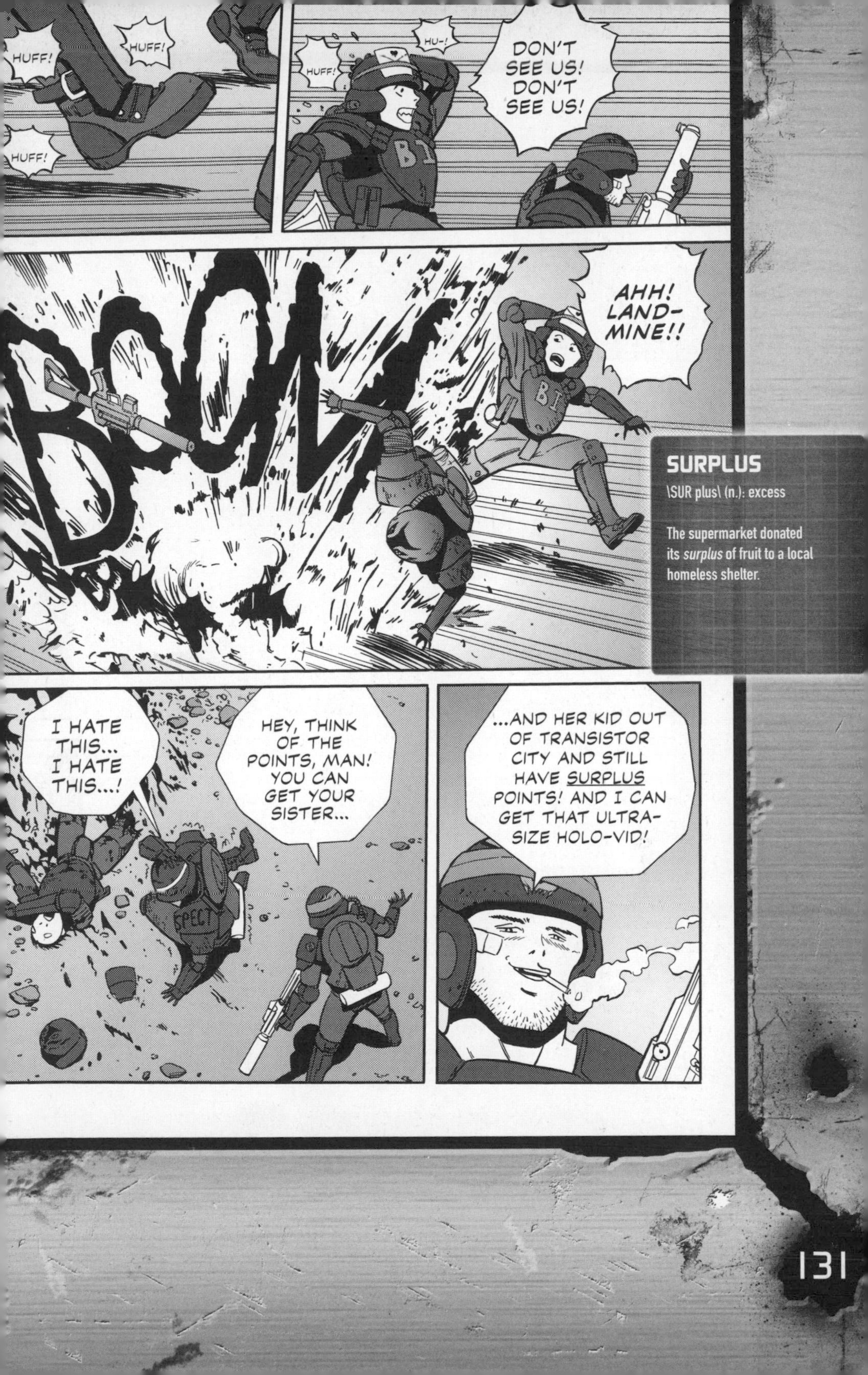
HUFF!
HUFF!
HUFF!
HUFF!
HU-!
HUFF!
DON'T SEE US! DON'T SEE US!
BOOM
AHH! LAND-MINE!!
I HATE THIS... I HATE THIS...!
HEY, THINK OF THE POINTS, MAN! YOU CAN GET YOUR SISTER...
...AND HER KID OUT OF TRANSISTOR CITY AND STILL HAVE SURPLUS POINTS! AND I CAN GET THAT ULTRA-SIZE HOLO-VID!

SURPLUS

\SUR plus\ (n.): excess

The supermarket donated its *surplus* of fruit to a local homeless shelter.

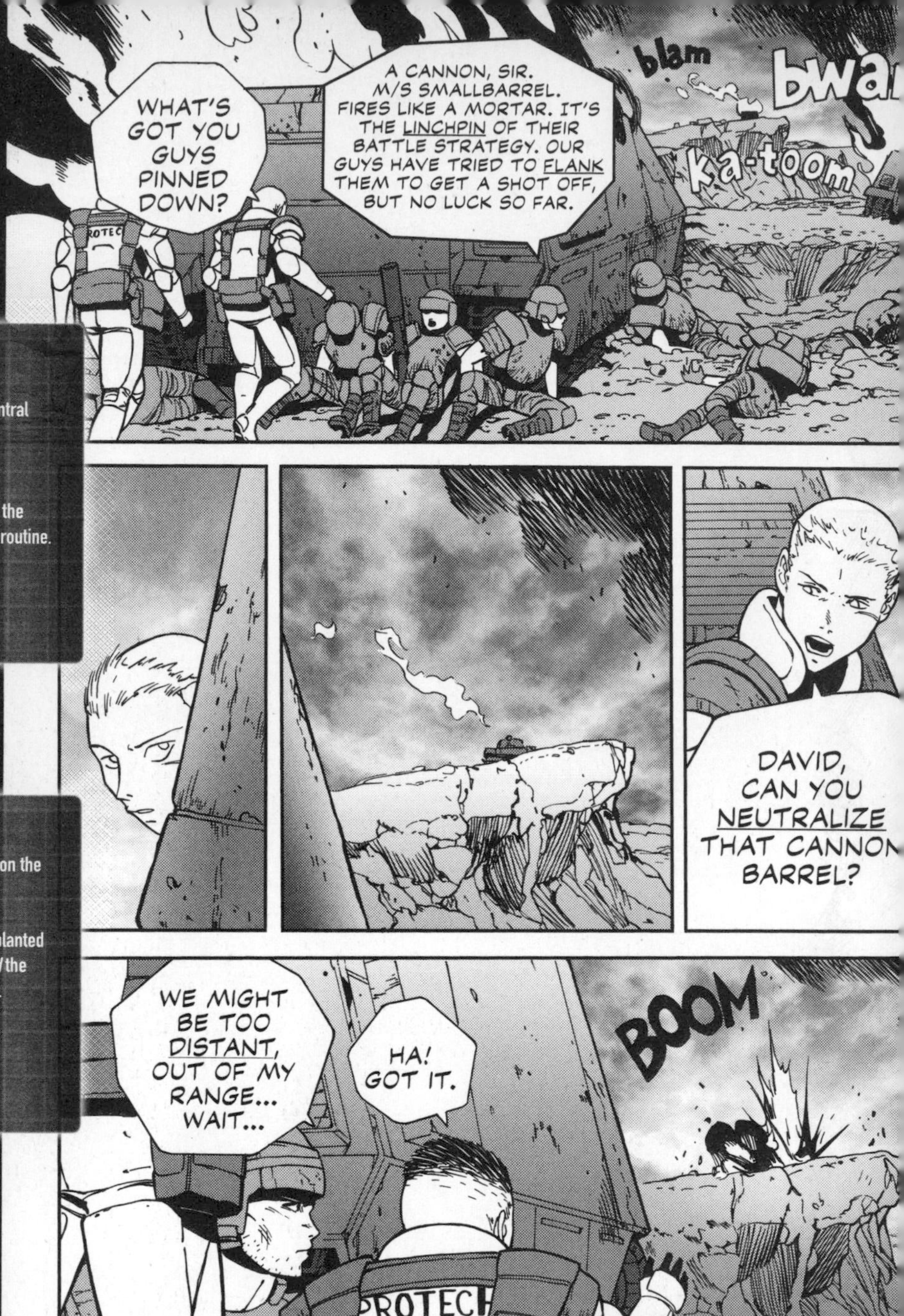
WHAT'S GOT YOU GUYS PINNED DOWN?
A CANNON, SIR. M/S SMALLBARREL. FIRES LIKE A MORTAR. IT'S THE LINCHPIN OF THEIR BATTLE STRATEGY. OUR GUYS HAVE TRIED TO FLANK THEM TO GET A SHOT OFF, BUT NO LUCK SO FAR.
blam
ka-toom
PROTEC
DAVID, CAN YOU NEUTRALIZE THAT CANNON BARREL?
WE MIGHT BE TOO DISTANT, OUT OF MY RANGE... WAIT...
HA! GOT IT.
BOOM
PROTECH

LINCHPIN

\LINCH pin\ (n.): central cohesive element

The school mascot was the *linchpin* of the cheerleaders' new routine.

FLANK

\FLANK\ (v.): to put on the sides of

The gardener had planted shrubs that *flanked* the steps and walkway.

NEUTRALIZE

\NOO truh liyz\ (v.): to balance, offset

Dr. Schwartz poured acid in the beaker to *neutralize* the basic solution.

DISTANT

\DIS tent\ (adj.): separate, far apart

Mary sounded very *distant* on the telephone, so her mother worried that she might be sick.

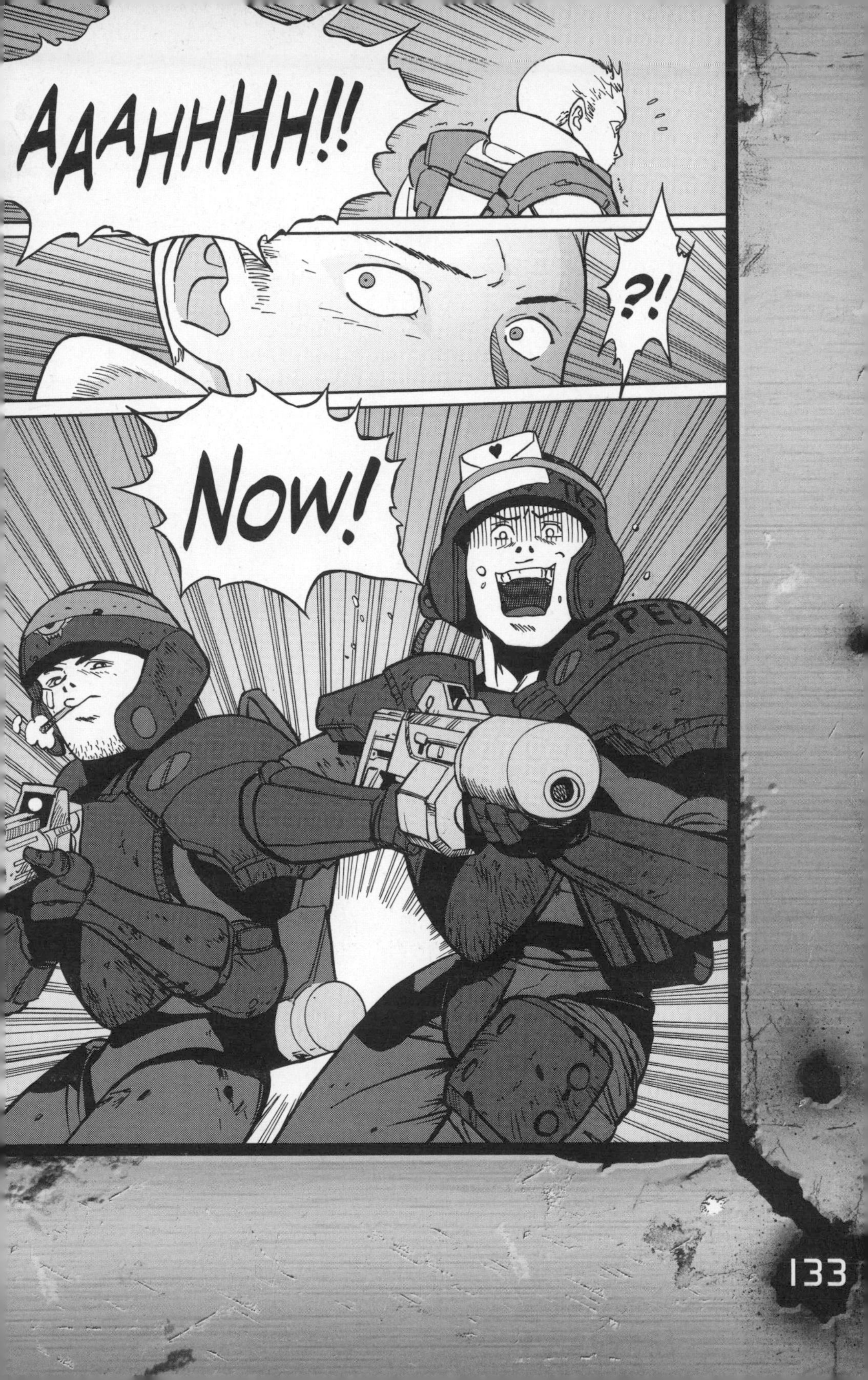
AAAHHHH!!
?!
NOW!
SPEC

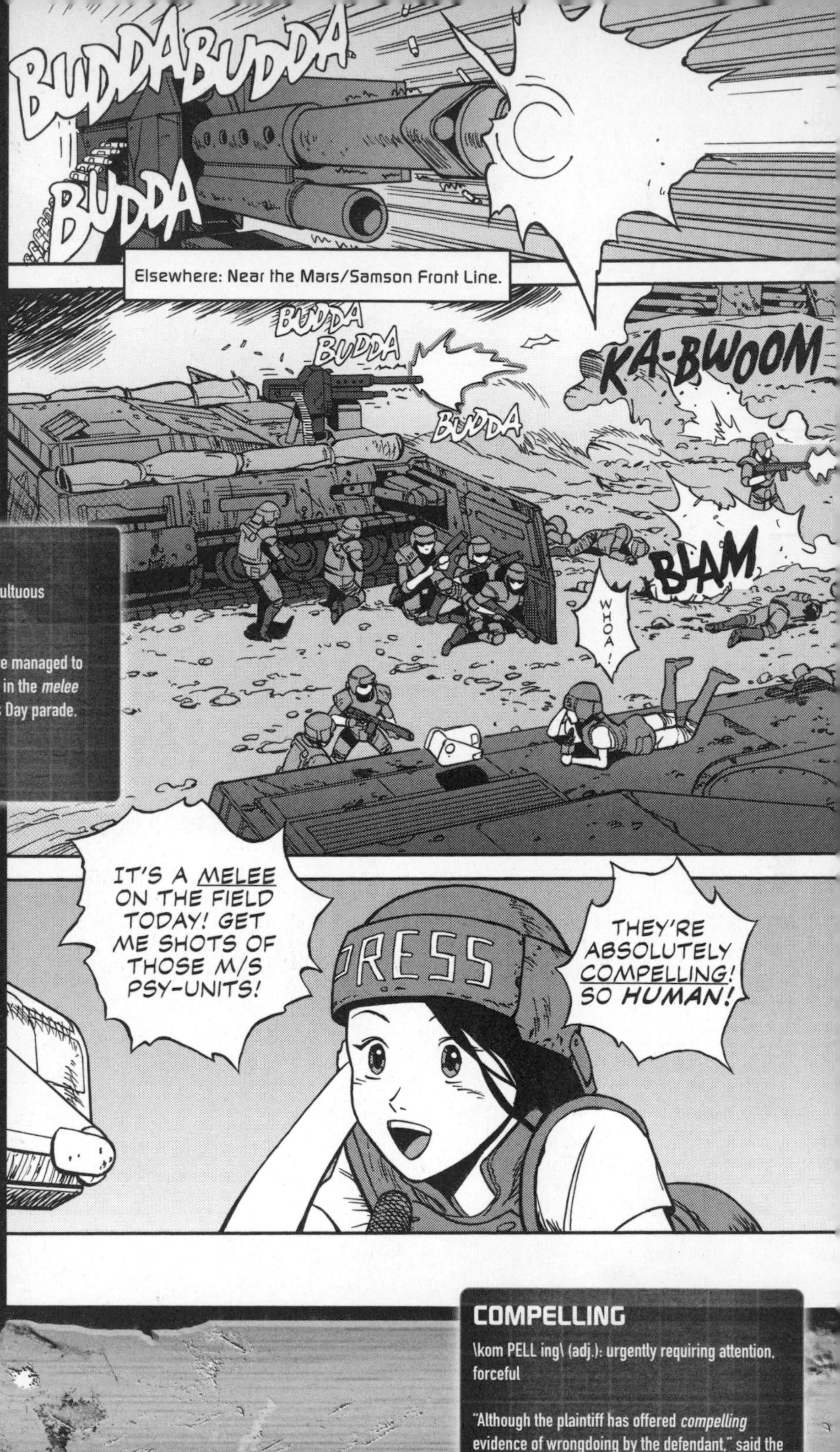
BUDDABUDDA
BUDDA
Elsewhere: Near the Mars/Samson Front Line.
BUDDA
BUDDA
KA-BWOOM
BUDDA
BLAM
WHOA!
IT'S A MELEE ON THE FIELD TODAY! GET ME SHOTS OF THOSE M/S PSY-UNITS!
PRESS
THEY'RE ABSOLUTELY COMPELLING! SO *HUMAN*!

MELEE

\ma LAY\ (n.): tumultuous free-for-all

The hunted fugitive managed to evade his captors in the *melee* of the St. Patrick's Day parade.

COMPELLING

\kom PELL ing\ (adj.): urgently requiring attention, forceful

"Although the plaintiff has offered *compelling* evidence of wrongdoing by the defendant," said the seasoned judge, "I have no choice but to side with the defense in this matter."

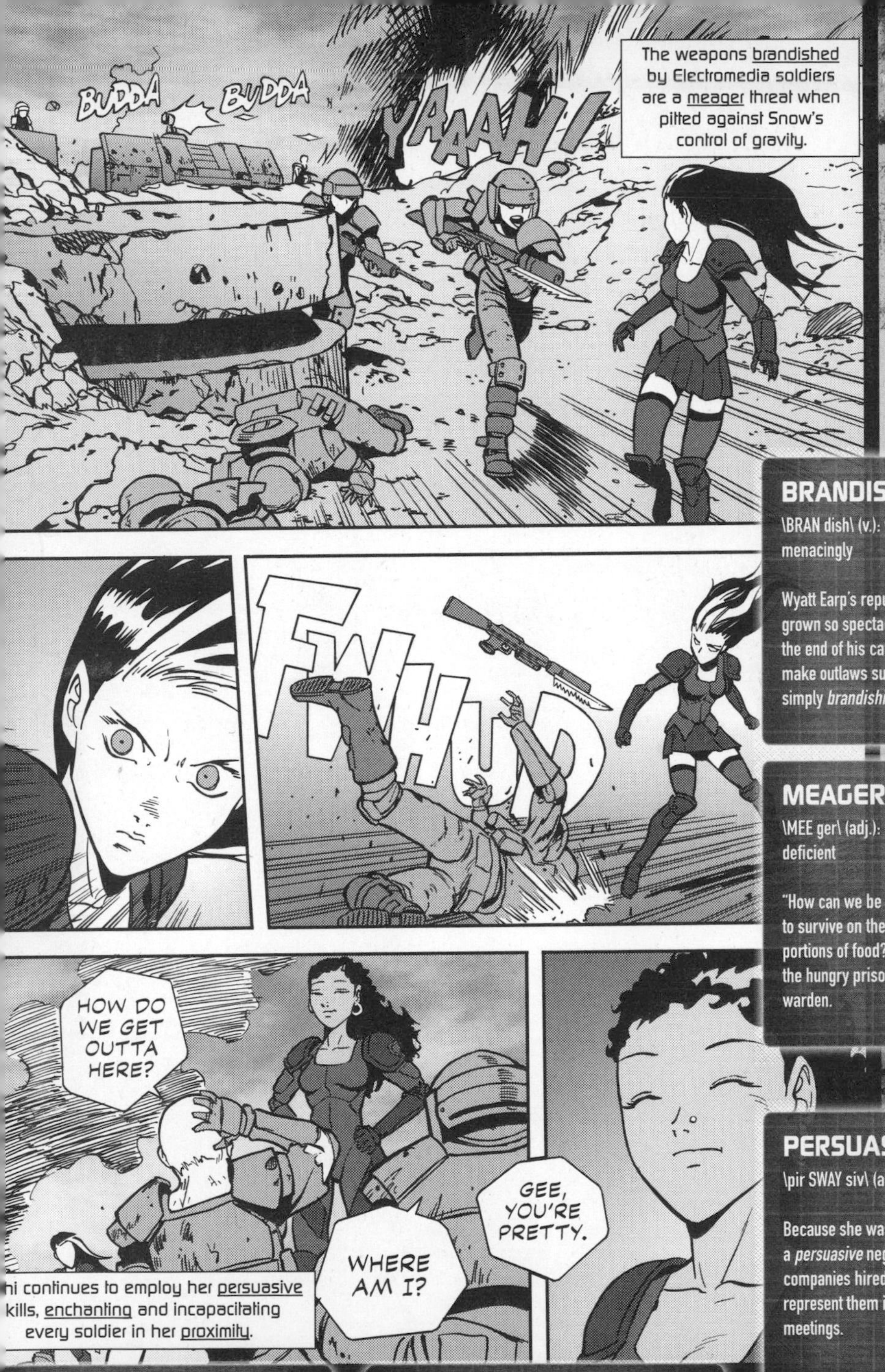
The weapons brandished by Electromedia soldiers are a meager threat when pitted against Snow's control of gravity.
BUDDA
BUDDA
YAAAH!
FWHUD
HOW DO WE GET OUTTA HERE?
GEE, YOU'RE PRETTY.
WHERE AM I?
hi continues to employ her persuasive kills, enchanting and incapacitating every soldier in her proximity.

BRANDISH

\BRAN dish\ (v.): wave menacingly

Wyatt Earp's reputation had grown so spectacularly that by the end of his career he could make outlaws surrender by simply *brandishing* his weapon.

MEAGER

\MEE ger\ (adj.): minimal, scanty, deficient

"How can we be expected to survive on these *meager* portions of food?" complained the hungry prisoners to the warden.

PERSUASIVE

\pir SWAY siv\ (adj.): convincing

Because she was such a *persuasive* negotiator, companies hired her to represent them in high-profile meetings.

NCHANT

n CHANT\ (v.): attract and delight

rna was dazzled by her first visit to the useum of Modern Art; the brilliant colors and ld paintings *enchanted* her.

PROXIMITY

\prok SIM ih tee\ (n.): nearness

Tim was careful to put the glass out of reach, since the toddler loved to yank down objects in her *proximity.*

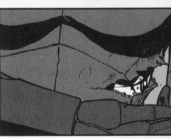

TRIVIALIZE

\TRIV ee uh liyz\ (v.): cause to appear insignificant

Rather than grant the legitimacy of her opponent's claims, the politician *trivialized* the question with a quick joke.

FORGE

\FORJ\ (v.): to advance gradually but steadily

Despite her intense workload, Sharon *forged* ahead and graduated at the top of her class.

RUN! THAT ONE DRAINS YOUR BRAIN-- URK!
ZOE, YOU'RE HURT.
HF
HF
HF
IT'S... UNH... NOTHING
OKAY, I'LL ABSORB THE PAIN, BUT YOU CAN'T TRIVIALIZE A WOUND LIKE THIS. GET IT LOOKED AT. YOU CAN'T JUST FORGE AHEAD.
!
FWOO

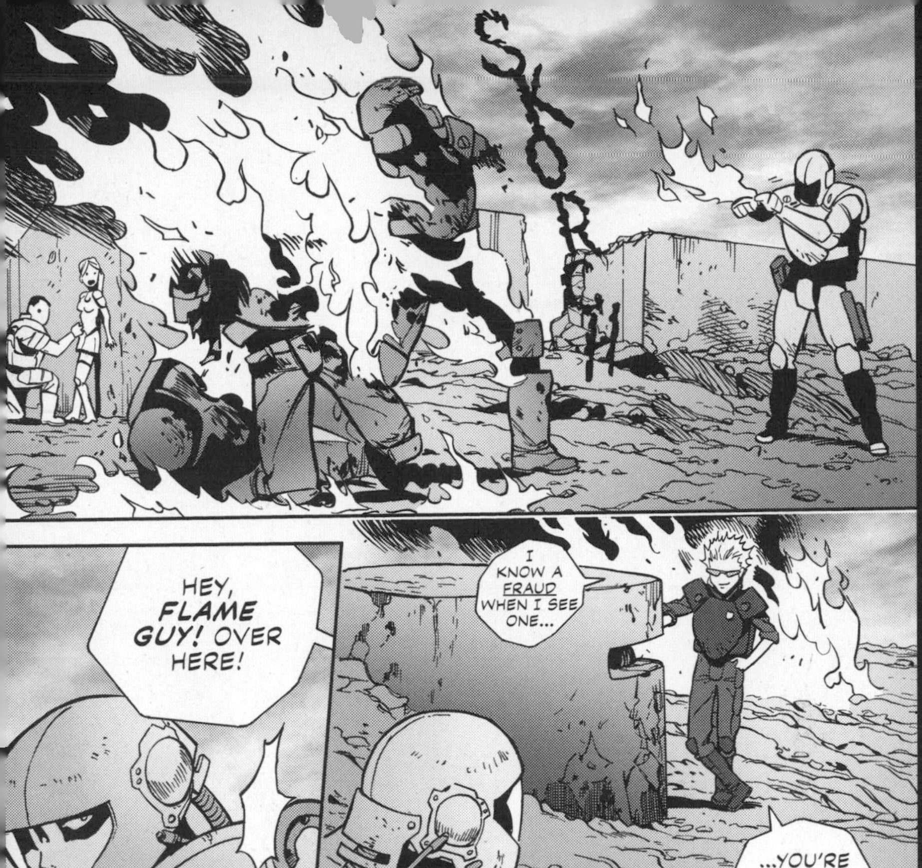
SKORCH
HEY, FLAME GUY! OVER HERE!
I KNOW A FRAUD WHEN I SEE ONE...
...YOU'RE NOT A REAL PYRO-KINETIC.
ZAP!
VZZT
ZZAP!
TAKE IT, NORMY!
YOU CAN'T USE SYNTHESIZED WEAPONS TO FIGHT POWERS LIKE MINE!

SYNTHESIZE

\SIN thi siyz\ (v.): to produce artificially; to create through combination of different elements

Because the guitar sounded so real, we were surprised to learn that the music had been *synthesized* in a computer.

FRAUD

\FROD\ (n.): deception, hoax

The salesman was arrested for *fraud* after selling 500 acres of mosquito-infested swamp, which he claimed was choice beachside property, to the senior citizens.

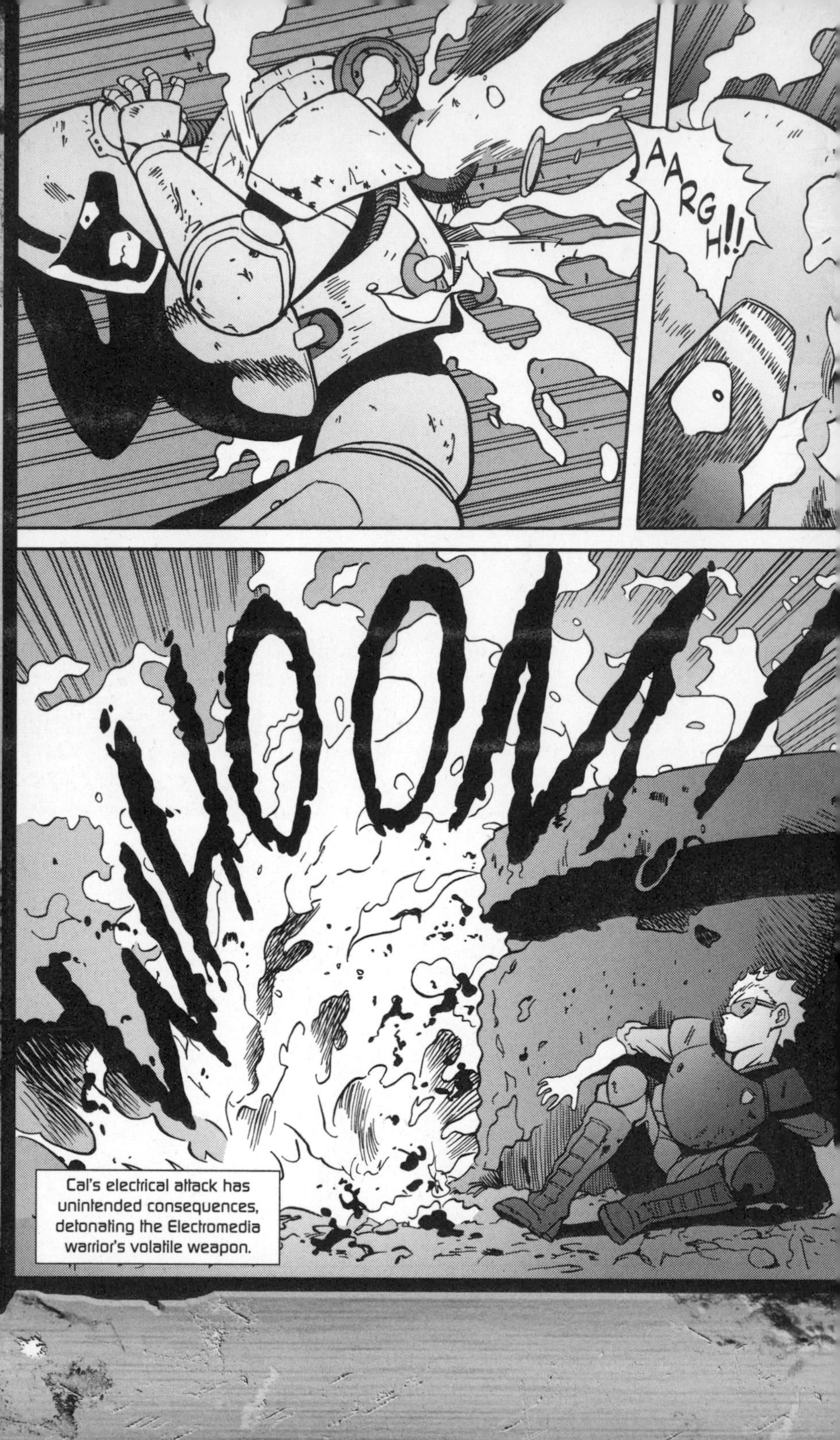
AARGH!!
WHOOM!
Cal's electrical attack has unintended consequences, detonating the Electromedia warrior's volatile weapon.

SPLOOSH
AHHH! PLASMA'S TOO CLOSE! CAN'T STOP IT!
SPAK
MAKE IT HEAVY-- HEAVY!!
WHAT'S THE MATTER WITH YOU, CAL?!
AIEE!!
DON'T EVEN THINK OF HELPING, PAOLO! HE'S TOAST!
YOU'VE GOT TO BE MORE CALCULATING IN YOUR ATTACKS! QUIT TRYING TO PROVE SOMETHING, AND GET WITH THE TEAM!

CALCULATING

\KAL kyu lay ting\ (adj.): shrewd, crafty

The *calculating* lawyer put the mother of his client on the witness stand in order to garner sympathy.

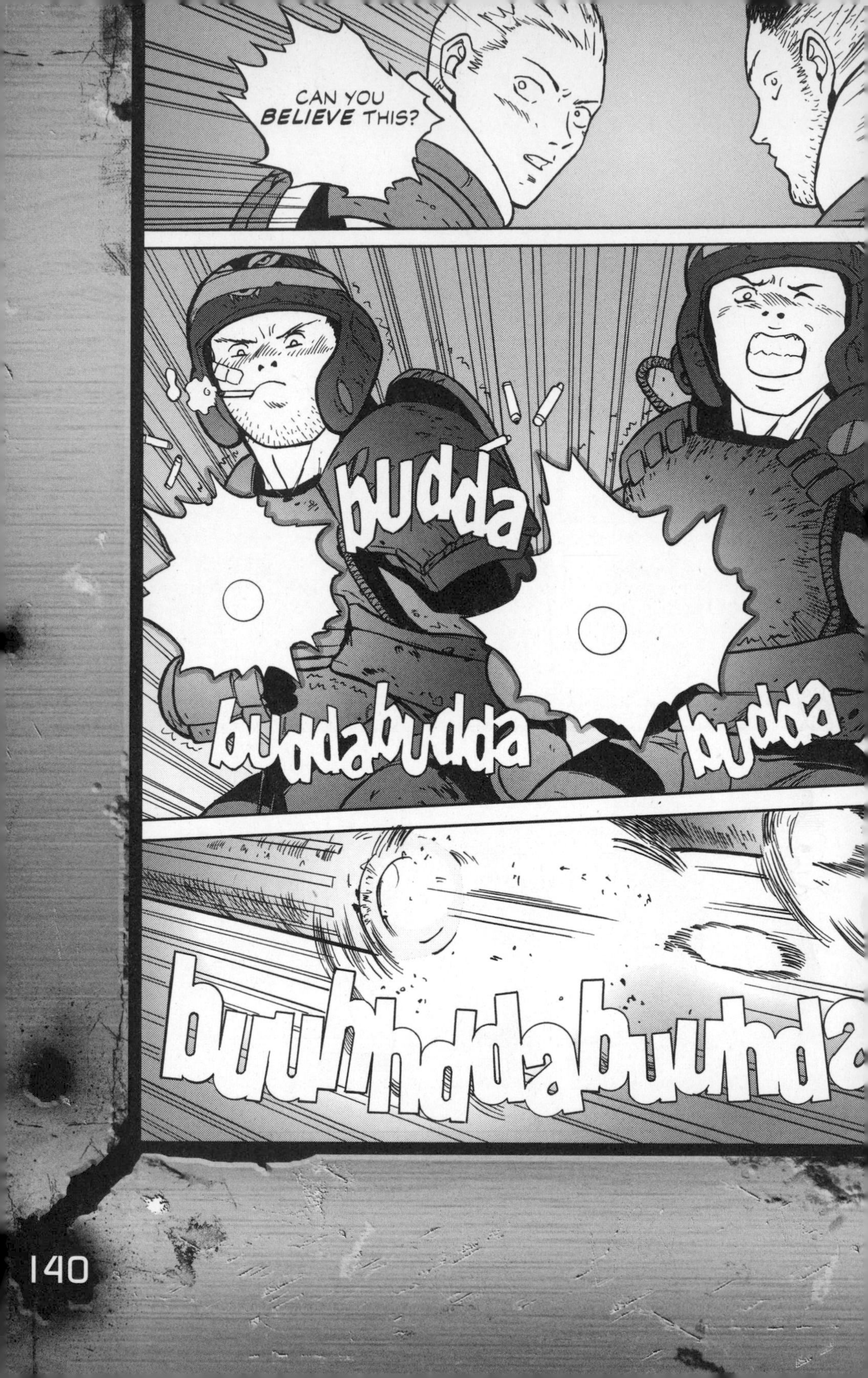
CAN YOU *BELIEVE* THIS?
budda
buddabudda
budda
buuhddabuuhd

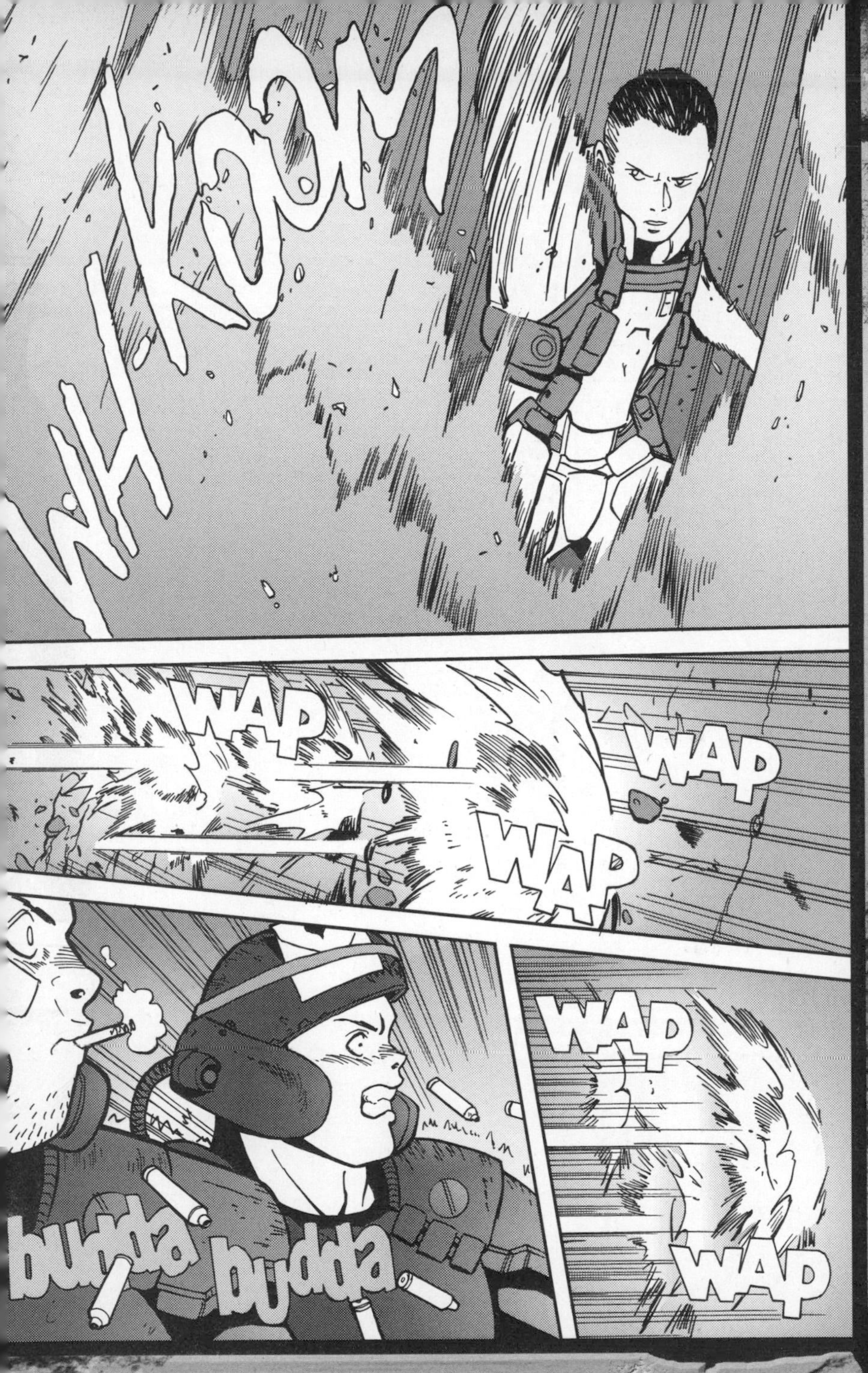

WHOOM
WAP
WAP
WAP
budda budda
WAP
WAP

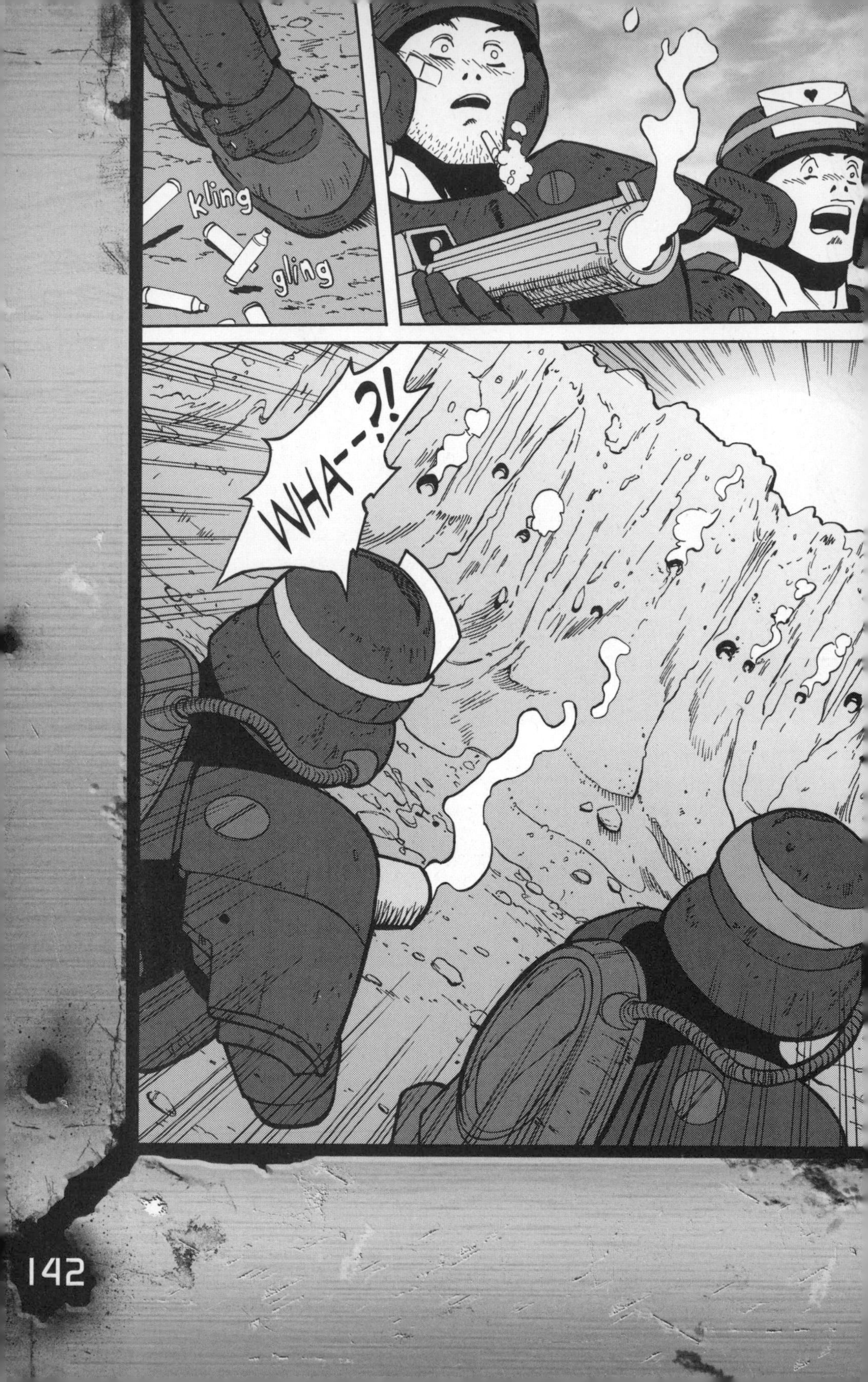
kling
gling
WHA--?!

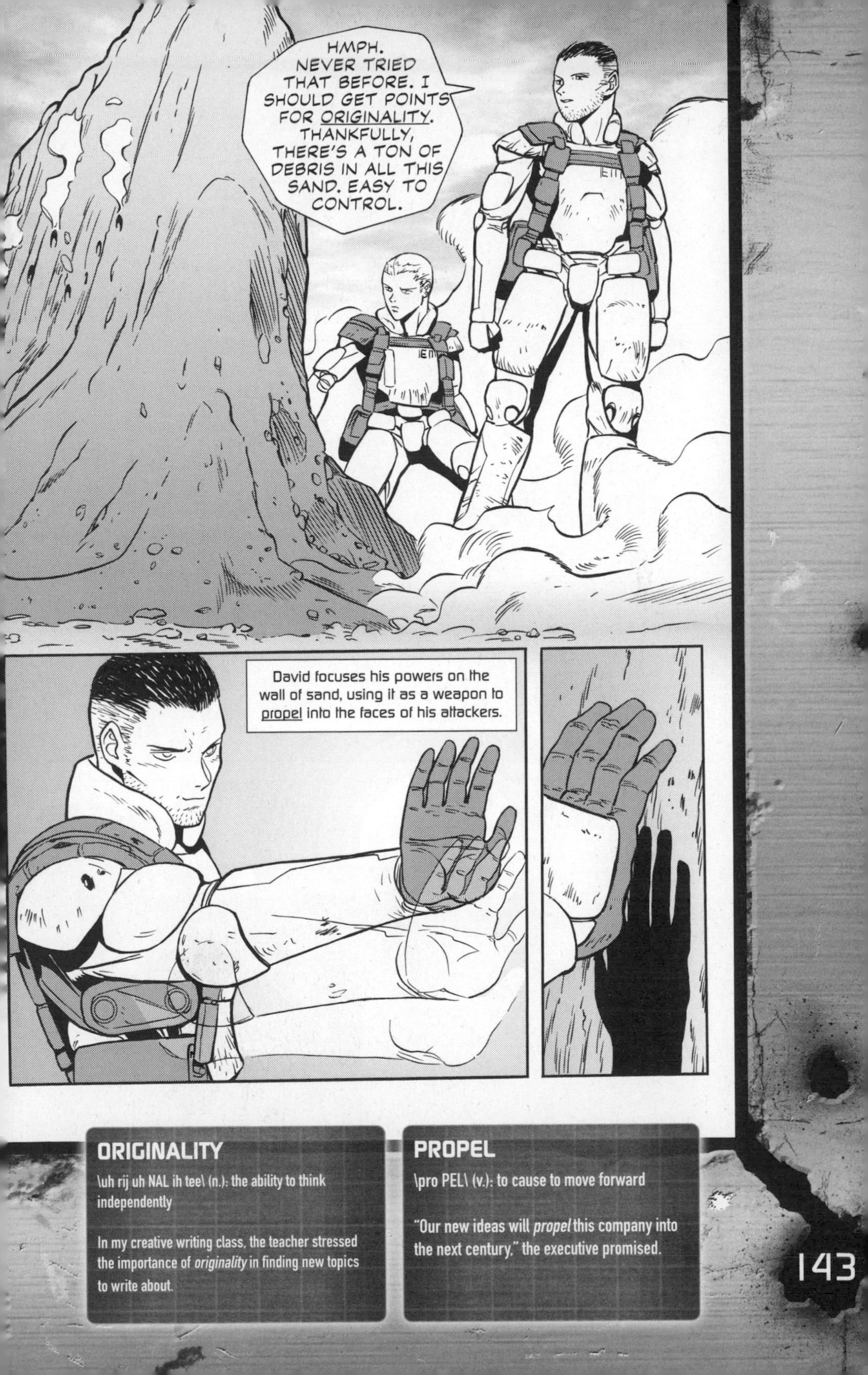
HMPH. NEVER TRIED THAT BEFORE. I SHOULD GET POINTS FOR ORIGINALITY. THANKFULLY, THERE'S A TON OF DEBRIS IN ALL THIS SAND. EASY TO CONTROL.
David focuses his powers on the wall of sand, using it as a weapon to propel into the faces of his attackers.

ORIGINALITY

\uh rij uh NAL ih tee\ (n.): the ability to think independently

In my creative writing class, the teacher stressed the importance of *originality* in finding new topics to write about.

PROPEL

\pro PEL\ (v.): to cause to move forward

"Our new ideas will *propel* this company into the next century," the executive promised.

BWOOSH

SliiiSShhhh

WE ADMIRE YOUR PLUCK. YOU'VE GOT TO BE <u>TENACIOUS</u> TO TRY TO BAG TWO PSY-COMMS.

OKAY, MARK, LET'S GO DESTROY SOME TANKS.

TENACIOUS

\ten AY shiss\ (adj.): determined, keeping a firm grip on

After losing his balance during the routine, the gymnast maintained a *tenacious* grasp on the parallel bars.

HEY.
K-chak
JUST STAY RIGHT THERE, **FREAK.**
I STILL GET THE POINTS IF I TAKE YOU ALIVE.
ACTUALLY, I THINK YOU MIGHT GET EVEN MORE. BUT THERE'S A FLAW IN YOUR PLAN.
IT'S NOT GONNA HAPPEN.
NO?
The soldier's demise is instantaneous.
WHAM
ED260
ETER
rrrmmmbb
YOU HEAR SOMETHING?
NOPE. NOT TODAY.

FLAW

\FLAW\ (n.): imperfection, defect

Because there was a *flaw* in the system, programmers had to rewrite the entire application.

INSTANTANEOUS

\\in sten TAY nee us\ (adj.): immediate, without delay

The new computer system was designed to offer *instantaneous* feedback to the user's questions.

LULL

\LUL\ (n.): relatively calm period

Although Sam ran into the tool shed when the hurricane started, he moved to the house during a *lull* in the storm.

RENEW

\re NOO\ (v.): resume, reaffirm, replenish

After a tense month of arguing, the two best friends *renewed* their pact to equally share the cost of maintaining the apartment.

CHERISH

\CHER ish\ (v.): to remember fondly, treat with affection

Despite the fact that Esther and Lily have barely had a chance to talk since college, they will always *cherish* their deep childhood friendship.

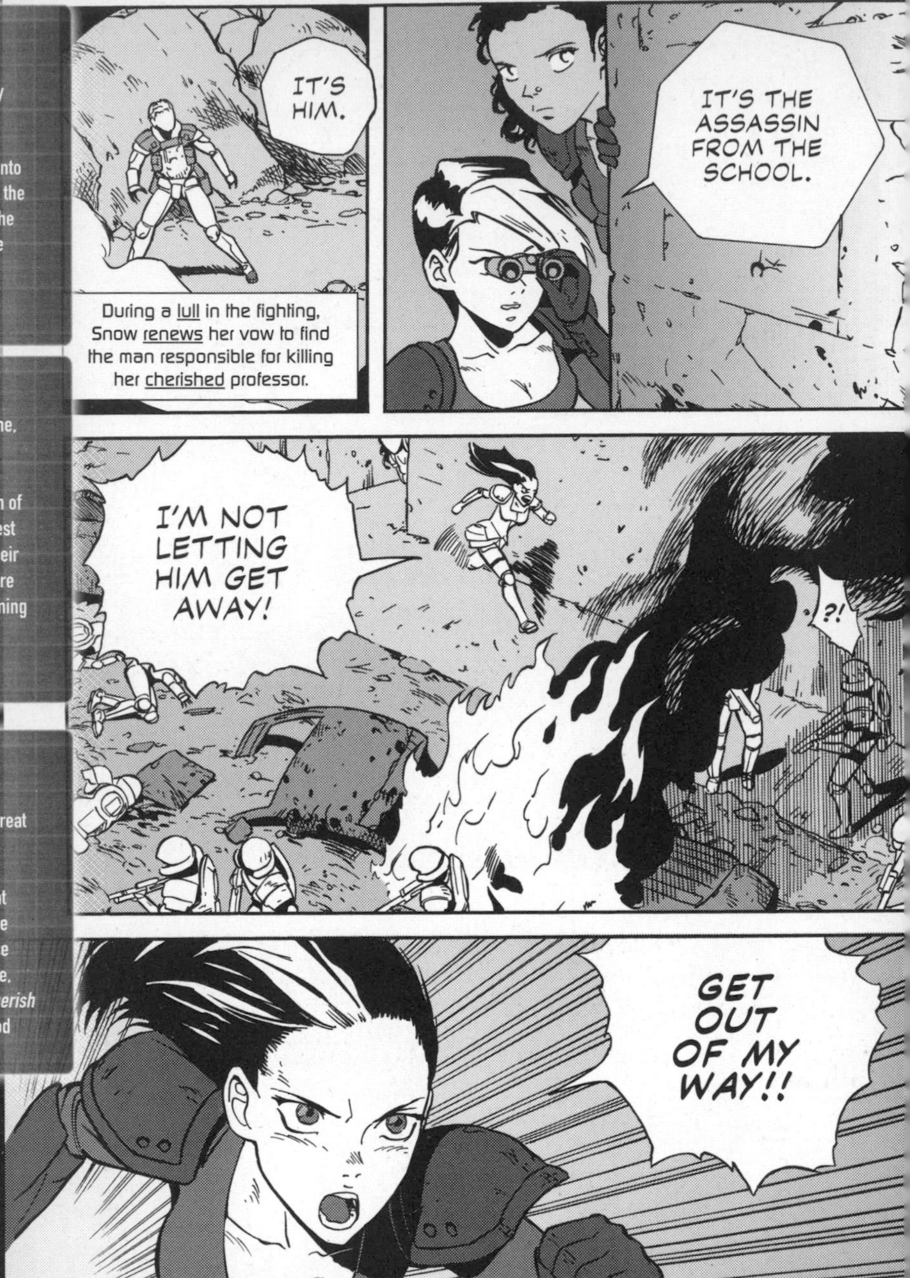

IT'S HIM.
During a lull in the fighting, Snow renews her vow to find the man responsible for killing her cherished professor.
IT'S THE ASSASSIN FROM THE SCHOOL.
I'M NOT LETTING HIM GET AWAY!
?!
GET OUT OF MY WAY!!

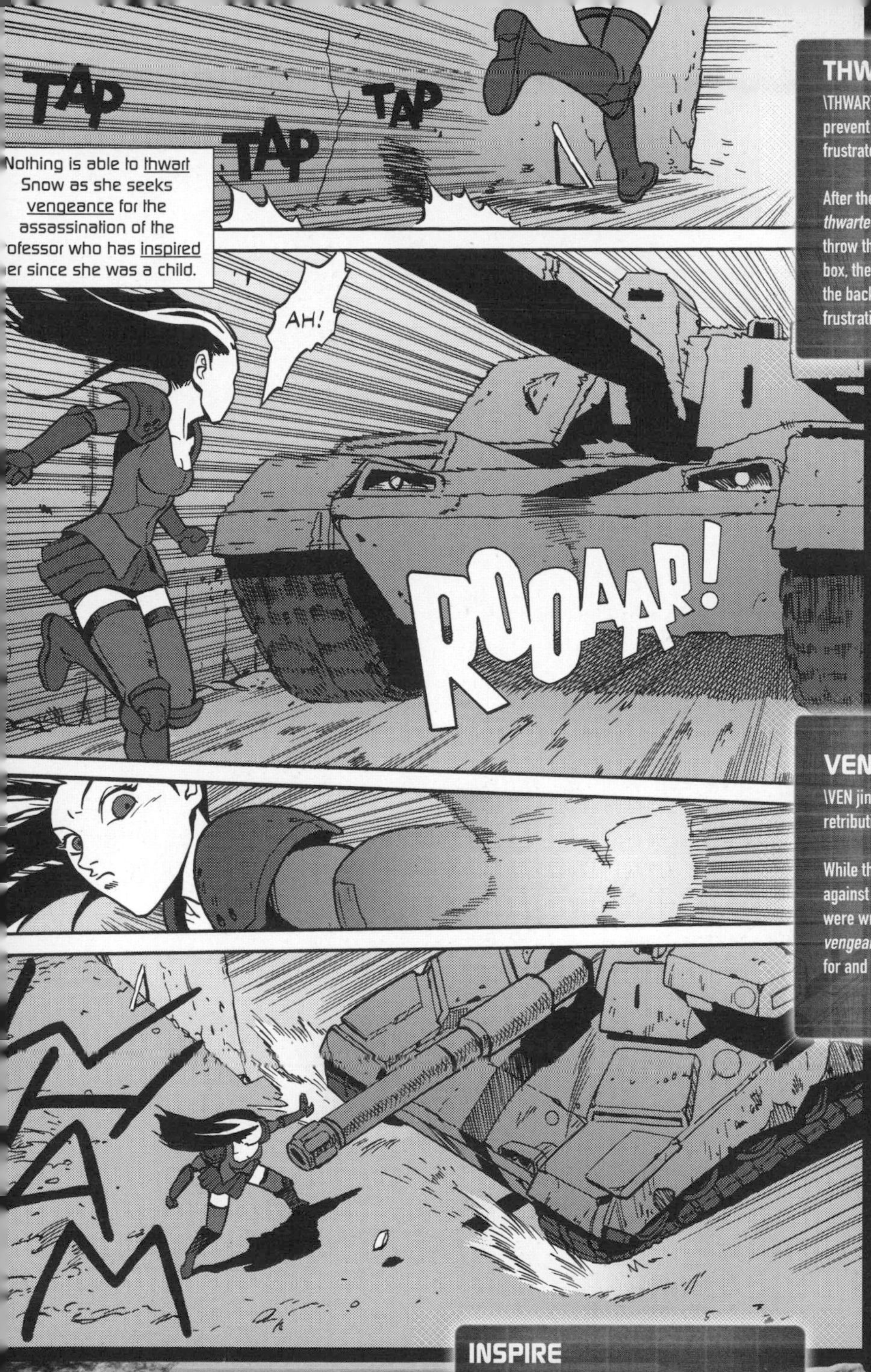
TAP
TAP
TAP
Nothing is able to thwart Snow as she seeks vengeance for the assassination of the ofessor who has inspired er since she was a child.
AH!
ROOAAR!

THWART

\THWART\ (v.): to block or prevent from happening: frustrate

After the tricky winds *thwarted* his attempts to throw the bag into the box, the chimp retired to the back of his cage in frustration.

VENGEANCE

\VEN jinss\ (n.): retribution

While their actions against the homeowner were wrong, his act of *vengeance* was uncalled for and overdone.

INSPIRE

\in SPIYR\ (v.): motivate, affect

Classical poets claimed to have a muse that *inspired* them to write great works of art.

IS IT TRUE YOU'RE SWITCHING ARMOR SPONSORS TO **ENDORSE** ANOTHER LINE?

NO WAY.

YOU DON'T MESS WITH PRO-TECH. IT'S TOP OF THE LINE, AND DOESN'T HAVE A SINGLE **DRAWBACK**.

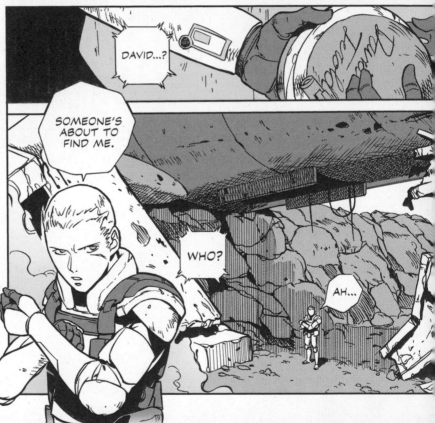

DAVID...?

SOMEONE'S ABOUT TO FIND ME.

WHO?

AH...

ENDORSE

\en DORSS\ (v.): to give approval to, sanction

The politician refused to *endorse* any group that wouldn't grant equal rights to all people.

DRAWBACK

\DRAW back\ (n.): disadvantage, inconvenience

The *drawback* to being famous is not having any privacy when you go out in public.

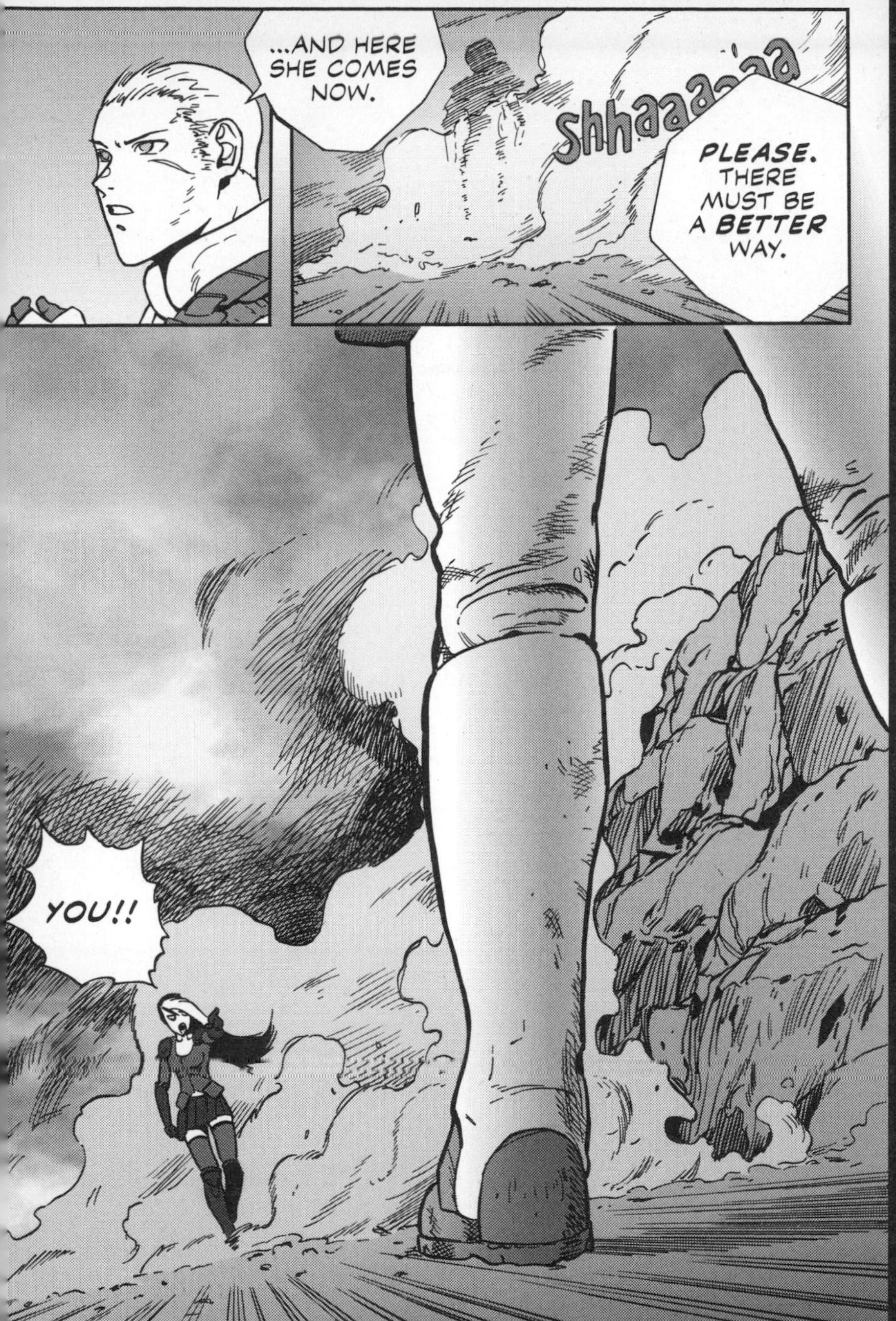
...AND HERE SHE COMES NOW.
Shhaaaaaaaa
PLEASE. THERE MUST BE A BETTER WAY.
YOU!!

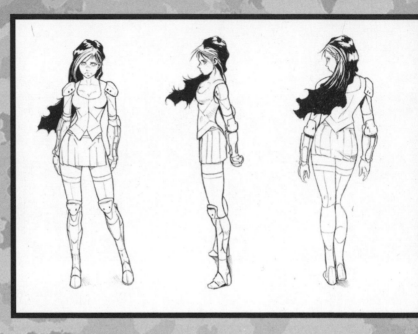

**EARLY DESIGN SKETCH FOR SNOW LUCENTE:
HER LOOK HAS REMAINED ESSENTIALLY THE SAME,
WITH THE EXCEPTION OF HER HAIR AND THE ARM-GUARDS**

PSY★COMM

CHAPTER [8]

PREVENT

\pre VENT\ (v.): to keep from happening

The Panthers tried their best, but they could not *prevent* the Patriots from winning the Super Bowl again.

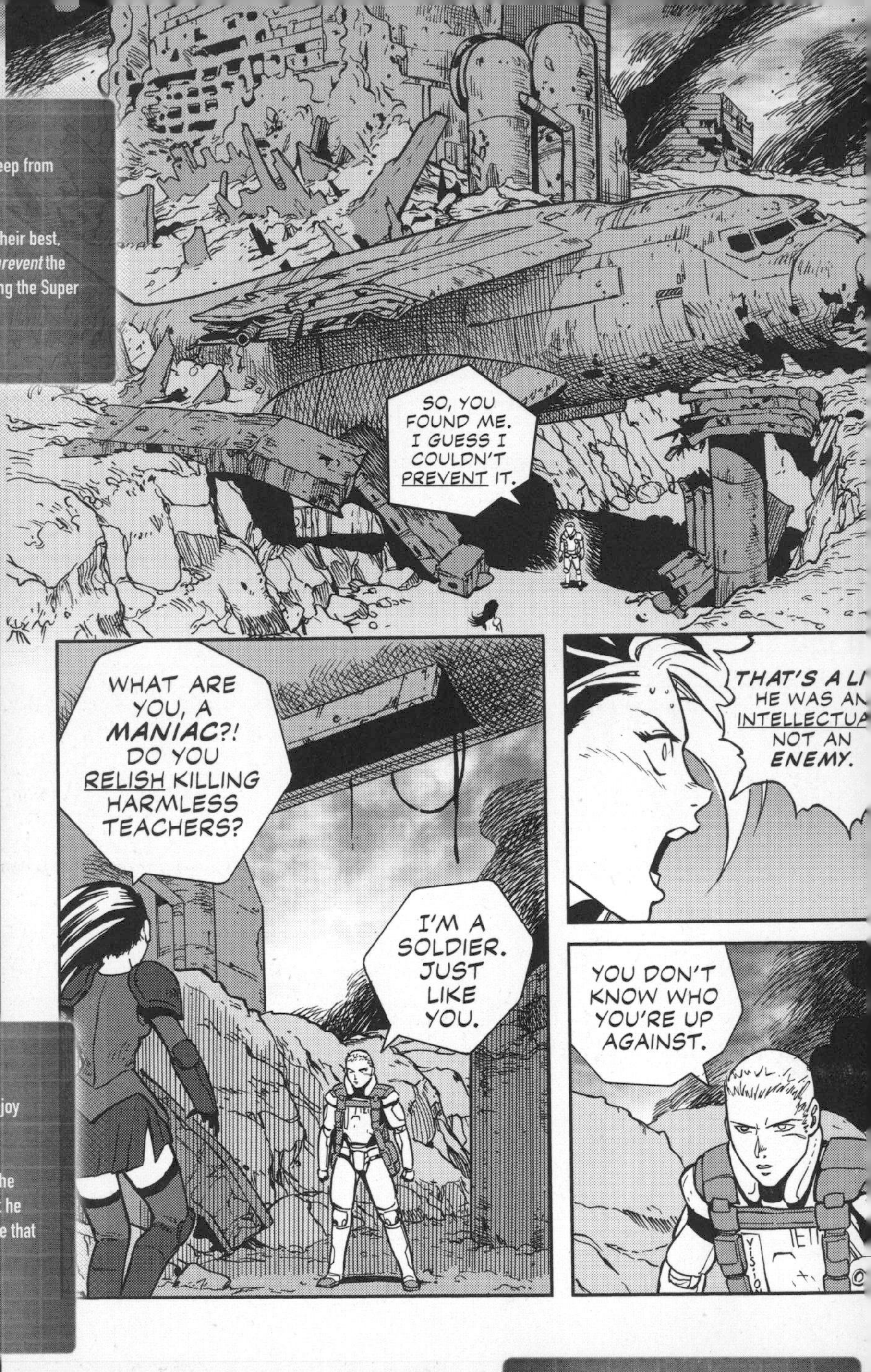
SO, YOU FOUND ME. I GUESS I COULDN'T PREVENT IT.
WHAT ARE YOU, A *MANIAC?!* DO YOU RELISH KILLING HARMLESS TEACHERS?
I'M A SOLDIER. JUST LIKE YOU.
THAT'S A LI HE WAS AN INTELLECTUA NOT AN *ENEMY.*
YOU DON'T KNOW WHO YOU'RE UP AGAINST.

RELISH

\REH lish\ (v.): to enjoy greatly

Cameron *relished* the tasty sandwich, but he didn't like the pickle that came with it.

INTELLECTUAL

\in te LEK shoo ul\ (adj.): intelligent, scholarly

Max enjoyed the *intellectual* aspects of football, analyzing videotapes of his opponents to discern their strengths and weaknesses.

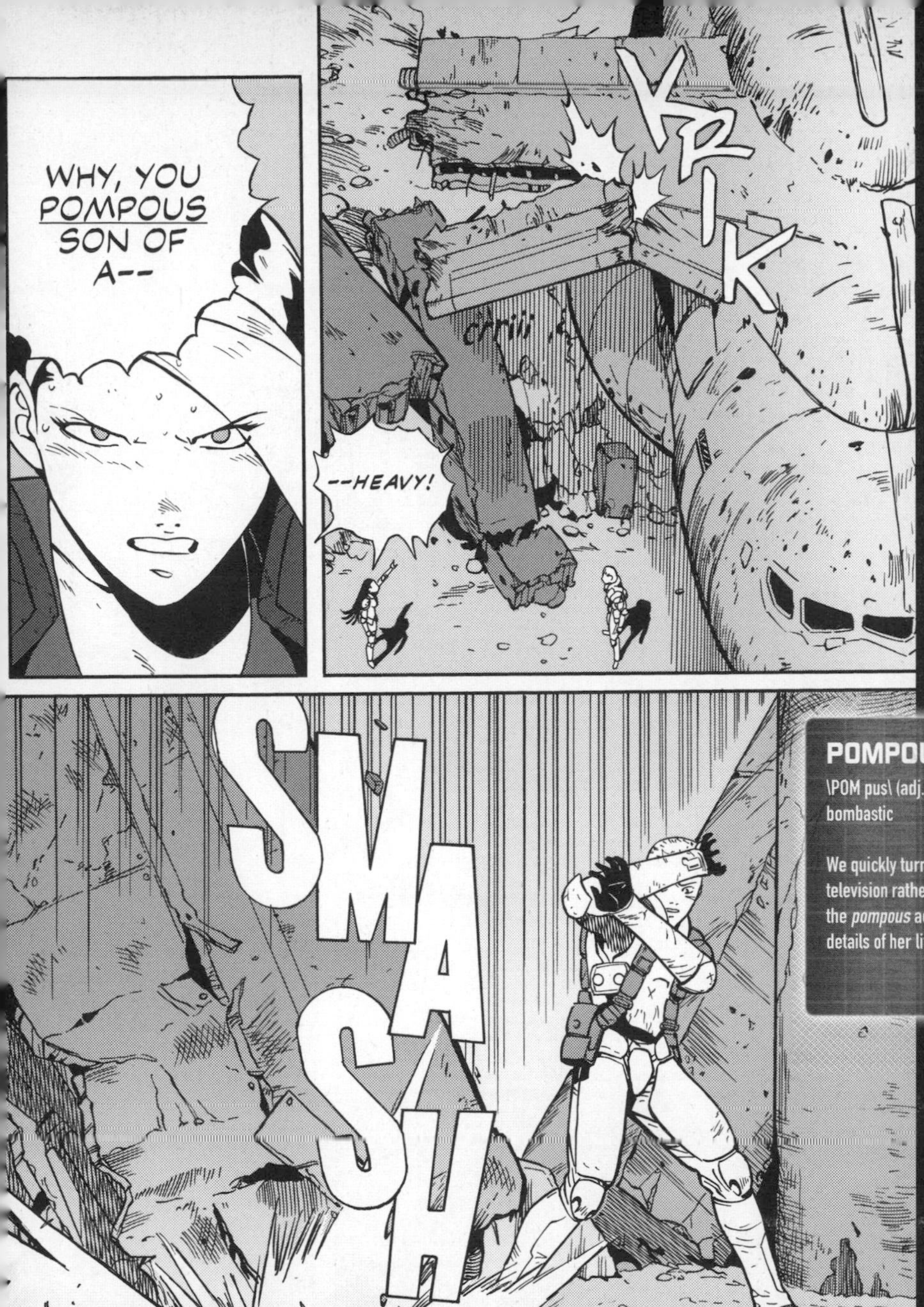
WHY, YOU POMPOUS SON OF A--
KRIK
crriii
--HEAVY!
SMASH

POMPOUS

\POM pus\ (adj.): pretentious, bombastic

We quickly turned off the television rather than listen to the *pompous* actress discuss the details of her life.

HEAVY!

ARGHH! LISTEN--GO BACK TO YOUR UNIT! WE DON'T NEED TO BE CONFRONTATIONAL!

KOFF--! GET OUT O HERE AND YOU'LL HAV LESS OF A CHANCE O GETTING KILLED!

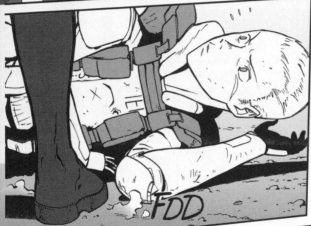

FDD

YOU KILLED THE PROFESSOR-- LIGHT!

WH U D

CONFRONTATIONAL

\kon fron TAY shun al\ (adj.): eager to defy, especially in a face-to-face encounter

Known by his coworkers to be *confrontational*, J.B. was elected to discuss the upcoming budget cuts with the company's president.

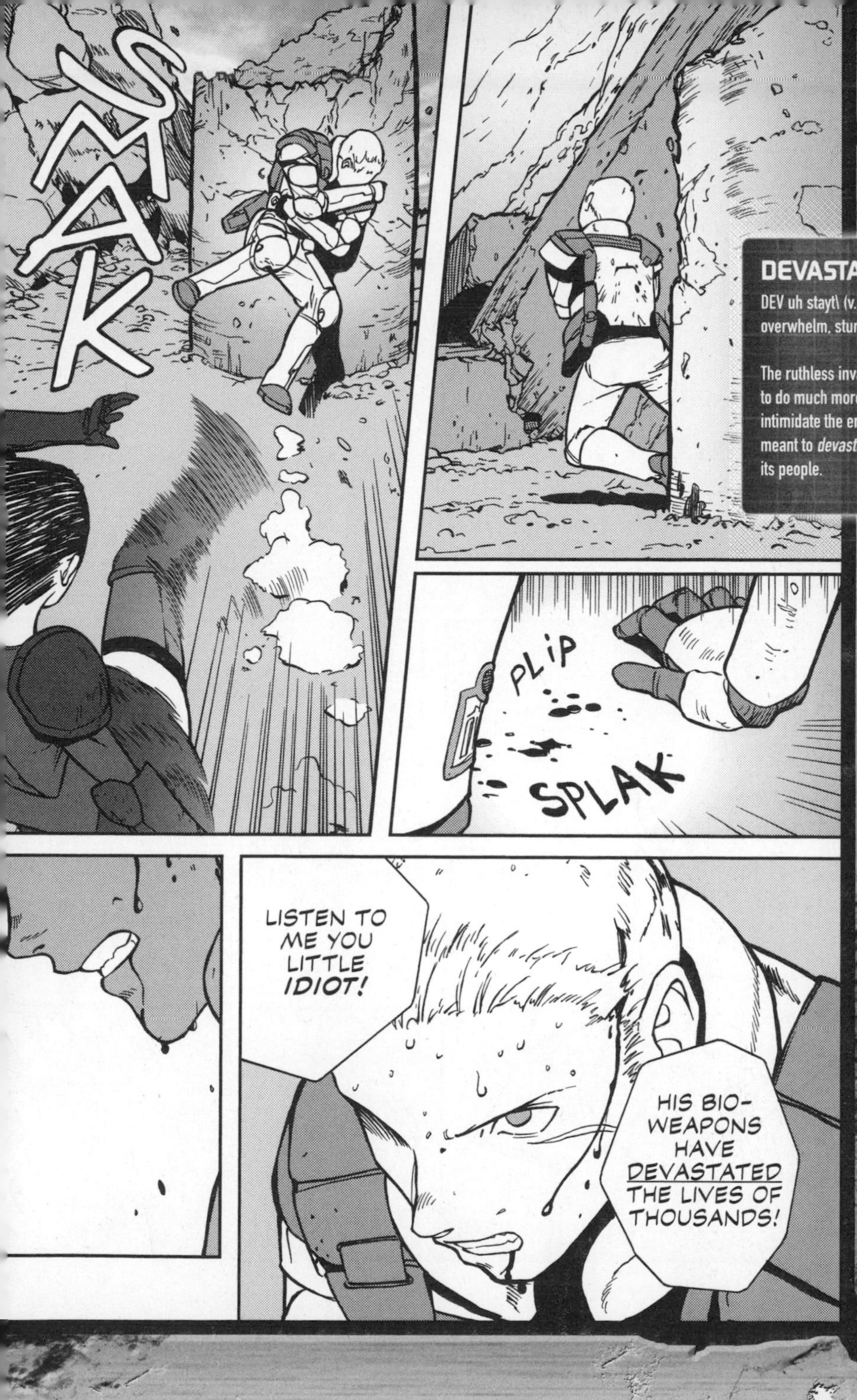
SMAK
PLIP
SPLAK
LISTEN TO ME YOU LITTLE *IDIOT*!
HIS BIO-WEAPONS HAVE DEVASTATED THE LIVES OF THOUSANDS!

DEVASTATE

DEV uh stayt\ (v.): destroy; overwhelm, stun

The ruthless invaders sought to do much more than simply intimidate the empire; they meant to *devastate* the land and its people.

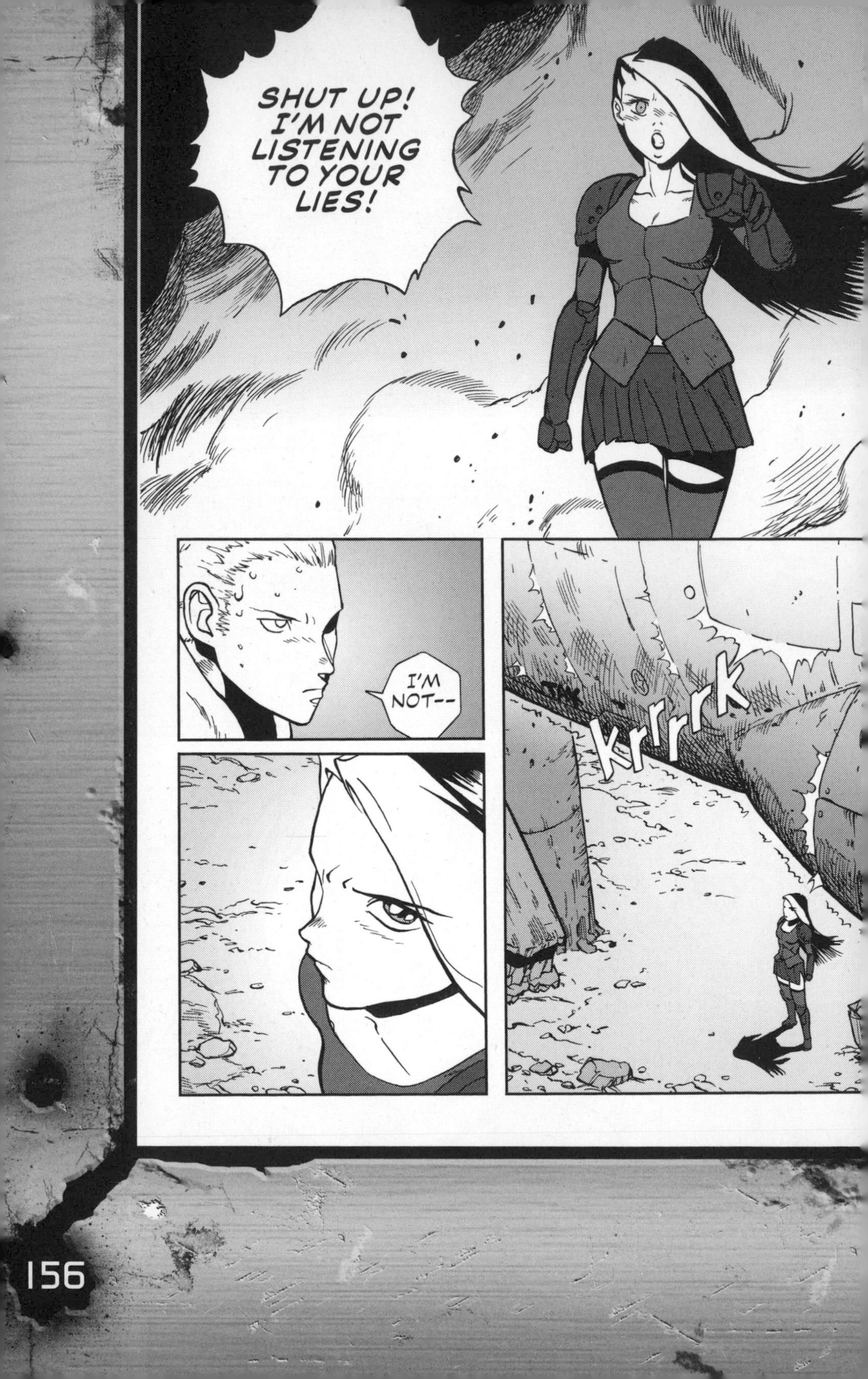
SHUT UP! I'M NOT LISTENING TO YOUR LIES!
I'M NOT--
Krrrrk

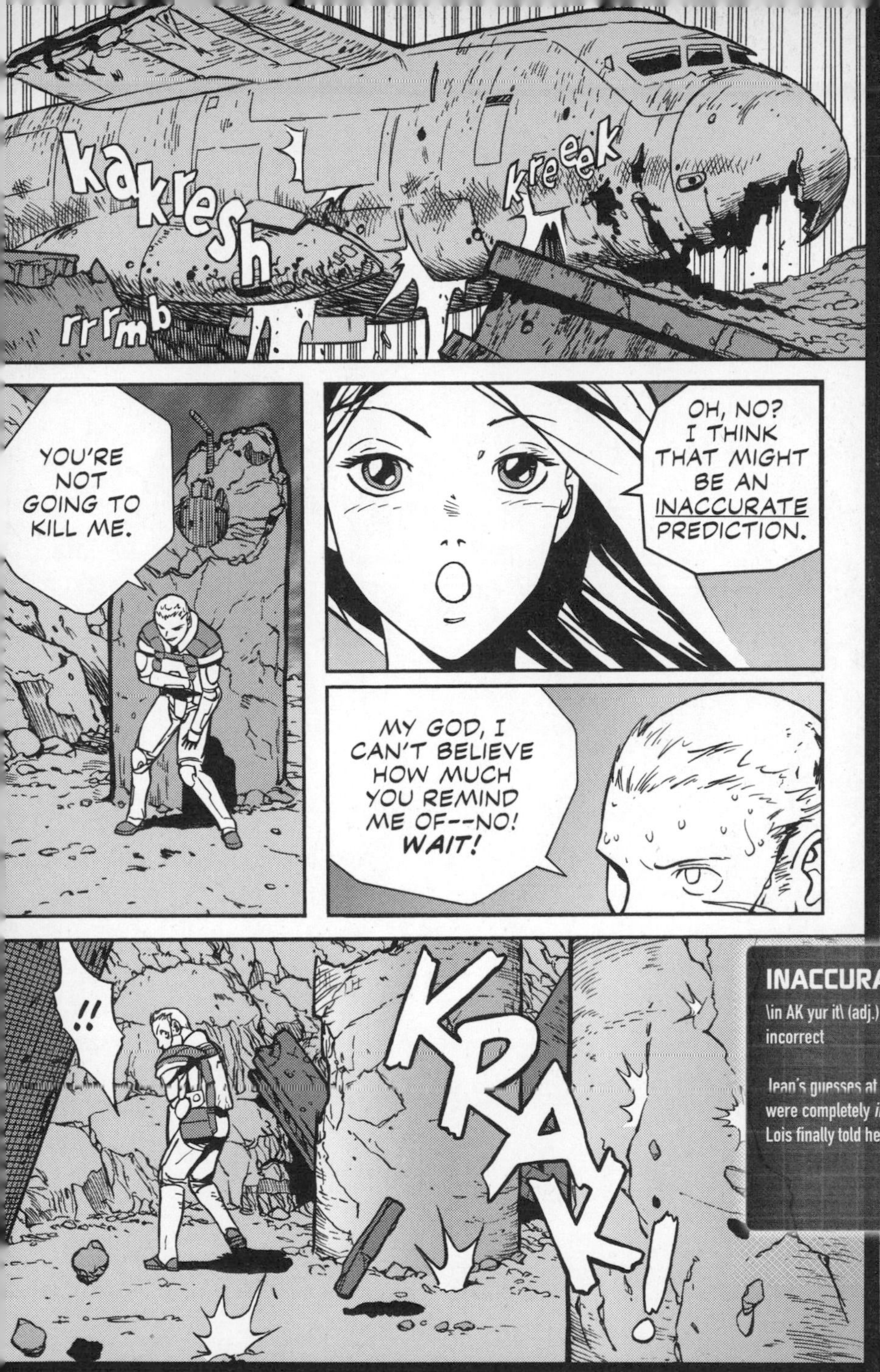
kakresh
kreeek
rrrmb
YOU'RE NOT GOING TO KILL ME.
OH, NO? I THINK THAT MIGHT BE AN INACCURATE PREDICTION.
MY GOD, I CAN'T BELIEVE HOW MUCH YOU REMIND ME OF--NO! WAIT!
!!
KRAK!

INACCURATE

\in AK yur it\ (adj.): mistaken, incorrect

Jean's guesses at Lois's age were completely *inaccurate*, so Lois finally told her the truth.

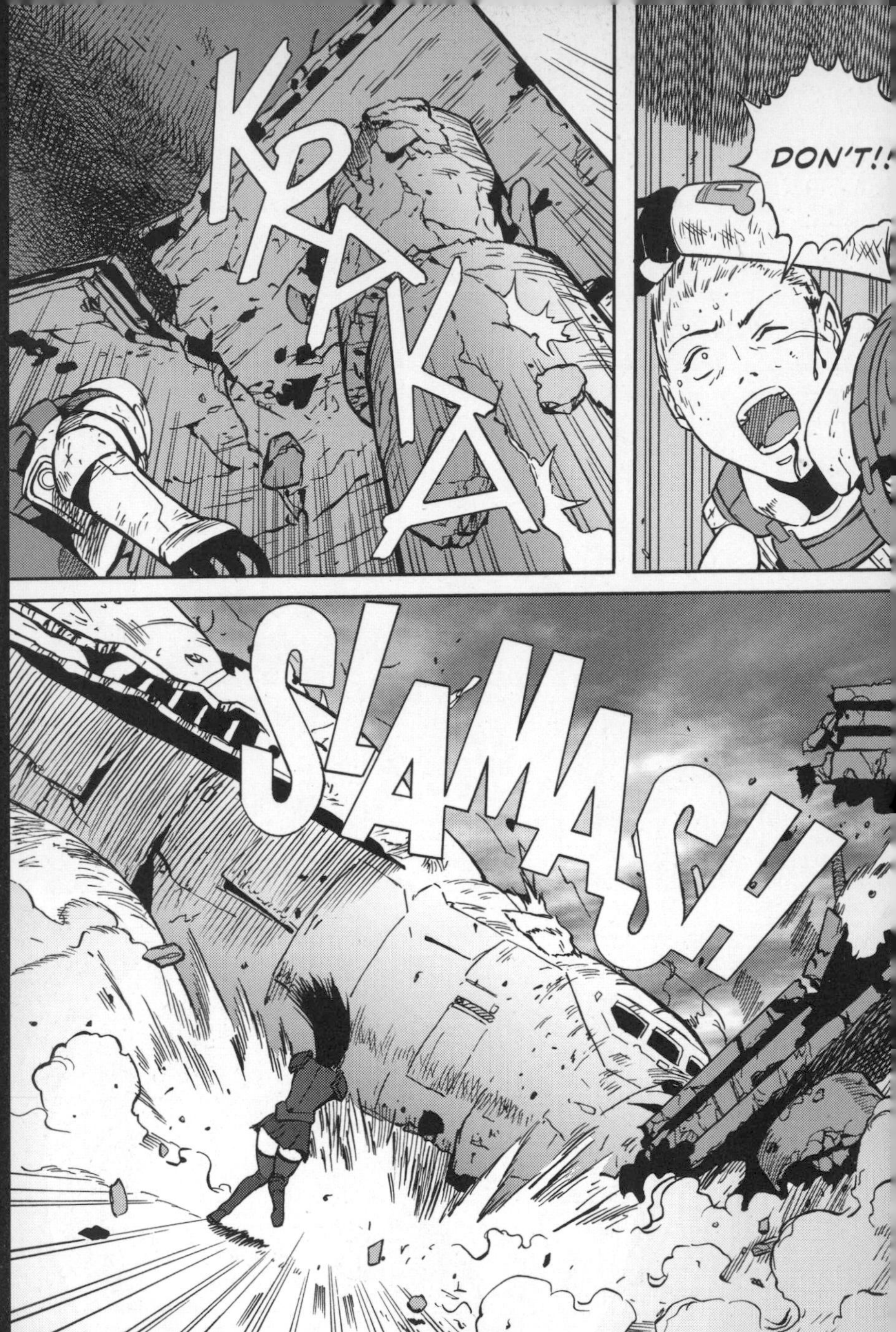
KRAKA
DON'T!!
SLAMASH

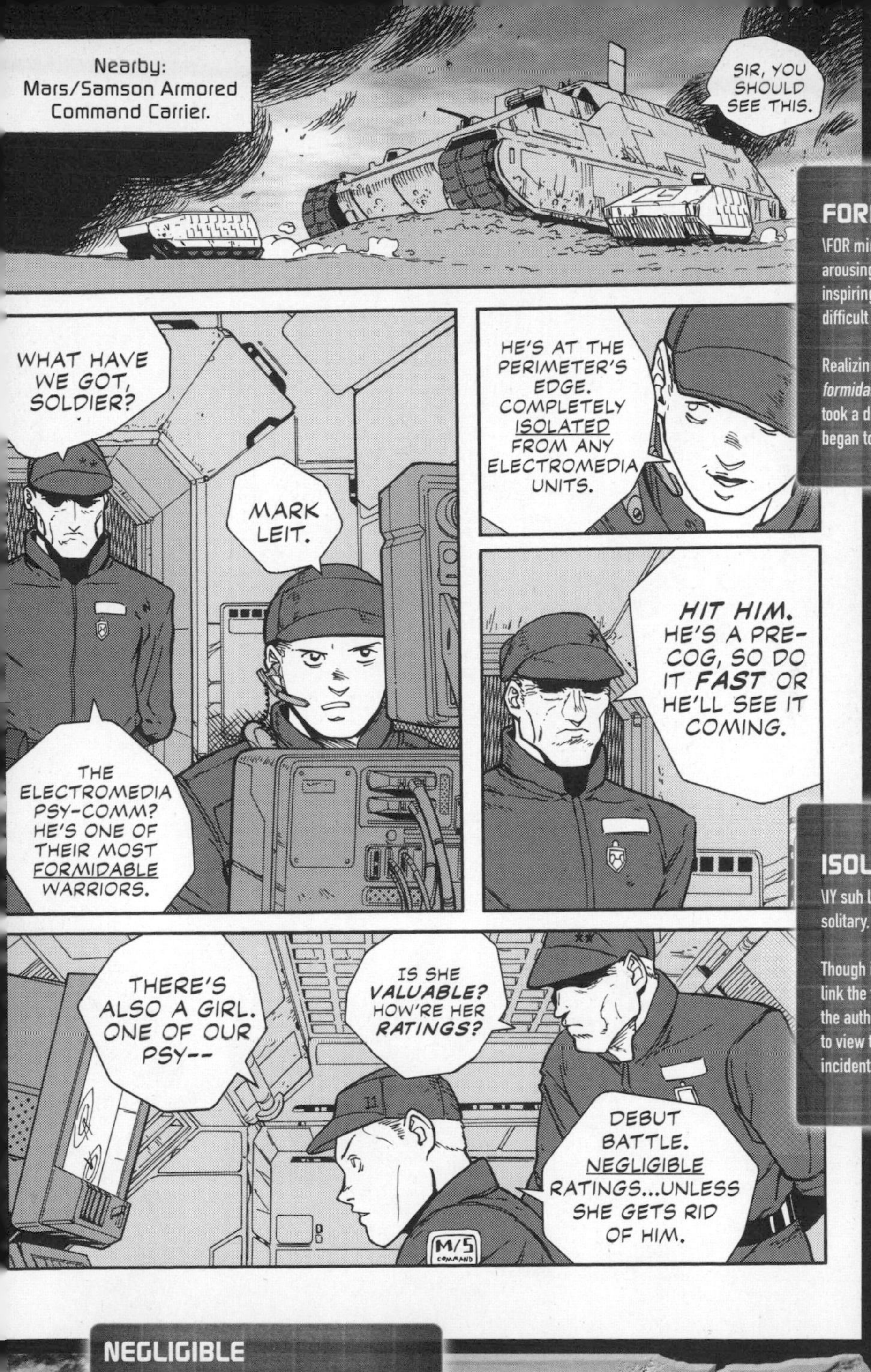
Nearby: Mars/Samson Armored Command Carrier.
SIR, YOU SHOULD SEE THIS.
WHAT HAVE WE GOT, SOLDIER?
MARK LEIT.
THE ELECTROMEDIA PSY-COMM? HE'S ONE OF THEIR MOST FORMIDABLE WARRIORS.
HE'S AT THE PERIMETER'S EDGE. COMPLETELY ISOLATED FROM ANY ELECTROMEDIA UNITS.
HIT HIM. HE'S A PRE-COG, SO DO IT FAST OR HE'LL SEE IT COMING.
THERE'S ALSO A GIRL. ONE OF OUR PSY--
IS SHE VALUABLE? HOW'RE HER RATINGS?
DEBUT BATTLE. NEGLIGIBLE RATINGS...UNLESS SHE GETS RID OF HIM.
M/S COMMAND

FORMIDABLE

\FOR mid uh bul\ (adj.): arousing fear or dread; inspiring awe or wonder; difficult to undertake

Realizing that she faced a *formidable* task, Barbara took a deep breath and began to clean her room.

ISOLATE

\IY suh lay tid\ (adj.): solitary, singular

Though it is tempting to link the three crimes, the authorities continue to view them as *isolated* incidents.

NEGLIGIBLE

\NEG lih ju bul\ (adj.): not worth considering

It's obvious from our *negligible* dropout rate that our students love our program.

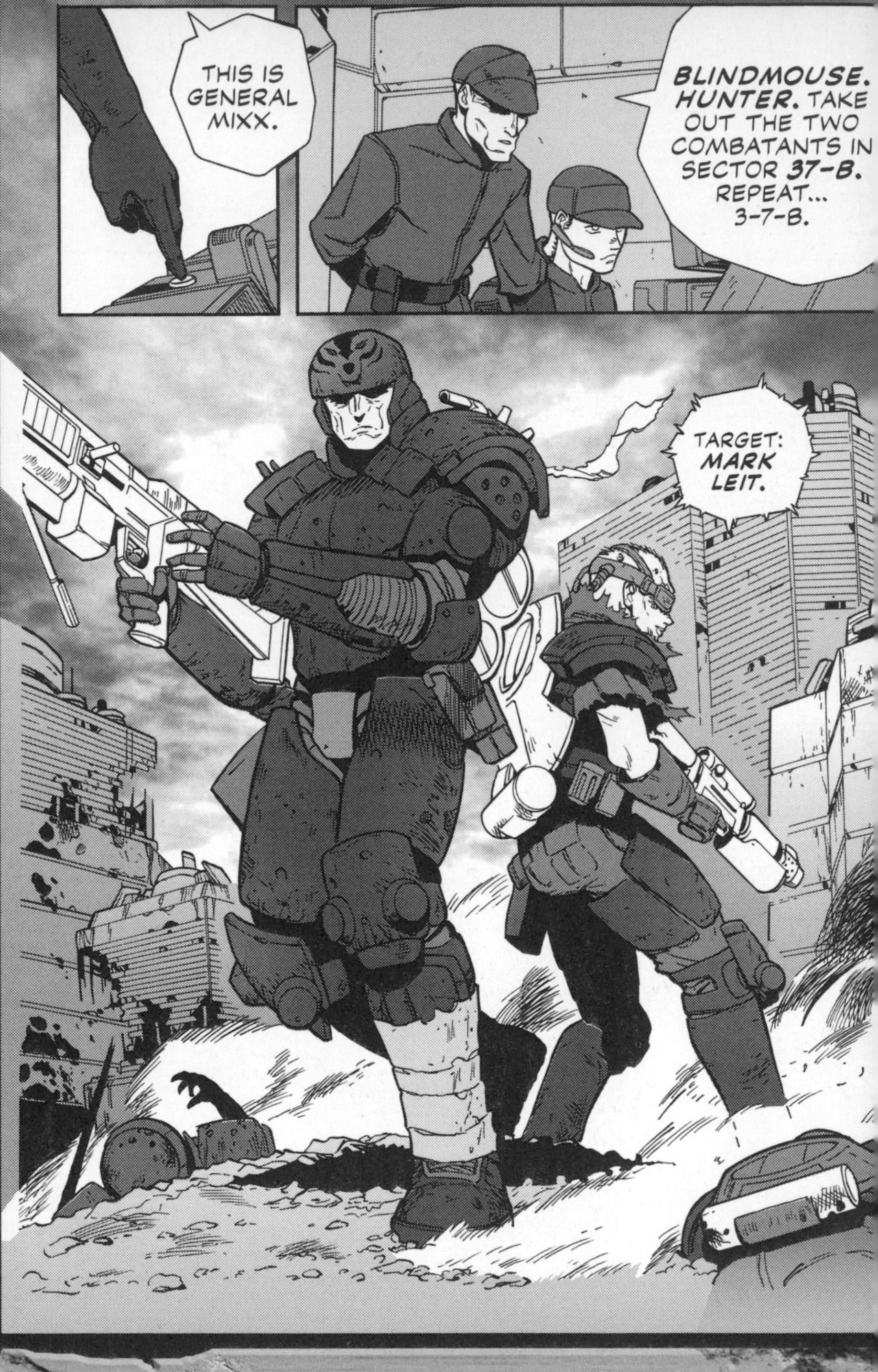
THIS IS GENERAL MIXX.
BLINDMOUSE. HUNTER. TAKE OUT THE TWO COMBATANTS IN SECTOR 37-B. REPEAT... 3-7-B.
TARGET: MARK LEIT.

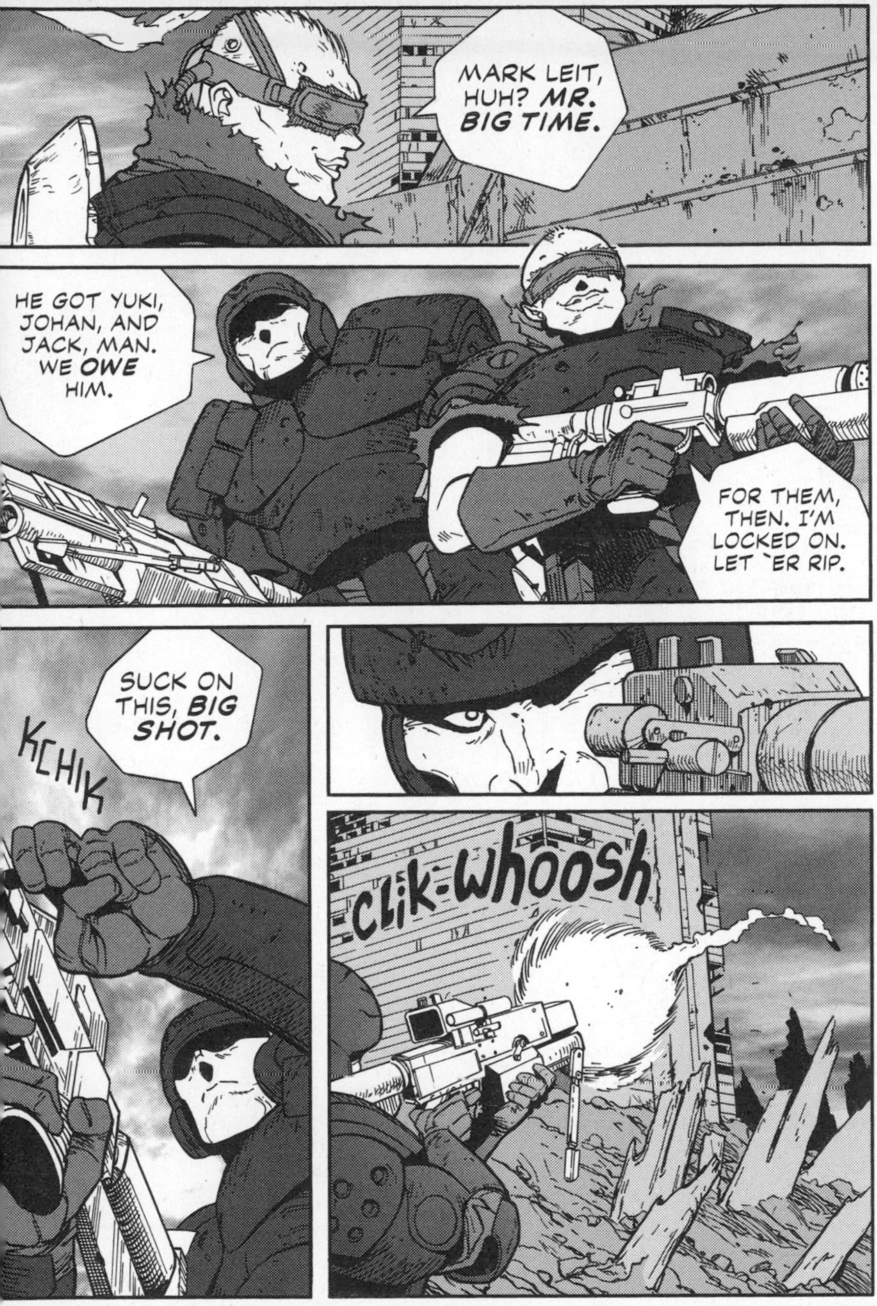
MARK LEIT, HUH? MR. BIG TIME.
HE GOT YUKI, JOHAN, AND JACK, MAN. WE OWE HIM.
FOR THEM, THEN. I'M LOCKED ON. LET `ER RIP.
SUCK ON THIS, BIG SHOT.
KCHIK
CLIK-WHOOSH

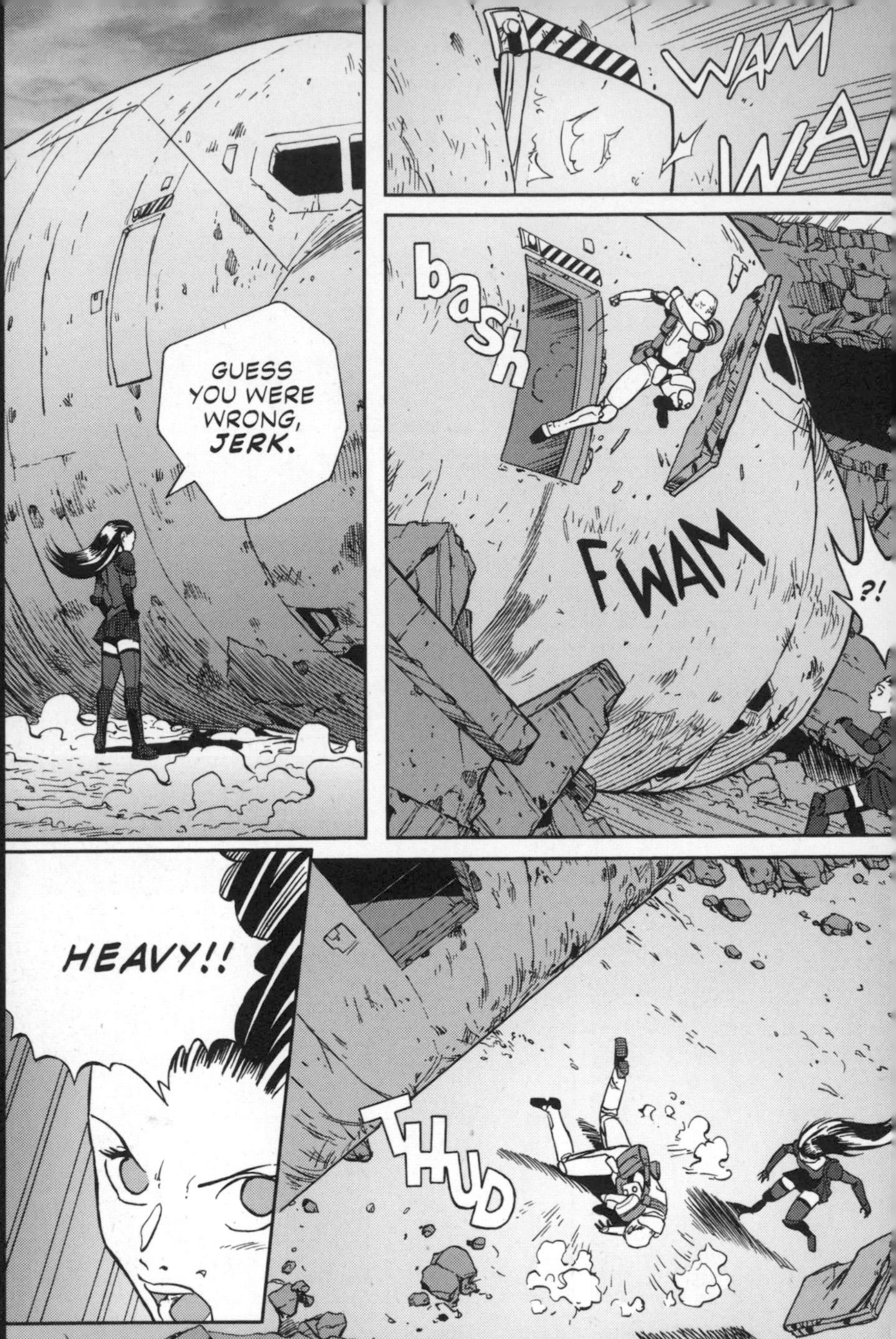
GUESS YOU WERE WRONG, JERK.
WAM
WAM
bash
FWAM
?!
HEAVY!!
THUD

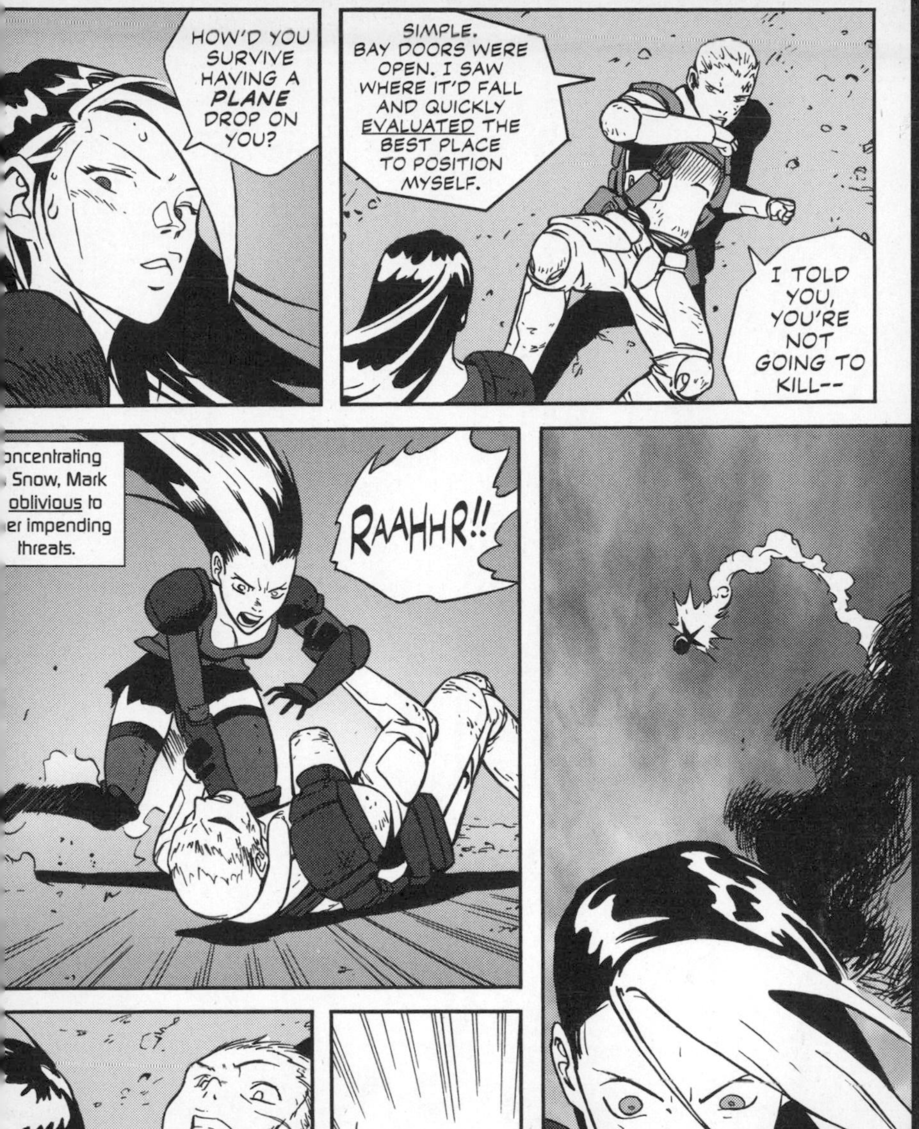
HOW'D YOU SURVIVE HAVING A PLANE DROP ON YOU?
SIMPLE. BAY DOORS WERE OPEN. I SAW WHERE IT'D FALL AND QUICKLY EVALUATED THE BEST PLACE TO POSITION MYSELF.
I TOLD YOU, YOU'RE NOT GOING TO KILL--
oncentrating
Snow, Mark
oblivious to
er impending
threats.
RAAHHR!!

EVALUATE

\ee VAL yoo ayt\ (v.): to examine or judge carefully

The judge instructed the jury to carefully *evaluate* all the evidence before coming to a conclusion.

OBLIVIOUS

\ahb LIV ee us\ (adj.): unaware, inattentive

The Police Commissioner calmly made his way through the crowd, seemingly *oblivious* to the angry rioters around him.

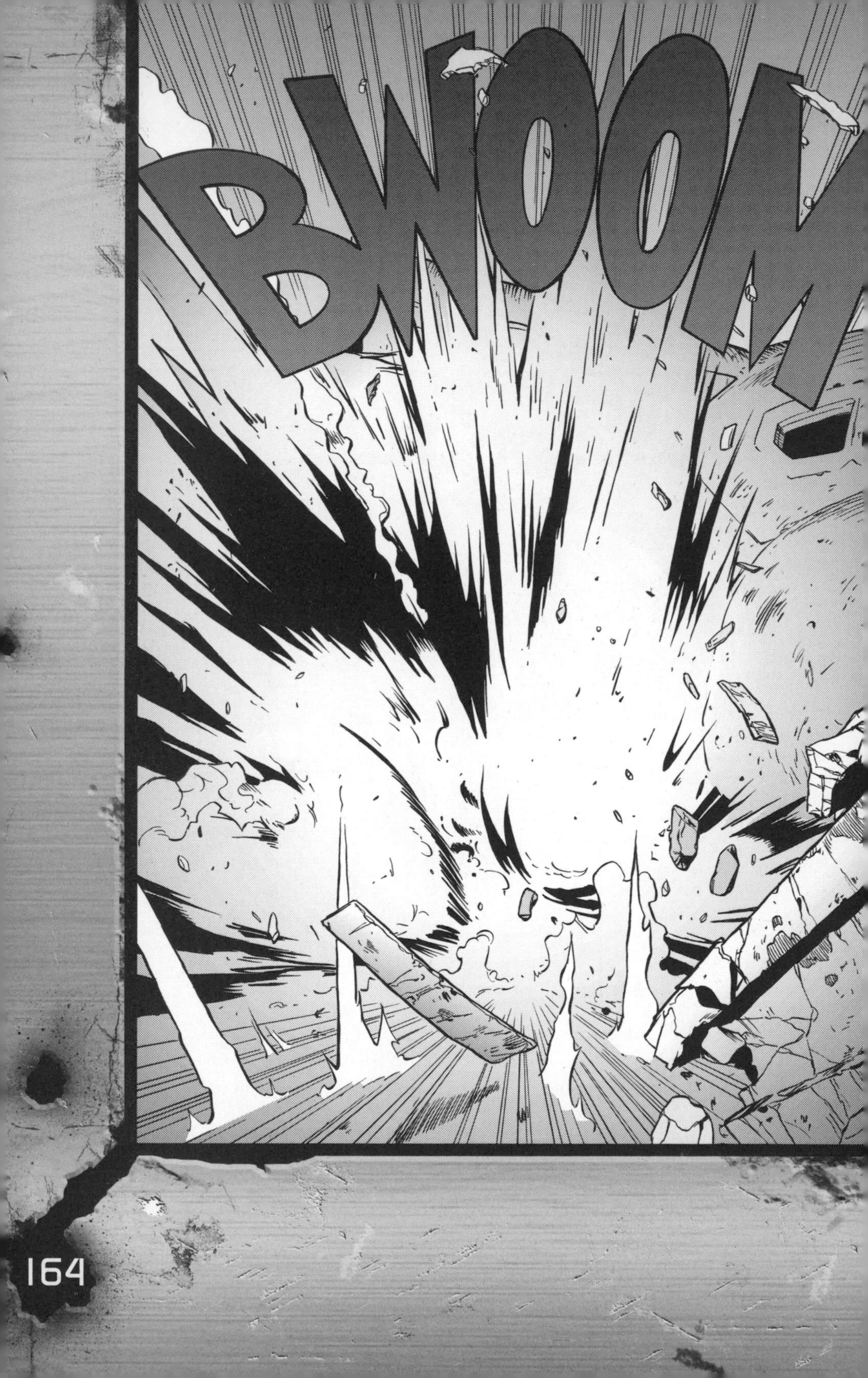
BWOOM

PSY★COMM
CHAPTER [9]

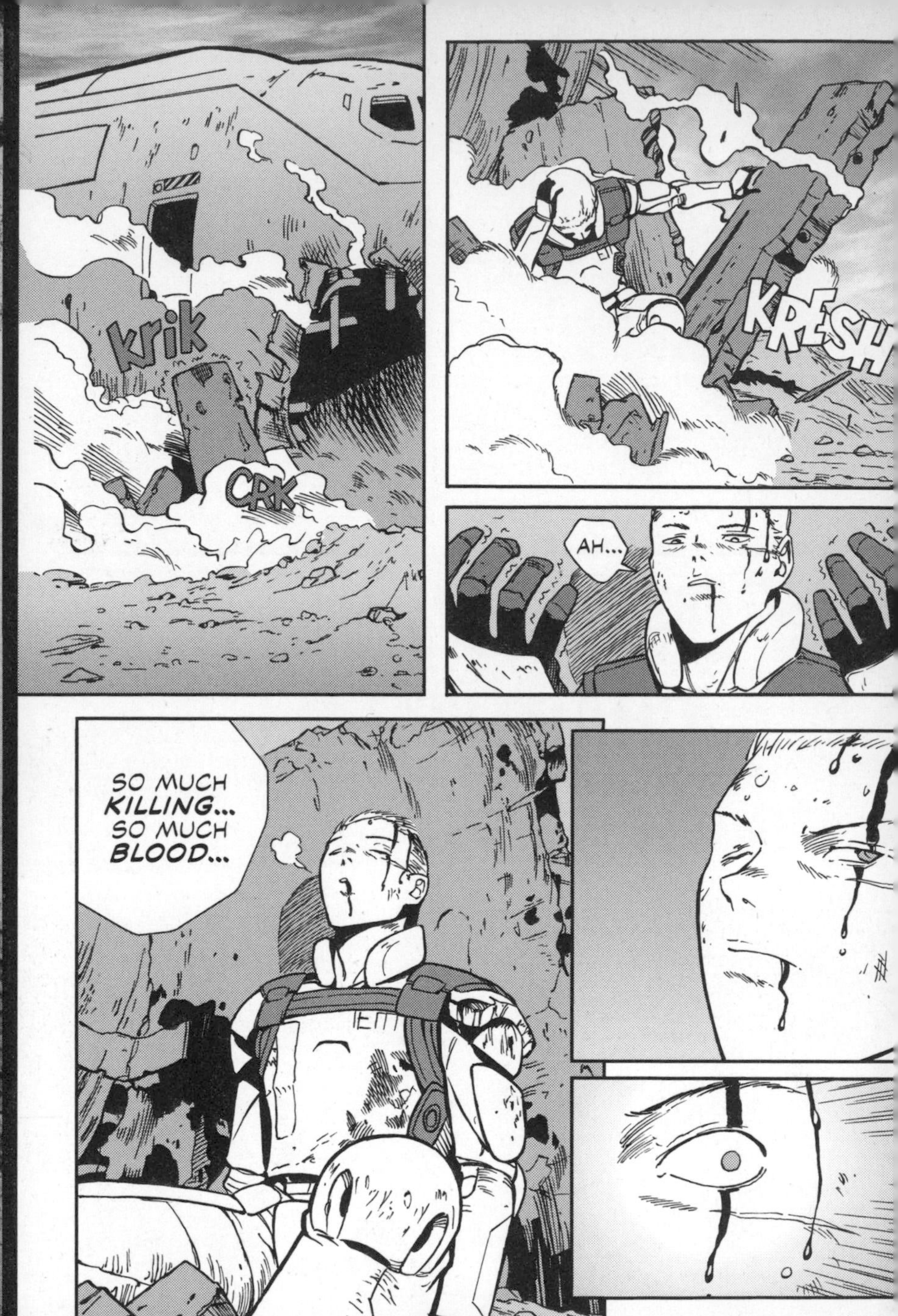
krik
CRK
KRESH
AH...
SO MUCH KILLING... SO MUCH BLOOD...

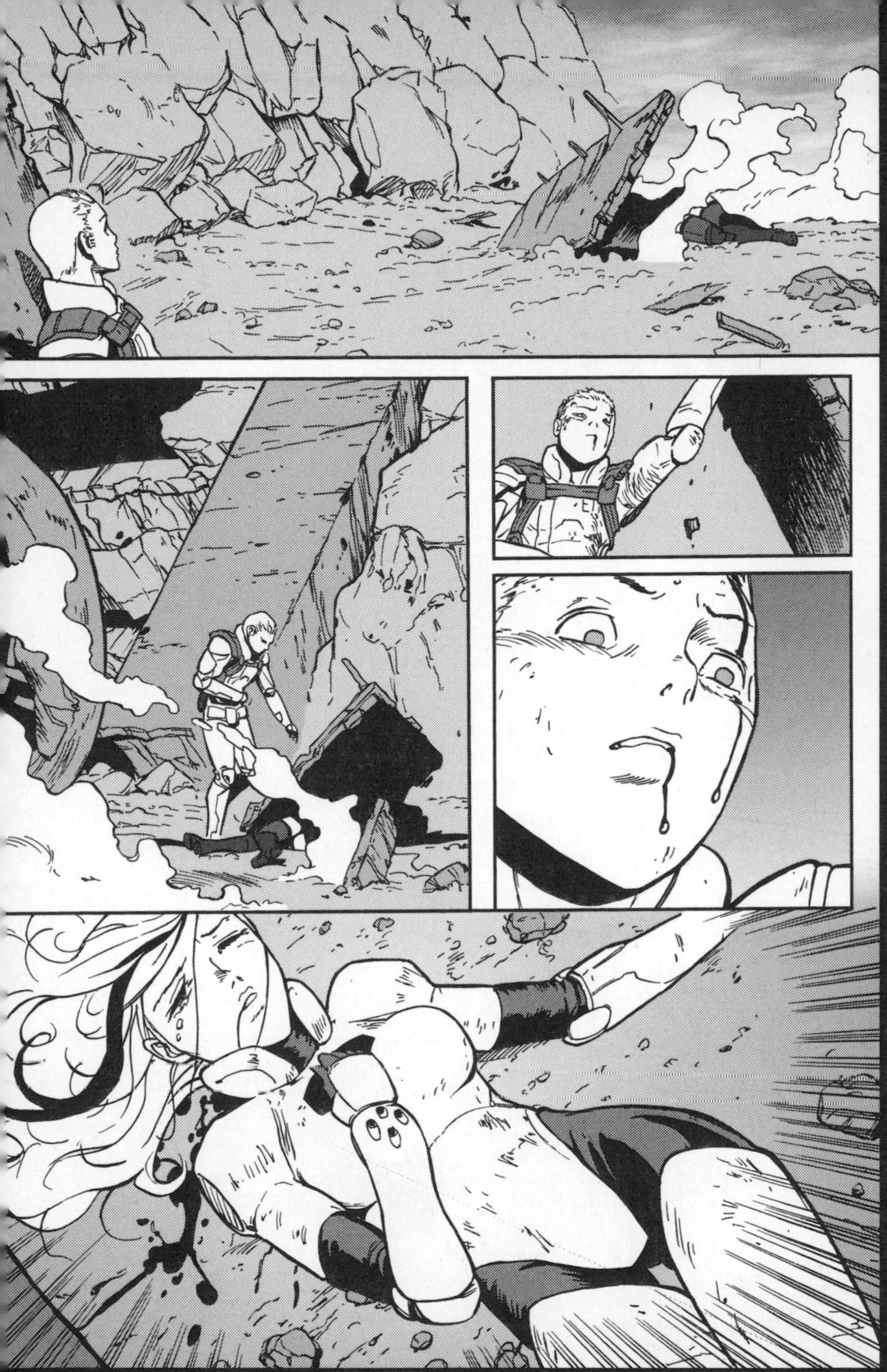

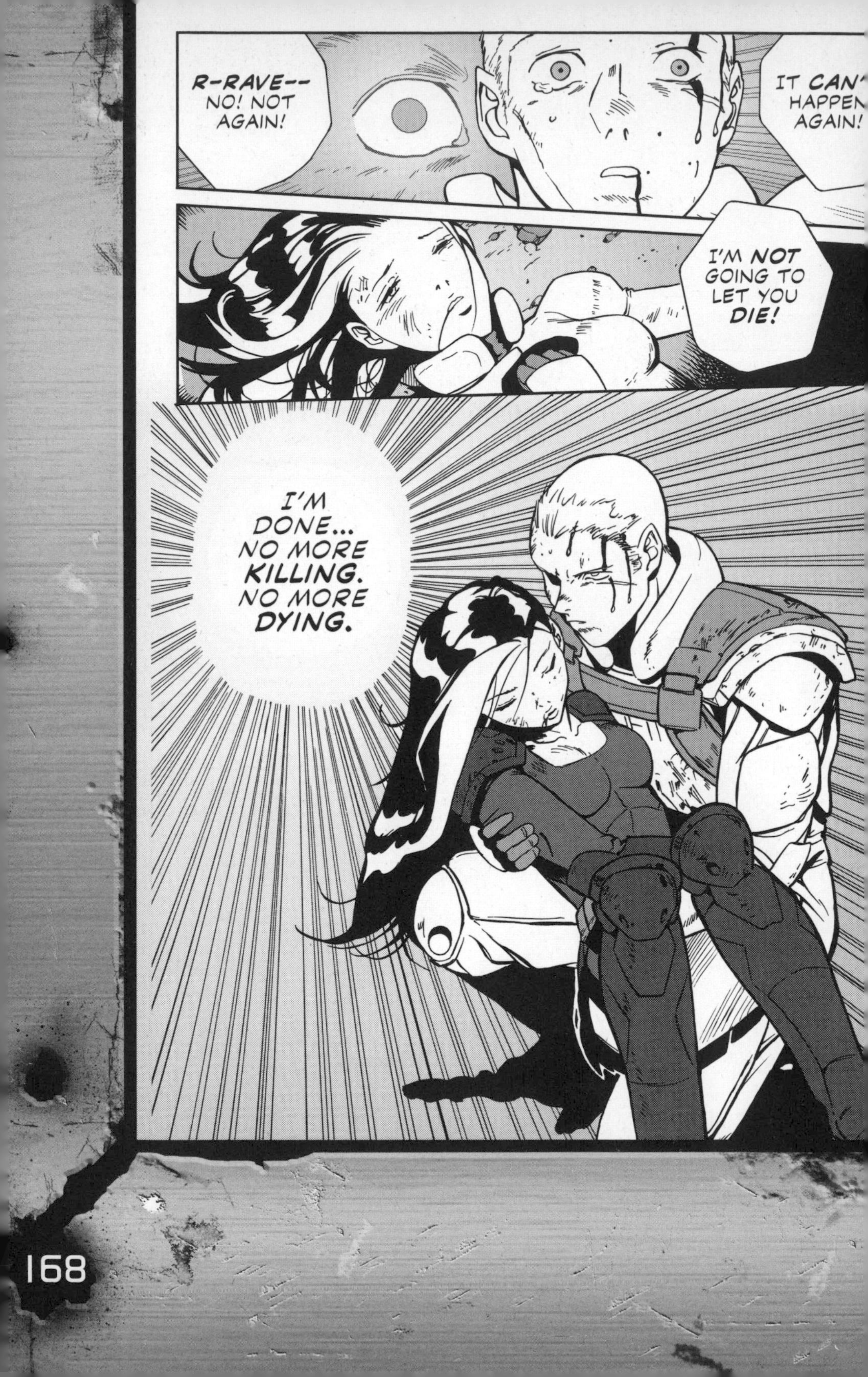
R-RAVE-- NO! NOT AGAIN!
IT CAN'T HAPPEN AGAIN!
I'M NOT GOING TO LET YOU DIE!
I'M DONE... NO MORE KILLING. NO MORE DYING.

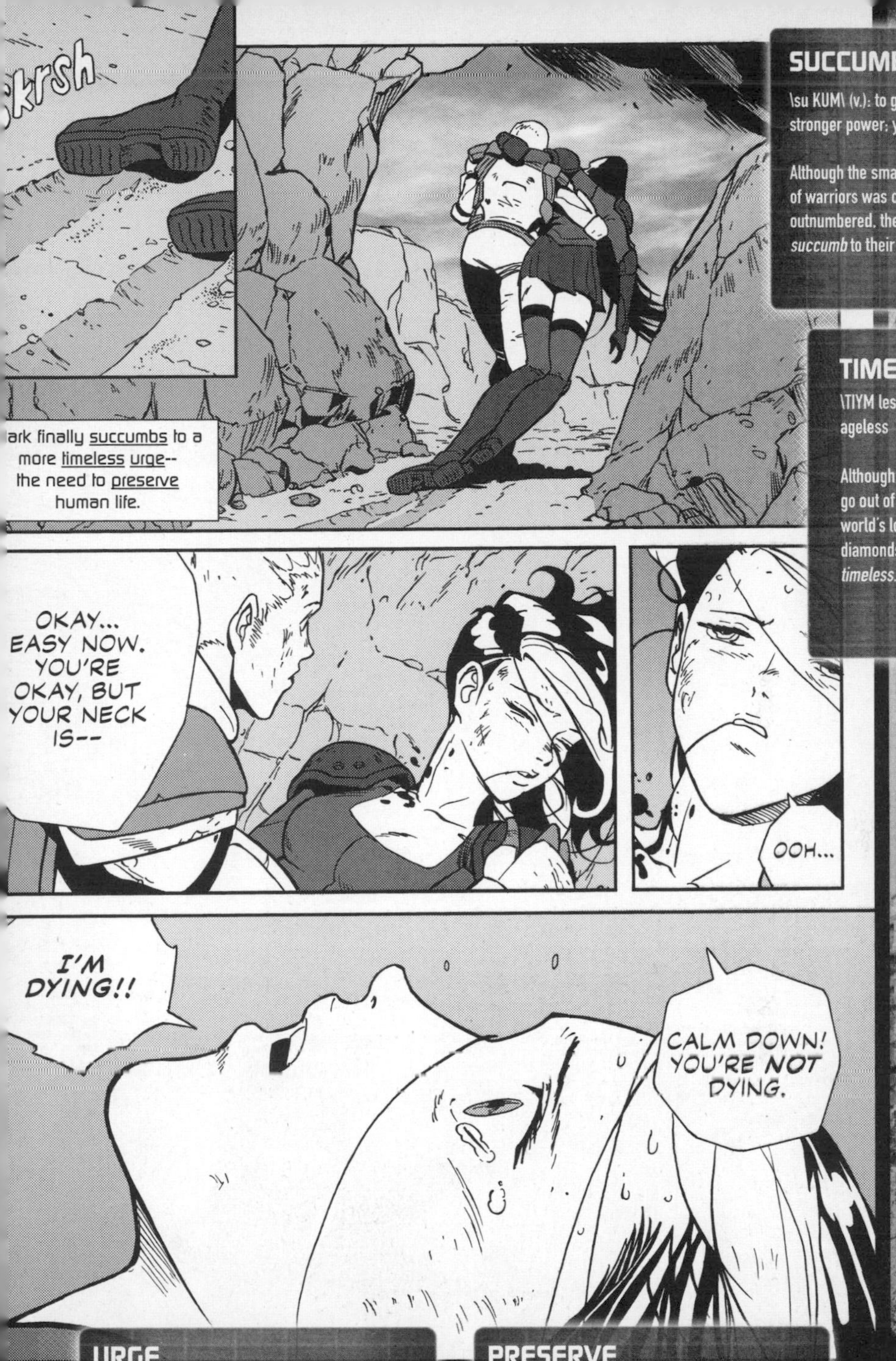

skrsh
ark finally succumbs to a more timeless urge-- the need to preserve human life.
OKAY... EASY NOW. YOU'RE OKAY, BUT YOUR NECK IS--
OOH...
I'M DYING!!
CALM DOWN! YOU'RE NOT DYING.

SUCCUMB

\su KUM\ (v.): to give in to stronger power; yield

Although the small band of warriors was clearly outnumbered, they refused to *succumb* to their enemies.

TIMELESS

\TIYM les\ (adj.): eternal, ageless

Although some riches go out of style, the world's love for diamonds seems to be *timeless*.

URGE

\URJ\ (v.): to impel, to exhort, spur to action

Principal Slater gave a passionate speech *urging* all students to take their schoolwork seriously.

PRESERVE

\pre ZURV\ (v.): to protect, to keep unchanged

The museum keeps the ancient manuscripts locked in airtight glass containers in order to *preserve* them.

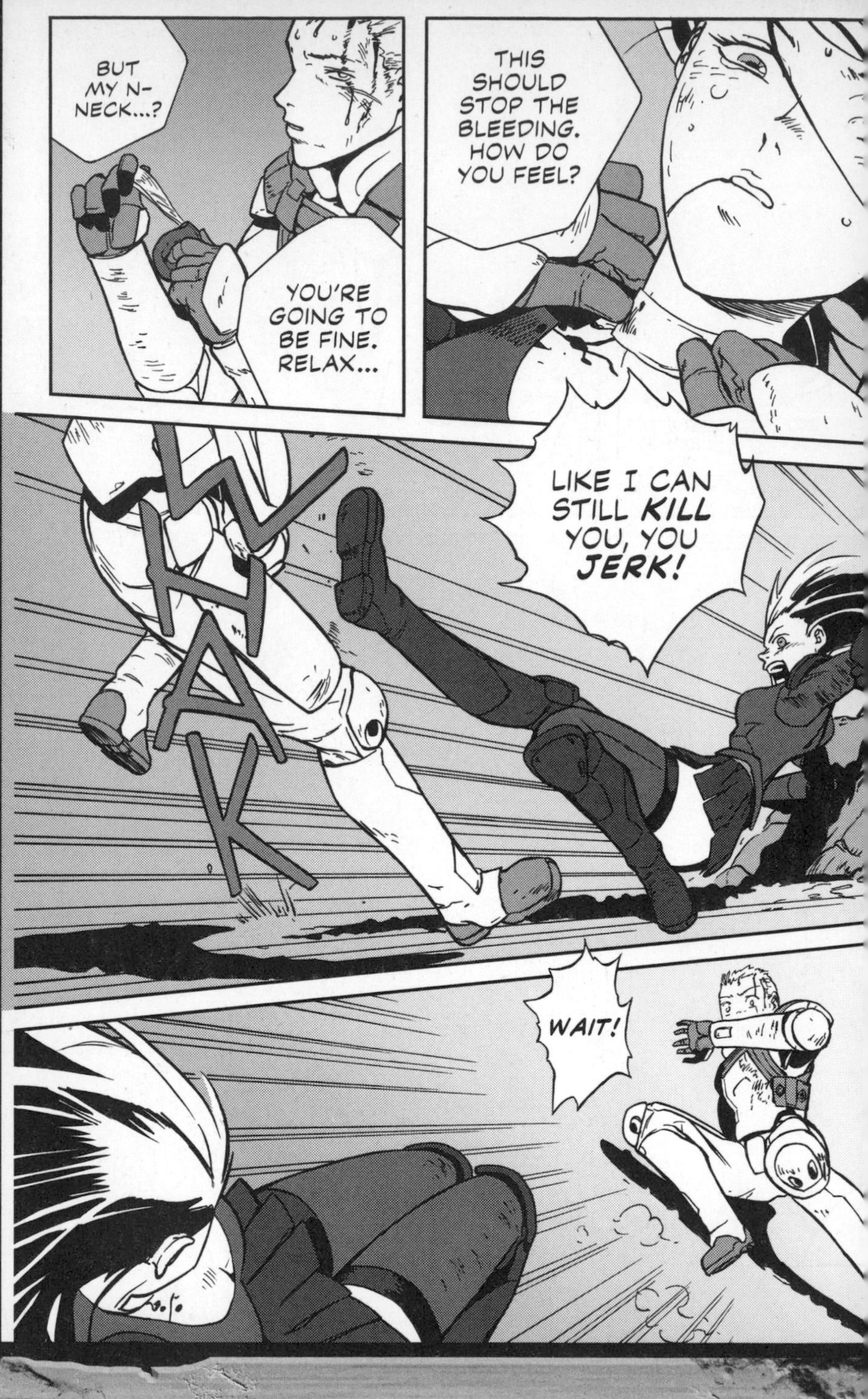
BUT MY N-NECK...?
YOU'RE GOING TO BE FINE. RELAX...
THIS SHOULD STOP THE BLEEDING. HOW DO YOU FEEL?
WHAK
LIKE I CAN STILL **KILL** YOU, YOU **JERK!**
WAIT!

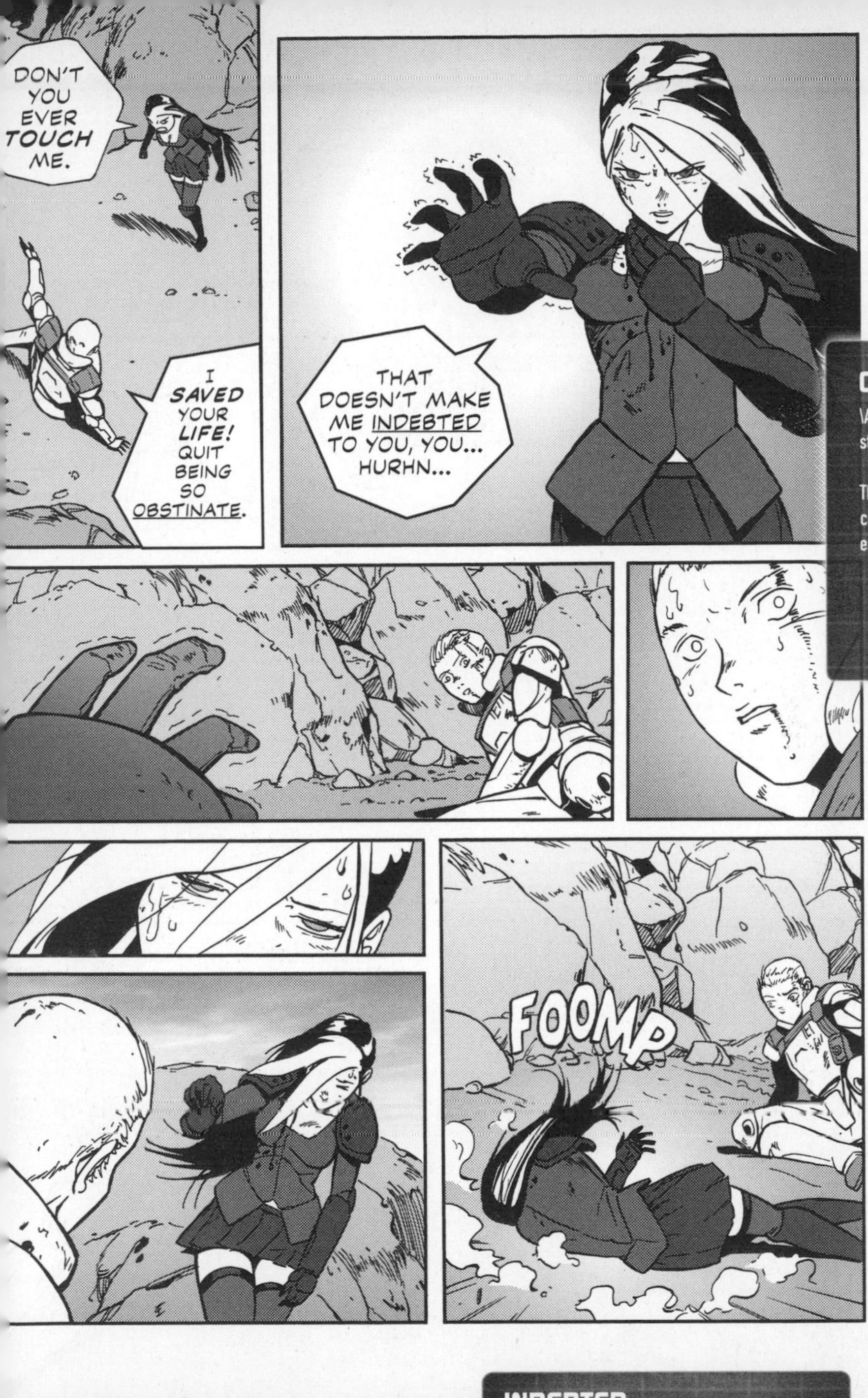
DON'T YOU EVER TOUCH ME.
I SAVED YOUR LIFE! QUIT BEING SO OBSTINATE.
THAT DOESN'T MAKE ME INDEBTED TO YOU, YOU... HURHN...
FOOMP

OBSTINATE

\AHB stu nit\ (adj.): stubborn

The *obstinate* child could not be forced to eat any vegetables.

INDEBTED

\in DET id\ (adj.): obligated to someone else, beholden

Tommy was forever *indebted* to his neighbor for introducing him to his future wife.

YOU WON'T MAKE IT IF YOU KEEP THIS UP.
WH-WHAT'S *WRONG* WITH YOU?
113M
SYS LINK:
bzzp
beep
GOTCH
boosh
boosh

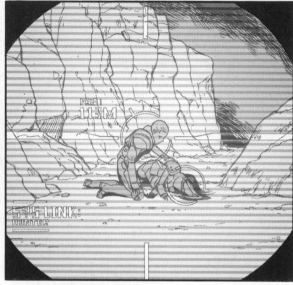

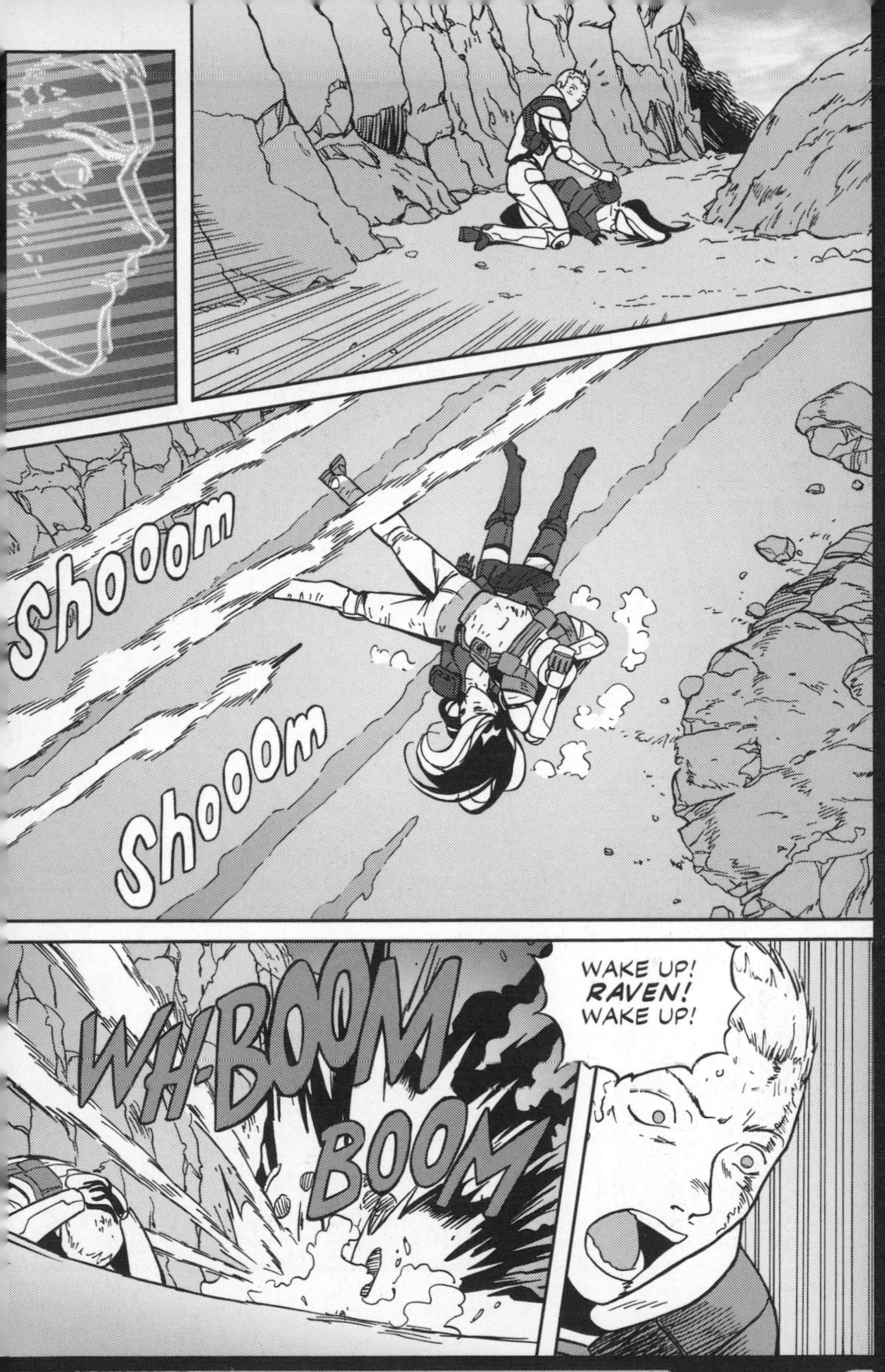
Shooom
Shooom
WH-BOOM
BOOM
WAKE UP!
RAVEN!
WAKE UP!

WHO?
UHH...
NOTHING. NEVER-MIND.
LOOK, I NEED YOU TO MAKE US A **WALL.**
WHA...?
BRING DOWN THOSE ROCKS! GIVE US A BUFFER WHILE I DO SOMETHING!
I'LL **KILL** YOU.
YOU DO THAT! BUT FIRST, MAKE THAT WALL, **SOLDIER!**

BUFFER

\BUFF uhr\ (n.): something that separates two entities

Miss Phillips placed Lenny between Rachel and Sari, as a *buffer* through which they couldn't talk during class.

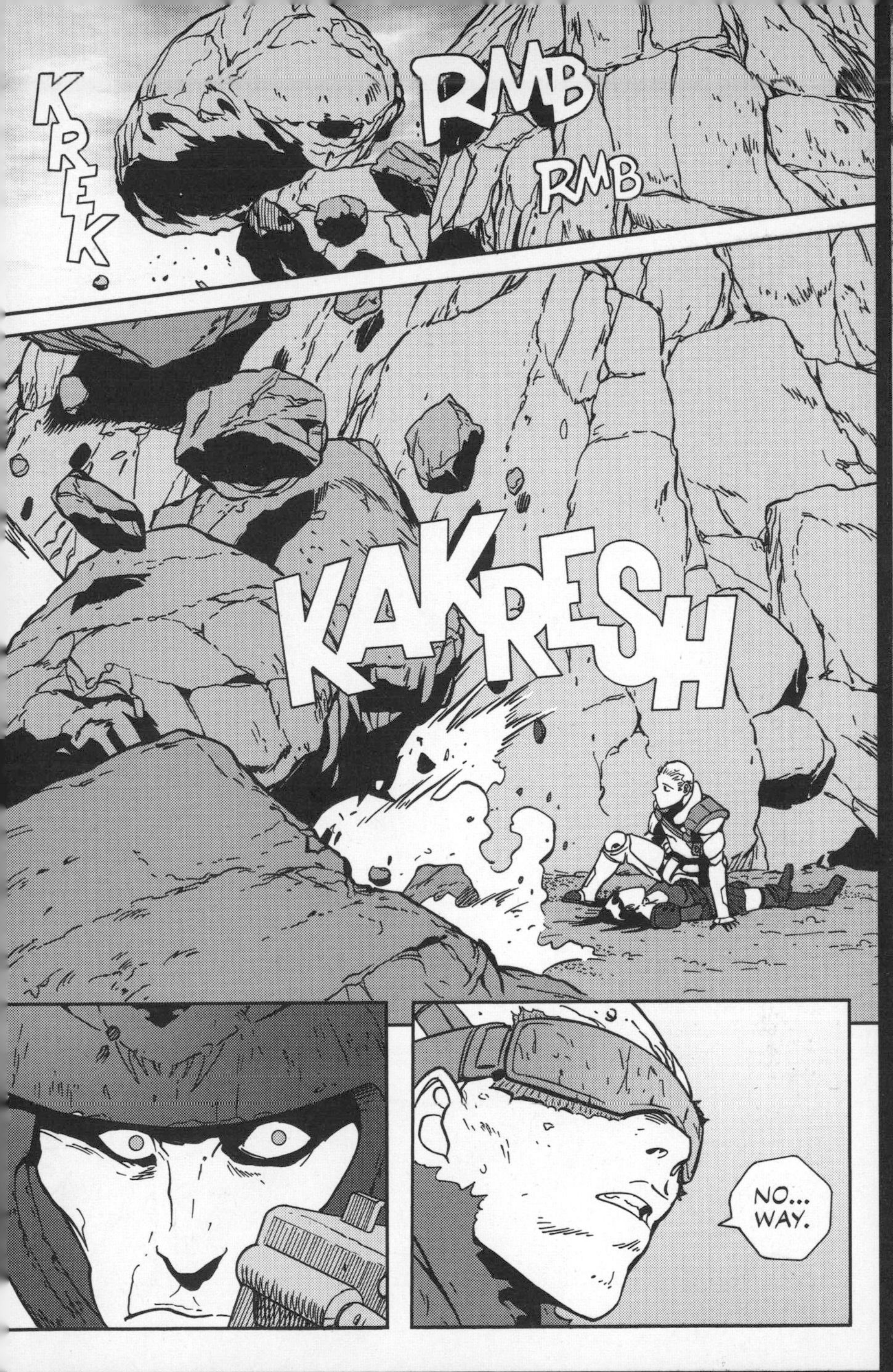
KREK
RMB
RMB
KAKRESH
NO... WAY.

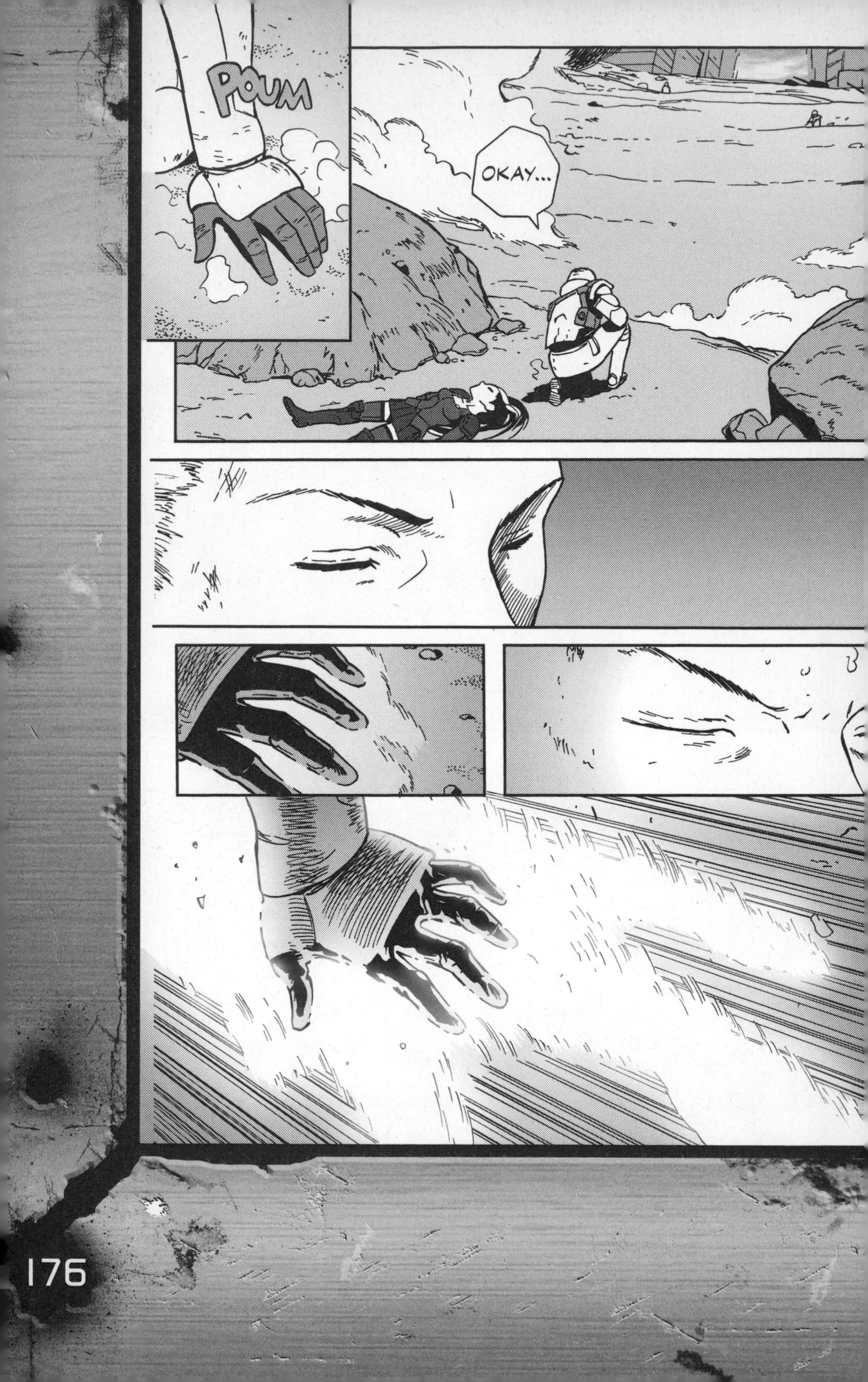
POUM
OKAY...

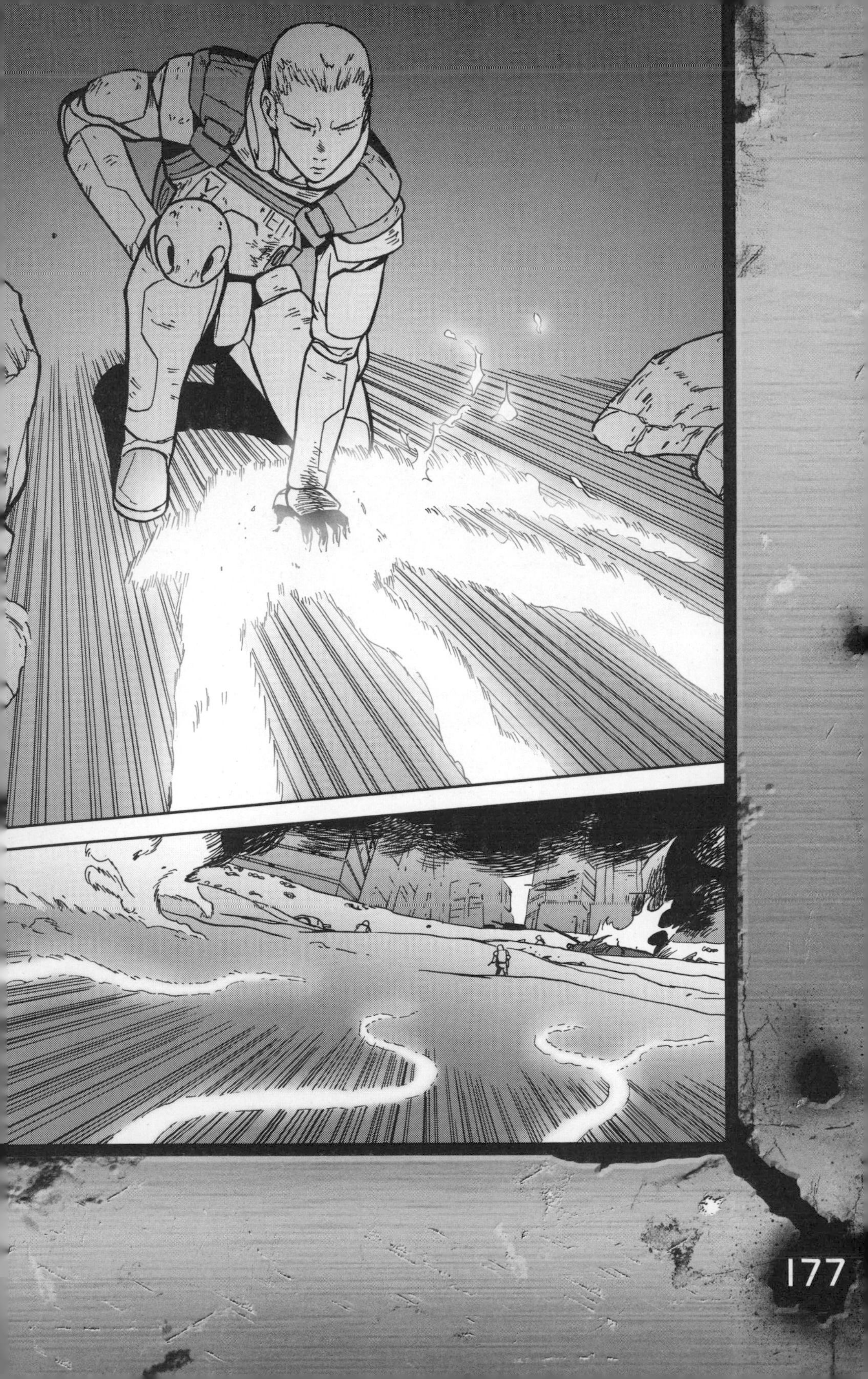

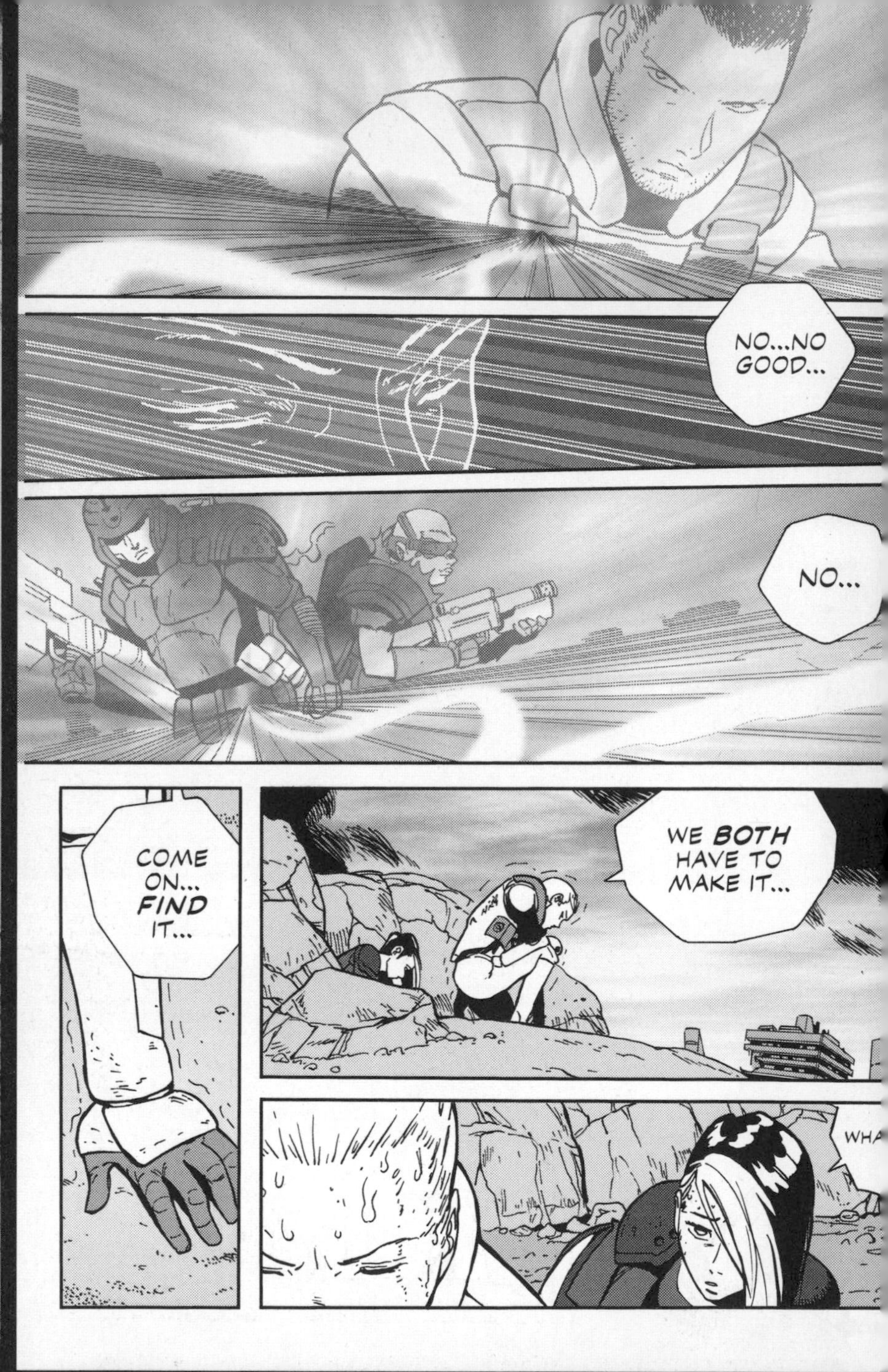
NO...NO GOOD...
NO...
COME ON... FIND IT...
WE BOTH HAVE TO MAKE IT...
WHA

Nearly drained of his last <u>reserves</u> of energy, Mark suddenly <u>determines</u> a route that will <u>liberate</u> both himself and his <u>reluctant</u> companion from the shackles of war.

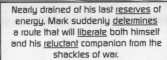

THERE! THAT'S IT!

RESERVE

\re ZERV\ (n.): something put aside for future use

I couldn't borrow the textbook from the library for more than two hours because it was on *reserve* for everyone in the class to use.

DETERMINE

\di TUR min\ (v.): to decide, establish

The scientists were unable to *determine* the cause of the strange ailment.

LIBERATE

\LIB uh rayt\ (v.): emancipate, set free

The politician promised to *liberate* individuals unjustly imprisoned during the current administration's tenure.

RELUCTANT

\re LUK tant\ (adj.): unwilling, opposing, hesitant

Florence was *reluctant* to believe the weather report that called for snow: the news had been wrong too often in the past.

17

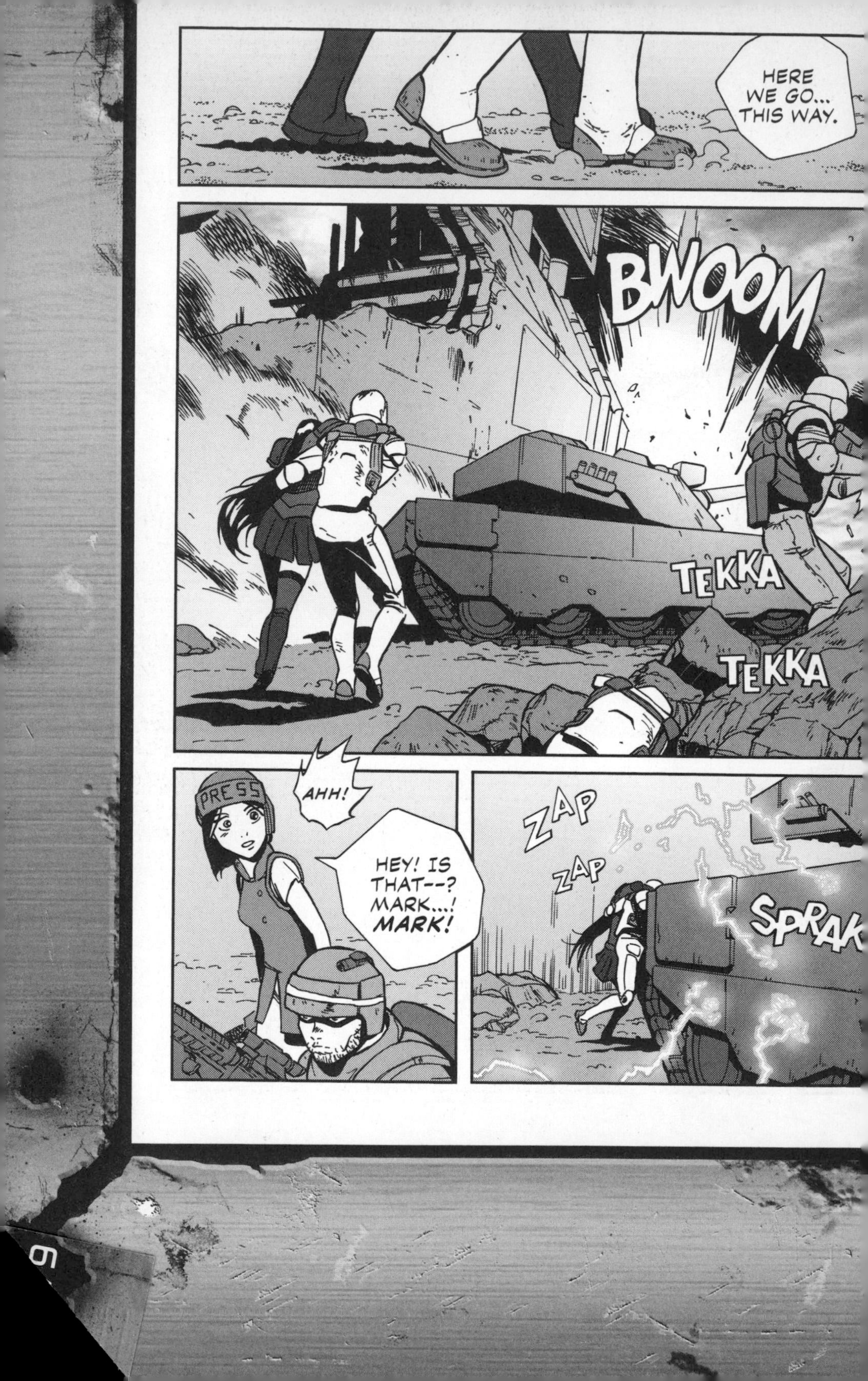
HERE WE GO... THIS WAY.
BWOOM
TEKKA
TEKKA
AHH!
HEY! IS THAT--? MARK...! *MARK!*
ZAP
ZAP
SPRAK

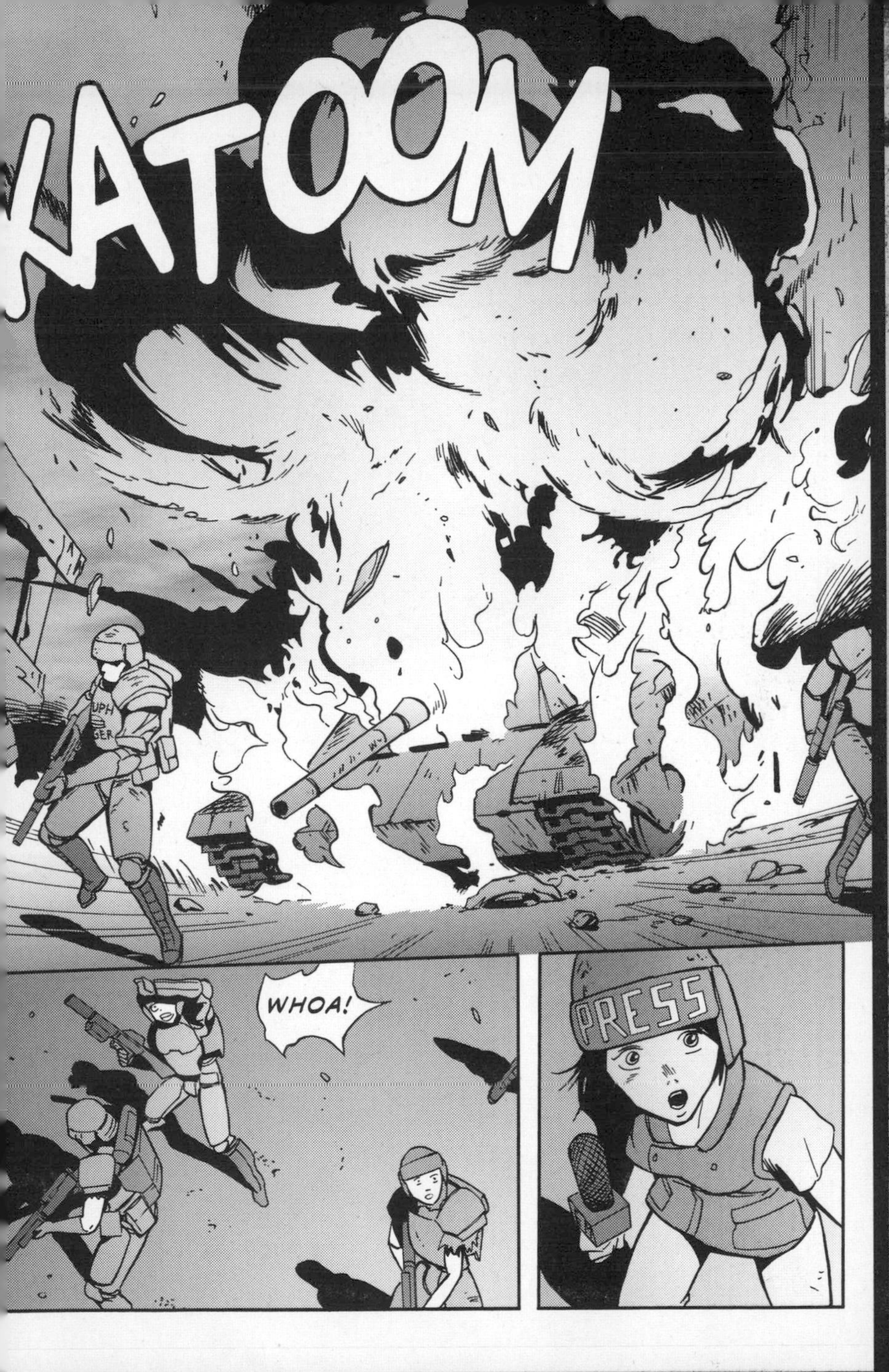
KATOOM
WHOA!
PRESS

MARK LEIT HAS JUST BEEN KILLED!
THIS IS SU BLAIR, AN WE'VE JUS CAUGHT T IMPLAUSIB CALAMIT LIVE!
ZAP
VZZT
ZZAP
NO... OH, NO...
I JUST WANTED HIM TO LET HER...I DIDN'T KNOW THE SHELLS WOULD...
I BLEW THE UP.
FSSHSSH
KRAK

IMPLAUSIBLE

\im PLAWS uh bul\ (adj.): improbable, inconceivable

A skeptical man by nature, Max found his neighbor's claim that he'd seen a UFO highly *implausible*.

CALAMITY

\ka LAM uh tee\ (n.): disaster, catastrophe

Last year's formal dance was a *calamity*: the band was an hour late and the food was spoiled.

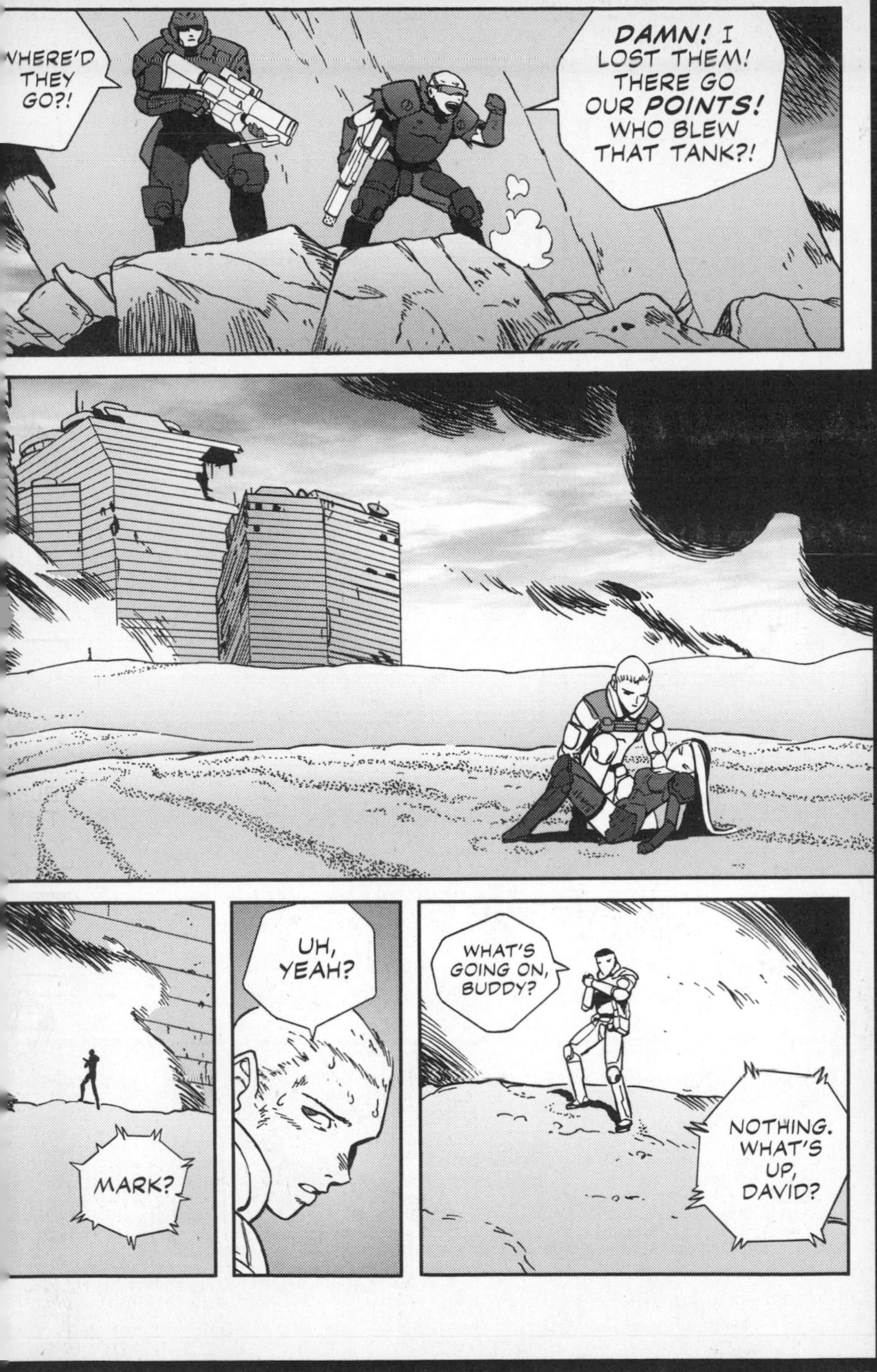
WHERE'D THEY GO?!
DAMN! I LOST THEM! THERE GO OUR POINTS! WHO BLEW THAT TANK?!
MARK?
UH, YEAH?
WHAT'S GOING ON, BUDDY?
NOTHING. WHAT'S UP, DAVID?

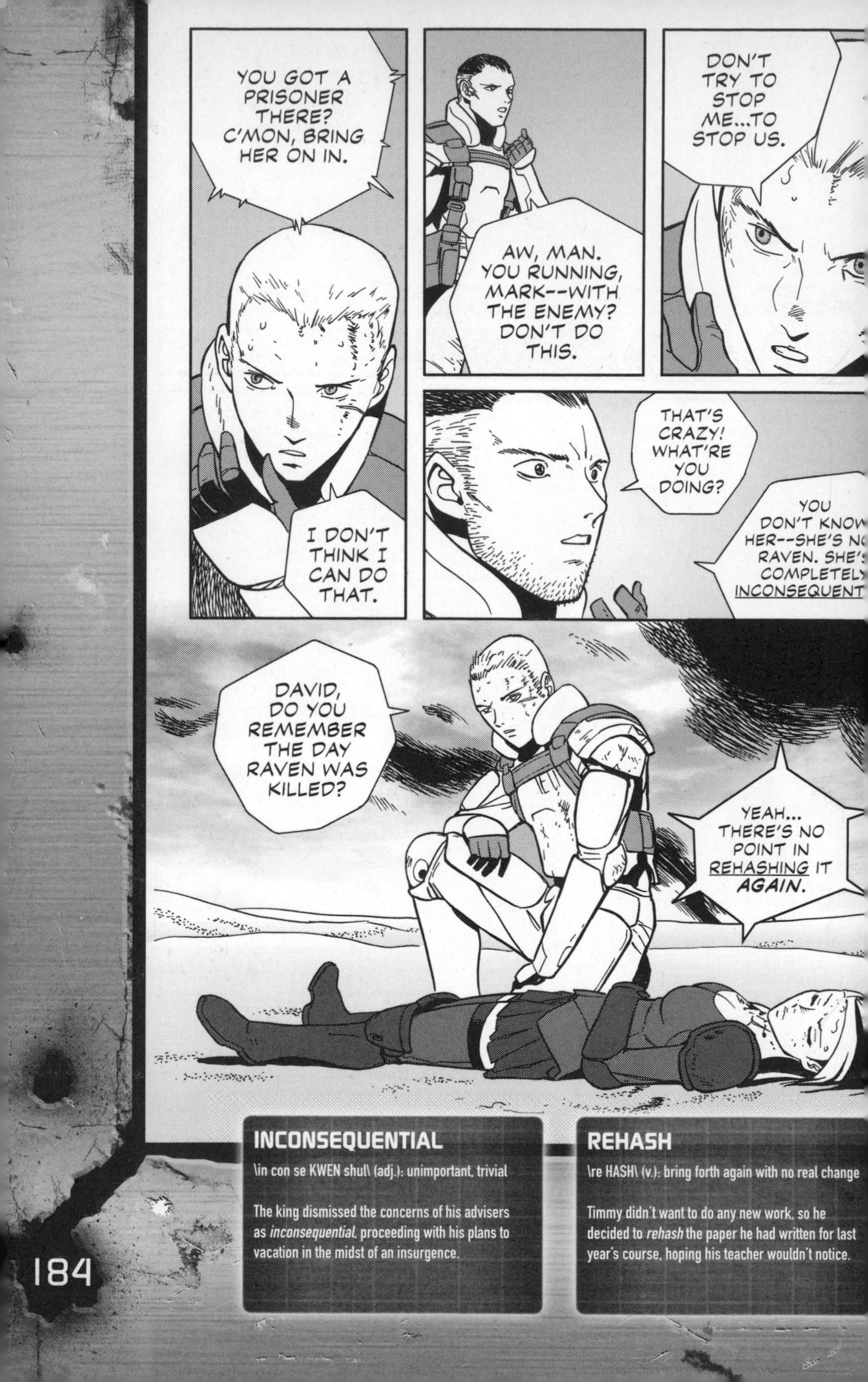
YOU GOT A PRISONER THERE? C'MON, BRING HER ON IN.
I DON'T THINK I CAN DO THAT.
AW, MAN. YOU RUNNING, MARK--WITH THE ENEMY? DON'T DO THIS.
DON'T TRY TO STOP ME...TO STOP US.
THAT'S CRAZY! WHAT'RE YOU DOING?
YOU DON'T KNOW HER--SHE'S NO RAVEN. SHE'S COMPLETELY INCONSEQUENT
DAVID, DO YOU REMEMBER THE DAY RAVEN WAS KILLED?
YEAH... THERE'S NO POINT IN REHASHING IT *AGAIN*.

INCONSEQUENTIAL

\in con se KWEN shul\ (adj.): unimportant, trivial

The king dismissed the concerns of his advisers as *inconsequential*, proceeding with his plans to vacation in the midst of an insurgence.

REHASH

\re HASH\ (v.): bring forth again with no real change

Timmy didn't want to do any new work, so he decided to *rehash* the paper he had written for last year's course, hoping his teacher wouldn't notice.

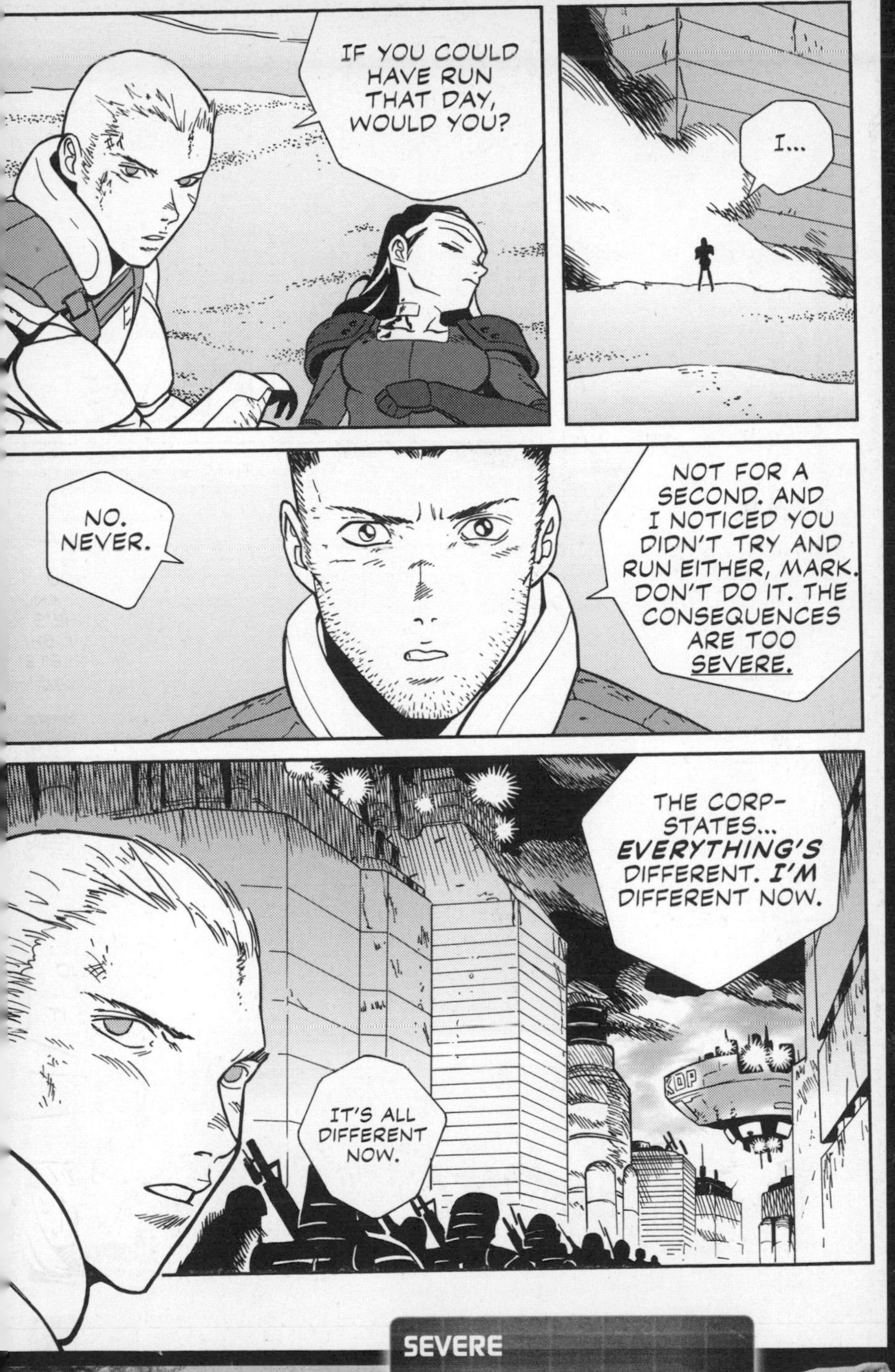
IF YOU COULD HAVE RUN THAT DAY, WOULD YOU?
I...
NO. NEVER.
NOT FOR A SECOND. AND I NOTICED YOU DIDN'T TRY AND RUN EITHER, MARK. DON'T DO IT. THE CONSEQUENCES ARE TOO SEVERE.
THE CORP-STATES... *EVERYTHING'S* DIFFERENT. *I'M* DIFFERENT NOW.
KOP
IT'S ALL DIFFERENT NOW.

SEVERE

\se VEER\ (adj.): harsh, strict, extreme

While the rest of the group went skiing, Morris stayed home with a *severe* case of the flu.

TREACHERY

\TRECH uh ree\ (n.): willful betrayal of trust

When the president's own advisor turned against him in the revolution, it was the ultimate act of *treachery*.

BETRAY

\be TRAY\ (v.): to be false or disloyal to

Unable to withstand the power of the dark side of the force, Darth Vader *betrayed* his teacher's confidence.

ARID

\AA rid\ (adj.): extremely dry or deathly boring

The *arid* desert could produce no crops.

REVIVE

\reh VIYV\ (v.): resuscitate, bring back to life; restore to use

The competent acting troupe *revived* interest in the theater among neighborhood residents.

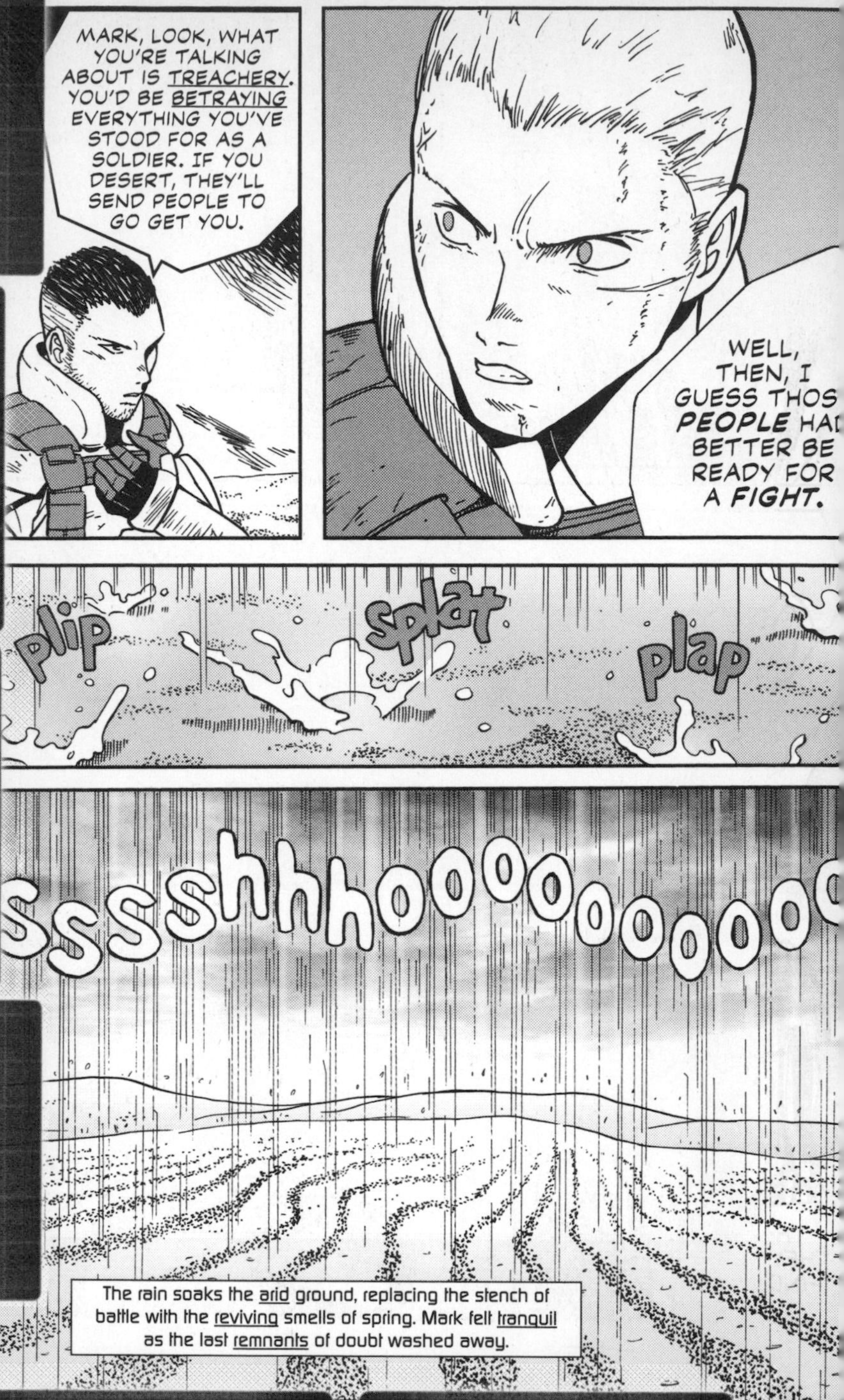
MARK, LOOK, WHAT YOU'RE TALKING ABOUT IS TREACHERY. YOU'D BE BETRAYING EVERYTHING YOU'VE STOOD FOR AS A SOLDIER. IF YOU DESERT, THEY'LL SEND PEOPLE TO GO GET YOU.
WELL, THEN, I GUESS THOS PEOPLE HA BETTER BE READY FOR A FIGHT.
plip
splat
plap
SSSHHOOOOOOOOO
The rain soaks the arid ground, replacing the stench of battle with the reviving smells of spring. Mark felt tranquil as the last remnants of doubt washed away.

TRANQUIL

\TRAN kwil\ (adj.): peaceful, calm, composed

The ship's captain looked over at the *tranquil* sea, motionless in the sun's setting sky.

REMNANT

\REM nent\ (n.): something left over, surviving trace

Although most of the food was finished before he arrived at the party, Mike managed to grab some of the *remnants* before the end.

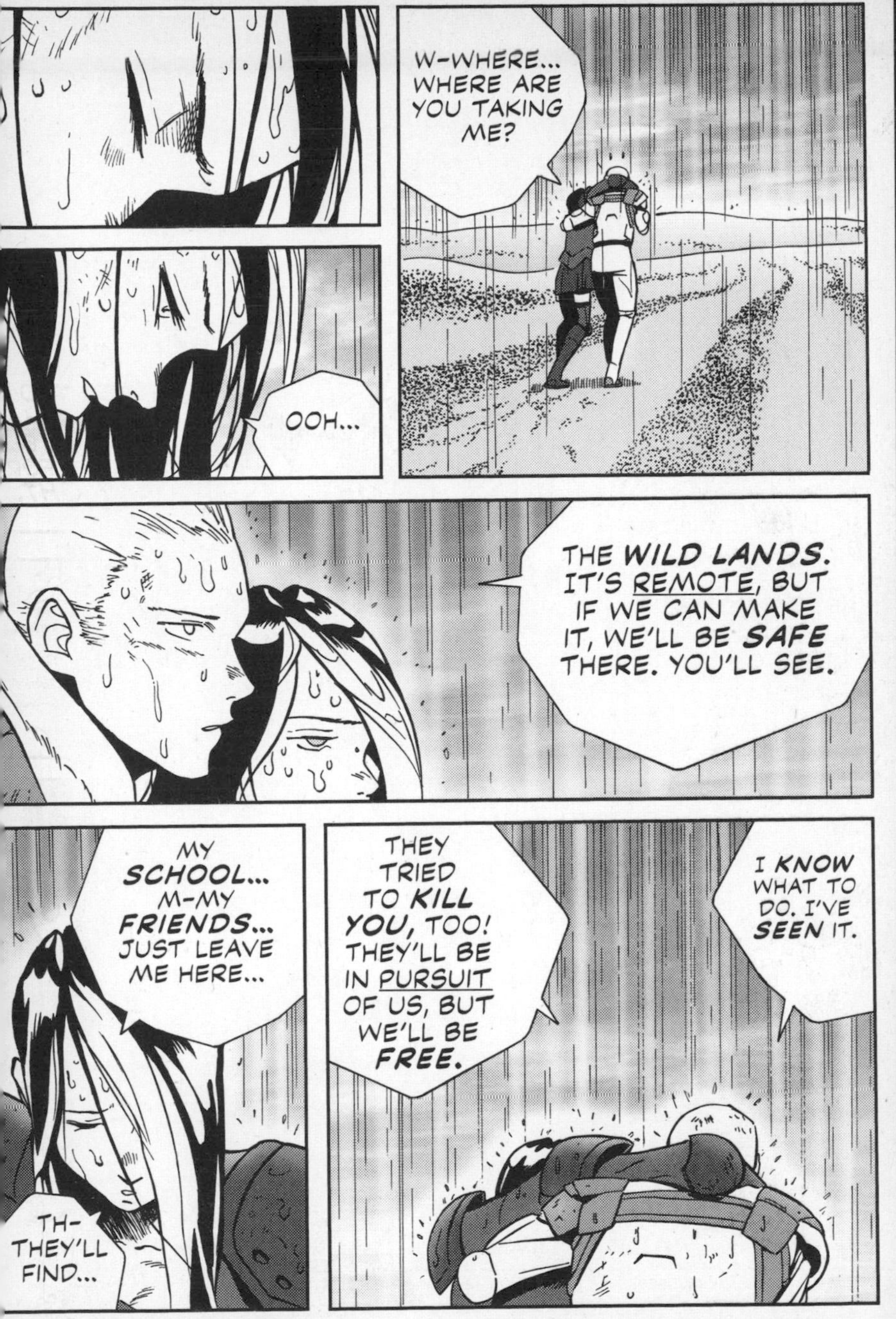
OOH...
W-WHERE... WHERE ARE YOU TAKING ME?
THE WILD LANDS. IT'S REMOTE, BUT IF WE CAN MAKE IT, WE'LL BE SAFE THERE. YOU'LL SEE.
MY SCHOOL... M-MY FRIENDS... JUST LEAVE ME HERE...
TH- THEY'LL FIND...
THEY TRIED TO KILL YOU, TOO! THEY'LL BE IN PURSUIT OF US, BUT WE'LL BE FREE.
I KNOW WHAT TO DO. I'VE SEEN IT.

REMOTE

\re MOHT\ (adj.): distant, isolated

The island was so *remote* that Chan's cell phone wouldn't operate.

PURSUIT

\pur SOOT\ (n.): the act of chasing or striving

While the *pursuit* of happiness is a basic right afforded to citizens in this country, the law limits it when one person's rights interfere with the wellbeing of others.

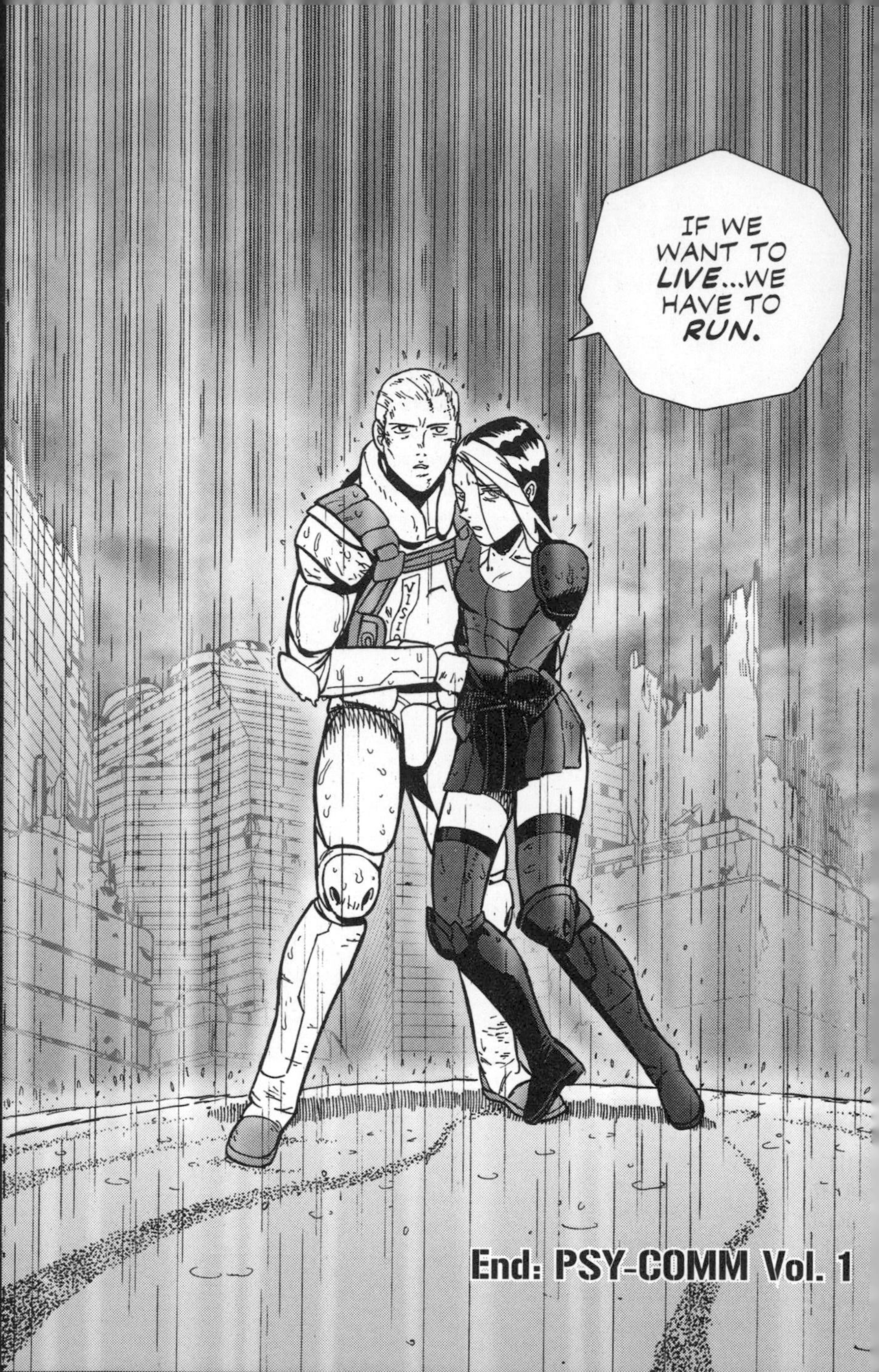
IF WE WANT TO LIVE...WE HAVE TO RUN.
End: PSY-COMM Vol. 1

t, 8
b, 118
erate, 85
nplice, 83
re, 13
t, 122
rsary, 51
essive, 54
107
te, 50
ity, 107
onist, 130
pate, 11
typal, 54
186
ss, 94
cious, 127

sh, 104
cade, 93
erent, 12
volent, 38
n, 88
y, 186
lder, 117
d, 59
t, 108
gart, 126
dish, 135
lity, 48
r, 174
onery, 42

e, 113
nity, 182
lating, 139
ap, 101
rated, 75
sh, 146
voyance, 9

clandestine, 58
clarity, 68
collaborator, 49
colossal, 114
combative, 127
commentary, 52
compassion, 88
compelling, 134
compensate, 120
complex, 14
composed, 16
conceited, 40
condolence, 34
conduit, 74
confident, 35
confirm, 82
conflict, 98
confrontational, 154
conserve, 123
consolation, 101
convenient, 106
conventional, 45
convicted, 59
counteract, 22
crass, 28
crude, 30
cue, 103
cunning, 9

D
daunting, 12
debilitating, 114
deceive, 110
defensive, 9
defiant, 8
demanding, 67
demeanor, 23
demolish, 16
derelict, 102
desolate, 6
determine, 179
devastate, 155
discern, 75
discourage, 51
disregard, 95
disseminate, 33
distant, 132

distortion, 52
distract, 50
divert, 99
divulge, 110
dominant, 81
drawback, 148
drub, 17

E
efficient, 70
eliminate, 14
embellish, 67
enchant, 135
endorse, 148
endurance, 97
enforce, 63
enhance, 28
enigmatic, 54
enormous, 8
entangle, 52
eradicate, 71
essential, 94
evade, 81
evaluate, 163
evaporate, 80
exaggerate, 53
exception, 88
exculpate, 60
exploit, 54
extensive, 56
extenuating, 98
exterminate, 20

F
factual, 51
fanfare, 27
fathom, 54
feign, 28
firebrand, 30
flank, 132
flaunt, 126
flaw, 145
flee, 92
foil, 51
foolhardy, 130
forge, 136

formidable, 159
fraud, 137
fundamental, 103
futile, 37

G
goad, 41
gravity, 82
gruff, 29

H
harangue, 41
harass, 72
hazardous, 59
heckler, 127
heinous, 100
hesitant, 44
hindrance, 60

I
implausible, 182
implement, 6
impotent, 81
impressionable, 124
inaccurate, 157
incidental, 112
incompetent, 7
inconsequential, 184
inconspicuous, 36
indebted, 171
indiscriminately, 116
indomitable, 17
inept, 66
inevitable, 80
inhibit, 49
insightful, 57
inspire, 147
instantaneous, 145
intellectual, 152
intrepid, 20
intruder, 92
investment, 41
irrational, 107
isolate, 159

J
jeopardize, 14

L
liability, 18
liberate, 179
linchpin, 132
lull, 146

M
maverick, 28
meager, 135
melee, 134
merciless, 38
milestone, 127
modest, 126

N
naïve, 80
narcissism, 127
negligible, 159
neutralize, 132
nitpick, 127
nonchalant, 36
nondescript, 67
notable, 74
notion, 82
novice, 46
nudge, 66
nurture, 49

O
objective, 127
oblivious, 163
obnoxious, 73
obstacle, 74
obstinate, 171
orderly, 75
originality, 143
ostentatious, 65
outcast, 59
overcome, 7
overpowering, 27

P
pariah, 59
peer, 80
perception, 40
perplex, 124
persistence, 7
persuasive, 135
placate, 7
ploy, 130
pompous, 153
postpone, 50
prank, 46
precedent, 52
precious, 103
predictable, 56
preserve, 169
prevent, 152
primary, 100
procure, 95
prodigy, 55
promote, 53
propel, 143
prosperity, 27
protégé, 102
proximity, 135
pursuit, 187

Q
quaint, 113

R
radical, 59
rascal, 73
reap, 63
reckless, 130
regale, 27
regurgitate, 53
rehash, 184
reinforce, 21
relevance, 119
relinquish, 12
relish, 152
reluctant, 179
rely, 15
remnant, 186
remorseful, 60

remote, 187
renew, 146
repel, 51
replicate, 54
reprimand, 29
reserve, 179
resilient, 124
revelry, 33
revive, 186
roster, 93
rude, 71
ruthless, 33

S
safeguard, 94
salvage, 19
sanctimonious, 16
scapegoat, 29
scholarly, 66
scurry, 33
sedative, 123
setback, 20
severe, 185
shabby, 124
signpost, 109
skepticism, 110
sluggish, 72
smug, 57
socialize, 69
solitary, 108
soothe, 50
stealth, 59
stifle, 62
stimulate, 69
subterfuge, 39
succumb, 169
sully, 102
superficial, 20
suppress, 32
surplus, 131
suspend, 63
swerve, 6
synthesize, 137

T
taunt, 73
tenacious, 144
tentative, 75
throng, 26
thwart, 147
timeless, 169
tolerate, 49
tourniquet, 118
trait, 54
tranquil, 186
treachery, 186
trigger, 71
trivialize, 136
turmoil, 30

U
undermine, 33
unfetter, 36
unparalleled, 53
urge, 169

V
vague, 63
vengeance, 147
verify, 39
vivid, 30

W
wary, 101
wrath, 98

With products serving children, adults, schools and businesses, Kaplan has an educational solution for every phase of learning.

KIDS AND SCHOOLS

SCORE! Educational Centers offer individualized tutoring programs in reading, math, writing and other subjects for students ages 4-14 at more than 160 locations across the country. We help students achieve their academic potential while developing self-confidence and a love of learning. *www.escore.com*

We also partner with schools and school districts through Kaplan K12 Learning Services to provide instructional programs that improve results and help all students achieve. We support educators with professional development, innovative technologies, and core and supplemental curriculum to meet state standards. *www.kaplank12.com*

TEST PREP AND ADMISSIONS

Kaplan Test Prep and Admissions prepares students for more than 80 standardized tests, including entrance exams for secondary school, college and graduate school, as well as English language and professional licensing exams. We also offer private tutoring and one-on-one admissions guidance. *www.kaptest.com*

HIGHER EDUCATION

Kaplan Higher Education offers postsecondary programs in fields such as business, criminal justice, health care, education, and information technology through more than 70 campuses in the U.S. and abroad, as well as online programs through Kaplan University and Concord Law School.
www.khec.com
www.kaplan.edu
www.concordlawschool.edu

PROFESSIONAL

If you are looking to start a new career or advance in your field, Kaplan Professional offers training to obtain and maintain professional licenses and designations in the accounting, financial services, real estate and technology industries. We also work with businesses to develop solutions to satisfy regulatory mandates for tracking and compliance. *www.kaplanprofessional.com*

Kaplan helps individuals achieve their educational and career goals. We build futures one success story at a time.